D0777649

the KING of BILLY GOAT HILL

To Sharron—
Very best always
[signature]
10.29.97

the KING of BILLY GOAT HILL

A novel by
Mark Stanleigh

Fallbrook Publishing Group
P.O. Box 3623
Sunriver, Oregon 97707
541-593-9343

Fallbrook Publishing Group
P.O. Box 3623
Sunriver, Oregon 97707
541-593-9343

Grateful acknowledgment is made to the following
for permission to reprint previously published material:

Epigraph: Excerpt from THE POWER AND THE GLORY by Graham Greene. Copyright 1940, 1968 by Graham Greene. Used by permission of Viking Penguin, a division of Penguin Books USA Inc.

Epigraph: Excerpt from Pen and Paper and a Breath of Air, BLUE PASTURES by Mary Oliver. Copyright 1995, 1992, 1991 by Mary Oliver. Used by permission of Harcourt Brace & Company.

Lyrics: From POOR LITTLE FOOL written by Shari Sheely. Copyright 1958, 1986 by Matragun Music, Inc. All Rights Reserved. Used by permission of Matragun Music, Inc.

Lyrics: From RUNAWAY written by Del Shannon and Max Crook. Copyright 1961, 1989 BUG MUSIC/MOLE HOLE MUSIC (BMI)/ Admin. by BUG MUSIC. All Rights Reserved. Used By Permission.

Lyrics: From MOMMA TOLD ME NOT TO COME, words and music by Randy Newman. Copyright 1966 (Renewed) Unichappell Music, Inc. All Rights Reserved. Used by permission of Warner Bros. Publications U.S. Inc., Miami, FL 33014

Book cover and title page design by DVA Advertising, Bend, Oregon.
Cover photo from the author's family archives.
Author photo by P. J. Morris.

Printed in the United States of America.
FPG First Printing, September 1996.

10 9 8 7 6 5 4 3 2 1

ISBN 0-9652888-0-3

dedication

For my brother, Paul,
whom I dearly love;

-and-

for Duke Snider,
my real-life childhood hero;

-and-

for children, young and old,
who just need someone to believe in
so that they might begin to believe in themselves.
* * * * *

In memory of:
John Norlin Morris
"lightbulb"
1955-1964

acknowledgments

The King of Billy Goat Hill came to life, in part, because of the invaluable support and encouragement given by the following special people, to whom I express my deepest thanks and appreciation: JoAnn Adams, Dan Almdale, T. Steven Brown, Dr. Anne Buttweiler, Bill Buttweiler, Mary Clizbe, Frederick Dellagatta, Todd "Breeze" Drange, Pamela Cosmo Gooch, Mary Ann Heathman, Jane Loebel, Kat Martin, William Morgan, Claudia Roseblade, Adrian Shields and Leann Thompson. I am also much obliged to Silver State Fiction Writers and the South Lake Tahoe Writers Group. As I walk the winding road of my life, countless good and giving souls enrich me with the manifold treasures of their hearts, and I am truly blessed. Forevermore, with love, this book is my gift to them.

For their kind and generous assistance responding to requests for information, I express my thanks to Robert Schweppe, Administrator, Baseball Operations, Los Angeles Dodgers Baseball Club; and Cynthia Hicks, Branch Librarian, Eagle Rock Branch, Los Angeles Public Library.

Finally, I am indebted to Michael O'Laughlin, an award winning writer, a talented teacher, and an extraordinary editor, whose warm and tender touch can be felt throughout this book.

There is always one moment in childhood when the door opens and lets the future in.
　　　　—Graham Greene,
　　　　　The Power and the Glory

After a cruel childhood, one must reinvent oneself. Then reimagine the world.
　　　　—Mary Oliver,
　　　　　Blue Pastures

prologue

They say what doesn't kill you makes you stronger. For most of my life this was not a self-evident concept. It didn't start out all that bad for me and Luke. Oh, we didn't have much, more than some. But it wasn't for a lack of material things that we suffered. I used to think it would have been better if there had been no love at all; to have it and lose it, I reasoned, must be worse. Before the bad things happened, there was some good. Our parents were together and happy, or so I believed, though Earl drank too much, and Lucinda probably would never be mother of the year. The sum of it, though, was that they made us feel secure. I guess you could say we were a family.

When our infant brother, Matthew, died, that feeling of family seemed to die with him. Lucinda fell into a long, sad silence, as though seeking refuge from the anguish of losing her baby. I think we understood that she couldn't help it. Earl, however, was a different story. He ran off forever...a fact we could never understand.

That left me and Luke to make due for ourselves. We were vulnerable, very much alone on the uncertain path through the nether world of childhood. Yet, considering the circumstances, we were doing OK. We had each other. We had a dog. We had our heroes. Until something bad happened, something far beyond our control, something, it would turn out, even worse than Matthew dying.

A part of me will always be eight years old...that voiceless, innocent child, the genesis of my imagination, my empathy, my passion. I am stronger now. What didn't kill me made me so. And, at last, I have found the words to set me free of the past.

My name is Wade Parker. Be well, my friends.

Peace.

one

Northeast Los Angeles
Spring, 1958

> *Eyes closed, mind in a groggy, neutral haze.*
> *Whine-chug-chuga...Varoom!*

I flinched as the distinct ignition signature of Carl's 1955 Chevy Bel Air pummeled the night calm. The cracked windowpane next to my bed rattled like a snare drum from the percussion of badly corroded mufflers. If I had fallen asleep, I was no longer. The firing up of the Chevy meant it was midnight, plus or minus one minute.

Our next door neighbor, Carl, a baker married to the night shift, the most punctual alcoholic I ever knew, never seemed very keen on the virtues of preventive maintenance. His Chevy, not yet three years off the assembly line, looked and sounded as decrepit as Betsy, our embarrassing-to-be-seen-in '40 Ford.

I sat up in bed and peered out the window as Carl put the poor Chevy in gear. The transmission clanked lazily and the car lumbered away from the curb, like a sickly sloth. A trail of smoke obscured the red glow of one working tail light. The window by my bed hummed louder, then gradually fell silent.

In the bed next to mine, my brother, Luke, slept on, snoring softly under his blanket, oblivious to the commotion of Carl's routine departure. Through the narrow dimness that separated our beds, I could just make out the top of Luke's red, fuzzy head poking out from under his blanket. It reminded me of the end of a hot dog sticking out from a bun. I must have been hungry. Sometimes I get that way when I'm feeling nervous. Luke was something else, able to fall asleep at the snap of a finger and remain there, comatose, until it was time to get up. He was like a light switch. Off or on. Awake or asleep. Nothing in-between. I envied him. He didn't lie awake worrying about things like I did, like I was now worrying about my imminent showdown with *The Crippler*. The coming danger loomed heavy on my mind, denying me rest, the precious energy I needed for any hope of survival.

I shivered visualizing *The Crippler*, as I listened to Carl drive off down the hill, absently anticipating the screech of brake pad rivets scraping against pitted and scarred metal drums, like finger nails on a chalk board. When Carl halted for the stop sign at the bottom of the hill, I felt it in my teeth.

Except for the slight intrusion of Luke's rhythmic wheezing, the night reclaimed total calm. I flipped my pillow over to the cool side, laid my head back down, and closed my eyes knowing there wasn't enough time left to sleep. Tossing and turning, listening to the approximate silence, I tried in vain not to think about *The Crippler*. When finally I couldn't stand it any longer, I got up and dressed as quietly as possible, daring not to wake our mother, Lucinda, whom we tiptoed around even when she was awake on account of her being sad or angry ever since our baby brother, Matthew, died. We hardly got to know him. He only lived 55 days. Lucinda worked all the time, I think, to keep her mind off of Matthew. Me and Luke looked out for each other. Mostly I took care of Luke.

"Come on, Luke, hurry up!" I urged with a poorly restrained whisper.

"Keep your shirt on," Luke hissed. "I can't find my other tennis shoe."

"Mac probably got it again," I half-cussed, one leg already hanging out of the bedroom window. "I bet we'll find it in the garage. Come on."

Mac was our dog. He was asleep at the foot of my bed. His ears twitched at the mention of his name and he lifted his head, mildly annoyed that we were once again stealing out into the night. It was two o'clock in the morning. Mac knew better than to bark, though. He was used to it. We did this kind of stealthy night crawling all the time. Depending on his mood, Mac would sometimes join us on our nocturnal adventures. On this particular night, he opted to break the triad. Mac was one of the smartest dogs that ever lived. He understood the concepts of culpability, accessory, and accomplice better than me and Luke ever did. And I swear, he knew when we were up to no good. Besides, he managed to get himself into plenty of trouble without tagging along with us.

"Dern grass is wet," Luke complained as I watched him hop on one shoe across the dew covered lawn. I loved him and all, in fact he was my best friend, but sometimes Luke could be a royal pain in the rump. I told myself all little brothers were a bother sometimes.

I opened the side door to the garage, pulling up as hard as I could on the door knob to silence the squeaky hinges. Garage smells wafting in the blackness, grease, turpentine, fermenting grass on the old push mower, filled my nose as I stepped through the doorway and flicked on my Flash Gordon flashlight. I moved the shaft of light to scan the oil stained floor, then smiled with satisfaction when I spotted Luke's shoe lying next to Betsy's front wheel.

"Like I told you, Red. There it is."

Luke balked, begrudging my intuitive powers. "You think you're so dern smart, Wade, how come you're not on Ed Sullivan?"

I swear Luke must have been a dang Myna bird in a past life. The way he mimicked Lucinda could drive me up the wall. "Maybe someday, Red." I jerked his brand new Los Angeles Dodgers cap down over his eyes. He swung at me in the dark, missing as usual. I picked up his errant sneaker, pooched out my mouth, planted my free hand on my hip and tried my best to sound like Ed Sullivan, "Tonight, ladies and gentlemen...we have a really, really, really big shoe."

"You don't even sound like him," Luke complained.

I tossed him his sneaker. "Come on Red...put your dang shoe on. They're probably already waiting for us."

Luke methodically made a bow with an over-long lace as I trained the flashlight beam on his foot. He was only six years old and had yet to fully master the art of shoe tying. Since I was the one who had taught him how to tie his shoes, I waited patiently for him to finish. I had learned not to rush or criticize his handy work unless I was up for contending with his prickly temper. The opposite of me, Luke wasn't shy about expressing himself. He was a redheaded firecracker, and making him mad was not a good idea at that moment.

Back in the yard, we both jumped when Mac instantly appeared in front of us. He whined a little, as if to warn us not to go, then disappeared into the inky black behind the garage.

"Dern dog. He's just going to do his duty," Luke blazoned.

"Shush! You wake up Lucinda and I'll tan you good, right after she tans the both of us."

He swung at me again.

Luke was quick to make judgmental or disparaging remarks about Mac. It was his way of clarifying his own position in the pecking order. I understood. But the fact was, Mac, having been the benefactor of the best genes of the German shepherd and Doberman pinscher breeds, could have made a snack out of Luke anytime he cared to. Fortunately for Luke, and me, Mac loved us more than, well, more than almost anything.

Our reason for risking the skin off our behinds that night had more to do with my shooting my mouth off, an unusual behavior for me, than anything that could be explained by reason or logic. You see, it wasn't enough for me to be the champion cardboard slider of Billy Goat Hill. Noooo, I had to brag that I could take *The Crippler* from top to bottom—IN THE DARK! Now, it's fine to make bold, daring statements to an audience of zero, but it's not a good idea to do it in the middle of a schoolyard when Guerrmo Francisco Torres SMITH, Gooey for short, is standing right in front of you.

"Is that so, Wade?" Gooey had said, challenging my outlandish claim. Instantly I knew that I had screwed up.

"Yep," I said, clearing my throat, unease causing my shoulders to tighten up.

Gooey was nine, a year older than me, and did not like the fact that I was a better slider than him. "In the dark, huh?" he repeated, grinning for effect, trying his best to make me squirm. I gave him a look that implored him not to push it. That was all he needed to drop the hammer. He flashed a meaner grin. "How about tonight then, say about, oh, 2:15 or so?"

A group of kids, many of them Billy Goat Hill regulars, had gathered around us sensing that something was up, making it impossible for me to back down.

"My old man's out of town again," I said, staring him down with steely-eyed, thespian couth. "Shouldn't be any problem...at all."

My own words pricked a hidden corner of my heart. I sorely missed Earl, our dissocial, usually drunk father. I guess Matthew's death had messed him up, too, and we hadn't seen or heard from him in nearly two months. Soon it would be my birthday, and I knew all the luck in the world wouldn't help him remember it. My eyes still locked on Gooey, I projected an overdraft of gratuitous nonchalance as a small volcano erupted in my gut.

The ethnically mixed crowd of grade school sliders ooh'd and aah'd, like old west townsmen roused by the threat of violence. Scenting blood on the malevolent parlance of gunslinger bravado, they stirred like nervous beasts in a herd. An excursion of thought had me scanning the onlooker's faces, expecting their devotion, their genuflection in the presence of their champion. But I found no loyalty in their lusting eyes, only the desire to be entertained, thrilled. They wanted to witness the lions eating the trainer, the fall of the unnetted trapeze artist, the fatal crash of the champion of Billy Goat Hill. Their aggrandized hero learned a quick but painful lesson: *Life is tough at the top.* I did, however, spot one friendly soul in the shifting crowd. Luke, his freckly face beaming with adoration, his chest swollen with pride, gave me the strength I needed to endure Gooey's relentless grin.

The Crippler was the longest, steepest, most dangerous run on Billy Goat Hill. Many of the kids wouldn't try it at all. It got its name when an out of town kid foolishly made a head first run and ended up on a permanent wheelchair ride. *The Crippler* ran a course of about 350 feet with a total vertical drop of nearly 200 feet, a sharply tilted minefield of natural and man-made hazards, any one of which meant disaster for the slider that veered off course. It was the perfect dare for young boys bucking for manhood.

Cardboard sliding was a poor kid's version of the sport of bobsledding. Our modest bobsleds were nothing more than sturdy chunks of cardboard cut from the large boxes used for shipping new appliances, and our snow was the thick, dry, weeds and grasses native to the hilly surroundings of Los Angeles. Unlike a real bobsled, our cardboard bobsleds had no runners, no brakes, and no steering mechanism. Directional control was minimal. You could shift the weight of your body by leaning left or right, or you could alternately drag your left or right foot using them as rudimentary rudders, but only if you wore boots or at least hi-tops lest you lose the meat off your ankles. Neither procedure did much to help steer. Mostly there was only one direction, down, and once you started down, with no brakes, there was no stopping. The most important objective was to stay on the cardboard. The other most important objective was to keep the cardboard on the run. Cardboard sliding was all technique. Thinking back on it now, those were probably the only moments in my life when I did my best to follow the beaten path.

The Crippler was one of a myriad of runs that scarred the variant slopes of Billy Goat Hill. The area looked very similar to the vitiated terrain swarmed over by "motocross" enthusiasts today. *The Crippler* was long and steep, but what made it dangerous was the jagged rocks, century plants, prickly pear cactus, stumps, car bodies and assorted other debris that had been dumped down the incline by people too lazy or too cheap to haul their discards to the city dump. You couldn't have designed a better run if you tried.

'In the dark, huh?' Gooey had said.

It was almost 2:30 by the time Luke and I made it to the top of Billy Goat Hill. I immediately went to work cutting to size the water heater box that we had tugged up the hill behind us. Luke sat on a rock next to me catching his breath. He suggested we should have brought Mac with us to help tow the box up the hill. Luke always came up with good ideas after the fact. I didn't say anything.

I was surprised that none of the other kids were there yet, especially Gooey, although it was common knowledge that his mom often had to throw cold water on him to wake him up for school.

With a razor knife I had indefinitely borrowed from Sal's, our neighborhood liquor store, I trimmed up the water heater box to form a bottom, two sides and a front. I wasn't planning to drag my feet. It looked like a square-nosed canoe with its back end cut off. Luke and I dragged it over to the top of *The Crippler* and sat down to wait for the other kids to show up. I tried not to think about the daredevil stunt awaiting me.

The low clouds hanging over the City of Angels that night were a disappointment; no stars, no Dippers to trace, no moon to make faces at. It was almost cool enough for long sleeves, but we were sweating after lugging the water heater box up the hill. We took our jackets off and let the night air cool us down. I looked at Luke in his sneakers, blue jeans, and horizontal striped T-shirt, and realized that except for his red hair, he was the spitting image of me. A couple of goslings away from the nest without leave. I tugged his Dodger cap down over his eyes again. He swung and missed again.

We were still buzzing from the excitement of seeing our first big league baseball game, the first game of the Los Angeles, by way of Brooklyn, Dodgers. It hadn't been easy. Absent Lucinda's permission, and with no tickets for the game, Luke and I, a pair of pikers with a plan, ventured across Los Angeles by city bus and snuck, like rats up a gangplank, into the Coliseum. *Rattis Gangplankus*. It had a nice ring to it, I thought. That, or something like it, is probably what my teacher, Mrs. Barr, would've called us. She aspired to be a Professor of Latin at UCLA and often practiced her gobbledygook on our class. Even the Catholic kids thought she was weird. I liked her though.

"Man, I've never seen so many people in one place before. That Coliseum is huge, huh?" Luke said.

"Yeah. Colossal. Man, were we lucky Davenport forgot to touch third base, because when Mays knocked in Kirkland it would have been tied up."

"Tough titties for the Giants."

"Yeah, Dodgers rule," I said, trying not to think about *The Crippler*.

"I used to like the Chicago Cubs best, but now we have our own team. Who's your favorite player?" Luke asked, then yawned without covering his mouth.

"Come on, you know the answer to that one...the one and only Duke Snider, the greatest player in the game today."

Luke smiled. "I like Charlie Neal the best. When I grow up I want to play second base like Charlie Neal."

I looked at Luke and laughed a little to myself. He was thinking about being as good as Charlie Neal and he couldn't even catch or throw well enough to play catch with me yet. Actually, I wasn't much better than him at that time, and, little did I know, before too long Luke would be a better ball player than me. He never was as good a cardboard slider, though.

I loved talking baseball with Luke, although sometimes it led to arguments.

"You know what's weird, Luke?"

"Nuh uh." Luke's eyes drooped as he pulled his coat over himself like a blanket.

"Hank Sauer hit two home runs for the Giants and he only lives a couple of miles from the Coliseum. He should be playing for the Dodgers."

Luke nodded his head indicating that he had heard my voice but I doubted that he was listening. A minute later his lids slipped shut and his mouth fell open. His chest slowly swelled and retracted with the well paced rhythm of sleep. I pulled his cap down softly over his eyes. He didn't swing at me.

My Howdy-Doody watch said 2:45 as I leaned back against the same rock Luke was nuzzling. He had started to snore in his typical cat purring way. I rested my head on the rock and gazed up at the charcoal sky. The expanse above was deep and dark, like the ocean. I watched from my weed covered crow's-nest, alert for whales, landfall, or maybe even pirates. Off to the southwest, the blanket of cloud cover faintly glowed, like a giant efflorescent night flower attracted to the nocturnal flame of downtown Los Angeles. I sat unafraid in the dark and watched the sky glow for a while. Luke's snoring seemed to call the crickets to sing and soon I was surrounded by a soothing chorus of nature's music.

A moment of loneliness set me adrift on thoughts of Earl. My arms went around me in a self-consoling hug, and remembering the last time I saw him, I began to smile inside. He had said I was shooting up faster than July corn. We wrestled on the grass in front of the house. He tickled me and tossed me up in the air so high I could see all kinds of stuff scattered on the porch roof. And I couldn't stop laughing because everything was great, even with his whisky breath blowing right in my face. I missed him more than I ever let on to Luke. Why had he fathered Luke and me and then wanted little or nothing to do with us? A swelling ache in my chest made me close the door on thoughts of Earl.

Gooey's goading me to run *The Crippler* in the dark, to put my cardboard where my mouth was, had caused my nerves to coil up tight. Now the tension dissolved in a wash of peaceful fantasy...me and Duke Snider taking batting practice, shooting the breeze, slowly gearing up to rip the hide off of anything dumb enough to be low and away. I wondered what it would be like to be Duke Snider's son?

A small break in the clouds appeared directly overhead just in time for me to see a shooting star through the opening. Shooting stars are wondrous things to me. Maybe it was Sputnik, I thought wistfully. After a moment I rejected the notion, reasoning that no satellite would be big enough for me to see without a telescope. I lay there next to Luke feeling oddly content for the moment. A red, flashing light wandered across the opening in the clouds. I quickly assessed it to be nothing more than a common airplane. Or, could it be...a Russian spy plane?

I thought about our next-door neighbor, Carl-the-baker. His passions were baking bread, drinking beer, singing patriotic songs and denigrating the Russians. He didn't like the Russians much. He called them rotten ruskies, cowardly commies, soviet bastards or just plain dirty reds. He claimed they were out to take over America. Carl was well known for sitting on his front porch, drinking beer, pontificating, warning ad nauseam about the Russians. Sometimes he'd curse out loud and then mutter that the only good thing about the bastards was that they made decent rye bread. His mournful complaining always grew louder and louder with each empty beer bottle. Finally, after ten or twelve empties, which he called dead soldiers, were lined up in a row on his porch rail, he'd launch into a medley of his favorite flag-waving odes. His deep, baritone voice, reminiscent of Tennessee Ernie Ford, boomed throughout the neighborhood. Eventually, his wife would convince him to come inside and go to bed, after which she would hastily collect up the beer bottles and close the drapes in her front windows. Embarrassing for her, but we thought old Carl was outstanding entertainment.

The hole in the clouds got bigger. I played connect the dots with the stars. Luke continued harmonizing with the cricket choir. Duke Snider whispered of baseball inside my head.

The cardboard canoe sat poised at the top of *The Crippler* thirty feet from where Luke and I nestled in the dark. I could just make out its shape. My watch now said 3:00am and I allowed myself to think that maybe Gooey, or anyone else, wasn't going to show up. I did show up though and that's all that mattered to me. Baloney! I was damn glad they didn't show up! Funny, though, as I sat there in the dark, I started to wonder if I really had the guts to make the slide in the gloom of night? But if I did it now, no one would be there to see. Nobody would believe me. Even if Luke was awake to watch, he wouldn't qualify as a reliable witness, on account of his being my brother.

The other kids not showing up was a psychological victory, but it left me with a feeling of disappointment. Did I really want to go down *The Crippler* in the dark? It's nuts! So this is why Gooey calls me *Poco Loco:* a little bit crazy. He's right. I seriously contemplated getting in the canoe and shoving off, until a picture of myself stretched out on top of a cactus patch, like an Indian guru painfully prostrated on a bed of nails, flashed through my mind. I did not get up. "How about them Dodgers," I muttered to myself.

Eyes back to the hole in the clouds. Wow! Another shooting star descended into nothingness. Next time I see Carl I'm going to tell him I saw Sputnik over Billy Goat Hill. I smiled and closed my eyes. I pictured me and Duke Snider sitting side by side in the Dodgers' dugout.

I was always a dreamer before Earl left and something inside me changed. I loved to dream. It was like delicious medicine. Tasty and good for you. Some people say they can go back to sleep and finish a dream if they wake up in the middle of it. I could actually decide about what I wanted to dream and then dream it, almost like picking out a movie before going to the theater. Sometimes the dreams didn't turn out exactly the way I planned them, though. For example, if I wanted to dream about flying on a magic carpet...I could end up on a braided throw rug with floppy pelican wings. It was a matter of concentration. Dreaming was better than a pocket full of money. And best of all I never had nightmares. Even my monsters would crack jokes. Mostly I dreamed about me and my teammate Duke Snider. I was always the youngest professional baseball player in history; I always played for the Dodgers, and any position I felt like playing was always fine with the team; and we always won in the ninth inning with me on base and Duke smashing the game winning homer. I closed my eyes and tried hard to make a picture of a ball park inside the lids. I heard the announcer reading the starting line up. As I walked out of the dugout onto the field, I looked up to see Earl in the stands, drunk, but clapping enthusiastically. Luke and the crickets droned on, as soothing as a cradlesong, and soon, I too, was sound asleep...*Dreaming.*

two

Seals Stadium, San Francisco.
Colder than a witch's tit.
*It was the top of the ninth. We were down by one run. I was
taking a cautious lead off first. Duke Snider was at the plate with a
count of 2 and 1. I caught the sign. He was swinging away....*

From somewhere deep within my dull slumber a jarring rumble
began. My neck muscles tensed and jerked banging my head against
the rock backrest that Luke and I had been sharing. Confusion
reigned as a cloud of choking dust blew over me. For a dizzy second I
thought I'd just got picked off, caught leaning the wrong way, dust
flying in a desperate lunge back to first base. *Dang! That's not
supposed to happen. Stop the dream!*

Lights lambasted my face overwhelming my groggy eyes. One
arm went up to ward off the brightness while the other slapped futilely
at the smothering dust. My ears itched and my entire body vibrated
from a bombarding roar. Luke was awake too, his finger nails like
talons digging hard into my thigh. I knew I was screaming, but the
sound was swallowed up in a terrible thunder.

The dust billowed away as a jet-black tire, snugged around a
chrome spoked wheel, stabbed out at me on a long silver fork no doubt
belonging to the Devil himself. The tire had stopped about an inch
from the toes of my well-worn sneakers, which now looked to me like
the witch's feet did sticking out from under the house that fell on her

in *The Wizard Of Oz*. And she was dead!

There was a flash of movement as Luke's feet snapped back under his butt. Defenseless against this unimaginable intrusion, we huddled together quivering with fright. Playing possum, except for my eyes, I scanned the periphery and quickly counted sixteen choppers belonging to a gang of murderous gargoyles known to us locals as *Satan's Slaves*. I had a powerful urge to urinate as Custer's ghost, thorny with arrows, smiling sympathetically, loomed out of the thickening background.

"Well lookie here. We got ourselves a couple of campers!" their leader barked, after the last Harley quit dieseling and choked itself mute. The chorus of crickets were already halfway to San Bernardino County. Now the silence was deafening.

The gang's leader looked like the drawings of Stone Age cave men that I had studied the prior year in second grade. Except this brute donned classic biker togs: black engineer boots, greasy blue jeans, no shirt, silver studded black leather belt with a matching scabbard sheathing a Buck knife as long as my arm, black leather jacket, and a red bandanna tied around his head, which somehow failed to keep his oily black hair out of his eyes.

I caught myself staring. He had the ugliest scar I'd ever seen. A puffy groove of recent origin slashed all the way from above his left eye, across the bridge of his nose, under his right eye, down his cheek and finally hooking under his right earlobe. The scar made his beard part in a funny way. No, not funny, scary. I was trembling.

"My name's Scar," he declared. "What's yours?" His black, heavily hooded eyes shot straight into my soul.

I had to look away. I was about a mile short on nerve and an inch away from tears. My throat was dry and as coarse as sandpaper. "My name—is—Wade," I squeaked. Minnie Mouse sounded like she was on testosterone injections compared to me. I could feel Luke squeezing himself back between me and the rock.

" 'Wade' you say?" He snickered in a way that I took as scorn.

Stomach squirming, eyes still averted, I said, "Uh-huh, *gulp*—Wade Parker."

Scar's eyes never left mine as he bit off the end of a new cigar and spat it to the ground. I took it he could just as easily do the same with my head. "What's that hiding behind you?" he demanded, shifting his gaze. He scrutinized Luke's exposed hindquarter like a vulture ogles carrion before the feast. His deep voice rattled me up and down with chills.

He flicked his eyes back on me, the more appealing hunk of sustenance, and jammed the cigar in his mouth. Magically, a Zippo lighter appeared already aflame, a living creature anticipating its master's every wish. I watched as Scar puffed hard, engulfing himself in a glowing fog of pungent amber smoke, the luminous cloud queerly pulsing in response to the capricious, licking fire of the lighter, my heart tripping strangely in sympathy with the hypnotic flame. The fissure dominating Scar's face caught and spilled the light, casting an evil liquid shadow across his face. Frankenstein's monster in the flesh, I thought, as he brandished his disfigurement like a weapon, a sign of absolute invincibility. Intimidation stabbed me with a syringe full of paralyzing fear, making me inert, incapable of speech.

A woman straddling the banana seat behind Scar looked over his shoulder at me. Her face captured some of the Zippo's flicker, startling me. I hadn't noticed her before due to the harsh glare of the motorcycle lights. Unconsciously, I squinted to get a better look and she immediately acknowledged me with a scintillating smile. I began to thaw, to relax. She was pretty, more than pretty—lovely. I couldn't help myself, I smiled back for a second or two, until a spurt of instinct, or just plain providence, made my eyes dart away. It couldn't possibly be prudent to smile at Scar's woman.

Scar grunted harshly, "What's the matter, cat got your tongue?" He was the sovereign wild boar barking a dismissive command to an inferior male.

The woman, her beauty, had distracted me, causing my comprehension to lag a couple of beats behind my hearing. "Pardon?"

Scar grinned, the expression making him look almost handsome. I wished he'd keep smiling, he didn't look so dangerous that way. "I asked you who that is behind you there." He cocked his head slightly to get a better visual angle on Luke.

The presence of the woman had somehow made me feel safer, less threatened. Now I could speak. "Oh. That's my brother, Luke. He's scared. He's only six."

"Look at them sitting there: oh, aren't they darling," the lovely lady gushed, further diluting the oppressive tension surrounding me. With a burst of female enthusiasm, she swung her long legs to the ground and lithely slipped herself off Scar's Hog. Now I could see her whole body awash in the motor cycle lights. Wow! She was more stunning than Bridget Bardot, her hair thick, golden blond, flowing nearly to her waist. She wore brown leather riding boots that ran up to her knees where white form-snugging pants took over and covered her up to her waist. A pale blue gypsy blouse, splayed wide open at her neck, plunged in a "V" that terminated behind a big glimmering belt buckle. Her silky mane glowed in an amorphous circle around her angelic face as she stood like a beauty queen basking in the motorcycle lights that encircled her, like lights focused on a stage. I felt a little woozy, spellbound.

She started toward us but Scar quickly grabbed her arm. "Better be careful, Miss Cherry," he said, patting her behind, "these squatters might be dangerous."

The gang enjoyed a hearty laugh while several more women riders dismounted and came toward us. I dared to stand up as she approached, Luke rising up with me like my shadow. Gosh, she was even prettier up close.

"How old are you, honey?"

Miss Cherry had spoken to me, but, in my instant-crush state of mind, Luke got the jump on me. "He's eight. He thinks he's some kinda big shot."

The gang laughed again. I gave Luke a discreet elbow in the ribs.

"What are you guys doing up here at four in the morning?" She stepped closer and I immediately noticed she smelled of nice perfume. Unlike the male members of the gang, Miss Cherry was clean and "lovely."

Luke let me answer this time. "We got up at two, ma'am. We were supposed to meet some of our friends up here."

"What on earth for?" she asked, casting an approving smile back to Scar.

Scar chimed in, "Yeah, what are you guys up to?"

"Nothing much really," I answered, but loud-mouthed little Luke stepped on my words again.

"He was gonna run The Crippler in the dark." He blurted it out before I could get my hand over his mouth. He shoved my arm away and glared at me.

"What is The Crippler?" Miss Cherry asked sweetly.

"It's over there," Luke said, pointing past me toward the cardboard canoe.

Scar got off his chopper and strolled over to the cardboard box, his heavy boots kicking up puffs of dust. He looked over the ledge and squinted into the black. Miss Cherry walked over next to him and peered down the slope. "Oh, my gosh!" she blurted. She carefully stepped back from the ledge and glanced toward me. My cocky smile showed up unannounced, the same one that had gotten me into this predicament when I mouthed off to Gooey. Miss Cherry started giggling. I couldn't help noticing the wonderful bounce of her full breasts in the glare of the headlights as she walked back toward me. I think that was the moment my preference—uh—let's be honest, my fetish for large breasts began. "Were you really gonna ride down there in the dark?" Her thickly painted eyebrows arched up into upside-down V's.

"Well, I was, but Gooey, the kid who challenged me, didn't show up." Several of the bikers chuckled suggesting I lacked nerve, but Miss Cherry spun around and hushed them. "I'm not afraid to go down that hill," I said, trying to stick up for myself.

Luke seemed a little miffed too. "Wade isn't afraid. He's the king of Billy Goat Hill."

With that the whole gang started laughing. Luke snarled at them, not understanding what was so funny.

"The hell you say?" Scar mocked, from behind us. "I thought I was the king of this turf."

"This boy is pissin' on your turf, Scar," said one of the gang members.

"Yeah. What are you gonna do about it, Scar?" chimed a big fat biker wearing a chrome Nazi helmet with a spear head on top. The gang passed around assorted snickers and guffaws. Even Miss Cherry couldn't resist a giggle as she turned to look at Scar.

Scar tried to be serious and play along with the gang, but when he looked over at me it was more than he could take. He let go and laughed out loud. I guess my failure to appreciate their humor had my face looking as stern as a constipated preacher, although, at that point I began to feel that we weren't in any real danger. Each one of them looked like they would slit their own mother's throat for a cold beer, but in my gut I didn't feel that they intended to do us any harm.

Scar finally got the laugh out of his system. "Hey kid, come over here. I want to ask you a serious question," he said, sucking hard to restart the cigar that had almost extinguished during his fit of laughter. I was very leery. I only moved a couple of little shuffles in his direction.

"Go on," Miss Cherry said. She gave me a little push. "He ain't gonna hurt you none."

Reluctantly, I eased myself over next to him. I felt as though I were about to lay my head in a guillotine. Luke, no longer my shadow, opted to stay by Miss Cherry. She promptly put her arm over his shoulders.

"Yes, sir?" I said, deciding it couldn't hurt to be respectful. I could tell that he liked being called sir, so I said it again. "Yes, sir?"

"That's one hell of a drop down there—in the dark." He gulped for dramatic effect and resumed looking down the pitch-black slope. "No telling what you might run into." He gave me an admiring glance and smiled. Then, quietly so the others couldn't hear, he asked, "Do you really think you can run The Crippler in the dark?"

"If I can't, nobody can. I'm the King."

He smiled again and with his eyes growing big, he said melodramatically, "You could get hurt real bad. Maybe even kilt." I giggled when he said *kilt*. He sounded like Fess Parker speaking as Davy Crockett. "Or even worse, you could get paralyzed," he added, almost whispering. Then in an explosive change of mood he yelled, making me jump so I darn near went down the hill right then. "Hey, Cherry! What's that called what happened to Moose Bachman when he crashed his Hog up on the Angeles Crest last summer? Para-something?"

"Paraplegic, baby," Miss Cherry answered.

Scar shook his head gravely. "Poor Moose, he can't get it up no more. He's stuck with a limp lizard. No more sugar for Moose." He sighed and his face shifted to a pained expression that made the ghastly gash fold in a zigzag across his cheek. Curiously, now I felt good. Mr. Scar was talking to me as if I were one of his gang members and not just a rambunctious, eight-year-old daredevil with many moons to live before I could begin to appreciate the significance of sugar. "I'd rather be dead," he abruptly volunteered, shaking his head some more.

His barefaced language had caught me a little off guard, but I noticed that Miss Cherry didn't seem to mind it. As a denizen of the wrong side of the tracks, I was familiar with most of the slang terms for sex by then. And I had also learned better than to make such utterances in the presence of a grown woman. A year earlier, Lucinda overheard me saying the "F" word, and being a woman inclined to apply proverbial remedies, I experienced first hand how long it takes to get the flavor of soap (made for external use only) out of one's mouth.

Bravely, I mentioned, "I don't know too much about—sugar, sir."

Scar choked on a puff of cigar smoke and laughed heartily. He playfully slugged my shoulder. "No, I don't guess you do, kid. Might not be too long, though. I wasn't much older than you the first time I dipped my willy."

I kinda got the drift of that one. "Is that a euphemism?" I countered, slinging him one of the few big words I knew. I tapped him back on the shoulder.

"Huh?" he grunted. "Hey Cherry!" He barked right in my face again. "What's a euphemism?" I didn't jump quite so much that time.

"An indirect way of saying something. To dip your willy is a euphemism meaning to have sex, darling." Her matter-of-fact answer came as natural as if she were commenting on the weather. She was beautiful, fragrant, and clean. But she definitely had a biker woman's mouth. I was shocked to hear a woman say the word sex in mixed company; after all, it was 1958, the Eisenhower years, the permissive '60s still a century away, and I was only eight years old. She definitely seemed to have a termagant's mouth, a term Lucinda used for those rough-and-tumble female skaters in the Roller Derby. Still, she struck me as being much too much of a lady to be hanging around with a motorcycle gang.

"Oh, OK," Scar mumbled, slowly absorbing the information. I had a sense then that Scar's intelligence was limited. Boy, was I wrong.

One of the bikers yelled from the back of the pack. "Hey, Scar! Cops are coming!"

Everybody turned to look.

In the dark-filled distance, a red, flashing light slowly crawled along a rutted firebreak that ran up the knobby, north side of Billy Goat Hill. Several of the bikers grumbled their displeasure over the impending visit with LA's men in blue, a few laughed; however, none made any effort to leave. My gut seemed to be telling me this was not a good sign. Scar showed no reaction at all, which, in itself, was a disturbing reaction. He turned his powerful gaze back on me. "You guys better make yourselves scarce. The cops wouldn't take kindly to finding you two out here with us, especially in the middle of the night like this." He nudged me to get moving.

I wasn't interested in the cops finding us out there period. Our nocturnal habits had thus far gone undetected by our most immediate form of authority, namely Lucinda Parker. If she ever found out we were sneaking out at night, there would be some serious hell to pay.

There was a small outcropping of rock about thirty feet down from the top of The Crippler, a nook custom made for hiding two young boys. I kicked the cardboard canoe over the edge and called Luke to follow me. Scar watched us as we slid on our backsides down to the rocks where we promptly secreted ourselves behind a jagged boulder. He patted his lips with a callused, heavily knuckled forefinger signaling us to keep quiet. I waved to acknowledge the universal sign of silence and lowered my head down like an Indian brave preparing to ambush a paleface cavalry scout. Luke bobbed up like a curious prairie dog sniffing the wind. I had to forcibly pull him down behind the rock with me. He loved the flashing lights.

That moment, a mere wink in time, forever burns inside my mind. A four-dimensional fantasia, crystal clear in every detail—the smell of the weeds, the gritty dust in my mouth, the break in the low hanging clouds directly overhead, and the shattering, red bursts of the police cruiser's emergency flashers igniting across Scar's muscular torso—jumps out live, as fresh in my senses as if it had happened just last night.

A black-and-white 1956 Ford pulled to a dusty stop among the enclave of two-wheeled rebels. From my vantage point, I could just see over the top of the rise above me and observe the upper bodies of the bikers and the top half of the police car. By now the crickets had returned, adding a dramatic, whirring meter to the scene. The air seemed hot, charged with electricity, as if the potential for violence was packing the oxygen molecules tighter and tighter, creating the heat of friction. The current skittered over my dampened skin giving me chills. My breath squeezed down into shallow rapid pants and my heart drummed loud in my ears, a frenzied drum, a drum of war. God, I was scared, but there was a sensation of pleasure, too. A libertine, spectator's grin beamed forth, revealing my jangled emotions. *Man oh man*, I thought, *this is better than a John Wayne double feature at a drive-in theater.* Even popcorn, bon-bons and a ten cent Butterfinger wouldn't have made it any better.

Everything stood still for what seemed like a very long time, as though the forces of nature had converged on this historic site to impose a pax, to hold the fiasco back, to force a reconsideration before untold tragedy laid waste to this no man's land. The group trance held, until two uniformed officers abruptly got out of the patrol car. They did not look happy, particularly the one that walked over to Miss Cherry. His rigid comportment and icy stare warned of vested anger aching for release.

"Lieutenant Theodore Kowalski. How nice to see you," Miss Cherry spewed. Her sarcasm was venomous. She defiantly threw her head back, tossing her long blond hair over her shoulders like a high-strung filly whipping its tail. Some of the bikers chuckled in a way that was clearly intended to needle the cops.

Scar had stayed at the top of The Crippler directly above where Luke and I remained cowering in the dark. I hoped he was standing guard to make sure nobody hurt us. Glancing nervously from the center of the action, to Scar, and back, I was very thankful he had chosen to stay close by. Suddenly, Lieutenant Kowalski grabbed Miss Cherry by the arm and roughly towed her over near where Scar was standing. I had to duck down quickly. For a second I feared the cop had seen me, but he was blinded by his anger, oblivious to everything except Miss Cherry and now Scar who stood unperturbed with his arms casually folded across his chest. The back of my neck bristled with anger, my cheeks hot. I did not like the cop one darn bit.

"How's it going, Kowalski?" Scar inquired dispassionately, outwardly not offended in the slightest by the cop's rough treatment of his girlfriend. I was dead certain he was ready to kill, though.

Miss Cherry screamed, "Let go of me, you asshole!" She struggled for a moment and managed to break free of the cop's humiliating grip. I was surprised she didn't move away. Instead she got right in his face and swore at him, something long and filthy that made me blanch, and then she plastered him with a haughty, defiant glare.

The other cop, a baby faced rookie, had stayed by the open door of the squad car, motor idling, occasional unintelligible squawks blaring out from the police radio. Everything about him—uniform, shoes, leather, even his haircut—looked new, clean cut, in a fresh out of the academy textbook sort of way. At that moment, however, he appeared as nervous as a puny mouse surrounded by a pride of pugnacious alley cats. My sense was that he was a nice young man, but clearly out of his element. His stance was tentative, his collegial face gaunt with fear, as if he were struggling to find the poise that had so recently been drilled into him. His eyes blinked and twitched as they darted around the group of bikers, all of whom remained steadfast upon their imposing chrome mounts. One of the bikers hawked up a wad of phlegm and deliberately spat it onto the hood of the police car.

I imagined the rookie cop cursing himself for not calling for backup when they first spotted the motorcycle gang. Even from the distance, I could see rivulets of sweat trickling down his forehead as he repeatedly brushed his arm against his side, double-triple-quadruple checking that his service revolver was where it was supposed to be. He reminded me of Mac during thunder storms, desperately in need of something to crawl under.

Lieutenant Kowalski ignored Miss Cherry's invective. He reeled around and faced down Scar. I could see the rage on his face, his malignant profile throbbing crimson with each slapping pass of the whirling emergency beacon. His eyes were death daggers, razor sharp with malice, eminently threatening. Furious, on the brink of detonation, he clenched his fists and stepped within punching distance. Scar just stood there twiddling like a bored third cousin at a family reunion. In vivid contrast to Lieutenant Kowalski's explosive manner, Scar was completely cool, apparently not worried in the slightest by the policeman's menacing approach. Like the poisonous spit of a viper, saliva sprayed from the irate cop's mouth as he railed at Scar. "I told you before, scumbag! I don't want my sister hanging around with the fucking likes of you!"

A chilly silence closed in.

Scar didn't move a muscle. Slowly, impalpably at first, his face gradually blossomed into a tantalizing smirk. And when he did finally speak, he spoke forthrightly and with volume exceedingly sufficient for all to hear, "Cherry does what she pleases...and she does *it* very well." The smirk ripened into an all-knowing grin that was so specific even I resented his salacious inference.

Lieutenant Kowalski's face flashed a gangrenous purple. He lunged at Scar. Miss Cherry screamed. Several of the bikers dismounted in blurs of motion, instantly ready for action. With the speed of a mongoose anticipating a cobra's strike, Scar shifted his weight and effortlessly pinned Kowalski's left arm behind his back. I bit down hard on my lip to squelch a cheer that nearly burst from my mouth. I tasted blood, and was transformed into one of the townsmen delirious with the thrill of violence.

Lieutenant Kowalski's look of shock turned into a painful grimace as Scar forced his arm farther north than it was designed to go.

A heartbeat passed.

The young cop panicked. He reached for his gun, then instantly checked himself when he saw that two sawed-off shotguns were already set to blast him in half.

"Funny thing about fear," Scar would later say. "It seizes you like some kind of two-part poison. A frigid-hot fever makes you shiver and sweat, and makes your brain skip like a broken record stuck between conflicting impulses to hide or jettison all cargo and flee."

Now I was squeezing Luke's leg, making him whimper. Realizing I was hurting him, I relaxed my quivering hand and fought back the urge to jettison the contents of my stomach. I wanted to run. I did not want to witness the cataclysmic, no-win conclusion of the big-league conflict rising only a few yards from where I hid shivering in the dark. But the tears welling up in Luke's little frightened eyes, and my keen awareness of the ominous hazards of the only escape route possible, forced me to hunker down, close my eyes, and wish that we were back home safe and sound in our cozy little beds.

Then abruptly, miraculously, the entire temper changed. It was as if we had been watching a Boris Karloff horror classic and, in the blink of an eye, Bugs Bunny appeared and stuck carrots into both barrels of Elmer Fudd's shotgun. Some creative film splicing had thrown us into another dimension, a sudden reversal in the action where absolutely nothing made any sense whatsoever.

Scar was laughing. Lieutenant Kowalski was laughing. Miss Cherry was laughing. Everyone was laughing except the rookie cop, Luke and me. The next thing I knew, Luke and I were standing at the top of The Crippler, and from the look of incredulity on Lieutenant Kowalski's face, we must have looked like matching pint-sized apparitions of the night materializing out of thin air.

"What the hell!" Kowalski blurted. He was not at all pleased that two young boys had just witnessed the hoax he had masterminded and that they all had perpetrated on the unsuspecting rookie cop.

I was dumbstruck, but Luke seemed to warm to the festivities. Somehow he already realized that the whole thing had been a joke.

"Meet the Parker brothers," Miss Cherry said. "That's Luke there with the Dodger cap, and next to him is Wade, a.k.a. The King of Billy Goat Hill."

"Hell fire! Damn it all Cavendish! These boys are gonna have to forget all about what they saw up here tonight," Kowalski grumbled, shaking his head in serious dismay.

Scar stepped over by me. "Don't worry, Ted," he said. "The Parker brothers are stand up guys. Ain't that right boys?"

"Yes sir," I replied, completely bewildered but certain that "yes" was the only reasonable response.

Lieutenant Kowalski walked back to the patrol car, slapping a few high fives with the bikers in his path. He got in behind the wheel, killed the flashing light overhead and testily looked at the nerve wracked rookie who now sat slumped down in the passenger seat.

"In case you were missing them, here's your bullets rook," Lieutenant Kowalski said. "Let's go find some coffee and talk about what we learned tonight."

Lieutenant Kowalski turned the patrol car around as the make-believe bikers slapped its hood and fenders to further taunt the chagrined young rookie, who had slipped even farther down in his seat. The cruiser slowly rocked back down the same rutted slope it had come up earlier. I watched it slither off into the darkness and struggled to accept that the whole thing had been a put-on to teach the young cop a lesson. But something about that Lieutenant Kowalski didn't sit right with me. His hatred had been too real. It left me shivering inside.

Miss Cherry sidled over and scooped Luke up in her arms. I rarely felt jealous of Luke, but at that moment I did. I wanted her to pick me up, too. Then Scar put his arm around my shoulder. "You OK, kid?" he furtively asked.

"Yes, sir." I did my best to keep a stiff upper lip, but he could tell I was upset.

Miss Cherry carried Luke over by the other bikers. One of them gave him a fist full of licorice. They included him in the celebration that had ensued after Lieutenant Kowalski drove away with his under-the-weather partner in tow.

A few minutes passed allowing my feelings to settle and my

thoughts to kindle. Scar stood by my side as I gazed listlessly at the distant twinkles of downtown Los Angeles, thinking, wondering what in the heck had happened. It was all too strange. Cops dressed up as bikers? And what they had done to that poor young officer? I thought it was out-and-out cruel.

As we stood there together, not talking, sharing the closeness of the dark, I began to feel a worrisome affinity for Scar. I felt as though I had known him before that night. Not as a biker though, or not even as a person. More like a spirit. A friend from a past life. The sense of familiarity made me feel both safe and unsettled. We were from different worlds. Maybe even different galaxies. No question about that. Yet, something about him, something mysterious, spoke to me in a way that defied explanation. Little did I know, the linkage that would begin that night would become the benchmark relationship in my life.

As I looked up into his face, into his dark, brooding eyes, he would reveal no hint of the mystery that would follow me far into the abysmal future. I wish I could have seen a clue. I would have done many things differently, for myself and for Scar, as well as the others. But that night I couldn't tell what he might do from one minute to the next, much less envision the profound impact he would have on my entire development. He was a man of many surprises, the next of which he was just then about to reveal. Boris Karloff couldn't have done it better.

"Hey, Wade, watch this," he said, and then deftly peeled the fake scar off of his face.

"Whoa!" I choked, backing away in astonishment.

He playfully laughed, at himself more than me, as stringy strips of ductile latex stretched and then snapped free of his forehead, nose and cheeks. A large part of the scar peeled away in one piece and he handed it to me. I accepted it reluctantly. I still have it. To this day it's in an airtight vial which I keep in a safe deposit box along with my stocks, bonds and other precious possessions. The initial shock had passed and I began to laugh which pleased him and made him laugh even more. He continued to pick the remaining pieces of theatrical adhesive from his face and then off came the beard. A good-looking face emerged. From a wild and woolly caterpillar to handsome butterfly in a matter of seconds.

"Who are you, really?" I inquired of the sorcerer, as I put the piece of rubber scar in my pocket.

"Can you keep a secret?"

"Scouts honor." I placed my hand over my heart.

He reached behind to his back pocket and pulled out a black leather wallet which he promptly flipped open to reveal a badge. There was just enough light to make out: *Sergeant, Los Angeles Police.* "I'm Sergeant Lyle Cavendish, Organized Crime Investigation Unit, Los Angeles Police Department."

A shocked "Oh," was all that I could muster. At that point I didn't know what to believe. But Scar, or rather Lyle, was indeed a policeman, as was everyone else on Billy Goat Hill that night. Except Luke and me.

Sergeant Lyle Cavendish went on to explain that what Luke and I had observed was called a hazing, part of the training ritual for rookie police officers. He was honest with me and said that the Police Department did not officially approve of hazing and that they could get in trouble for doing it. He said it was an old tradition that had been in practice for many years. He said he was hazed when he was a rookie.

"Do you understand, Wade?"

"Yes, sir. Luke and I won't tell anybody." I knew I wouldn't say anything, but whether Luke could keep his trap shut was something else. I had my doubts about that.

Dawn lay shimmering on the dewy grass when Luke and I climbed back through our bedroom window. Mac, stretched out on the floor between our beds, ignored us as we stripped down and slipped back under the sheets. I pulled up my blanket and listened to the crickets fade in inverse proportion to the sunlight that slowly peeked into the room. My mind was still tingling, still numb, quarreling over whether or not any of it had been real. I had never before returned from a dream with a piece of latex scar in my hand, though. It was real. It happened. Jeez Louise!

Luke's Dodger cap hung from the bedpost above his head. He was already snoring softly with a secure smile on his face, the happy hot dog tucked back in its bun. I imagined he was dreaming that Miss Cherry still had him tucked tight to her ample bosom.

"You should have come with us, Mac," I whispered. "This time it was great." Mac thumped his tail once and opened a tolerant eye.

"Come here," I called softly. He obediently jumped up on my bed and plopped his head next to mine on the pillow. We lay there nose to nose. "I'm gonna be a motorcycle cop when I grow up, Mac." He sighed, and licked my chin. I held out the piece of latex scar and he gave it a series of thorough sniffs, his wagging tail gently rocking the bed with somnolent motion. I closed my eyes. Soon I was a great king sailing up and down *The Crippler* on a cardboard magic carpet, the beautiful Miss Cherry, the object of my eight-year-old's crush, my queen, riding behind me with her arms wrapped tightly about my waist.

Two years would pass before I would see her again, and if not for that wonderful dream replaying now and then, I'm certain I would not have survived the storm looming just over the horizon. I still have that dream once in a blue moon.

three

"Ah pooh!" Luke grumbled. "They should have done better. I expected them to at least win the pennant."

We were sitting cross-legged on top of a towering, weather-beaten promontory known as Eagle Rock. Luke and I often climbed up there to chew the cud on issues of family, school, neighborhood and, of course, our beloved Dodgers. Unfortunately for me, the serenity of this high-up place was often interrupted by my concern for Luke's safety. More than once he had forgotten where we were and nearly slipped over the edge.

Mac sat a cautious ten feet or so behind us. He had followed us up the rock once when he was just a pup and had nearly fallen. Ever since that scare he never went near the edge. He sat on his haunches content to watch us from his position of safety, his moist, black nose pointing and sniffing incessantly toward the cloudless sky.

The October wind swirled, stirring up dust and leaves on the valley floor below us. A newspaper lying in the gutter down on Figueroa Boulevard flapped in the wind. I watched it finally come apart, the pages streaming across the pavement like darting little phantoms playing tag with the traffic that zoomed by in both directions. The vision was pleasant, hypnotic. It made me feel drowsy.

Eagle Rock was a notable landmark. It jutted dramatically from the side of a hill above the northeast corner of Colorado and Figueroa Boulevards. It was said to have been a sacred place of Indian worship.

Its name derived from a curious eagle-shaped shadow that appeared at midday on the western face of the rock and gradually disappeared as the sun arced slowly overhead. Like the Indians before us, we were fascinated with Eagle Rock. We hiked up to its top as often as we could get away with it. It was a dangerous trek and kids had been known to take a plunge now and then. Fly like eagles they did not. Their landings were always fatal.

The potential for danger added to the mystical allure of Eagle Rock. No doubt, if the rock had been a man made object it would have been declared an "attractive nuisance" and been torn down long ago.

"Don't worry, Luke," I said. "Mr. Alston will see to it they do better next year."

I had been infected with Brooklyn optimism since the day my team, the Los Angeles Dodgers, had arrived. Luke didn't share my positive outlook. He grumbled some more as I lay myself back on the hard surface and delighted in the glorious Dodger blue sky. My legs in a lotus pretzel, I clasped my fingers behind my head and stretched out my spine to get comfortable, just like Mac often did. Mac looked at me looking up, licked his nose with a long pink slosh and hooked his snout skyward again. He didn't mind sharing the Dodger welkin with me.

Luke muttered begrudgingly, "Yeah, Walter Alston is a good manager..." His wistful gaze converged on the same stream of newspapers I had been watching. "...but don't you wish he'd get mad at those dern umpires sometimes?"

"Nah," I said, grabbing the opportunity to get in a dig. "I'm glad he's not a hothead like you."

Luke grinned, acknowledging he had a temper.

We sat not talking for a while, pretending we were Indians paying respect to the holy rock of the great and wise eagle. Soon Luke got bored. He started prying off pieces of weathered granite with his pee wee pocket knife and tossing them over the edge.

As was happening often since our encounter with Sergeant Cavendish and Miss Cherry, I began to think about that night on Billy Goat Hill. Many times I thought about trying to contact them. I didn't have the confidence to do such a thing and let myself off the hook by reasoning that they probably wouldn't remember me anyway. Still, I thought of them nearly every day. They had both touched me. I wanted more of the Sergeant's strength and camaraderie. And Miss

Cherry's sympathy and tenderness had flavored my dreams ever since. Whenever I felt sad I thought of them and that crazy, unbelievable night. I had felt everything except sadness that night.

Mac watched with curious interest as Luke picked and pried with the knife. He timidly shuffled a couple of inches closer to Luke, clicking and scraping his nails on the brittle rock, coming only so close to the edge, then promptly back-pedalled to his original position.

Luke tossed another piece of stone and counted out loud, "One-thousand...two-thousand..." until the rock hit the ground below. Sometimes the rocks would make a thud and sometimes the impact sounded more like a ping. We'd try to guess which noise each piece of rock would make, inevitably arguing over whether it was a thud or a ping. I shut my eyes and listened to the soothing, repetitive measure of Luke's voice as he timed each stone's descent. "One thousand...two thousand..." My inner voice warned that this was absolutely not a good place to take a nap. I kept my eyes closed anyway and pictured the beautiful Miss Cherry.

Luke had been pinging and thudding for some time, when all of the sudden his brilliant, crimson crown came under attack. He had carelessly forgotten to put on his Dodger cap, and like blood-thirsty Zero's diving on Pearl Harbor, a pair of mockingbirds made a daring high-speed pass at his delectable, bright-red hair. They came from behind to avoid detection, swinging low at a cowardly, ignoble angle, thus preventing poor Luke from initiating evasive action. I heard the sinister *whoosh!* of their slicked back wings a fraction of a second before they screeched and pecked.

Luke yowled like a scalded dog and instantly started slapping his arms wildly over his head. Caught in a whirlwind of flapping feathers, squawking beaks and clutching claws, he looked like an Indian medicine man gone mad. It was as if the great, winged spirit of Eagle Rock had been conjured forth to rid the ancient sanctuary of the impious palefaces whose vulgar presence was a blasphemous desecration of that hallowed place. The birds squawked furiously as they swooped and dove, clawing and pecking at Luke's head. They were not dissuaded by the flailing arms and terrified yelps coming from the boy below the enticing red hair. Nor were they bothered by the half-breed Doberman that barked and growled but came no closer.

"Help! Ahgh! Help me!" Luke screamed.

I was momentarily stunned and didn't know whether to laugh or scream myself. Then I saw a spot of blood. It began to trickle down from the hairline on the left side of Luke's forehead. Suddenly I realized the birds could hurt him badly if they hit his eyes. Luke was in a total panic and had quickly become hysterical. Tears were streaming down his cheeks mixing with the blood that now ran all the way down to his chin. The birds weren't letting up at all. Mac was all snarls and fangs, but didn't dare come any closer to the edge. I quickly looked around the barren rock for something to use as a weapon, knowing there wasn't a twig to be found. Luke was completely out of control, spinning, ducking, screaming and slipping dangerously close to the point of no return. I realized the birds were no longer the most immediate threat...Luke was about to go over the ledge. I dove on my belly and grabbed Luke's pant leg just as his feet slipped out from under him. He was so frightened by the birds, I don't think he even realized he was falling. I got both of my hands around his left ankle and hung on. My heart was a locomotive chugging against an impossible load. Gorged with adrenaline, I fought not to let go or be pulled to certain death. I looked from side to side, frantic, desperate for something, anything to grab onto. Nothing. Nausea, vicious as a cross-cut saw, slashed at my gut.

I weighed maybe ten pounds more than Luke, just enough to keep gravity and friction in equilibrium. I laid on my stomach, the toes of my sneakers anchoring against the gritty slope, and tried to think. "Hold still, Luke!" I grunted. "I won't let you fall!"

Luke's reply was barely audible—faint, wheezie whimpers of dread. His leg trembled within my grasp, but he stiffened his body, as I had ordered, and didn't squirm.

The seriousness of the situation hit me with a blast of fear as the unconquerable forces of gravity began to overcome the lesser forces of friction. Ever so slowly, we began to slide forward, like hunks of helpless iron summoned by a giant, evil magnet. At that moment, I thought of Reverend Bonner, the pastor of the church we once upon a time regularly attended. I tore through my memory searching for the Sunday school lessons that had gone in one ear and out the other. Fractions of both testaments flared and faded as a refrain of *Onward Christian Soldiers Marching Off To War* rattled my skull. To hell with it—I started to pray: Dear God and Jesus in heaven, please call off your birds. I'm sorry for sticking my gum in the hymnal book and

I'm sorry for letting Gooey take the blame for putting the green dye marker in the Highland Park public pool last summer and I'm definitely sorry for telling our next-door neighbor Carl that eating Rye bread means you are a communist.

Ever since that moment of revelation, I have, on occasion, resorted to prayer and blanket confessions, because at that precise instant we stopped sliding and Mac started tugging on my pant leg. The birds were suddenly gone, too. I was a believer. Divine intervention had clearly saved our lives.

I clamped my hands around Luke's ankles, like Popeye would after a big gulp of spinach, and with Mac's help pulling and tugging at my trousers, I began to push backward with my elbows. In my mind, I became a scared but heroic soldier crawling under strafing machine-gun fire to rescue a wounded buddy, except I was crawling uphill and backwards. Connected by arms and legs, we undulated caterpillar style making slow, painful but steady progress. My long sleeves did little to pad my elbows and after three or four thrusts of bony skin against rasp-sharp granite, I saw red smudges slowly pass in front of me and disappear under Luke's shaking legs. I felt no pain. Instead, I realized only dry-mouthed fear and a surging desperation to survive. "Pull, Mac—*Pull-l-l-l!* " I screamed into the rock grinding against my sweaty face. "PULL! PULL! PULL!"

Then I felt something shaking me, something more than Mac pulling at my trousers.

"Wake up, Wade! Wake up!"
"What?"
Luke shouted, "Wake up ya big donkey!"
"Cri-ma-nee sakes alive," I spluttered, squinting as I cracked my eyes open. I sat up in amazement expecting to see blood all over Luke's face. No blood? Not even a tiny scratch. Nothing but freckles.
"What's the matter with you, Wade?"
"God-all-mighty...was I dreamin'?" I winced as a drop of salty sweat stung my left eye.
"I guess so. You started yelling something about a pool," Luke said, concern showing on his face.
"It was *pull*," I muttered, feeling my elbows for shredded skin. "Dang." I rubbed my eyes. "Are you OK, Luke?"
"Shoot, yeah. But I think we might be in a little trouble."

"Huh?"

Luke's eyes narrowed as he nodded in the direction behind me. Mac started to growl, real low, like he always did when something wasn't right.

four

I looked over my shoulder and immediately spotted a policeman clambering up the back side of Eagle Rock. "Uh oh," I murmured under my breath. There was no place to hide and no way to escape.

"We're busted," Luke said, stating the obvious.

The cop quickly scrambled up to the top of the rock. He said nothing. Standing fifty feet away, he paused to catch his breath. We said nothing in return. He began peeling off his black leather gloves. Then he removed his aviator style sunglasses, the kind motorcycle cops wear, and hung them from the breast pocket of his black leather jacket. There was an efficiency, an elegance about him. No wasted motion. A correctness.

Luke and I stood still, watching like passive creatures relying on highly evolved camouflage to fool an approaching predator. But we were as naked and exposed as baby turtles in the sand at low tide. The cop grinned, his eyes holding steady, unblinking, as he moved toward us. Something seemed queer for a moment and then I recognized him. It was the Sergeant—Lyle Cavendish. I was thrown off at first by how different he looked from that night on Billy Goat Hill. His smile gave him away. When he finally spoke it was the same voice, just softer and more refined than the raspy-throated speech of Scar. He kept his eyes trained on Mac. "I bet your folks don't know you're up here." Mac returned the Sergeant's stare, but had quit growling. I wasn't quite sure what he would do. Slowly, he folded his ears back and tucked his tail between his legs, as if the Doberman part of him were ashamed of his uncropped-unbobbed appearance. Not afraid, more submissive, he glissaded over and charily stretched to sniff at the Sergeant's boots.

I answered. "Yes, sir. That's right. They sure don't know we're up here."

It didn't take Luke long to spout off. "Our father's a drunkard. He don't care diddly what we do. But Lucinda would skin us good, if she knew." He flashed a punctuating grin. I winced with embarrassment.

"You guys know who I am?" he asked, casually looking down at Mac who had just plopped his rump down on the toe of one of his boots. Mac looked up and accepted a caress from one of the Sergeant's leather smelling hands. This was a curious thing as Mac rarely took to strangers. Then I remembered the piece of latex scar I'd let him sniff. It had been six months but Mac was smart enough to remember that scent and conclude the Sergeant was OK.

"No, sir," I lied, remembering that we were supposed to forget that we had witnessed the hazing of the rookie cop. Under the circumstances I thought it was best to play dumb.

Luke on the other hand was true to form. "Sergeant Scar," he said with biblical sincerity.

The Sergeant was momentarily taken aback, then blurted out a healthy chortle. Luke reacted with a squeaky, nervous laugh which he cut short when he caught the stern set of my face. He complied with the look I gave him, but it was clear that he didn't quite get it.

"You look different," I said.

"Yep. This is what I normally look like. And, by the way, I'm glad you remembered you weren't supposed to remember." He gave me a solemn wink.

I warmed to the kudos and flashed a lofty smile at Luke, which sailed by him without notice. He still didn't get that we were supposed to have forgotten all about the hazing we had witnessed. *Patience.*

Mac got up and padded over to the only piece of green on the top of Eagle Rock, a scrubby little shrub rooted in a crack in the granite. He gave it a procedural sniff and then lifted his right hind leg. Mac was a right legged pisser. Always the right leg, which made for a lot of U-turns in his life.

"Dern dog," Luke said. He was just feeling superior. He and I had used that bush many times.

"How come you think your dad doesn't care about you coming up here?" He posed the question directly to Luke.

"Earl? Why he's nothin' but a drunkard. He's never around much anyway."

Fine way for a boy to speak about his father. I interjected, "Earl is a traveling salesman."

"Yeah? So was my old man. What's he sell?"

"You know all the supplies they sell at truck stops?"

"Not really. Like what?"

"Oh, you know—trinkets, gadgets, books, shaving kits, stuff truckers need when they're on the road."

"Oh. Well, then I can understand why he'd be gone so much," the Sergeant agreed.

"He sells the rubbers they put in those machines in the bathrooms, too," Luke added, matter of factly.

I was shocked. How did he know about rubbers? I only had a vague idea about them myself.

"Yeah, I guess truckers need those, too," the Sergeant said. He chuckled out of the side of his mouth as he scanned the valley below.

Luke and I just stood there looking at him, waiting for the lecture we were sure was to come. Mac finished relieving himself and then did one of those vigorous stretch-strut-scrape-the-ground-with-the-feet maneuvers that dogs like to do afterward. His nails scratched and clicked loudly on the hard surface which seemed to annoy him—no soft dirt or grass to fling in the air.

"Dern dog," Luke said.

I grew tired of waiting for the lecture. "Are you mad at us for coming up here?"

"No. But I am worried. This can be a very dangerous place to play. A few kids have fallen from here."

"Did they die?" Luke asked.

"No one has ever survived a fall from Eagle Rock, that I know of. I remember a kid named Jakey Blume." He looked away. "He fell to his death going on thirty years ago."

"Did you know him?" I asked.

Sergeant Cavendish suddenly looked very sad. "Yes. In fact, he was my best friend."

"How did he fall?" Luke asked, now very interested.

The Sergeant looked away and gazed far off in the distance toward downtown Los Angeles. He didn't say anything for a long while, as if he were trying to remember exactly what had happened all those years ago. Finally, he sat down on the rock as though thinking about it had made him weary. Mac came over and nudged the Sergeant's shoulder with his nose. He wanted to hear the story, too. Luke and I sat down, one on each side of the Sergeant, while Mac curled up a few feet behind us where he felt safe back from the ledge.

"It's been years since I thought about Jakey Blume. You boys would have liked him. He was a good guy. He was funny, too. A real character." The Sergeant smiled, cheering himself. "We met in first grade at Garvanza Elementary School."

"Hey, that's where me and Wade go to school," Luke said, surprised that a grown man would have gone to his school.

"Yeah, I know. I happen to know both of your teachers."

Hearing that made me feel a little nervous. "So what about your friend Jakey?" I asked, and instantly the mention of his friend's name made him look sad again.

"Jakey liked to pull crazy stunts. Like I said, he was a real character. You didn't dare dare him to do anything, because, by golly—he would do it. He was a little crazy I guess." *Poco Loco, like me,* I thought. "But I sure liked to hang around with him. He wasn't boring to be with.

"I remember one time we had a May Day festival at our school, and..."

"We have those, too," Luke interrupted.

I leaned forward, caught his eye, and gave him the shut up look.

"...Jakey had secretly dressed himself up in the image of our Principal, Mrs. Hackworth." The Sergeant grinned and then added, "Giant gazzangas and all."

Luke didn't get it, then did get it when the Sergeant positioned his hands, arthritic-like fingers curled in front of his chest, to illustrate his point.

"Hundreds of parents were bunched up in herds around the edge of the schoolyard. When it was time, one of the teachers started playing marching music real loud on one of those great big Victrola machines that we used to have in the old days." The Sergeant could see that we didn't know what a Victrola was. "Anyway, first the kindergarten class came marching out in costumes they had made themselves for the special parade."

Luke nodded and grinned having done the same thing himself.

"They marched around the yard, smiling and waving, sometimes yelling out to a parent or relative in the crowd. Then the first graders came out with long paper streamers, every color you could imagine waving and floating in the wind. Next came the third grade, fourth grade, and so on," the Sergeant laughed, "none keeping any better step to the music than the younger kids in front of them. They made a big circle around the schoolyard and then were lined up by their teachers and told to sit down on the black-top in front of the audience." Luke, a new veteran of the May Day Festival tradition, kept nodding as the Sergeant painted the scene. "In the middle of the yard there was a small wooden platform where..."

Luke interrupted, "...the Principal stands," he said proudly.

"Yes." The Sergeant grinned and buffed his knuckles on the top of Luke's head. "She was smiling generously and nodding encouragement to the students as they slowly circled around her. Finally, the sixth graders made up the caboose. They were showing off, marching real cool, like they were in the army or somethin'."

Luke blew out some air in disgust. "Those dern sixth graders always think they're big shots." I just listened intently while the Sergeant's charismatic voice worked me over like the expert hands of a masseuse.

"Then," he chuckled, "when the Principal wasn't lookin', out came Jakey, smiling and waving to the crowd like a movie star. I was sittin' with my third grade class in a fluffy sea of red, white and blue pom-poms. I wasn't too thrilled to be carryin' pom-poms around like that, you know, in front of people and all." I nodded, knowing the feeling exactly. "Anyway, Jakey was all dressed up to look just like our beloved Principal. He was somethin' else all right, complete with her peculiar pigeon-toed waddle, blue tinted hair and her goofy, condescending smile. At first, most of the people over on my side of the schoolyard didn't see him. But it didn't take long for the laughter to start. Pretty soon, most of the people had spotted him struttin' along right behind the last sixth grade class. That is, everyone except Mrs. Hackworth.

"It was priceless. Jakey was a great actor—the specific walk, the hair, the highfalutin smile, and, of course, the trade-mark gazzangas. Well, let's just say it was obvious who he was lampooning."

Luke interrupted, "What's lambdoonie mean?"

"Lam-poon-ing," the Sergeant repeated. "It means to make fun of."

Luke grinned. "Thought so."

The Sergeant nudged Luke in the ribs and continued. "Mrs. Hackworth still had not turned around, but she was beginning to get this real confused look on her face, not understanding why so many people were laughing. Jakey was really getting into it, and so was the crowd. He started walkin' kinda crazy-like, pigeon-toed, except real exaggerated. You know, kinda like Jerry Lewis?"

"Yeah. That Jerry Lewis is really cool—he cracks me up!" Luke enthusiastically agreed.

Mac was sitting up now, listening in, his head cocked to one side.

The Sergeant shook his head slightly, nostalgia drifting in his eyes. "Jakey Blume was the type of kid that just didn't know when to quit." I thought of Gooey—his calling my bluff about riding The Crippler at night. "He started to lose control of his performance. You might say, he was overcome by the awesome forces of femininity." Luke and I exchanged blank looks. "The gazzangas kinda took off on him—kinda swinging and swayin'—get the picture?" We did, and we grinned accordingly.

The Sergeant's mood had gone from sad to happy as he recalled and related the story to us. He was throwing around a few big words to describe the scene. None-the-less I had managed to form a clear image of this Jakey Blume character making a total spectacle of himself. And judging from the way Luke was laughing, he'd accurately sized up the situation, too. He was giggling at about mach two but managed to say, "I don't think the Principal liked it much when she finally turned around and saw your friend, Jakey, making fun of her like that."

"What happened?" I queried.

"Well, you're not going to believe it." The Sergeant looked up at the sky, big-eyed, as if he still couldn't believe what ever it was that had happened.

"What?" I urged.

"Tell us!" Luke demanded.

Woof! Mac barked, making us all jump and then start laughing again.

"Dern dog. He thinks he knows what you're talking about," Luke said.

I wanted to hear the rest. "Come on. Please finish the story.

What happened?" I was beginning to get a little irritated.

"Be patient," Luke said. Then mimicking one of my own little catch phrases, he added, "Duke Snider waits for his pitch you know!" Luke loved to aggravate me by repeating my material back to me.

"Oh crimanee! Would you *please* hush." I gave him my best deluxe-evil-eye-glare and he stuck his tongue out at me. The Sergeant had been ignoring us. That sad look had taken him over again. Now I was exasperated. "Please, finish the story. What happened next?"

"Well, the gazzangas were actually large rubber balloons that he had filled with water. He had tied a length of heavy-duty twine to the balloon ends and looped it around his neck to hold them up. The dress he had on must have been about ten sizes too big for him, so there was plenty of room in there for Jakey and the water balloons. When his pigeon-toed cake walk got out of hand, the balloons started rocking from side to side until they somehow crisscrossed and flung all the way around to his back. He looked like a hideous cross between a badly deformed camel and the Hunchback of Notre Dame."

Luke and I were laughing so hard now we were lying on our backs screaming at the sky.

"At about that moment, Mrs. Hackworth turned around to see just what in tarnation were all those people staring and pointing at. By then Jakey's dress had crept up around his waist exposing his naked scrawny legs and worn out Hi-tops. The blue tinted wig had twisted around and now dangled sideways off one side of his head. He no longer resembled Mrs. Hackworth at all and she looked at him with total incredulity. He was a terrible sight to behold, looking like some tortured little creature not of this world. Thank God he was wearing underpants."

Luke and I yowled with delight, tears now streaming down our faces. And the Sergeant was laughing, too.

"One of the teachers ran to Mrs. Hackworth's side and hurriedly explained what had happened. Her expression slowly shifted from dismay to horror as she absorbed the teacher's explanation. Then the wig finally slipped off of Jakey's head and fell to the ground. Now it was a sombrero for Jakey's private little Mexican Hat Dance. Around and around he went—prancing, bobbing, weaving—and inadvertently stomping on the wig every other time his foot came down. It was absolutely hilarious. However, my friend Jakey was no longer trying to be funny. In fact, there was now a look of terror in his eyes. The water balloons had swung every which way and the twine had become twisted and tangled around his neck. The weight of the liquid filled balloons kept pulling the noose tighter and tighter until his mouth gaped open. Struggling for air, he desparately clawed at his neck.

"Strangely, the crowd was convinced that Jakey's frantic struggling was just part of the act. They were into it good and had begun in unison to clap their hands and stomp their feet, countering the warped, spastic rhythms of poor Jakey's death dance. Jakey's face, a smeared mess of lipstick and rouge, started to turn a noticeable blue. He fell down to his knees, slapped aimlessly at his neck for a few more seconds and then slowly laid over on his side, like a groggy wild animal that had been shot with a wildlife biologist's anesthetic dart."

Luke and I had stopped laughing.

"Jeez Louise," I said. "What in the heck happened to him?"

"Yeah, did somebody stomp on the gazzangas?" Luke said, as if it was a boa constrictor that had wrapped around Jakey's neck.

"Come on, Luke!" I yelled and laughed at the same time. "Let him tell us!"

The Sergeant had to catch his breath from laughing at Luke's stomp on the gazzangas remark. "Well, then somebody shouted from the crowd, 'Hey! He's choking to death!' Some of the women started screaming and a bunch of people ran over and crowded around him. I couldn't see through the crowd, and a couple of minutes went by while nothing seemed to be happening. Boy was I worried, until, all of the sudden, Jakey squirted out of the crowd and took off running for home with nothing but his underpants on."

The Sergeant had finished his story, and was back to that distant mood, the one I now took to be grief. We all sat silently for a few minutes, immersed in a pensive reverie of solemn reflection. My eyes kept drifting down, wondering where Jakey Blume's body had landed.

The afternoon winds had gone leaving Eagle Rock still and peaceful, save for the murmured sounds of the traffic that forever hummed below this ancient place. I felt close to the Sergeant at that moment, the same feeling I'd had that night on Billy Goat Hill. He had shared a personal part of his life with us. It made me feel good, important, satisfied. I needed that kind of connection with a grownup. I just didn't know how to express it.

He had made his point. Telling us the story, getting us to feel like we had known Jakey Blume, had made us feel the loss, feel a little of what we would suffer if one of us should fall off Eagle Rock. I looked at Luke as he cautiously stared over the ledge and could see that the story had gotten to him, too. He looked over at me and smiled. It was a trusting smile that, to me, said that he thought it was OK to be up there on the rock because he was with me, his big brother. I looked away quickly but it was too late. I could not abate the stinging constriction of sorrow that seized my throat and moved down across my chest. Unconsciously, I began to flex my fingers, then touched forefingers to thumbs and rubbed them together nervously, involuntarily. I strained hard trying to fight off a wave of sorrow, but a single rebel tear broke free and tumbled down my cheek in full view of Luke. It was an odd, foreign emotion, not the crying, the reason I was crying. The saga of Jakey Blume had wrapped me up tight in the realization that I was failing at my responsibility to protect my little brother, to prevent him from being hurt. *Jeez. Damn!* What kind of irresponsible idiot was I? My recklessness was constantly placing Luke in harm's way, and to make me see that, I believed, was the purpose of Sergeant Cavendish's story.

"What's the matter, Wade?" Luke said, his little pink chin already starting to quiver. It was automatic that Luke would cry if he saw me crying. I was the same. We had always been simpatico like that. No rhyme or reason to it. It was the strangest thing. We just couldn't stand to see the other one in a state of tears. 'Symbiotic brats,' Lucinda called us. She couldn't handle it when we both set off like civil defense sirens. The truth be told, Luke and I had figured out our stereo wailing technique had great tactical value. It tended to keep us in close proximity to each other and had saved us from countless spankings. I'm not sure, but I think Lucinda eventually put two and two together and noticed the correlation, because we were clearly much better behaved when we were apart. I suppose Lucinda had adequate ears and nerves for one crying brat. Luke was already starting to tear up, his mouth inverting into a frown causing hundreds of freckles to bunch into orange blotches where laugh lines had been.

"Nothing's wrong. I just got some dust in my eyes," I lied. Mac knew better though. He came over and put his head in my lap. I hugged him around the neck and could tell he was uneasy being that close to the ledge. I could hear the scrape of his nails pressing hard into the rock and could feel the weight of his body pushing against mine, away from the ledge.

Luke seemed to accept my fib and changed his expression to neutral, his freckles slowly returning to where they belonged. "Yeah, I think I got a little dust in my eyes, too," he said.

Sergeant Cavendish shifted his weight and slid a little closer to me. He put his arm on my shoulders, his leather motorcycle jacket groaning with the movement. The noise of the leather registered slight interest with Mac. He twitched his ears but did not lift his head from my lap. We stayed like that for a good while. I felt secure in a way I don't think I had ever felt before.

five

Sergeant Cavendish took his arm off my shoulder, unzipped the
front of his jacket and reached inside for something in his inner
pocket. The tightness in my throat had subsided under the comforting
feel of his arm. I was relaxed and in control again. Mac could tell I
was OK. He got up and returned to where he had been sitting before.
I heard the faint squawking of a police radio and realized the Sergeant
had parked his motorcycle somewhere down below. I couldn't tell
from what direction the sound was coming and wondered if Luke had
been throwing his pebbles down on the motorcycle. Would the
motorcycle make a ping or a thud?

Luke resumed picking at the rock with his pocket knife. Mac
resumed watching him with curious interest. The two of them could
go on picking and watching for hours. All seemed back to normal.
We had been sitting there with the Sergeant for over an hour and I was
surprised, intrigued, that he had been content to stay with us that long.
He wasn't preparing to leave and had yet to say anything to us about
getting down off the rock. I think he realized it would do no good to
order us to stay off Eagle Rock, but he had made his point about the
danger. We sat in silence for a moment or two longer, no doubt each
of us thinking some more about poor Jakey Blume.

"That's a good dog you have there," the Sergeant said, his hand
still in his pocket seemingly toying with something.

I glanced at Mac and then at the Sergeant. There was an insight-
ful glint in his eyes that said he knew Mac would kill to protect

us, or die trying, and that he found great honor in that. "Yes sir," I said. "Mac takes good care of us."

It was a Friday in late October. Luke and I had come up to the rock after school. We had stopped at home first to gobble down peanut butter and jelly sandwiches, and to take the telephone off the hook. The routine plan was to blame Mac for knocking the phone over if Lucinda later bawled us out for not answering. Lucinda would be home at about 6:30 and I reminded myself that we needed to allow at least forty-five minutes to make the return trip home. The sun was slipping low to meet the horizon, leaving the valley below us in shadow as I started to think about the long walk home.

"You guys seen your father lately?"

"He came home for my birthday last month," Luke answered.

I knew Earl's appearance on Luke's birthday had only been a coincidence. I had let Luke think otherwise. Earl wouldn't even know what day was Jesus' birthday. He sure knew when to celebrate Jack Daniels' birthday though. Every day! "We haven't seen or heard from him since then," I said.

The Sergeant pulled an Abba-Zabba out of his pocket and handed it to Luke. "Happy birthday," he said, smiling.

Luke sat up straight and grinned a mile. His freckles stretched so thin they were almost invisible. "Wow! Abba-Zabba's are my favorite!" He had the wrapper off and the candy in his mouth in three seconds.

"Would you like one, too, Wade?" He reached back inside his jacket.

"No, thank you. I only like Butterfingers."

As clever as a magician, smiling slyly, he slid his hand out from his jacket and handed me a Butterfinger. The sly smile burgeoned into a broad grin. The sleight of hand amazed me, as much so as if he had pulled a live squirrel from his sleeve. My reaction was a catalyst for him and he laughed out loud, just like Scar did that first night we met.

"How did you know?" I managed to ask, laughing along with him.

"Trained policeman," he answered mysteriously.

We chomped on our candy bars and laughed until chocolate streaks ran down our chins. Our confection painted faces made us look like descendants of the great Shoshone Gabrieleno who first sat on Eagle Rock and laughed, as we did now partaking in the timeless magic of innocence.

Luke finished his Abba-Zabba. "You know what?" he said. "I heard Lucinda jawing on Earl the last time he was home. I woke up the night of my birthday. I got up to go to the bathroom. I didn't turn the light on so they must not have known I was up."

"Yeah, so?" I said, offering the last bite of my Butterfinger to Mac. It was gone instantly.

Luke said, "Ever hear of some place called Barstow?"

"Nope."

"It's a little town out in the desert on the way to Las Vegas," offered the Sergeant.

"Oh. Well, I heard them say Las Vegas, too." He wiped his sticky chin on his shirt sleeve. Then he asked, "What does *da-borse* mean?"

He had my full attention. "That's just kind of a funny word grownups use sometimes. What did you hear them say exactly, Luke?"

"Hmmm," he murmured, then sat quietly for a bit thinking. "I think Lucinda was mad at Earl. She sounded mad, cursing and all. She said, 'I know about the one in Barstow, Earl. Her name's Trudy. Don't even try to deny it.' Then Earl said, 'OK, if that's the way you want it. We'll get the *da-borse* in Las Vegas'." Luke, appearing content, finished wiping his chin on the other sleeve.

I was thinking that little Matthew never wanted any of this to happen. I looked at Sergeant Cavendish and read the sympathy in his eyes. He put his arm across my shoulders again. We were all quiet for a little while longer. Luke started picking at the rock again. His question was left unanswered, and I was left feeling depressed. The inevitable event had come and Lucinda had apparently opted not to tell me about it. I was old enough. She should have told me. I squinted at the sun. Watched it settle lower and lower.

Soon the Sergeant's leather groaned as he moved to get up. He took his time. Stretched his legs. Did three deep knee bends. "Maybe it's time we thought about heading for home, boys." He made it very clear he wasn't leaving us up on the rock.

I looked at my watch, 5:30. It was time to go anyway. Luke and I stood up, following veiled orders. Mac got up and went through his stretching routine. Luke looked over the ledge and tossed one last pebble before we headed for home. One-thousand, two-thousand... "Hey," he said, turning to face the Sergeant. "How did your friend Jakey fall off this rock anyway?"

"You wouldn't believe me if I told you," the Sergeant said. He looked sad again, staring off toward the sunset.

I was a little irritated that Luke had brought up the subject of Jakey Blume again. At the same time I was also interested to know exactly what had happened.

"I'll believe you," Luke said.

"You'll be the first one then," the Sergeant replied, still looking off in the distance.

For a second I thought he was about to cry. He looked so alone, as though we weren't there with him. Down below, half of the cars had their lights on casting soft glowing arcs on the pavement in front of them. I watched them for a second or two and then looked back at Luke and the Sergeant. Luke had moved and now stood close to the Sergeant with his back to the ledge. Their forms were silhouettes centered in the remaining half-round shape of the dwindling sun. Luke, with his head tilted back, looked up innocently at the Sergeant. "I'll believe you," he repeated.

The Sergeant's eyes drifted down to meet Luke's trusting gaze. He slowly placed his hands on Luke's shoulders. He smiled...almost grimly. Mac stiffened and started to growl, very low, very tentative. Something seemed wrong. But what? My heart kicked hard and accelerated. My legs suddenly felt rubbery, disconnected from my body.

Then, almost in a whisper, the Sergeant said, "To be completely honest with you guys, some people actually thought maybe...*I*...pushed him."

Oh, God! No!

I couldn't move.

Terror.

I was helpless to do anything to stop the unthinkable thing that was most certainly about to happen. I tried to speak, but couldn't form the words. What words? What could I say? Help? Who would hear? Who would help? Nobody. *Oh, God—NO!*

"I know you couldn't have pushed him. He was your friend. No way would you do that," Luke said. "What really happened? How did Jakey fall?"

I willed my legs to step closer. The gap between us was closing and I sensed movement like I was floating, but I couldn't feel my legs taking actual steps. Instantly, my eyes focused on the holstered gun hanging from the Sergeant's left hip. What an impossible thought, but what else can I do? *I want that gun!*

"Let's move back from the ledge," the Sergeant said, "and I'll tell you what really happened."

Mac relaxed and I slumped down, took a deep breath, and began massaging my legs hunting for feeling. Luke and the Sergeant sat down next to me. "God, I can't take this," I mumbled to myself.

The Sergeant started, "It happened on a day just like this, a little cool, a little windy, so clear you could see all the way downtown. Jakey and I had climbed up on the rock after school. We liked to come up here and sit. We talked about stuff, you know, anything and everything, whatever came to mind. I remember Jakey was excited about going to Catalina Island with his family the next day. It was to be his first visit to Catalina. I had been there twice before so I told him what I knew about the island. I remember he was especially interested in seeing the buffaloes and wild goats.

"I also told him about the bright red Garibaldi fish I had seen through a glass bottom boat at Emerald Bay. Funny, I remember telling him the Garibaldi fish had been named after a famous Italian General whose soldiers were known for their distinctive bright red shirts, and not knowing for sure whether the story was true or not. Huh, isn't that weird? Oh yeah, and Jakey wanted to know all about the glass bottom boat. I think he was nervous about being on a boat with a glass bottom. Jakey didn't like the water much."

The Sergeant's voice choked to a stop, the memory of his last moments with Jakey Blume obviously difficult and painful to recall. He took a deep breath and resumed his story with more emotion in his voice than before.

"Jakey and I had been sitting for an hour or so right about where we're sitting now."

"Right here?" Luke asked, placing his palms down on the rock.

"More or less. Anyway, here's the part nobody ever believed. Suddenly, out of nowhere, two mockingbirds swooped down and started attacking Jakey." The Sergeant averted his eyes and looked off toward the sunset like he was expecting one or both of us to laugh at him. But what he said hit me like a sledge hammer right between the eyes.

"What happened? Tell me. I'll believe you," Luke repeated, tugging on the Sergeant's sleeve.

I felt a chilly curtain drop around me as the blood drained from my face. I already knew the story. *God!*

"At first I thought it was funny. The birds were after him and weren't bothering me at all." He failed at an effort to smile. "They swooped, and screeched, and dove at him, pecking and clawing at the top of his head like something crazy. Jakey scrambled to his feet. I'll never forget the terror in his eyes. He was swinging his arms over his head and he just took off running—right over the edge. He was gone. Before I really knew what was happening he was just plain gone. His scream still haunts me. It just faded away into the sky."

Luke turned pale, close to tears. "I believe you," he said. "I believe you."

The Sergeant gave up a weak smile. "Thanks," he said softly.

The sun retreated below the ridge line leaving a wake of pinkish-purple brush strokes across the sky. It was so quiet, so still, I could hear my heart pounding hard, deep, deep down in my ears. I leaned back and rested my head on Mac who had curled up behind me. Numbly I asked, "What color hair did Jakey Blume have?" I closed my eyes and waited to hear what I already knew.

"Bright red," he said. "Just about like Luke's."

Dreams, including daydreams, are strange and powerful things, I thought. I wondered what Duke Snider would say about that?

six

It happened on a Saturday afternoon in the middle of July, 1960.

Luke shook my pillow at the first expectant pulse of false dawn and insistently repeated, "Get up, Wade. I want to go to Three Ponds early today." I was feeling sluggish from a long fitful night and he had to pester me awake. Mac wanted to go, too, and had joined in the pestering. I got up in a bad mood and slowly moped my way toward the bathroom.

It seemed as though Lucinda hadn't been around in days. Wondering if she were home, I brushed my teeth and thought about peeking into her room, until I spotted a note she'd left on the kitchen table. 'See you guys tonight,' was all it said. No: *I love you, Mom.*

With Earl completely out of our lives, now residing in Barstow with someone named Trudy, and Lucinda working more hours than ever, Luke and I were left to entertain ourselves. What we lacked in material things we tried to make up for with imagination. Still, our devices were limited. Only three weeks into summer vacation and we were already trudging through periods of tedium and restlessness, the onset of the devil boredom. The devil's plucky partners (phone pranks, trespass, petty theft, and other minor transgressions) were whispering in our ears with the zealousness of overstocked drug dealers. Luke, the master of pluckiness, kept pestering, and soon, against my rumpled humor, we were on our way to Three Ponds.

Three Ponds was a long way away from where we lived; at least it was to us in 1960. Neither Luke or I owned a bicycle until the summer of 1963. Walking affords one great freedom to notice and appreciate detail, which, in the case of kids, can foster a predictable amount of mischief. From where we lived on Ruby Place, a block north and a block west of the intersection of Figueroa Boulevard and Meridian Avenue, it was quite a trek to Three Ponds. I suppose it was only a thirty or forty minute walk. That is if one were to take the most direct route and not dawdle along the way, which was impossible for us to do.

Luke had something in his hand. "If that dern Molly barks, I'm gonna throw this rock at her."

Molly, a rather pretty, but dumb, Irish Setter, belonged to Mrs. Robinson, who lived half way down the hill from our house. Mac managed to impregnate Molly on a regular basis. A female in heat within five miles turned Mac's hind legs into powerful pogo sticks. Our six-foot high fence was useless to keep him in. Mac was a horny bastard. Now, some twenty-five or thirty generations later, I would imagine his descendants are leaping fences and scratching fleas on all seven continents. Molly barked when she saw Mac. I noticed Mrs. Robinson looking out her kitchen window just in time to restrain Luke. Molly, not being in heat at the moment, was ignored by Mac.

Luke finally dropped the rock when we rounded the corner. "Think Jake will be open?" he said, looking down the boulevard.

"Naw. It's too early," I grumpily replied.

Jake's Barber Shop sat across the street from Luther Burbank Junior High School. Jake, no relation to Jakey Blume, was a great guy, if not a great barber. Jake was a barrel-chested giant of a man. His huge Dizzy Gillespie cheeks shook when he laughed or growled as he loved to do whenever we showed up. Plainly speaking, Jake loved people. Especially kids. He was a good story teller and always had a funny yarn to share. It was impossible to walk past Jake's Barber Shop without stopping to say hello. He wouldn't allow it. "Hey you!" he would yell like thunder if you tried to pass by without at least waving to him.

Jake gave Luke and me our first haircuts, and at least a hundred more before we were forced to move away. He was a friend of Earl and Lucinda's and might have shared a cozy time or two with Lucinda after Earl left. I'm not sure about that, though.

Luke and I had a passion of our own. We called it "sneaking" which was code for sneaking in through Jake's back door. We'd secret our-selves in Jake's supply room and peek through a curtained doorway waiting for the most opportune moment. Seeing our chance, we'd dash through the barber shop and out the front door, whooping and hollering like a couple of drunken cowboys letting loose on a Saturday night. If we managed to scoot past Jake without him grabbing us, he'd reward us with a wad of Bazooka bubble gum. It was quite a challenge. Jake was big, but he was sure of foot and lightning quick. If he caught us he'd sling us up into the chair and, lickity split, what little hair we had grown since the last time he caught us was buzzed onto the floor and ready for the sweeper.

We were poor in those days but were never in need of a haircut. Thanks to Jake's army-style butch cuts, Luke and I looked like a couple of cue balls most of those years. Lucinda never had to pay for any haircuts, as far as I know. Sometimes I think back on it and wonder if maybe I should have gone to Jake with my problem. I think he would have understood. He would have known what to do. I guess it wasn't in the cards to go to Jake though. Not in the ones I'd been dealt anyway. We stopped and looked in the window. No Jake.

Down the block from Jake's was a pedestrian tunnel that burrowed under Figueroa Boulevard. It came up on the other side of the street in front of our school, Garvanza Elementary. The tunnel always intrigued me. Nothing exciting ever happened down there, but I always felt different underground—safe and secure. Maybe I was a mole or a woodchuck in a past life. On this particular day we would take our chances aboveground dodging the traffic to get across the street.

The school playground slowed us down. Luke was determined to throw something, and dirt clods began to fly over the fence at no apparent target. I stood and watched him, figuring he couldn't hurt anything, letting him get it out of his system. He threw one last dirt clod, looked up at the sky for a moment, and then turned to me. "Wade, is Matthew in heaven?"

"Yes."

"H-*m-m*. Does Lucinda know that?"

"Well, yes. But she still wants him to be here with us."

"Is she mad at us?"

"No. I guess she's mad at God."

"Oh."

Past the school, our next stop was Kory's Market at the corner of York and Figueroa Boulevards. I suppose the term "supermarket" would have applied to Kory's in the following decade, because of its ample parking and multiple check-out stands. To Luke and me, Kory's was the best place to steal a free look at the latest comic books. Kory's was a busy place, so it was relatively easy to snatch the new issues, sit on the floor behind the magazine rack and catch up on our favorite two-dimensional heroes. Often we'd get away with this for ten or fifteen minutes before being noticed and sent on our way. Nowadays kids need a pocket full of quarters to play video games. No such thing as a free peek anymore.

At Luke's insistence, we skipped Kory's and beat an expeditious path the rest of the way to Three Ponds—left off York Boulevard, down the hill on San Pasqual Avenue, and straight ahead to the overpass at San Pasqual Creek. Most days would have presented something to ignite a digression and take us off on another tangent, but this day was to be like no other.

A secret known only to a few privileged locals, Three Ponds was an oasis in the middle of urban desert, a hidden wilderness, the last holdout against reinforced concrete channels that grew like fingering roots up every last little natural drainage in the great Los Angeles basin. Flora and fauna abounded untouched and somehow protected from encroaching civilization. A peaceful, restful, place where time, lulled by a meandering stream towered over by spectacular trees, seemed almost to slow to a stop. The stream set the pace, never in a hurry to commingle with the larger flow of the Arroyo Seco which fed the larger-yet Los Angeles River. The great Pacific could abide, its volition would ultimately prevail.

The cool, shadowy, fern laden environment was a natural habitat for a host of furred and feathered species. Early morning and late afternoon, when the animals came to drink and play, were my favorite times. If you hid downwind and crouched very still, the experience was more fun than visiting the jailed animals at the Griffith Park Zoo.

The sun-timed retreat of unseen nocturnal hordes left a catalogue of muddy footprints, a cryptic record of a night's worth of frolic. The tracks dispersed from the ponds like wheel spokes from a hub. Fascinated by the mosaic, I would look at the print trails and imagine the little creatures snuggling in their cozy, surreptitious lairs.

The birds were just the opposite. The first hint of daybreak magically unlocked the doors to a huge natural aviary, commencing a flurry of action overhead. I enjoyed the constant aerobatic display and interminable chatter of the jays, robins, sparrows, and finches. All of them frequently visited the water's edge to sip, bathe, preen and vainly stare at their immodest reflections. Sundown brought the end of a cycle and the beginning of the next. Luke and I cycled with the birds, preferring the non-jungle terrain of Billy Goat Hill for our after dark fantasies, motorcycle gangs notwithstanding. The empyrean environment of Three Ponds was the most fertile of all grounds for our youthful fantasies and Luke and I were drawn there almost daily.

The occasional appearance of an aggressive mockingbird invariably disturbed the otherwise harmonious interaction of the other birds, and forever reminded me of my bad dream and Sergeant Cavendish's story of Jakey Blume's fatal fall from Eagle Rock. I did not like the mockingbirds and swore for the longest time that one day I would bring a sling shot with me and do away with as many of them as I could. A ridiculous thought for a boy who would avoid stepping on an ant.

We had whiled away the morning sitting with our pant legs rolled up, bare feet dangling in the stilling coolness of the middle pond. We had been looking at the animal prints in the mud and speculating as to what kind of animals had preceded us that day. I had tired of throwing sticks into the pond for Mac to retrieve, but continued on because it was the only way to keep him from barking, which he would do until he was ready to quit.

"Dern dog," Luke chided, as if Mac belonged only to me. "He thinks he's some kind of bird dog."

I smiled devilishly, sensing an opportunity to rile Luke. "You'll be wishing he's a bird dog, if those dang mockingbirds come to visit your head again."

I had told Luke about my dream of him being attacked by the mockingbirds up on Eagle Rock. It had really unnerved him. He seemed to watch the sky all the time now. He reached up and tugged on the visor of his Dodger cap just to make sure it was there.

Luke knew we were heading deep into mockingbird country and had insisted that I lug my slingshot and two pocket loads of ball bearings to Three Ponds that day. I had to work to keep my pants up all the way there. I fondled the bulging supply stuffing my pockets and checked to see that the slingshot crammed into my back pocket was still there ready for action.

Luke looked at Mac for a moment, then begrudgingly, but with new found civility, said, "He's a good dog."

Mac finally tired of playing "get the stick" and decided to ignore my last throw. It was a prank of his that rankled me. He couldn't just go get the stick, return it politely, and say thanks for the game. Nope. He had to make me throw the stick one more time just so he could ignore it, and thereby have the last word. I wished I had the power to make myself invisible so he would run back to where I had been and stand there with the stick in his mouth looking stupid.

Mac sat down in the mud, his rump in two inches of turbid water, tail swishing from side to side like a thick black water snake. He arrogantly gaped at me. I held his stare for a bit, then looked away and spat into the water. "Chase that," I said. He put his head down, closed his eyes and ignored me.

"Who do you think is better...Drysdale or Koufax?" Luke casually asked. He was lying on his belly drawing a baseball diamond in the mud with his finger.

This was how most of our arguments started.

"Duke Snider is the best," I answered, knowing full well he was talking about pitchers, not power hitting center fielders. Already I caught a whiff of smoldering cordite.

"I'm talking pitchers, fire throwers, masters of the mound—you big dumb donkey!"

It wasn't easy, but I ignored his insult, as Mac had ignored me. "OK. Who do you think is better?"

"I asked you first," he spouted, looking up from his handy work. He was miffed that I had dishonored him by answering his question with a question.

"I asked you second!" I shouted back, louder than him.

Now my fuse had been lit, too. We were angry, pint size versions of Abbott and Costello. Who's On First? Except we rarely found any humor in this non-comedic sibling ritual.

Being the older brother, I tried very hard to be patient and take the long road with Luke. Admittedly though, now and then I made a wrong turn and got stuck in a quagmire on the low road. I knew he did it on purpose. Of course he did. He relished challenging me with captious queries—black or white, hot or cold, up or down kinds of questions—so that no matter what I said, he could automatically jump on the contrary side of the fence. The best I could do was throw off his rhythm by detouring around the question and asking him what he thought. He didn't like that, which made it fun for me.

I had decided not to antagonize him any further, but then changed my mind. "OK...Drysdale's the better of the two. But I'm glad we have Perranoski in the pen," I said, not because I necessarily thought Drysdale was better, but because I knew he liked Koufax.

Smart-alecky as he could be, Luke looked up from the mud and glared at me. "No way! Sandy Koufax is an Ace!"

"Oh yeah! Well Don Drysdale is the King of Diamonds..." I pointed angrily at the mud "...Including that mucky mess you're making with your stupid, dinky little fingers!"

Luke got to his feet and shouted, "Drysdale's the King all right! The King of the bean ball!"

In reaction to the rising tension, Mac's tail started churning the water, but he didn't open his eyes. He'd heard this a thousand times before.

"It wouldn't take a Drysdale to brush you back from the plate you little twerp!" I screamed.

I had made a mistake. I allowed him to get me mad. I moved suddenly, deliberately stepping right where he had placed his pitcher's mound. I mashed my foot into the mud as if I were squashing out a cigarette butt.

Luke gasped, then screamed, "Hey! You big donkey!" He clamped onto my leg, like a monkey to a vine, knocking me off balance.

"Whoa-a-a-a!" I spluttered, arms flailing, struggling not to fall. I made one futile, spastic lurch to right myself before I landed front down in two inches of fetid water, burying my face up to my ears in the mud. Luke jumped on my back landing hard enough to force a loud *Umph!* from my lungs and started shoveling gobs of slimy goo onto the back of my head. It felt like he had knocked the wind out of me. I couldn't get any air, putrid, muddy scum filling my mouth and nose. Mac was now barking furiously at the rough-and-tumble action. Through my moss clogged ears, his barking sounded like someone was beating on a muffled gong.

I panicked.

Frantic for air, charged with the might of fear, I thrust my back upward in a powerful bucking arch propelling Luke ass-over-appetite like an over-matched, tenderfoot bull rider. He landed head first in the deepest part of the pond.

Dazed and gagging, I stood up and wiped the goop away from my eyes. I coughed up something wiggly. A big tadpole. Yuk! I opened my eyes and blinked away the stinging organic residue clinging to the insides of my eyelids. I tried to focus. Through burning, squinting slits, I thought I saw Luke's Dodger cap floating away in the center current. The vague, blue dot disappeared down a lazy, granite flume enroute to the shallower pool of the lower pond.

seven

Where is Luke?

First I choked on a hard lump in my throat, a different kind of panic, then dove into the water like Johnny Weissmuller rescuing Maureen O'Sullivan from flesh-craving crocodiles.

The middle pond was about twelve feet deep at its center. I had touched the sandy bottom only once before and that was with my foot. I kicked my legs as hard as I could, grabbed arms full of verdant liquid and descended faster than I thought possible, until I realized it wasn't because of my powerful strokes. I was sinking. My ball bearing laden pockets were pulling me down faster than a pair of concrete boots, and all I could think about was how I had ignored Luke when he asked me to teach him how to swim. Nearing the bottom my ears began to ache from the pressure. Then my feet touched down harder than I expected, startling me into action. Eyes open, I glanced up through an emerald glow and strained to see the faint, rippling sheen of the water's surface. My mind shouted at me: *What a way to go, lying face up at the bottom of a huge vat of lime Jello!* Straight out in front of me my arms waved uselessly, fading at the elbows into handless stubs swallowed up by a murky, greenish gloom. There was so much area to cover, too much, and not enough oxygen to feed the frenetic exertion of every muscle in my body.

I snatched something in my grip that felt like it could be an arm or a leg. A surge of hope. I tugged it to my face only to see a water logged piece of wood, part of a tree root, not part of Luke. Angry, I kicked my legs and wildly swung my arms searching the area around me, and knew that I had started to cry.

Underwater tears.

Underwater sobbing.

Underwater doom.

On the verge of drowning myself, I had to turn and kick off the bottom and pump hard toward the light. The sinkers in my pockets held me down like a baited hook. It took forever, but at last I reached the surface. As my head came out of the water, I heard myself screaming for help. I sucked my lungs full of life and immediately began sinking back down into the gruesome watery prison that held Luke captive. I felt powerless to save him, but I kicked hard to get my face back above the water and worked furiously to replenish my breath. I had to have more air before resuming my hopeless search. I tried to dig the ball bearings out of my pockets, but it was no good. The second I stopped paddling with my arms, I started to sink.

More air!

More air!

Gasping, choking, fighting to catch my breath, I dog-paddled furiously, the stronger kick of my right leg slowly pushing me in a wide, lazy circle. Entangled in a mile long moment of indecision, "LUKE! LUKE!" I sobbed. "I'm sorry Luke!"

Arms and legs working at full throttle but rapidly diminishing in thrust, I slowly came around to face due west, looking straight into the glaring afternoon sun.

Why God? Some fall off cliffs...some drown in ponds? But I'm the one that threw him in. Don't take him. It's not his fault. It's my fault. TAKE ME! LUKE! LUKE!

The sun beat down on my face with slaps of hot defeat. I squinted, imagining I had seen something move just below the lower fringe of the sun's glare. I blinked. There it is again, shapes, two shapes...

"You swim worser than Drysdale pitches, you big dern donkey!"

There, on the muddy bank, with Mac proudly stationed at his side, stood a very angry Luke. I blinked again, harder, and tried to raise a hand to shield my eyes. Coming around slowly, my face drifted under a merciful shadow, only to leave me wide open to the blunt force of Luke's petulant glare. His freckles seemed to be radiating the energy they had absorbed from the sun, which towered over them like a giant, tangerine sparkler. And there amid my fear and desperation, I was, for a fleeting moment, so greatly, wonderfully relieved to know he was safe.

Mac barked, a muffled gong again.

Now spent beyond all endurance, I made one last, pathetic attempt to yell, "I'M *DRO-O-OWNING!*" But my dire plea gurgled out in a swirling nebula of bubbles as the pond poured inside me and sent me spiraling, spiraling...down. I could only watch as Luke's ghostly form got smaller and smaller, corkscrewing up, away, gone.

It felt as if a school of slimy eels were wagging their tails in my face. Terrified, my eyes fluttering half open, I swatted out blindly, missing whatever was there. And then I discovered I was eye ball to eye ball with Mac and the eels were actually one, big, pink, sloshing tongue. I held still for a moment and let him keep licking. It affirmed I was still alive.

"What happened?" I groaned. I felt sick to my stomach as I feebly raised myself up to a sitting position. My legs seemed to weigh ten tons. The ball bearings must have turned into bowling balls.

"I think you drownded," Luke said, cautious, keeping a step out of arms reach. He was not quite sure if I was mad or not. "But me and Mac saved you." He grinned triumphantly, but still kept his distance.

"You mean you jumped back in the water and pulled me out?"

Luke's grin softened. "Well—uh—not exactly."

I looked around half expecting to see Sergeant Cavendish, thinking he must have showed up again. But I didn't see him or anyone else for that matter. My head was pounding. My ears were full of water. And the way my stomach was twitching, I thought I might have swallowed a few tadpoles. Then I belched real loud— *Moss flavor*—and Mac gave me one of those head cocked sideways, eyebrows raised, curious looks like he did whenever Luke or I farted. "Chase that," I said.

His tail instantly went into motion.

My stomach suddenly felt much better.

"What do you mean, not exactly? Either you saved me or you didn't." I shook my head from side to side but my ears remained plugged. Mac looked at me strangely again.

Luke stared at his feet trying to cover his embarrassment. "I don't know how to swim. You know that."

"Well? How did you get me out of the pond then?"

"I didn't," he said, chuckling softly. "Mac did."

"Huh?"

"Mac saved you, ya big donkey!"

I was incredulous. "Well I'll be a bluenose gopher. How in the name of Pinky Lee did you get him to do that?"

"Easy, I just yelled: 'GET THE STICK!' and pointed at you."

"Well I'll be dogged!"

"You were," Luke proudly proclaimed.

Physically, mentally and emotionally exhausted, I lay on the bank of the middle pond and let a large shaft of afternoon sun bake me dry. With considerable effort, I moved twice to remain in the warm, rejuvenating spotlight. When finally I had the energy, I pulled the slingshot from my back pocket and methodically unloaded the near deadly ballast from my front pockets.

Still feeling stupefied, shaky, I mindlessly counted the ball bearings and arranged them into letters on the muddy ground in front of me. I gave it my best effort, trying to polish up my downbeat mood. But soon one hundred and sixty-six silver marbles spelled out the word STUPID in six-inch capital letters. Feeling very down on myself, I thought: *It's a wonder that I ever came up from that first dive.* I was not as smart as Tarzan. Jane never would have survived with Wade Parker running around bare-chested in nothing but a loincloth. With my luck, she probably would've gotten tangled up in one of my vines and strangled to death.

Luke seemed to be enjoying a new level of kinship with Mac. For once Mac had done what he had asked him to do. *Thank the Lord for that!* And Mac knew that he had done something important. He was showing off, retrieving everything Luke could find to throw with great verve and enthusiasm. I'd only seen him behave that energetic when Molly the mindless Irish Setter was in heat.

I watched them play while my sapped strength slowly regenerated. My temper, and my anger at Luke, had been washed away in a proselyte's conversion. I was damn lucky to have Luke as a brother, and Mac as a friend. Turning it over and over in my mind, I kept coming back to how stupid I had been to place Luke in yet another hazardous situation. I really thought that he had drowned. *Will I ever learn? Maybe. In the meantime I can't let him see how scared I am.*

"Hey, twerp, what happened to your hat?"

Not realizing his hat was missing, Luke reached up to his head and then flinched. In a reflex, his eyes snapped skyward, like a cottontail reacting to the blip of a hawk's shadow. "It must have come off in the water," he uttered stonily, eyes to the vertical, his hand still feeling around on the top of his head. Mac barked, impatient for Luke to throw the stick dangling from his other hand. "Dern dog," Luke cussed, instantly reverting to his old ways. He tossed the stick away without looking down. Mac watched the stick sail to the far side of the pond. Put off by Luke's lack of sincerity, he turned around twice and sat down in the mud. Game over. I smiled. "Dern dog," Luke muttered.

"Don't worry about your hat. We'll find it in the lower pond on our way home."

"OK," he said weakly, feeling naked, vulnerable.

I had a thought. Like Luke, old ways are hard to change. A small smile began to multiply. "You know what I would do if I was you?" I said, trying to sound serious.

"What?" He was still looking for con-trails or maybe a message in the clouds.

"I would smear mud all over my head just in case there are any mockingbirds in the area." My eyelashes fluttered dramatically. Yes, I was feeling much better. I felt a little impulse of cockiness and decided to push my devilish thought over the line of fairness. "You know, with your hair, it might be more dangerous out here than walking into a bull ring with a red suit on." He never looked down, just kneeled, scooped and smeared. In a matter of seconds he looked like a lost gopher popping up in the middle of a peat bog. Maybe I wasn't so stupid after all.

The looming shadows had turned the pond from an iridescent green to the color of over-ripe guacamole. Luke had been content to sit next to me and repair his earthen head gear whenever I noted that pieces had dried and fallen off, while I played a lazy game of word-spell with my one hundred and sixty-six ball bearings.

I had just discovered that there were enough ball bearings to spell M-I-S-S-I-S-S-I-P-P-I if I didn't dot the I's, when I heard Luke squeal like somebody had pinched him. "What?" I said, wondering if I could make smaller letters and have enough ball bearings for *Massachusetts*.

"Look," Luke whispered, rapidly patting more mud on his head.

"What?" I looked up, hearing the fear in his voice.

He kept smearing as he spoke. "Over there." His lips scarcely moved as he hoisted a crooked, muddy finger and pointed across the pond. "Two mockingbirds just landed—*whimper*—in that bush over there." I choked back a giggle and looked where he was pointing.

"Get your slingshot." Now he had the voice of a greedy pirate sniffing the wind for hidden treasure.

"Where? I don't see any birds."

"Get your slingshot!"

"OK, OK. Take it easy."

I forced myself not to laugh at the streak of goop working its way down his forehead. I picked up the slingshot and took a ball bearing from the second S in Mississippi. I prepared the ball snugly in the leather sling and pinched the load firmly between my thumb and forefinger, thinking—*I've never hit a darn thing that I've aimed at with this stupid thing, and now I'm supposed to hit a bird I can't even see from a hundred feet away? Right.*

"Where are they?" I repeated, believing I had about as much of a chance of hitting a bird as I did to meet Duke Snider. I would have bet anything those birds were safer than raw liver crumpets at a Shirley Temple tea party.

"They're right across the middle of the pond. On the top branch of the smallest bush above that L-shaped rock." He couldn't have been more precise.

"O-o-o-h yea-a-a-h. I see 'um." I squinted. "Two of 'um. And they're looking right at your head, I think."

Luke's neck disappeared down inside his T-shirt. Now he looked like a turtle. A mud turtle. "Kill them," he whispered, oblivious to the little chunks of mud now slipping off the end of his nose.

Mac had dozed off earlier. He was whimpering in his sleep, dreaming of Molly no doubt. It was just as well that he didn't see my shot miss anyway. He could be very judgmental at times.

"Hurry up!" Luke implored.

I propped my left elbow on my knee and raised the slingshot to eye level. The birds looked to be a mile away as I positioned their faint little shapes at the center of the yoke. Slowly, I pulled back on the black rubber straps, back, back, as far back as I could. My arm trembled, the muscles in my forearm bulging from the strain.

The birds are so small and I'm so big—it doesn't seem fair. Goliath aiming the slingshot at David?   That's not how Reverend Bonner told the story.

"Shoot! Shoot!" Luke hissed.

Aw, heck, I ain't gonna hit them anyway.

I closed my eyes and let go. THWACK! The ball bearing sizzled forward, singeing the air over the water. Instantly a puff of feathers floated in suspension around the bush and slowly settled on the leaves, like fake snow in a Sears Christmas window display. The recoil of the rubber straps snapped the slingshot out of my hand and flung it into the pond where it slowly floated away in search of Luke's Dodger cap.

"You got 'um!" Luke roared. "You got 'um both!"

I was stunned.

He was right.

No more birds.

I'm a murderer!

Mac opened one eye, winked at me, and then went back to sleep.

Luke danced around in a circle, a fearsome warrior celebrating a fruitful hunt, and then took off upstream toward a spot where he could cross over to the other side without having to swim.

"Wait up, for crying out loud!" I shouted, still fazed with a strange mixture of amazement and regret. I hurried to catch up with him.

On the other side of the stream we made our way back down to the middle pond, until finally we stood side by side at the feathery bush. There were lots of feathers, but no birds. We pushed our way into the thicket, scouring the branches and ground as we went.

"Some bird dog," Luke said disgustedly. "He ain't even interested. Dern dog."

Across the pond Mac snoozed in the mud.

"They gotta be back here somewhere. They can't fly with that many feathers missing," I said guiltily. I was sure they had to be dead, at least one of them anyway.

We pushed our way through the brush maybe thirty or forty feet and came upon a small open space.

No birds.

"Dang," Luke said warily, fearing some kind of counter attack. Retaliation. Revenge of the mockingbirds.

"What could have happened to 'um?" I said, thinking out loud. I couldn't imagine that they had flown away.

"Hey, what's that?" Luke pointed to a piece of cardboard big enough to use for sliding at Billy Goat Hill. It stood on end leaning against a waist high rock, looking quite out of place in these undisturbed surroundings. Noticing something more peculiar, I stepped closer and observed a perfectly round hole in the cardboard, exactly the same diameter as my ball bearings.

"Look at that," I said, pointing to the little hole.

We stepped closer. I leaned down to peek through the hole. Luke reached over and grabbed the cardboard. The cardboard fell over. We both screamed.

My face wavered four inches away from a man's face. He sat on his butt, legs outstretched, torso leaning back against the rock. His mouth hung open as if frozen in mid-speech, glazed eyes staring in disbelief, and there, for all the world to see, was my killer ball bearing buried down a bloody vent in his forehead. I could see its shimmery roundness lodged one knuckle deep in a finger size hole. Flies were already flitting around the wound, excited by the early smell of death.

What I had become came in a mental roar, hitting me first in the pit of my stomach, then slamming up my spine to my brain where a silent scream tried to split my skull open from the inside. *I AM A MURDERER!*

A moment later Mac stood bracing against my weakening legs, sniffing cautiously at the dead man's shark skin pant leg. He looked up at me, worry filling his big brown eyes, as if to say—*This is not good, Wade. This is not good at all.*

Before I fainted, there was an instant of revolting sickness, then a sense of softly descending, as I imagined I was falling into the safe, comforting arms of Miss Cherry. Instead, my head crashed hard on the rock next to the dead guy.

eight

Two weeks had passed. Each seemed like a century. Rampant guilt consumed me from the inside out in a lonesome, protracted torture of conscience. Methodically, like ants hauling away a carcass bit by bit, I was being dismantled. Everything positive about me melted away, shriveled down to nothing, absorbed by the gluttonous sponges of fear and remorse. I longed for Earl to show up and beat a confession out of me, knowing I would feel so much better after it was over. And if he killed me? Well, so much the better.

The knot above my right eye was gone. A faint bruise remained that looked as harmless as a smudge that wouldn't wash off. That my injury was only minor added to the guilt. I should have at least lost an eye.

Luke was making progress. The day before he had come out of the house and sat on the porch for twenty minutes. His eight-year-old conscience was bothering him for running away and leaving me lying there. I told him not to worry about it and that I was proud of him for not fainting, like I did.

The scene churned in my mind, like flipping through photographs from a homicide file—the card board shifting, the gaping mouth, the horror filled eyes, and the shiny ball bearing staring, staring, glaring out at me, looking like an angry silver bumblebee snugged down a bloody hole in a cadaverous telephone pole.

It was nearly dark when I came to. I had no idea how I had gotten from the middle pond out to the overpass at San Pasqual Road. I must have gotten up on my feet and stumbled out there on my own power. When I woke up, Mac was sitting next to me, but he can't talk. Mac is an amazing animal. Maybe he dragged me that far and then got tired? I was dizzy and my head hurt, but I was OK. I got up and started walking home. Mac and I hadn't gone far when a patrol car pulled up behind me and stopped at the curb. I was too scared to run, but certain I was about to be arrested for murder. The cop said they had received a report of somebody lying by the road. "Yeah," I told him, "It was me. My dog accidentally tripped me and I bumped my head. I'm OK though. I'm just on my way home now." The cop seemed satisfied and drove off. If he had been the Sergeant, I think I would have told the truth. As it was, I threw up on the sidewalk.

Lucinda bought the story I made up about me banging my head on a low branch. She was very upset at us for losing our tennis shoes though. Luke had panicked, I had fainted, and we both had ended up at home barefooted. I lied again and told her some big kids swiped our tennis shoes. Luke wasn't talking at all.

Later that night, Lucinda took the coffee can down from the crawl space in the hall ceiling. She didn't know I was in the bathroom with the door cracked open. I saw her crying and knew there wasn't enough money to replace the tennis shoes and still buy the new pair of high heels she needed for work. I stayed in the bathroom for a long, long time trying to work up the nerve to go back to Three Ponds for our shoes.

I couldn't marshal the courage until a week later, when, with my heart quaking to rival the San Andreas, I crept back to see if our shoes, and the man, were still there. It was awful, a stabbing pain in my stomach nearly forcing me to chicken out half way there. When I finally came upon the scene everything was gone—our shoes, Luke's Dodger cap, my sling shot, all of the ball bearings, the piece of card board with the hole in it...and the dead man. The knot of nerves in my middle finally came up in a sick whoosh, dropping me to the ground in the thicket of bushes amid the only remaining physical evidence of my crime, a scattering of dull, lifeless feathers.

The nightmare wouldn't quit. It was always the same: I dive into the pond to save Luke. A chrome-eyed Cyclops wearing Luke's Dodger cap grabs my feet and pulls me down to the bottom. I try to swim but I can't. Somehow my tennis shoes are snugged onto my hands with the laces tied together like handcuffs. At the end I'm drowning with Mac swimming circles around me underwater. He's barking furiously, but what I hear sounds like he's screaming...Get the stick, murderer!...in perfect English. I cry out for help and billowing streams of steaming mockingbird feathers flow from my mouth. I wake up drenched and shivering.

All of this banged around in the ten percent of my brain not yet petrified by ravenous guilt as I leaned over the railing and looked down at the unforgiving concrete spillway glistening in the dawn two hundred feet below. I knew how the bridge had earned its name. Now I knew how the dozens of tormented souls that had gone before me felt just before they...solved their problems.

Suicide Bridge looked the part. Constructed with two, Model-T width lanes of sculpted, discolored concrete, it loomed high above a deep gorge. The architecture was hideous, what I would call classic Gothic horror. Not a cheery place. Perfect for those in an "end it all" state of mind.

A short way up the draw was a venue famous for some of the most jubilant celebrations of modern times, The Rose Bowl. From where I stood, I could just make out the top of its magnificent oval protruding up above the mist. I remembered when Earl took me with him to the '55 Rose Bowl game. I was going on five at the time. Two minutes into the third quarter I announced that I had to go to the bathroom. Earl was already drunk. It angered him that I hadn't gone to the rest room during half time. Not wanting to miss any of the action, he sent me off to find the latrine by myself.

I got lost in the crowd. At first I was scared, but after a few minutes of aimless wandering it became an adventure. I probably circled the stadium two, maybe three times. The game was nearly over when I finally spotted Earl and sat back down on the bench next to him. He barely glanced at me, probably never missed me. That was Earl for you. How could someone who looked so much like me not care about me? The bridge seemed to understand.

The majestic vision of the Rose Bowl vaporized when the dead man's face flashed into my consciousness, a pasty-gray contorted version of Ricky Ricardo's face. Who was he? Did he have any children? Did he love them? Did he ever take them to the Rose Bowl?

What was he doing there under that piece of cardboard? Was he sleeping? He didn't look like a hobo, well dressed, suit and tie, expensive shoes. Wincing pain throbbed behind my temples, like it does when you eat freezing-cold ice cream too fast. I couldn't get the dead man out of my mind. I needed to throw up again.

I had been awake since Carl, right on time, fired up his Chevy and headed off to bake and wrap his daily quota of twenty-thousand loaves. After I finally got up, it took me almost an hour to decide not to leave a note. I left Luke snoring peacefully, ordering Mac to stay with him before I eased myself out into the moonless night. I looked back through the open window one last time and silently granted Luke full dominion over the room and all of its contents. Mac whimpered softly when, at length, I carefully slid the window shut.

My sandals did little to keep my feet dry as I tiptoed across the dewy grass. I had left my brand new tennis shoes, half of Lucinda's sacrifice, behind for Luke to grow into.

It was so dark.

I had made my decision, yet sadly, as I stood on the sidewalk looking back at the house, I wished that Luke and I were sneaking out once again to bask in the nocturnal beatitude of Billy Goat Hill. We had some good times, Luke and I.

Walking down the hill of Ruby Place I felt more alone than I'd ever felt before, like the last boy on earth. At Mrs. Robinson's fence Molly barked once. She was stupid but not deaf. It occurred to me that it was a sound I would never hear again. The dead man's face flashed through my mind. He was already there, where dogs don't bark...I guessed.

I crossed Figueroa Boulevard to the east side of the street and trudged north. Like a captured soldier, head down, prodded along by my abusive captor, my own fate, I leaned forward at a disconsolate angle and marched. Wretched, pitiful, forlorn, I marked a steady pace toward my eerie, self-imposed conclusion. At some point, I looked up and caught myself longing for that sparkling miracle, that beautiful, tangerine sun that had delivered Luke back to me that day at Three Ponds. No such luck. Not even one last shooting star to light my deserted path. "No matter," I said to my feet. There was no need for beacons, bench marks, or moonlit maps...they knew the way to Suicide Bridge. The ebony sky sealed my loneliness within me.

At each cross street I called out its name from memory: Myosotis, Roy, Springvale, Albans, Delphi, Oakcrest Way, La Prada, Hillandale, Burwood, Strickland, Poppypeak, Annan Way, Tipton Way, Crestwood Way, Vista Terrace, Glen Arbor, Yosemite Drive, Rockdale, Lanark, La Loma Road and, at last, Colorado Boulevard. Eagle Rock loomed in the darkness above me as I pushed on up the hill toward the bridge.

I sat down on the curb in front of Henry's Rite Spot to catch my breath. A faint light shimmered inside the front window. I was thirsty and thought about Henry's quart size strawberry shakes. Earl used to treat us to those shakes once in a while, back in the "good old days," when he and Lucinda got along. Earl had his good points. I missed him, but I never let on. I didn't want to make things worse for Luke. No sense crying over spilt milk shakes anyway.

The lights on the bridge snapped into my field of vision, warm and inviting, waiting patiently, like faithful candles in a window. As bright and disarming as Miss Cherry's lovely smile, but dangerously insincere, the lights were a clever disguise obscuring a grotesque monster; a huge dolmen tomb for an exquisite covey of wayward souls. Now the youngest to take the solemn oath, I was drawn to its willing arches, compelled by anguish and despair, seeking solace and comfort in the ultimate capricious act. Funny how I wasn't scared.

I plodded out to the middle of the bridge, sure that there was nothing else to do but wait for the sun to appear as my witness. I had arrived too early. Waiting for the box office to open had always been painful for me and here I was, the first one in line again. I leaned against the railing and willed the dead man out of my mind. I didn't want him to jump with me. This was private and personal, and I didn't even know his name. Minutes passed. Nobody got in line behind me. The bridge lights shut off making the first glow of daybreak more noticeable. Sounds in the distance signaled the end of the city's slumber. I looked down again. A morning mist had crawled out from the rocks covering the channel bottom, a fresh-smelling sheet on a bed custom made for my weary bones. It wouldn't hurt, I thought. I'll just pull the covers up and go to sleep.

A tear rolled down and dripped off the tip of my nose. I watched it plummet away and prepared to follow. My wounded mind closed in on itself, incapable of distinguishing anything except the final critical task...and one last selfless thought. My lips trembled over the

words..."I'm sorry Luke." Overriding the oppressive sorrow, I began
to form the intent, the mental instructions. It was time. The muscles
in my right leg began to respond...to lift up over...the rail....

"Hey! You're out and about kind of early, aren't you?"

A car had come across the bridge and pulled to a stop not six feet
away from where I stood. I was mired so deep in my gloom, I didn't
hear it. The voice, loud over the drone of the motor, had startled me
out of my dark trance. My leg slumped back down on the deck. I
turned around and saw an unfamiliar car. It was big and bright-white
in color. An ivory stallion out on a morning run. My face must have
been an obvious display of pain and sorrow. I sat down and put my
head in my hands. I was ready to kill myself but not ready to cry in
front of a stranger.

"What's the matter? You got problems?" the man asked, leaning
across the front seat to the open passenger window. I nodded my head
up and down without showing my face. I must have looked like a silly
toddler playing a game of peekaboo. He shut off the motor and got out
of the car. I stole a look and then quickly wiped my eyes.

He was in his uniform. He looked out of place, strange, driving a
civilian car. I stared at the familiar spit-shined, black knee boots as he
approached from around the back of the car. It had been a year and a
half, but he recognized me right away. "Wade Parker? Kind of far
from home aren't you?"

I nodded. It was good to hear that sympathetic voice again. It
warmed me a little. "What are you doing over here," I asked weakly.

"I live in Pasadena. Got a little place off Fair Oaks." He pointed
over my shoulder to the southwest.

"Oh, I thought you had to live in Los Angeles."

"Used to. Not anymore. Say, you're not related to Chief Parker
are you?"

"No, I'm not an Indian." I wasn't in a joking mood, it just came
out. I chuckled sarcastically, my emotions split wider than the Grand
Canyon. He looked at me kind of sideways then got it and smiled.

A car started across the bridge in the same lane he had stopped his
car. He would have to move or let the car pass. "Come on, get in," he
said, opening the passenger door. I hesitated for a moment, then one
step and I was in. He slammed the door, hurried around the hood and
got in behind the wheel. He gunned the engine and put it in gear.
The rear wheels yelped. "She's got great traction," he said, as if I

knew what that meant.

I looked out the back window at the bridge as we crossed into Pasadena. My solution had been stolen away from me.

He made a few turns and within five minutes swung the big white car around to the back of a restaurant called *The Den*. He turned the motor off and set the brake. "Just got her yesterday," he said proudly, referring to the car as if it were his first born child. "She's a 1956 Buick Special; not brand new, but just barely broken in. Got her for a pretty good price from a *White Rock* beverage salesman over in Highland Park." He grinned. "Like her?"

"I've never been in a car this big before."

He grinned some more and stroked the big steering wheel. "Haven't picked out a name for her yet." He looked at me, inviting me to make a suggestion. I shrugged my shoulders. "I know," he said. "I can't think of anything either." He rolled up his window and asked me to do the same. "Come on," he said, "let's get some breakfast."

I moved slowly. My stomach wasn't interested in food. My mind was still back on the bridge.

nine

Like a mindless drone carrying out a rote assignment, I slogged along behind the Sergeant. We entered the building through a service door and tramped down a dim hallway that smelled of animal fat and stale produce. A couple of turns later, we emerged through a swinging door into a cramped but clean, well-ordered, brightly lit kitchen. My eyes narrowed to adjust to the light. My mind, still mulled from the scene at the bridge, lagged far behind.

An elderly, baldheaded man, no more than an inch taller than me, thin as a rail, stood at a stainless steel sink full of bobbing potatoes. His back was to us and he turned abruptly, startled by unexpected visitors. I immediately noticed the naked lady tattoos on his wet forearms. It was impossible, even in my spiritless mood, to look at the man and not smile.

"Well I'll be a gelded stud—how ya doin', Lyle," the little man cackled. He quickly wiped his hands on an apron tied below a miniature beer belly that looked huge on him. He flashed a smile that looked way too big for his elfish face, displaying a set of choppers yellower than an old plow horse's teeth. I watched with fascination as the tattoo buttocks jiggled on the arm he stuck out to shake hands with. The other arm displayed a frontal pose of the same naked lady.

"Couldn't be better, Rodney. How in the hell are you?"

"Don't do no good to complain, Lyle. Just keep shoveling. That's my motto!" He cackled again.

Inside myself I was still very distraught, but I couldn't keep from smiling. Rodney wasn't a dwarf, but his high pitched laugh and spunky disposition reminded me of the Munchkins in *The Wizard Of Oz*, my favorite movie.

"Who's this young colt?" he asked, turning his grin on me. He hobbled over and thrust the buttocks at me. His walk propounded the presence of an invisible barrel between his legs. His knees were three times farther apart than his ankles. To say he was bowlegged would be an understatement.

"Wade Parker, sir...pleasure to meet you."

"Rodney Bernanos," he fired back. "Nice to meet you, too, Wade. Just call me Rodney, if you please. You're as tall as me so you can save the *sir* for teachers, preachers, and jail keepers."

"Huh?"

He clipped short another cackle when a gray cat leapt from some unknown springboard and landed gracefully on his right shoulder. The cat sat perfect as a parrot on a perch. Intrigued by the man and the cat, I watched them as a trace of an impression tickled my consciousness. *Bernanos? Why does that name sound familiar?* Rodney reached up natural as could be and commenced scratching the cat behind its ears as if the cat had been there all along. This motion stood the tattoo of the front facing woman in an upright position and made her pelvis thrust and boobs jiggle like an animated pornographic cartoon. My stare was flagrant.

"Like my tattoos do you?" Pride of ownership twinkled in the little man's eyes.

Caught in the act, I flushed red and giggled nervously. I was at that age that young males find so perplexing; that in-between stage when females, much less naked ones, start to make your blood race in a strange new way, but you're not quite ready to admit it yet, especially to your peers. But I was with grown men now, even if I did outweigh one of them. I pictured Miss Cherry, her breasts bouncing under her blouse as she walked toward me that night on Billy Goat Hill. I resumed staring at Rodney's arms and promoted myself up to their level. "Yes, sir, those are dandy tattoos."

Rodney cackled with delight and held both arms up for inspection. I leaned in for a closer look. "Meet my former wife, Doris. She was a six-footer," he said clearly bragging. "I like tall women. Good for dancing with, if you know what I mean." His eye brows wiggled lecherously as he freed a mirthful snicker.

The cat furtively eyed Rodney's eyebrows as though it were spying baby birds in a nest. Its mouth twitched as it readied to pounce. I glanced at Sergeant Cavendish. He had noticed the cat, too, his face a mixed bouquet of smile and grin.

Rodney wasn't finished with the subject of his ex-wife. "Good old Doris. Helluva woman...but my God," he shook his head sharply, "she used to ride my ass harder than a starving jockey." *Jockey? Rodney Bernanos? He used to be a Jockey.* "But I have to be honest with you, Wade. I miss that magnificent body of hers something fierce." He held his arms out in front of him and gave the fore and aft of Doris a long, wistful look, his animated face slackened by the heartswelling tug of lost love. Then he jumped on a fresh horse faster than a Pony Express rider running behind schedule. "But by God, you could seal that mighty mouth of hers in a burlwood box, bury it with the Pharaohs, and I'd STILL be able to hear her nagging." I stepped back, a little shocked. He grinned. "Don't regret the tattoos though, no sir-*ree*, not one darn bit."

"Yes," I said, feeling I should agree. "Those are real fine tattoos."

He held his arms up facing toward the Sergeant and me and cackled again. The cat hunched low on Rodney's shoulder watching his eyebrows for any sign of movement.

"Good Lord, I can hear her right now: 'Rod-*neee!*'" he screeched, mimicking the voice of Doris, I gathered. "That's just how she'd say it: 'Rod-*neee!*'"

Rodney was something to behold, bald head, bowling ball belly, cat on his shoulder, all the while cackling like a chicken that just laid a three yolker. The cat, seeming mildly annoyed, glanced at us briefly and then re-focused on the eyebrows. I had to sit down before I fell down and scooted onto a stool next to the sink full of potatoes.

"'Rod-*neee!*'" he continued, "'You don't know which way you're going unless you're on a damn horse running in a circle! Rod-*neee!* Them damn horses are smarter than you!' She was right about that," he said grinning, breaking character only for a split second. "'Rod-*neee!* You can't even ride me right, lessen I turn you around and point you in the right direction!' GOD that woman could hurt a man's feelings when she wanted to.

"Well, you know what, Wade?" he said, finally calming himself, returning his fingers to the back of the cat's ears. I shook my head sideways, holding my breath to suppress the laughter, unable to talk.

"Old Rodney always knows where he's going now. And if ever I do get lost, I'll just hold up an arm, right or left, and old Doris will point the way." The eyebrows wiggled again. This time the cat was ready.

Pow!

Thwack!

Boom!

The cat gave him a hard left jab, followed by a slashing right cross, then another hard left jab before leaping from Rodney's shoulder to my lap where it promptly curled up into a tight ball of purring fur. The pummeling sent Rodney's gray-brown eyebrows scattering like dandelions in the wind, leaving him stunned and completely baffled. I couldn't take it. I slid to the floor in a heap of laughter, the stool toppling over to the side. The cat rode down to the floor with me without budging from my lap one inch. The sergeant was practically gagging, he was laughing so hard.

Rodney tried to appear dignified as he spat on his fingers and began smoothing his eyebrows back into place. "Now you know why I named him Rocky," he said, looking at the cat with sincere respect. "You ain't never gonna find any rodents hang'n 'round with a cat named Rocky Mouseano in the ring, ah, *Cackle*, kitchen I mean."

It was impossible to hold my breath any longer.

The Sergeant and I sat on the floor, Rodney standing between us flexing the likeness of Doris to the beat of a silent rhumba, all of us acting silly. Composure came slowly to the raucous gathering. I looked at the Sergeant sitting there laughing and smiling as much or more than me; the same man that had led a motor cycle gang to the crest of Billy Goat Hill and had ripped a latex prop from his face as we stood in the dark at top of The Crippler; the same man that had appeared at Eagle Rock like a friendly ghost sent to reveal a mysterious message of caution and responsibility. Now the same man shows up again, as a guardian angel might, and whisks me off of the bridge of no return. *Stuff like that only happens in the movies*, I thought.

That was the magical moment, sitting there on that kitchen floor, alive, wanting to be alive, glad to be alive. And I felt sure, looking at him, not seeing the uniform but only the man, that a special bond had been forged. The Sergeant looked at me and smiled. I knew he was reading my mind. He gave me the thumbs up. I returned the signal.

To me, the deal had been sealed. The bond would change the course of my life, and forever be remembered in my heart and in my dreams.

Rodney Bernanos, by his own account, cooked better than he ever raced horses. Already well past seventy by then, Rodney's best rides had occurred long before I was born, but he certainly proved his mastery of the culinary arts that morning. The Sergeant kind of hung back and let me and Rodney get acquainted.

I learned how to make "Horsecakes."

Buttermilk batter with a palm of oats, diced apples and four sugar cubes mixed in thoroughly, tail up when you plop them on the griddle and a whinny when you flip them over. The whole procedure is carried out set to an adolescent rhythm resembling the great American classic, The Hokey-Pokey.

Rodney claimed that his secret horsecake recipe had helped him bed Doris the first time. "She fell in love with my cooking, then she fell in love with me," he said, holding up his arm and giving Doris' shapely fanny a tender smooch.

Rodney supervised me at the stove while he told stories from his racing days. He critiqued some of the more famous jockeys like Eddie Arcaro, Bill Hartack, Willie Shoemaker and Johnny Longden. He claimed he taught Longden everything he knew about jockeying, plus some.

Years later, while working at the Huntington Car Wash in Monrovia, not far from Santa Anita Race Track, I would actually meet Johnny Longden. He drove into the car wash one day in a big Lincoln rigged with extensions on the brake and accelerator. I was working the gas pump that day. He opened the car door and said, "Fill'er up, Giraffe." I was well over six feet tall by then, though I'm certain he called most people Giraffe. He was amiable and friendly, chatting with me while I filled the gas tank. I told him about Rodney Bernanos and Mr. Longden confirmed that Rodney had indeed been a big influence on his career. Mr. Longden watched me struggle with his modified foot controls and laughed like hell while I pulled the Lincoln up to the vacuum hoses with my knees touching my ears. He gave me a five dollar tip which was about three times more than my hourly wage. I asked him to autograph the fiver which he did. I still have it. It's in the safety deposit box with the fake scar.

Rodney talked horses with pure passion. His little eyes glowed like flares as he reminisced about the great ones—*Kelso, Round Table, Carry Back, Nashua and Citation*—none of which he had ever been blessed to ride. He particularly raved about *Carry Back*, known for his sensational late rushes in the stretch.

His all time favorite was a horse called *Silky Sullivan* which he claimed was the greatest come from behind thoroughbred of all time. He made a wisecrack of a sexual nature, something about Doris claiming he was too much like *Silky Sullivan*. The Sergeant chirped out a lascivious snicker. I didn't quite get it.

The three of us sat in an upholstered leather booth in the main dining room of The Den. I caught on that we were special guests when I saw that there were no other customers or employees present. The Den was strictly a dinner house open for business at 4:30 p.m. seven days a week. It was an upscale place catering to the type of clientele that appreciated candlelight and linen napkins. The Den's atmosphere was stylish, but well broken in. A decor of uncultured elegance sat like bait in an alluring trap. It captured the fancy of artful horsemen and rueful gambler alike. Thoroughbred memorabilia owned the theme. Each booth was dedicated to a famous horse or jockey as evidenced by a tasteful display of framed photographs and oil paintings. We sat in the Sir Gordon Richards booth and ate horsecakes smothered with apple butter and hot maple syrup. At Rodney's insistence I drank coffee for the first time in my life. I pretended I liked it.

Halfway into the meal, my thoughts drifted during a short lull in the conversation. Maybe an hour had passed since I leaned over the bridge railing and watched that tear drip from my nose and fall like a tracer bullet leading the way. I envisioned myself lying in a bloody, mangled mess, cold meat and crunched bones waiting for some hapless mortal to come along and be marred for life by the grisly discovery. I shivered at the thought. I should have been concerned with thoughts of a guilt-ridden Lucinda, torturing herself with blame, second guessing every child rearing decision she ever made, having to locate dental records after failing to positively identify what was left of me; and, oh God, poor Luke, how he would have floundered through years of resentment, his broken heart festering, raw, the wounds of desertion and betrayal refusing to heal; and Mac, my most trusted confidant, my noble protector, loyal beyond death, forever waiting for the boy that said "stay" and then never came home. A day, a week, a year, however long it took, he would follow my scent through a thousand nuclear battlefields to get to that point on the bridge. From where, with his tail wagging, heart filled with love, he would jump. I closed my eyes and thanked God that none of that would happen.

Because instead, I was being fed and entertained by a joke cracking, ex-jockey restaurateur who almost needed a booster chair to see over the stack of horsecakes piled on the plate in front of him. I sat there radiating energy like a crystal in the sun. Instead of recrimination, I felt perfect, in harmony with the universe, my symmetry complete, as if molded from the purest of elements by the hands of a loving and forgiving God. A short ride in a four year old Buick Special captained by a Sergeant named Lyle had delivered me from the balustrade of despair to the open gates of nirvana. I felt special. I felt chosen.

"Want some more horse—*Argh!*—cakes?" Rodney grunted, belching loudly, then shoveling in the last bite from his plate.

"Just one more," I answered, making him cackle again.

He got up and went into the kitchen. Rocky trailed after him with his tail straight up in the air like an antenna alert for important signals.

"Pretty neat guy, huh?" the Sergeant said once Rodney was out of ear shot.

"He's wild," I said enthusiastically. "How did you meet him?"

"He kind of saved my life a long time ago."

A small chill ran down my spine. "Really, how did he do that?" *If he says 'He saved me from jumping off a bridge'...I'm leaving.*

"It's a long story. Maybe I'll tell you about it sometime."

"You've known each other for a long time?"

"I've known Rodney all my life. He knew my mother and father. They died in a fire when I was little. I guess you could say Rodney looked after me from then on."

There was something in his voice that told me he didn't want to talk about his parents. "Did Rodney save your life by pulling you out of the fire."

"No." He seemed defensive, concerned that I would make that connection. "Rodney had nothing to do with the fire."

What an odd answer. Did Rodney set the fire? No way would I think that.

Rodney reappeared with one final horsecake big enough to choke a horse. "That's the last of it, gents. Eat what you can," he said, setting a large platter down in the middle of the table.

The three of us picked at the pizza size pancake. Rodney fed small bits of it to Rocky who sat on the floor performing for his master. "He's not as smart as a horse, but he's a good animal," Rodney said. "Have any pets, Wade?"

"Got a dog named Mac. He's very intelligent."

"What kind of dog is he?"

"Shepard and Doberman mix."

Rodney thought for a moment. "Still got his ears and tail?"

"Yeah, but he doesn't like us to tease him about it. We couldn't afford to get him clipped and cropped."

Rodney cackled. "No, I don't guess he would. Animals have feelings, too. I learned early in the game not to bad mouth horses." He grinned, another story about to begin. "Least not to their faces anyway. *Cackle!* Caught a ride once on this hot blooded three year old named *Abdulla*. She was fighting the gate real hard and we were about to get disqualified. Out of frustration I told her she wasn't fit to make dog food. *Cackle!* She threw me in the mud two lengths out of the gate and won the race without me. Best not to antagonize animals. Ain't that right, Rocky." He gave the cat another little morsel and thought a little bit longer. "This dog of yours, Mac you say?"

"Yes, sir. Mac."

"He wouldn't happen to have a noticeable scar on his right hindquarter would he?"

The Sergeant looked at me. He had noticed the scar that day at Eagle Rock.

"Why, yes, he does," I said, more than curious. "How did you know that?"

"I heard a racket in my neighbor's back yard one night a few months back. I knew my neighbor wasn't home so I grabbed my flashlight and went out in my shorts to investigate. I saw your dog Mac playing connect the dots with a lovely young Dalmatian by the name of Antoinette. My neighbor paid a stud fee the next day hoping for a lucrative litter of mascot pups for the Glendale Fire Department." Rodney had us laughing again. This time on a full stomach. "You should see the little buggers. *Cackle!* They look like Picasso's worst nightmare. I told my neighbor he ought to try to sell them to the police department. Maybe they could use them as undercover dogs."

He gave the Sergeant a chilly look. "They'll make fine cop dogs...they'll probably change their spots."

I didn't get Rodney's meaning. I glanced at the Sergeant. He looked a little funny, pale. He didn't respond to Rodney's jab. Something was odd. Strange.

"Might keep one myself now, though," Rodney said, turning back to face me. "Now that I know they were sired by your Mac."

"You live in Glendale?" I asked.

"I sure do. Right below Adventist Hospital. *Cackle!* Mac covers a lot of ground doesn't he?"

"He's a horny bastard," I said without shame.

Rodney crowed like a rooster. He freely identified with Mac's debauchery. "Couldn't put it more forthrightly than that myself, kid!" he roared.

The Sergeant just shook his head. He'd been very quiet since Rodney made the crack about the puppies.

ten

It seemed to me that the first decade of my existence contained enough trials and tribulations to fill ten lifetimes. I needed a long, smooth straightaway in my road. The bumps and turns had nearly killed me, literally. Rodney Bernanos was to become a willing participant in my life for the next few months, a fact for which I was eternally grateful. Had he not died so soon, I'm sure things would have been different, and probably better. We promised to get together again soon, said our good-byes, and loaded our full bellies back into the Buick. I had started to worry about Luke being home alone, even with Mac on guard. The Sergeant offered to give me a ride home.

The sun was out in full glory as we crossed back over Suicide Bridge. The mist in the Arroyo had been driven back to where ever it comes from. I felt queasy about beating the odds, not understanding any of it, but naively believing that understanding of such things would come to me later. I watched uneasily as we passed by the spot where I had stood barely two hours earlier. I turned and looked back over the seat gazing at the diminishing spot that seemed a lifetime ago.

"Never look back, Wade," the Sergeant said, breaking my reverie.

Slowly letting go of my thoughts, I turned to look at his face. "What do you mean?"

The corner of his eye crinkled as he bestowed me with a warm, gratuitous smile. I was mesmerized. I knew that all knowing, didactic look from before. I felt he knew why I was there on the bridge. He saved my life. There was nothing to say. I was completely humbled.

We drove on in placid silence, the soft vibration of the big Buick engine settling my emotions back to neutral. I felt his eyes on me several times but I could only look ahead and watch the street signs go by in reverse order of the litany I had earlier chanted to the dark, death march sky. I had expected that I would never see any of this again. Now, in the healthy light of day, every tree, every house, every blade of grass sparkled with the invigorating shine of renewal.

The experience of meeting Rodney had a tonic effect on me, but it was more than that. The Sergeant had literally saved my life. I'm sure I would have jumped if he had not come along. I knew deep in my heart his showing up on the bridge couldn't have been a coincidence. It was part of a plan. It had to be.

"Ruby Place," the sign said. To me the word Ruby had always conjured up visions of a boisterous black woman with big painted lips. Now the word whistled from my lips with reverence for the precious gem that it was. Isn't that something. We live on Ruby Place. Wow! The Buick ascended the hill like a flirtatious gull embracing the thermal lift of an amorous westerly. Regal curb feelers fore and aft trumpeted the arrival of the royal coach.

"Queenie," I said.

The Sergeant looked at me. "What?"

"She is a girl isn't she?"

"Who?"

"I thought you were a trained investigator."

"I am," he said, with a little frown.

"You asked me to think of a name for something." I patted the seat to give him a big hint.

He grinned. "Yeah. Queenie. I like it. Queenie it is."

The screen door slammed open and Luke bounded off the porch as if he were greeting rare company. "Hey, ya big donkey. Where ya been?" His smile made me feel like I was the Good Humor Man giving out free Popsicles.

"I went for a walk this morning. The Sergeant gave me a ride home." It was the truest lie I ever told him.

"Hi, Mister Scar. Cool car."

"Thanks, Luke. You can call me Lyle or even Mister Cavendish, if you like."

"OK," Luke said.

"Hey. How 'bout you guys let me take your picture in front of Queenie."

"Queenie is the car's name," I informed Luke, proudly adding, "She's got great traction."

The Sergeant got out of the car. He went around to the back and popped the trunk. He pulled out a camera case and ushered Luke and me to the front of the car where he positioned us in front of Queenie's massive grill. He made us feel special, like two little Buick Specials posing with the Queen Mother herself. Lucinda could never get us to stand still and have our picture taken, but Luke and I stood there like trained professional models patiently standing by while the photographer fiddled with the camera.

Luke watched him preparing the camera and innocently asked, "Do you take pictures of dead bodies with that camera?"

The shutter clicked.

The flash bulb exploded inside my brain. Reality drove home, not in a *Body-by-Fisher* pride of General Motors piece of the American dream, but more like a sledge hammered wedge of tempered steel pounding into petrified oak. I split in half. Dry me, stack me, burn me, and scatter my ashes to the wind. I'm still a murderer!

The picture the Sergeant took would show a boy who by all appearances looks well-balanced and happy. A picture is worth a thousand words? No one has ever looked at that picture and said anything other than "cute kids" and "nice car."

"Yes, as a matter of fact I have," the Sergeant answered.

It sounded like an accusation to me. Luke must have been on another planet because he seemed to make no connection between Lyle, Mr. Policeman, taking pictures of dead bodies, and our real life horror show at Three Ponds. I must have looked whiter than Queenie as I stared off into space, my short-lived hold on happiness suddenly frozen dormant, repressed by living, breathing fear.

"What's the matter, Wade? You look like you just saw a ghost," the Sergeant said.

In my mind his words were marinated with innuendo. *Do they handcuff ten-year-old boys?* "I guess I ate too many horsecakes." Luke looked at me funny. "I'll tell you about it later, Luke."

The phone rang inside the house.

"I'll get it," Luke said. I couldn't move if I wanted to. "It's probably Lucinda calling to see if you showed up. She was in a snit about going to work and leaving me at home by myself." He darted inside the house.

The Sergeant put the camera back in the trunk and slammed it shut. "Well, Wade, it's been quite an experience. But I better say so long for now."

Suddenly I was flooded with adrenaline. I didn't want him to go. I wanted him to come into the house, sit on the sofa, and hear my confession. But I couldn't speak. I was scared to death, afraid he wouldn't like me anymore, fearful the government would ship me off to Sing Sing, or Alcatraz, or worse yet, to the bottom of a pond filled with the syrupy, green blood of a million Martians where I'd live forever breathing in goop through gaping gills like a giant carp.

He started up Queenie.

I wanted to scream "WAIT!"

Luke yelled from the front door. "Wade, it's Lucinda! She wants to talk to you!"

I couldn't move.

The Sergeant rolled down his window and motioned me over to the car. I rocked closer on numb stilts, barely functioning. He held out his hand to give me something. I presented my palm and looked for speckles of forgiveness in those all-knowing eyes. He held his closed hand over mine, said, "You boys ever been to Mississippi?" and then let it drop.

I think I said no as he slowly drove away. For a second I saw his eyes in the rear view mirror. Then I looked down at my outstretched hand and saw a shiny silver ball bearing, the one from the second "S" in Mississippi, the gouged out eye of the Cyclops. I wanted to throw it into the next galaxy, but it wouldn't let me. In a stupor, I involuntarily put it in my pocket and glanced at Queenie making her stately descent down the hill of Ruby Place.

The Sergeant waved.

I waved back.

"Wade! You better get the phone. She's madder than a hornet."

I went into the house and picked up the receiver.

"Hello...Yes...I'm sorry...OK...I promise...Bye." I hung up the telephone and walked like a lobotomized zombie toward the bedroom. Mac, sitting exactly where I had ordered him to stay hours before, wagged his tail. "Come," I whispered. He jumped up and plopped his head on the pillow. I laid down next to him. "You be Toto and I'll be Dorothy." He licked my cheek.

There's no place like home.

Never look back, Wade.

No longer in control of my dreams, I closed my eyes and repeated the words over and over, deathly afraid that the nightmare was waiting for me. I was still a murderer, but it seemed that my chance meeting with Rodney had changed things for the better, because for the next twelve hours Doris and I did the Rhumba all the way back to Kansas.

eleven

Many years later I read this passage in one of those self-help type books. It spoke volumes to me.

It is a rare man that faces his darkest hour so full of sanity that thoughts of self-destruction escape his battered consciousness. Is it nasty lunacy or noble reason to plunge the dagger of mortality deep into one's own heart? It is also a rare man, who once afflicted with suicidal notions, plays out the hand to tragic end. Most of humanity falls somewhere between the extremes.

The Grim Reaper's scythe had come close enough to shave me, if I'd had any whiskers that is. The bridge was a tool of my guilt. It had lured me, as Reverend Bonner would say, to the brink of eternal damnation. Inexplicable forces had intervened and all I knew for sure was that I wanted no more of that business.

I had gone way beyond harmless contemplation. Indeed I had readied myself, the "dagger of mortality" poised, all nets of rationality removed, nothing in the way save the final impulse. Only to be pulled back from the edge of darkness because of some larger plan to which I was not privy, nor remotely equipped to understand. Gradually, understanding or not, I realized I had to face my demons squarely. Unfortunately, knowing and doing were not the same thing. I found progress wherever and whenever I could. Most importantly, I never ever thought about killing myself again.

Yesterday John Fitzgerald Kennedy was elected the 35th President of the United States. If I had been old enough to vote—ten didn't qualify me—I would have voted for Richard Milhous Nixon. I remember it clearly because Earl had showed up, got into an argument with Lucinda, made her cry, and swore out loud that he'd sooner vote for Nixon than pay another damn dime in child support. Of course, I misconstrued his meaning. I thought he meant he had voted for Nixon, when, actually, Earl hated Nixon and his Republican Party. It was a rich man's club, which disqualified him from membership for life. Kennedy's victory meant, to my prepubescent mind, that there were more people out there like Earl than not like Earl. This sowed within me a slow germinating seed of conservatism. I was powerless to compel Earl to give Lucinda more money, but by God I was certainly free to identify with and strive to be worthy of a slot with the Young Republicans, if the opportunity ever came.

This type of twisted irony had become the dominating theme of my life. Had I been a ten-year-old boy living in early Nazi Germany my bitter and vulnerable state of mind would have made me a likely recruit for Hitler's Brown Shirts. Thankfully, I was born in another decade, near the Arroyo Seco, not the Danube, Elbe or the Rhine.

I had managed to shore up my collapsing world due in large part to frequent visits with Rodney at his restaurant. We had quickly developed an extraordinary friendship, without which I never would have survived the psychological machinations, the quick-fire fear that tormented me during August through November of 1960. The Sergeant was around some, making me feel special when he was, though remaining a mystery in most respects. *He's looking out for me, protecting me,* I repeatedly reassured myself. I needed to believe that. To me, he was as real as real can be—I believed in him. Or was our relationship just a fantasy, a pathetic creation of my needy heart? I had no idea just how omnipresent he really was. Nor did I sense how complicated, how dangerously entwined, our lives had become; nor how singularly responsible he was for shaping my collapsing world. The truth would not shine until all those years later, when the only thing left in his Pandora's Box was a dying man's conscience.

The lumbering but lovable trolley cars of Los Angeles had gone the way of the dinosaur, driven to extinction by a conspiratorial tire-and-rubber company. I retain a vague but fond image of those old Red Cars, but the free-wheeling, fume belching, rubber-tired buses that now scurried over the landscape like fleas on a mongrel suited me fine. They gave me mobility at an age when the system works against you. I took full advantage. I knew the routes of northeast Los Angeles better than some of the bus drivers, and getting to Rodney's house in Glendale by bus was almost as easy as walking to Suicide Bridge. Sadly, I was to make only one visit to Rodney's little house on Stanley Avenue off Chevy Chase Drive.

It started out as one of those rare days of smog-free splendor that almost justifies living in Los Angeles the rest of the year. Rodney had invited Luke and me over to see Kirk, the spotted son of Mac and Antoinette. Kirk was named after Rodney's favorite actor. Believe it or not, we actually had Lucinda's permission to make the trip. It was a Saturday. She was working, as usual, and couldn't give us a ride.

We arrived just before noon, laughing and hamming it up as we found Rodney's newly repainted house. Coming up the front walk, I glanced through a large undraped window and could see all the way through the interior of the house to an open back door and a sun-drenched yard beyond. Rodney was out there, and in an instant I could tell something was wrong. I stopped cold, confused, unsure. Luke collided into me and I lost the bright, sunshiny, image of Rodney. I could have sworn he had just swung his arm out, as one would do to slap someone in the face. Worse yet, I thought I saw a figure retreating from Rodney, only a blur of motion, but enough to associate with the unmistakable outline of the Sergeant. *What is happening?* This was to have been Luke's first introduction to Rodney. He was very excited about meeting him. On the bus ride over I had repeated all of my favorite Rodney stories for Luke, psyching myself up as well in the process. All of that was gone now, replaced by uncertainty. If I saw what I saw, how could it be so? I looked again, saw Rodney standing alone, his back to me now, staring off at some unknown corner of his yard. *What did I see?*

"Come on," Luke said. "What are you waiting for?"

I held him back for a moment, trying to gather my wits, then allowed him to move ahead to the porch. He looked at me with a question, I nodded, and he rang the door bell. We heard a puppy bark, followed immediately by Rodney's trademark cackle, and I was tremendously relieved. Disavowing any need to know, I willingly let go of my fears, and waited with a heart full of joy as the nicest, funniest friend I ever had hobbled to let us in. What a great day this was going to be, after all. A moment later the door opened. "Hi, guys," Rodney said, smiling.

Then suddenly he grimaced and squeezed his eyes shut strangely. He clutched his chest and bent his knees with a jerky motion, as though he'd been clipped from behind by an unsportsmanlike tackler. He hadn't yet unlatched the screen door and it stood between us like a barrier separating inmate from visitor. In stunned disbelief, I stared at him as he dropped to the floor, his body rigid against the screen door, hands pawing at his chest and neck, fighting to breathe. A moment of futility passed during which I thought, hoped, prayed that he was just kidding around, perhaps playing an outrageous prank as though the sight of Luke had given him a heart attack or something. But it wasn't a joke. He was in serious trouble, awful pain, and there was nothing we could do except linger at a standstill, dumb, ambushed.

"Neighbor next door!" Rodney gasped.

I screamed at Luke to run next door and he took off like a shot. From a stupor, I pleaded, "Rodney, what's the matter? What's wrong?"

"Wade!" he called out from some distant dimension, his eyes rolling around as though disconnected from their sockets.

My throat now constricted in sympathy with his tortured breathing, I wheezed, "Yes, sir?" as I knelt down as close to him as I could get. My face and hands pressed hard against the screen, I tried in vain to reach him, to touch him. Tears of agony flooded down and off my face, pelting the newly painted threshold I wanted desperately to cross.

His whole body trembled as he struggled to speak. For just a brief moment he focused on me, his pained eyes conveying how desperately sorry he was, and said, "Remember, Wade, never...look...back." Then his eyes rolled up leaving white blanks between fluttering lids. From inches away, I watched him let go, the terrible pain softening, the tenseness in his body slackening, his face drifting to an expressionless, non-existent state. Last, his arms fell away from his chest, one final breath hissing slowly over his lips as he peacefully laid over on his side. It happened that fast.

Seized by panic, unable to move, mouth opening and closing with the convulsions of silent screams, I looked on in horror as Kirk the puppy whimpered and nudged Rodney's limp hand. At some point, before Luke came back with the man from next door, my mind halted, shutting off like a burned out lamp. I could feel myself rocking back and forth to an inner, pulsing, pounding rhythm. I felt nothing else.

* * * * *

The ambulance drove away slowly, no siren, no lights, no hurry. Luke would have preferred emergency flashers and squealing tires. I sat on Rodney's porch, weeping, not understanding, wanting to lash out at something, anything, everything. The man from next door was inside Rodney's house talking on the telephone. He was nice. He said he had known Rodney for over twenty years. He said Rodney had told him all about me. He said Rodney liked me very much. Filled with a longing I had never before felt, I sat with my head in my hands, my chest painfully aching with the worst of all things—a broken heart.

Kirk scratched at the screen door, whining, wanting to come out and play. He was young and did not yet know how to behave at a time like this. His father, Mac, would know. I wished Mac would come and comfort me. The man hung up the telephone and came to the door. He let Kirk out on the porch, Rodney's porch, and Luke started playing with him. Luke was eight now, old enough to realize what had happened, but he didn't know Rodney. Somehow, perhaps because he was in his own kind of shock, he didn't cry. It was better for me that he didn't cry.

The man came out on the porch and sat down next to me. "Someone is coming to pick you guys up."

I nodded, unable to speak.

The man had been crying, too. His eyes were red and puffy like mine. "Rodney's heart gave out. He had two heart attacks last year," the man said sniffling. "I'm going to keep Kirk for him." He put his arm around me. "Rodney was my best friend, too." I nodded, shaking uncontrollably from the staggered gasps and bitter chills that come from the cruelest of all things...the unanswerable *why* of life and death. The only rationale my mind could convey was beyond unbearable: *God had taken Rodney Bernanos away from me as punishment for killing that man at Three Ponds.*

Stuttering badly, I whispered, "Who is coming for us?"

"Sergeant Cavendish. They reached him on his radio. He happened to be close by."

It must have been him in the back yard. But how can I possibly ask him about it?

Luke took good care of me. He didn't run away this time.

twelve

The Sergeant met Lucinda for the first time, in person, the Wednesday following Rodney's heart attack. I suspected they had spoken on the telephone before that, although neither one had said so. Lucinda agreed to let me attend the funeral with the Sergeant. She made a point of being there to meet him when he picked me up. I sat in Queenie while they chatted on the porch for a couple of minutes. Seeing the two of them talking face to face made me nervous. The Sergeant knew things. One wrong word from him, an innocent slip of the tongue, and Lucinda could easily turn into the *Scourge of God*...Attila for short.

We were well on the way to Rodney's funeral when the Sergeant spoke for the first time. We had shared a respectful quiet up until then. "Your mom is pretty," he said, his cheerful tone as much for his own benefit as for mine.

"She works too much," was the only reply I could come up with. I was too depressed to see or hear the bright side of anything. Caught up in my own grief, I didn't realize how much the Sergeant was hurting, too. I had only lost a new friend. He had lost his closest loved one. I didn't think about it that way.

Miss Cherry was conspicuously absent. When I asked why she hadn't come, he said she didn't know Rodney, had never met him. I thought that was strange. I was surprised Miss Cherry, as close as she was to the Sergeant, had never met Rodney. And that certainly wasn't a reason for not coming along. I thought she should have been there, at least to lend moral support. I sensed it was a sore subject with the Sergeant, so I didn't push it. My curiosity slowly dispersed in a somber cloud of fresh memories of Rodney. Queenie glided on.

The funeral looked like a reunion of Gulliver's Lilliputians. Twenty-five jockeys entered the church dressed in full riding gear. It was a colorful tribute to their departed friend, though quite a bizarre sight. It pleased me to witness such admiration, to know Rodney was liked and respected by the people who knew him from his horse racing days. I only knew Rodney for a brief four months, yet his friendship had made a deep and lasting impression on me. To this day I can't look at a horse without thinking of him.

The infamous Doris showed up at the funeral. She was old but it was easy to project that she had once been a beautiful woman...even with her clothes on. Regardless of his jokes, Rodney had never stopped loving Doris. He took her likeness with him forever. Front and back.

Beautiful Queenie, polished to an ivory sheen, looked out of place in the funeral motorcade. A white sheep in a family of black sheep. We rode along solemnly, the minister's powerful invocation still governing the mood. The Sergeant tried to cover his tears so as not to upset me further. It was a long, sad ride to Forest Lawn. A little too long for me to keep quiet. I wanted to tell him I saw him at Rodney's house, see what he had to say, but the nerve wouldn't come. My desire to speak up, combined with my gutless reticence, made the trip excruciatingly long. When finally we turned in the main gate at Forest Lawn, there was no relief from the multiple layers of melancholy besetting me.

Quiet stayed between us as the long procession of cars wound slowly up a grassy, headstone crowded hill. We stopped, Queenie the eighth car back from the long, black hearse carrying Rodney, while the crawling procession of vehicles stretched far back down the hill. The people at the end of the line had a long walk up to the grave site. Funny how I still have a clear picture in my mind of Rodney's friends and family mournfully trudging up that hill. All of them, except the jockeys, wearing the drab, black apparel of death.

I stood at the grave with all of those people, feeling like a stranger, like I didn't belong, but glad I was there. I went numb as they lowered the casket down in the hole. It was so final. I waved good-bye to the descending coffin and wondered if Rodney would look up Matthew, maybe say hello for me.

I visit his grave and pay my respects every Christmas. His marker says: *Rodney Luis Bernanos, 1884-1960...In The Home Stretch.*

Back in the car, neither of us had much to say for awhile, both of us thinking to ourselves how much we already missed Rodney. I almost asked the big question, and then chickened out. I turned the car radio on instead. The dial was full of Christmas music and commercials touting the appearance of Saint Nick at a dozen different places at the same time. It only served to further set the pessimism solidifying within me. I turned it off in the middle of Bing Crosby's *White Christmas.*

"I'm not in a Christmas mood either," the Sergeant said.

Finally I spoke up. "Remember that morning at Rodney's restaurant when I first met him. You said sometime you would tell me about when Rodney saved your life. How about now?" I would try to work my way up to the hard question.

The Sergeant looked at me. His face lit up with a warm smile. "You're quite a kid, you know that. You reading my mind?"

"Nah," I said, smiling back at him. "I guess maybe we both were thinking about the same thing, about Rodney I mean."

"You wanna hear the story, huh?"

"Yes, sir."

"OK...ahem," he said, clearing remnants of emotion from his voice. "When I was about your age, I guess it was a year or two after Jakey Blume died, I got myself into a real jam one day." He laughed heartily. The atmosphere of the funeral vanished. "I mean a *real* jam," he repeated, laughing harder yet, his eyes growing big as saucers.

"What?" I had started to giggle.

"OK. A friend and I were walking down York Boulevard one April day. It had been drizzling just enough to keep things damp for two days, so we paid no mind that the sky had turned angry, black with pregnant clouds just aching to burst."

Pregnant clouds? Who got them pregnant?

"I had a silver dollar my dad had given me. I carried it around like a good luck charm. You know what I mean?"

I nodded as I reached into my pocket and touched the ball bearing.

"Well, I had been flipping the silver dollar in the air and my friend was calling heads or tails. You know, just goofing off, something to do. I kept trying to toss the silver dollar higher and higher, and finally I dropped it. Off the sidewalk it rolled, over the curb, into the gutter and disappeared down a storm drain."

"Oh man," I said. "I lost a couple of baseballs that way."

"That's just the thing. I was determined not to lose my good luck charm."

"Tough luck."

"Nope. I went down the drain after it."

I wasn't sure whether to believe him or not. He seemed serious though, absent that little give away twinkle in his eye that I had come to know so well.

"Are you talking about those funny, skinny openings in the gutter where the water from the street goes?"

"Water and everything else that people don't want, but most important, my silver dollar."

I was skeptical. "I don't think I could fit my body through those openings. How could you?"

He smiled crisply, his lips pinched tight in the middle. "Don't believe me, huh?"

I thought I might have made him mad. It knocked down the nerve I had been building up to ask him if he was in Rodney's back yard. I tried to rephrase. "Well I'm just saying..." He cut me off.

"I was a skinny little runt. Much smaller than you. More the size of Luke."

I bristled inside. *Luke's not a runt!* "Oh. OK," I said. It was obvious he didn't appreciate being doubted. "Isn't it dangerous to go down in there, garbage, spiders and stuff like that?"

"Isn't The Crippler dangerous?"

"Yeah. But it's fun."

"My point exactly," he said.

"Huh?" My nose crinkled. For a second I thought he meant it like he had scored a point. Then I thought I got it. "Oh—*uh*—OK."

"Like I said, you're quite a kid. You're smart enough to figure these things out."

"Figure what out?"

"Confused?"

"Yes...a little, I think."

"What I mean is, sometimes when we're kids we know when something is dangerous, but we do it anyway. It's when we don't know that something is dangerous that we can really get into serious trouble." He had me going in circles. "OK, forget about that for now," he said. *Forget what?* I felt stupid. "Anyway, the gutter opening dropped down into a concrete box. The box was about four feet long, three feet wide, and deep enough to stand up in. It was very wet down in there, but I easily saw my silver dollar lying on the bottom. I squeezed through the opening and dropped down into the box. That's when my problems started." He grinned, glanced over at me, then turned his eyes back to the road.

"What?"

"When I dropped to the bottom I accidentally kicked the silver dollar. It slid into the drain pipe that empties the water from the box down to the big storm drain pipes that lie thirty feet or so below the street."

"That's where my baseballs went I suppose. So long silver dollar, too, huh?"

"Nope. I went down the pipe after it."

"Jeez! Were you crazy or what?"

"No. I just failed to think clearly and realize the danger."

A light went on in my head. "OK, I get it. So what happened?"

The Sergeant nodded with satisfaction. "The pipe was just big enough for me to squeeze my shoulders in. It was dark. Spooky. I was nervous, but I figured my silver dollar hadn't gone very far. So I pushed with the toes of my shoes, inching my way along with my arms outstretched in front of me. All the while my fingers were feeling around for my good luck charm. I got in there about six or seven feet and finally found my silver dollar."

"Boy, you were lucky," I said, shaking my head.

"Nope."

"What?"

"I was stuck. Which might not have been so bad if the clouds had held their load. The rain started coming down in buckets."

"Jeez Louise!"

He looked at me for a moment, then said, "We just finished burying the guy that saved me from that storm drain."

I was stunned. *How amazing.*

Then, almost against my will, the words jumped from my mouth.

"Sir?" My stomach flip-flopped. I stopped breathing.

"Yes?"

"Were you in Rodney's back yard right before he had the heart attack?"

Clearly startled, he looked at me with a hardness in his eyes that I had not seen before. "No. Why?" he said, looking away.

He was there. "I thought I saw you, saw Rodney slap you in the back yard."

"Well, that's kinda ridiculous. Isn't it?"

"Yes, I guess." *Why is he lying?*

"I don't know what you think you saw, but I even had some detectives...well, everything looked normal at Rodney's house. After he passed away, I mean. You know?"

"I guess. What ever you say, sir." It was no use pushing it.

He cleared his throat again, quite differently from the way he had cleared it a few minutes before. "How about I finish the story now?"

"OK."

Shifting moods like a chameleon changes color, he gave me one of those careful cryptic grins, like that night on Billy Goat Hill. Instantly I thought of Miss Cherry. Thoughts of her seemed to visit me whenever I was feeling low or when the Sergeant displayed one of those mannerisms or expressions that I associated with that first time we met. Like the grin just now.

Not at all intending to change the subject, but relieved to be on to something else, I said, "It would be nice to see Miss Cherry again sometime."

"I thought you wanted to hear the rest of the story."

"I do. It's just when you smile that certain way it always makes me think of Miss Cherry."

"You know, just the other day she asked me about you and Luke."

"She did?" My spirits took an immediate boost upward. The look on my face gave me away.

"You like her, huh." It was a declaration, not a question.

A tingling blush crawled all over my cheeks. "Yes, sir. I think she's real fine." It no longer mattered that he was in Rodney's back yard. I trusted that he had his reasons for not telling me the truth.

"Me, too," he said, pausing for a moment, then adding, "I plan to ask her to marry me."

I turned sideways in the seat to face him. He looked so happy.

"Really?"

He nodded seriously. "You're the first one to know...well, not counting Rodney. I told him last week."

I was pleased on all three counts: that he wanted to marry Miss Cherry, that Rodney knew about it before he died, and that he liked me enough to tell me.

"Think she'll say yes?" he asked tentatively.

I would learn the feeling years later when I prepared to ask a raven-haired goddess named Melissa Hoover to marry me. I cleared my throat for dramatic purposes. "No. I think she's going to marry someone else."

He choked once and fought off a coughing spasm. Red faced and watery eyed, bona fide worry etched deep into his brow, he blurted, "What! *Cough!* Who?"

Gotcha! That'll teach you not to lie to me.

I turned away from him and gazed out the side window, trying my hardest to look like a person struggling to find the least painful words to express some terrible news. Queenie hummed along sharing a silent giggle with me. I could feel him glaring at the back of my head. Finally he couldn't stand it any longer. He slapped me on the shoulder, harder, I'm sure, than he meant to.

I flinched.

"Spit it out, Wade."

I turned back around and faced him squarely. "Well, sir, as you well know by now, I get around this part of town pretty darn well. For a kid anyway."

"Yes, you certainly do. Too much for your own good I fear."

There was a faint threat in his eyes. That, combined with the inference I found veiled in his words seemed to make the ball bearing in my pocket vibrate, like a vane signaling the approach of bad weather. He threw me off balance for a second. "Well—*ahem*—Luke and I—uh—well, sometimes we like to hang out at the Highland Park Police Station." A light-hearted, ah shucks, changing the subject aloofness came over me. I gave him a false smile. I was going for the gold. "Maybe one of us will turn out to be a police officer when we grow up, like you, sir."

"Yeah, so what's that got to do with Cherry?"

"Miss Cherry works with you at the O.C., uh—whatever you call it, doesn't she?"

"O.C.I.U., Organized Crime Investigation Unit. So? What about it?"

I had definitely found his weak spot, his athlete's heel, or whatever you call it. Anyway, he was starting to fume. I delighted in the fact that he was getting sucked in by a ten-year-old kid. "Well—uh—sir, I guess a lot of the officers at the Highland Park Station know you O.C.I.U. people, including Miss Cherry."

Queenie turned the corner at Ruby Place.

The Sergeant was blistering now, his imagination flinging his temper wildly away from its normal realm of cool and calm. I allowed a lengthy pause just to needle him.

"Get to the point, Wade," he said bluntly.

Queenie glided to a graceful stop at the curb.

Mac was napping on the front porch. He raised his head, visually verified that the car and its passengers were authorized objects, then returned to his previous state of slumber. Luke's head popped up in the bedroom window. He waved. I smiled at him while I discreetly moved my hand to unlock the car door, then casually lowered it down to the door handle.

"Well, sir, I overheard some of the officers talking a couple of weeks ago." I was beginning to impress myself with my acting. The seriousness in my voice might even have fooled Lucinda.

"Talking about what, Wade?"

"Not what. Who."

He looked like he was ready to choke me. Then he deliberately relaxed himself and forced a smile. Calmly he said, "OK, Wade, about whom did you overhear my fellow officers at the Highland Park Station talking about?"

I wanted to say 'Pardon me?' but I was sure he would smack me. "Miss Cherry," I said solemnly, playing the bearer of bad news to the hilt.

He tensed noticeably. "What about Miss Cherry?" he asked, while forcing his face into another genuine artificial smile.

I glanced toward the house. Luke, still standing in the window, was motioning to me to come in the house. I returned my attention to the Sergeant and gave him my most sympathetic look. "I'm really sorry to be the one to tell you this, but I think you should know so you don't end up making a fool of yourself."

He looked like he was about to cry. "Go ahead...tell me."

"They were talking about Miss Cherry being in love with someone other than you." I reached out with my left hand and gave his arm a comforting squeeze. He gasped and recoiled from my touch. His face instantly contorted into prunelike folds of dismay.

I felt wonderful, giddy, soused on an exhilarating libation called sweet revenge. I was paying him back for all of the roller coaster rides he had taken me on—the unnerving scene that night on Billy Goat Hill when Scar and his gang challenged the cops and scared me and Luke half to death; and that moment of horror when he peeled away his face like a half-human lizard shedding its skin; and the time up on Eagle Rock when he told us the heart-tugging tale of Jakey Blume, mockingbirds, crimson red hair and all, as if he were a gypsy fortune teller revealing the hypnotic visions of my dreams from his mystical crystal ball. But most of all, it felt like I was handing him back that atrocious ball bearing, erasing all of the bad and keeping all of the good. Instead of all that, it was just a joke. No, not just a joke—a *great* joke. The kind of joke that close friends use as building blocks in the construction of trust and respect.

"Did they say who the other guy was?"

"Yes...they did, sir."

I touched his arm again.

He flinched.

"Who is he?" he asked, closing his eyes to lessen the sting.

I went for the kill.

"*ME-e-e-e-e*!" I squealed.

I bounded out of Queenie, slammed her door, and sprinted to the house. I wanted to stop on the porch and turn around to look at him, squeeze out all the pleasure I could, but I couldn't find the nerve. I didn't dare even glance over my shoulder as the back of my neck prickled from the deadly glare of a rancorous male Gorgon painfully hankering to turn me into a pre-acne, towheaded, pillar of salt. I hid in the bedroom until I heard the soft thrum of Queenie fade down the hill.

Oh, well, I guess I'll hear how Rodney saved him another time. Then, like a Drysdale fast ball, high and inside, it hit me. If it was the last thing he ever did...he would get even with me. God help me! Regret closed in faster than Mac on a scent leading to Molly's house.

thirteen

Christmas 1960 came and went like a train passing through an abandoned station. Lucinda did her very best, I'm sure, but Luke and I were less than grateful for our meager bounty. Luke complained the loudest. I had to get a little tough with him when he made Lucinda cry. *Tis' the season to be jolly...what a bunch of crap!* I missed Rodney terribly.

I was disappointed that the Sergeant didn't come by to say Merry Christmas. A card showed up in the mail about a week late. It was a religious one, which surprised me because I never thought of the Sergeant that way. There was no return address. I decided he was mad at me. Some of us can dish it out and some of us can take it. I wondered if he'd told Miss Cherry what I had said.

There were times that I was sure the Sergeant was near. I'd get a spooky feeling once in a while standing in the schoolyard, walking on the sidewalk, hanging out at Billy Goat Hill. I never spotted him though. Here it was the middle of April already and I hadn't seen him since the day I slammed the car door and ran into the house. I missed him. Him and Rodney. I planned to say I was sorry, if I ever saw him again.

The ball bearing banged around in my pocket. And as the weeks limped along, it gradually took on a different significance, transforming itself into an object of remembrance, a cherished keepsake. It seemed I couldn't go anywhere without it, and constantly checked my pocket for fear that I might lose it and have my only connection to the

Sergeant fizzle away. That haunting little silver ball had managed to make itself invaluable. It had become *my* silver dollar, and I vowed I would never let it fall into a storm drain. Moreover, I would slide down a hole to Hell, if necessary, to keep it. Ever so slowly, I was learning that there was a hole to Hell, but I did not know its sides were greased with deceit.

Most of the first quarter of 1961 went by in a sun up to sun down drudgery of existence, punctuated by frequent flashes of anxiety about the mysterious *Dead Man of Three Ponds*. Two highly unusual things occurred in April, however. One was provoked by the Russians, the other inspired by Sergeant Lyle Cavendish.

Our next door neighbor, Carl-the-baker, got blitzed on Blatz and walked out into the middle of Ruby Place with his tarnished but venerable antique rifle. He put on quite a show until the cops came and hauled him away. Luke and I sat on the porch with Mac watching and cheering Carl on. 'Yuri Gagarin you red bastard!' Carl had yelled between long pulls on his long-neck bottle. 'Come down from there!' Staggering badly, he pointed the rifle up at the smog and peered through the sights like he was actually aiming at something. Then he let the old bolt action single shot rip...*BOOM!* Mac howled and Luke and I roared our approval every time Carl fired off a round. Given the odds against one of the slugs falling back down on us, which were worse than the odds of old Carl actually hitting the first man in space, we were never in any danger.

The best part was getting my name in the newspaper. A reporter from the Los Angeles Herald-Examiner showed up just in time to snap a picture of four very nervous cops engaging and disarming Carl. Wouldn't you know, out of all the people standing around watching the show the reporter picked me to ask questions about the incident. I swear I was misquoted: '...Wade Parker, age ten, said his neighbor, Carl-the-baker, was (envious, ed.) of the Russian's high quality Rye bread...' Go figure it.

The other exciting thing that happened was Luke and I completed our network of candles along the walls of our new Shangri-La, the storm drains under northeast Highland Park. Cavendish Caverns became the code name. Luke captured the phrase after seeing pictures of Carlsbad Caverns in a back issue of *National Geographic*. I liked it the moment he said it. I felt it was most fitting that we christen our new playground in honor of the man that gave me the idea. I had found a different moral in the Sergeant's story about how he had rescued his silver dollar from the storm drain. Adults should be mindful of the stories they tell to children.

Our first challenge had been to find another way into the storm drain system. Going in through a curb drain was a physical impossibility for me. And I was not about to send Luke down in there to reconnoiter. I was positive the curb drain route posed some terrible hazard, the nature of which wasn't quite clear. The Sergeant hadn't been around to tell me the rest of the story. I don't know what I was thinking. I didn't really know how the storm drain system actually worked. All I knew was that water drained from the streets into the openings in the curb and disappeared, for all I cared, down a deep hole to fill the rice paddies in China.

The challenge of trying to figure another way into the storm drain helped keep my mind occupied. The loss of Rodney, my apparent disaffection from the Sergeant and Miss Cherry, and, most important, the dead guy, had all compiled to form a burden too much for a young boy to bear. I badly needed a remedy, and somehow I knew I had to step outside myself in order to find something with restorative power, in order to survive. Perhaps some magic medications could be found in the dark, fortress-like dispensary of Cavendish Caverns?

We discovered the discharge tunnel opening in the concrete side slope of the Arroyo Seco quite by accident, literally. The discovery came about when two cars collided on the York Boulevard Bridge, which traversed the Arroyo Seco and the Pasadena Freeway.

Luke and I had just gotten the boot from Kory's comic book section for the umpteenth time. We were standing outside the store, miffed that we had been invited to leave so quickly, making rude faces at the manager through the storefront window. Then the red flashing lights of the police cruiser stopped in the middle of the bridge caught Luke's attention. "Lookie there," he cooed. I was mad at the store manager and didn't give Luke my immediate attention. He tugged my shirt sleeve.

I could take them or leave them, but Luke was always mesmerized by those flashing emergency lights. The cyclical flicker of the strobes had a Pied Piper effect on his brain. Like a moth to a flame, as long as those lights were on, there was no stopping him. The fireworks of

Independence Day were a veritable lust feast for him. For some arcane reason, the flickering flames of fire did not have the same effect. Thank God for that or I might have spent my childhood even more demented than I was as a permanent member of a bucket brigade.

Anyway, the next thing I knew, we were standing on the bridge staring with morbid fascination at two mangled cars. The drivers, dead or alive, we didn't know, had already been whisked off in ambulances. Traffic had been routed away from both ends of the bridge. As we stood gaping at the carnage, two rattletrap tow trucks appeared like half-starved mongrels scenting the waftures of road kill. The drivers crawled out of the rusted wreckers and ambled over to inspect the auto carcasses, which appeared to be fused together by the head-on impact. The tow truck drivers were a rueful sight. They looked like inbred cousins from some distant hollow. Poster boys for the...oh, never mind, you get the picture. They stood scratching their heads as if the friction would warm their wits enough to figure out how to separate the cars.

Suddenly Luke walked over to them. The flashing lights had been turned off and the euphoria had cleared from his eyes. I followed him, staying three steps behind. I didn't want to get too close to Festus and Jethro. They looked diseased. Luke stepped right up to them and performed one of his priceless Lukisms, as I had come to call them, an outlandish absurdity of the type I had previously strove to discourage, but recently had developed an appreciation for. Call it an acquired taste, a term I had learned from drinking Rodney's coffee.

"You gentlemen give me a quarter each and I'll tell you exactly how to solve this problem," Luke said.

Christ, the little mercenary sounded like he had a Ph.D. in mechanical engineering. I started to reach for his arm to pull him back. I was afraid they might smack him one for being a smart ass. Then I saw them both digging down deep in their greasy coveralls, smiling kind of goofy like, oozing makeshift cleverness like they were only being charged half price at a fifty-cent peep show. They each deposited two bits in Luke's little pink hand.

The taller one of the two, a Tennessee Valley baritone, spoke first. "OK, young feller..." He snorkeled a cubic foot of air in through hair clogged nostrils, which sounded like the snore of a congested whale, and then expelled something from his throat so vile I couldn't possibly describe it. "...tells us how ta untangle these mules." The man's parched lips retreated revealing a slovenly grin, a greenish tangle of broken teeth. I took a couple of steps to the west to get out of the stream of his breath. Luke stood his ground.

"Yeah," the other tow truck driver chimed in, "hopes we don't haffs ta put the A-cet-a-lean turch to 'em."

Luke peered up at them with his angelic baby blues and spoke with the sincerity of Billy Graham. "Put a hose on them. It works with Mac every time." He deposited the quarters in his pocket, turned smartly, and walked away.

I busted a gut.

Festus and Jethro resumed scratching, pondering at a snail's pace whether or not they had received fair value for payment rendered.

Luke hadn't an inkling how funny he was. The perfect straight man. He wasn't serious and moody like I often was, always far freer with his thoughts and feelings than me. His mind traveled a zone that I could never enter. Even during a phase in the late 60's when I hitched a few rides on mind-bending vehicles affectionately known as Blue Barrel, Rainbow, and Sunshine, I never gained access to Luke's easy going realm of inner peace. As the months and years flowed by like the steady flow of the Arroyo Seco, I began to look up to Luke, at times even envying him for his steely nerve and philosophical armor. That he could fearlessly approach two men and advise them on the art of strategic uncoupling, two men that looked like they ate little kids as in-between meal snacks, that he could get away with something like that just dazzled me. And I envied his immunity from nightmares. Certainly he had cause to entertain ghosts same as me, what with his plight with the mockingbirds, not to mention our shared encounter with the dead man. Yet, such was not the case. Luke's armor seemed impenetrable to the same emotional bullets that mowed me down every so often. God, I admired and loved him for his crazy daring. I mused about it as we walked over to the bridge railing. Behind us, Jethro and Festus began to tinker with the mangled autos.

Luke stood at the railing casually looking down at the Arroyo Seco, like anyone else would. I was only reminded of that morning on the "other bridge" when I stared down into the inviting mist. I wished I could find a way to be less affected by things, to be more like Luke. He usually seemed so at peace. In balance. I had remained the oldest chronologically, while (somehow) Luke had grown beyond me, in a spiritual sense. Of course, it was not until many years later that I came to think of it that way.

About then is when we made our great discovery.

"Look," Luke said, pointing downstream toward a county flood control truck parked on the concrete coated bed of the lazy Arroyo Seco.

"Well, well, well," I said. "I think we may have found the entrance to King Tut's tomb."

"Nope...it's Cavendish Caverns," Luke proclaimed, stretching his freckles to the limit.

That's when he told me about the article he saw in *National Geographic*.

fourteen

Luke could walk upright with plenty of freeboard. I had to stoop slightly, crook my neck, and tuck my chin to my chest or I'd end up with a bald spot.

A continuous trickle of contaminated water moistened the bottom of the tube. Some kind of invidious, slimy life form marked the concave walls, its various stages of hydroponic metabolism staining the concrete with striations that reminded me of the horizontally scarred shoreline of a fickle lake. We observed the strange phenomena with passive curiosity, ignorant of its foreboding message...just indecipherable hieroglyphics decorating the walls of an ancient cave. Such obvious signs of a changing water level should have triggered a warning.

We had observed the flood control workers use a special tool to open the massive metal discharge cover. The cover was designed, I supposed, to make it next to impossible for tunnel rats like us to get in. It was like the door to the nest of a giant trap-door spider, free swinging, and actuated by force applied from the inside. A giant cast-iron poker chip suspended from a single monstrous hinge. It blocked the opening tight as a sphincter until enough water came along to force it open. A little water opened it an inch or two. A lot of water would push it open several feet.

The first time I got a close-up look at the door I thought it was a hopeless idea. It seemed it would take a miracle tantamount to the resurrection of Christ to open that door. As it turned out we were not to be defeated. The tire jack from Lucinda's trunk worked perfectly, for a while.

Animals may not possess the highly evolved logic based reasoning ability that we humans supposedly have, but they often display remarkable instinctive judgment that some of us, namely me, could do well to observe. Mac quickly demonstrated that he was no relation to *Cerebus*, hound of the underworld, as he absolutely refused to enter the storm drain. He took one look at the precarious way we had propped open the huge discharge door and slammed his rump down on the ground, like a pack mule on strike. Admittedly, Lucinda's car jack was equivalent to a toothpick propping open the mouth of a great white shark, a giant bear trap with a vicious hair trigger, and if the toothpick ever snapped during ingress or egress there wouldn't be a second chance. (No more hazardous than a late night showdown with The Crippler, I reasoned.) And as each expedition into the bowels of the catacombs took us deeper and deeper beneath the city, and further and further away from the portal of the man-made maze of tubular stone, Mac was invited along, each time declining, insisting on taking up a post just outside the tunnel opening. There he'd sit, humorless, stoic, rigid as a carved stone gargoyle, and, without question, the best looking mixed breed sentinel in all of the Arroyo Seco.

We tested our nerve on the first trip. Apprehension marked each step as we edged our way into the darkened crypt. An ominous semblance hung in the dank air, like a sign saying *Danger-Go Back!* But we proceeded into the crypt anyway, plodding ever so slowly, imagining we were knowingly going against the wishes of the dead. Behind us the circle of light slowly dimmed giving inverse rise to a growing unease. My Flash Gordon flashlight, an unreliable gadget at best, wasn't near enough to make us feel secure.

Luke hooked a finger through my rear belt loop and shuffled along behind me, his sneakers making sucking noises each time he lifted his feet. I stopped after we had penetrated the hole about the length of a football field. I glanced back toward the dwindling spot of light and tried to absorb a few additional rays of courage. Seeping blackness had nearly closed the void behind us and I continued forward a little slower than before. Soon my flashlight began to flicker. I could tell Luke was beginning to feel panicky, as judged by the increasing resistance pulling my pants back against my middle.

Already leaning forward to keep my head from scraping the top of the tunnel, I shifted my center of gravity a little farther forward offering more tug, and encouragement, to help Luke along.

Luke could stand face to face with those tow truck drivers and bamboozle them without batting an eye, but delving into this kind of unknown was a different trick altogether. Suddenly he put the brakes on. My belt loop snapped and Luke fell backward landing on his backside with a sloppy splash. I sailed headlong in the opposite direction. All of my momentum to the forward, I tried in vain to catch my balance but ended up gliding to the horizontal and executing a full-stretch landing that was almost graceful. My flashlight took it much harder hitting the deck like the lights-out-loser in a Sonny Liston fight. I slid on my belly for thirty yards, like a wet seal on oily ice, and thus we had made another fantastic discovery.

A slick solstice encompassed me with a strange sense of security, back in the womb, Blindman's bluff without the blindfold. Exhilarated by the unexpected foray into the slithery, wet blackness, I blurted, "Wow! That was fun!" *Wow! That was fun!* a hollow but happy echo immediately agreed, launching me into a much needed giggle. I sat up soaking-slimy-wet and squinted back in the direction of Luke. As my eyes adjusted to the new darkness, it seemed as though I were looking up from the bottom of a fathomless well. Far away, a wanton circle glowed, flirting with the darkness like an impassioned, but very demure moon. At some inestimable distance in the foreground, a starkly contrasted silhouette, Luke, shifted like a geometric shape imprisoned in the cylinder of an infinite kaleidoscope. I laughed out loud, attempting to curb a new wave of anxiety, and thought...there is light at the end of the tunnel.

"I'm OK!" I yelled.

"I'm not," Luke instantly replied, his silhouette rapidly retreating toward the safety of the loving moon.

Expedition number two yielded the concept of placing candles in the tunnel. Luke came up with the idea and his freckles seemed to glow in the dark when I complimented him for thinking of something good. Every fifty feet or so we'd locate little imperfections in the otherwise smooth wall of the tube and use them as sconces to hold the candles. We'd find a crenation above the midpoint of the circum-ference, melt some wax on it for stickum, and post a candle. Pinpoints of flame licked at the concrete, leaving odd, tear-shaped soot marks, while swaying flares of light, embracing shadowy partners, silently danced on the curvilinear walls. The crepuscular ambiance fit my imagination like a glove—we had become masters of an endless medieval dungeon.

An instance of Darwin's theorem accelerated, we were fully adapted by the end of our third trek into Cavendish Caverns. We moved about with sure-footed confidence, firmly in command of our strange new environment. I had found the perfect escape from the surface world, a world that had revoked my right to happiness, a world where I felt far more dark in its light than in the light I had found in the darkness below ground. Down here I felt privileged. Down here I felt free from the haunting images that resided in the scenery above ground. Those gruesome images of the dead man that only showed themselves to me. There was no scenery in Cavendish Caverns.

Luke seemed happy enough just to be wherever I was, however, Mac, stubborn beyond all belief, had not altered his position on tunnel frolicking one iota. We had started calling him Mr. Party Pooper, but he was immune to childish insults. Wise beyond his years, he continued to lord over the storm drain opening with suppressed trepidation, while Luke and I had become mercurial in our actions, buzzing in and out of our honeycombed hive like bees jazzed with the feverish pace of spring. Overriding Mac's obvious displeasure, a great period of emotional prosperity ensued.

By the time the dreary, overcast, mid-June skies over Los Angeles had once again tarnished the myth of *Sunny California*, Alan B. Shepard, Jr. had restored Carl the baker's pride, Sam Yorty was preparing to move into City Hall, Chavez Ravine was synonymous with Dodger Stadium, and Luke and I were spending more time in our cave than hibernating bears in the dead of winter.

While the surface dwellers suffered through the furnace of summer, we enjoyed the cool, damp, darkness of our secret hideaway. We had become moles, shunning the light of day and the attendant clatter of the normal world to enjoy the serene isolation of our exclusive subterranean kingdom. We cavorted in a carefree universe of peace nestled deep below all of the terrible things that plagued us. For me, the tons of compacted earth overhead served as perfect shielding from everything that was bad. And Luke, well, he was just glad there weren't any mockingbirds in the storm drains.

On one particular day, Lucinda had to go to work very early in the morning. This afforded Luke and me a quick start on the day, a lucky break, we thought, because of the rain showers that had been forecast to hit late that afternoon. I had enough sense to know we did not want to be down in the storm drain during a flash flood. I told Luke we would have to call it quits at the first sign of rising water. That was fine with him.

We wolfed down some Wheaties, the breakfast of champion cardboard sliders and tunnel riders, and hastily packed some munchies in a knapsack. We grabbed a fresh can of motor oil and Lucinda's tire jack from the garage, and headed out.

We kept our tunnel riding gear squirreled just inside the tunnel opening. In our riding outfits we looked like a couple of drillers after a good day in the oil field. We wore old sweat shirts and dungarees soaked with motor oil, a kind of slick, friction-free dunnage worn between skin and concrete. Luke called our slimy getups greased pig skin. Many years later it occurred to me that oil soaked clothes, candles and matches must have been a dangerous combination. I guess we were lucky. Human Molotov cocktails were one of the few things we never became.

"I'm tired," Luke announced, after a couple of hours of vigorous riding. "Can we stop for a few minutes, maybe have some munchies?"

"OK, but let's walk back up to the starting gate so we'll be ready to go again after we rest." I was also out of breath and hungry.

The "starting gate" was the name we applied to an inclined section of the pipe. The storm drain system was designed to utilize the force of gravity, rather than pumps, to move the water. The entire network was laid out with a slow downhill gradient that routed the water toward outlets that discharged directly into the Arroyo Seco. After much exploration, the starting gate turned out to be the optimal point from which to start a run. It worked like a Pinewood Derby ramp or a ski jump ramp and we used it as such with a good running start to boot. We probably achieved speeds on the order of twenty-five miles per hour at the bottom of the ramp and then slid down the pipe for nearly a quarter of a mile. It was pure fun. An exhilarating sense of freedom. Blasting like a projectile down the longest cannon barrel in the world.

Depending on how fast your start was, you would finally come to a stop anywhere from two to four hundred feet from the tunnel outlet, feeling all charged up and raring to run back to the starting gate and do it again. We did it all: feet first, head first, belly down, belly up, sitting up frontwards and, weirdest of all, backwards. Sometimes we even hooked together in tandem like a two man toboggan, although this was much slower than making the run by yourself. We had an occasional collision, too, when the one walking back up the tunnel failed to spread his legs in time for the one coming down. Boy did we have fun. Marvelous, carefree, timeless fun... *'twas a life not for the fainthearted. But such innocent foolishness, when compounded, leaves young rascals well confounded, or...maybe even with the dear departed!*

We sat at the top of the starting gate leaning against the wall of the tunnel with our legs arching over the silent trickle that flowed continuously—the perpetual life-blood of the eventide sanctuary we devotedly called Cavendish Caverns.

Resting.

Munching.

Talking.

At times we just sat quietly and listened to the cavern's voices, manfully nodding or smiling when we heard noises that we hadn't heard before. The caverns spoke frequently. Mysterious, invisible, sourceless rumbles. Echoes softly sailing on still tunnel winds. Different sounds that after a while all sounded the same. I wondered about the tunnel voices. They came like messages traveling across time from unknown universes. Communications neither understood, nor answered. In time I came to enjoy the sounds. They were my sounds—distant manhole covers groaning under the weight of passing trucks, or maybe the resonant vibrations of misplaced baseballs yearning for the game, or the chimelike knells of silver dollars calling heads-or-tails like forlorn loons lost in the dark. The heartbeat of the mother city, I thought. It was wonderful—Luke and I, didymous midges of the underworld, nestled together deep in her womb, soothed by the symphonic rhyme of her gentle heart. Yes, life was good down below.

I sat there looking at Luke reposing opposite me. My younger brother. My only brother. He looked so innocent, so unaffected. I wondered if he wondered about things like I did. He realized I was looking at him and grinned, his freckles shimmering in the quivering candlelight. *Did Luke ever have such convoluted thoughts as I?* He had problems, too. I knew he did. Some of the same ones as me, in fact. Yet, he seemed so able to take things in stride. Another convoluted thought...*Maybe if I had an older brother, if I weren't the oldest, I would be able to do that, too?*

Luke was human of course. He'd react at the time that something happened. But he seemed to have the ability to not complicate things by dwelling on them, like I did. He was lenient with the world, with life's imperfections. I sat there resting, looking at him, admiring him, wishing I knew how he did it.

Luke stared back at me with no specific focus, apparently deep into his own confidential accounting. After a little while, he said, "I think I should get a new cap."

It was a pronouncement that, after my long rumination, seemed ridiculously profound. While my feeble mind was lost in a kind of metaphor-seasoned philosophical soup, Luke deftly whipped up a tasty baseball cap broth. *How convoluted can I get?* We had never retrieved his Dodgers cap from Three Ponds. He had been hatless since.

"Why?" I asked.

"Because I can't stay down in these tunnels forever."

I thought about it for a moment. "True enough," I said, knowing that he was leading up to something. "Are you worried about the mockingbirds?"

"I've realized that I need to be more practical about that," he replied, as if that was an answer I should be happy with.

"What do you mean?"

He smiled judiciously making me feel as though I had asked him to reveal the secret of life. "Well," he said, "I've been doing some research on my problem." The careful smile reappeared. "Did you know that mockingbirds are also sometimes called catbirds?"

"No, I didn't know that." *Maybe he is as strange as me?*

He nodded his head enthusiastically, affirming the validity of his own statement. "Have you ever noticed that their call sounds like the meow of a cat?" He didn't expect me to answer him. "Meow, meow," he said, attempting to mimic the sound of a full grown cat, but sounding more like the *mew, mew* of a tiny kitten. Nonetheless, it vaguely resembled the annoying squawk of a mockingbird.

I fought off a laugh. He was being far too serious to see the humor in this. "Ahem, yes I see what you mean, Luke. Would you like to stop off at Kory's on the way home and see if they have any Dodger caps?"

"Ah, well, actually I don't want another Dodger cap," he said a little sheepishly.

That surprised me. "Wait a minute," I said testily. "If you think you're gonna wear a Giants cap, well, dang, you can't be my brother anymore."

He laughed hard at that one. "No way, Wade. I want a cap from that university down in Georgia. The kind that has a bulldog on it."

"Why?"

"No catbird is gonna mess with me with a big, mean, ugly looking bulldog on my head." He was deadly serious.

I laughed so hard I nearly wet my pants. Jeez, what a comedian. He had absolutely no idea how funny he was, naturally funny, without even trying to be funny, funny. At first he was offended by my irreverence, but the virus of laughter is very contagious and soon he was laughing along with me. It took a while for us to calm down after that.

We were about to get up and make another slide run, a tandem one, when we were startled by a tremendous BANG!

fifteen

I was badly shaken. A surge of adrenaline had left my skin
tingling with the feel of static electricity. The noise had come from
the direction of the tunnel opening. It reverberated up the tube, a
wicked metal-against-metal scream that made the fillings in my teeth
squirm. The candles near us flickered and swayed. I felt a shift of air
brush by my face.

Luke gave my arm a desperate shake. "What was that?" he
urgently demanded.

"I don't know," I said, denying the creeping hunch that had
already throttled through my mind. I could almost feel my brain
hardening, like some yet to be discovered organism whose only
defense against the perils of the wild is to turn to stone to keep from
being eaten.

*Here I go again. Why can't I just react? Why does my mind
launch itself into some kind of out of control hyper-thought that pulls
a total vacuum on my very being, sucks the marrow right out of my
bones?*

Get a grip on yourself, Parker!

I could smell my own dread. It oozed from me like blood from a
body riddled with holes. An aching urge to repent enshrouded me, a
hardening crust closing me in, locking me in, a Chrysalis prison for
my petrified mind that might not open for a thousand years.

Get a grip, Parker!

We had trespassed in the medieval mines of Mephistopheles, the worst of the seven devil chiefs. Now he hath come to exact a toll! Death to the transgressors!

Get a grip, Parker!

I became conscious of my own labored breathing. I focused on it, slowed it down, steadied myself. Gradually my body relaxed, but tremors of fear still tempered my hapless thinking.

Then, in a calm, normal voice, Luke said, "Don't you think we better go see what made that noise?"

I swallowed air as deep as I could. "Yes."

Loosening my arm from Luke's grip, not wanting him to feel me trembling, I consciously conjured up my real, imaginary friend, Duke Snider. I pleaded for guidance and strength. Power of the mind gave me a quick burst of resolve upon which I braced myself and bravely stood up.

A big mistake.

I was so rattled, I had forgotten the first rule of Cavendish Caverns. I bumped my noggin on the hard ceiling overhead and sat back down faster than an obsessed competitor in a game of musical chairs. I saw twinkling, silver ball bearings, not stars.

Luke cringed. "Jeez, are you all right?"

"Ugh!"

"Your head sounded like Lucinda testing musk melons at Kory's, except at least ten times louder."

Watery eyes squinting with pain, bile bubbling in my throat, mouth wide open as if to scream, I reached up and delicately felt for an egg. An ostrich egg. "God. I dang near busted my head wide open," I whined, confirming the obvious. "Ouch! Ooo-ah! Hold on a second, I need to sit still for a bit."

"OK," Luke said. He sat down next to me, patient.

I took some deep breaths and decided my head was OK, but a fierce soreness rising from my shoulders told me I'd jammed my neck. Soon Luke saddled up behind me at the starting gate. We slowly pushed off, cautious, not a fast running start like we normally did. We slid along at a sightseer's pace, half speed, like a steam locomotive out of steam coasting in neutral, trying to stretch it out to the next water tower. I scanned the narrow, pinpoint horizon ahead. Luke did the same stretching to see over my shoulder. Our perception of distance was thrown off by the reduced rate of speed, or so I tried to convince myself. But when at last we came to a stop, I knew we were in trouble.

We were close enough to the tunnel outlet that the absence of that glorious spectral beacon that had always been there waiting with Mac could only mean one thing. The worst had happened. Denial went down in one big gulp of stomach punching reality. My head throbbed with each titan pulse of my quaking heart. Luke clung tight to my back, his breath hissing in my ear, short gasps of fear, long wheezes of terror. A desperate SOS stabbing deep into my failed sense of responsibility.

Get a grip, Parker!

Motionless silence closed around us. At length, Luke released me from his backwards bear hug and stood up. I turned sideways and leaned against the wall, dejected, hopeless to resist the charge of guilt percolating in through all of my pores.

"The jack must have broke," Luke said, finally.

The truth ripped me wide open. I looked up at him and saw that he was nearly smiling. His face, softly aglow in the lusterless hue of the candlelight, reminded me of the picture of Jesus in Reverend Bonner's office. The Son of God posed in serene earth tones, smooth, muted, as if the painting had been done by candlelight.

Maybe Luke is Jesus?

Maybe he will save us?

Oh God, Parker, get a grip!

We walked to the end of the storm drain, now sealed shut by a cast-iron monster. A sliver of light rimmed the outside of the circular barrier. Mac was out there, very angry, barking incessantly. The jack must have taken off like a rocket. Thank God Mac sounded OK, that it didn't hit him. He was whining, sniffing, listening. He knew we were huddled there just on the other side of the door from him. I put my mouth close to the door, called his name loud, then yelled at him to be quiet. Even under the duress of the circumstances he obeyed, like a well trained dog of the silver screen. But this wasn't a movie. Mac wasn't Rin-Tin-Tin or Lassie. He wasn't going to valiantly run home and bring back help. There was no intermission, no commercial break, and probably no happy ending.

"Tell me the story again, Wade."

"What story?" My throbbing head and sore neck were competing with each other.

"About how Rodney saved the Sergeant from the storm drain."

I was wound up tight and I lashed at him before I could think.

"Jeez, Luke! I told you before...HE NEVER FINISHED THE STORY!" Screaming made my head throb worse.

"I'm sorry," he said, then muttered, "You big donkey."

"I didn't mean to yell at you, Luke."

He sat down next to me. After a bit he said, "Don't worry, Wade. We're going to get out of here. We'll be OK."

Luke spoke so confidently he almost sounded cocky. Damned Parvenu tunnel rat. Suddenly he was above the line and I below. Luke the numerator. Wonderful. Maybe he has a plan? Right. The catbird boy and his magic bulldog hat will gladly work a little legerdemain. Maybe he wants us to wear ground hog hats so we can find our way out of here by the first day of spring. Meanwhile I'm the one responsible. The oldest. The one who should have known better. Great. Why not go ahead and strangle him? Yeah, why not? When they eventually find our bodies I'll be blamed for the whole thing anyway. Let the big donkey's record show it: *Convicted, 1961, Fratricide, (Posthumously). Get a grip!* I sat there thinking myself into bigger and tighter knots.

Then I heard a different sound. I put my ear to the cast-iron monster. "Listen. Do you hear something, Luke?"

"Yes, I do."

"What does it sound like to you?"

"Rain."

"Uh oh," I mouthed.

"It's raining hard, Wade. Mac doesn't like to be out in the rain you know."

Great. Now the dog's getting wet and I'm to blame for that, too. How am I going to explain this to him? "Luke, listen to me. We've got a real serious problem here. It's raining outside. I don't want to scare you, but do you know what that means?"

"Yes, Wade. I do."

"What do you think is going to happen?"

He smiled. "Pretty soon this tunnel is going to fill up with water."

He floored me completely. "And you're not scared?"

"No, not really." He extended the smile. The candlelight made him look like a subterranean gremlin, full of mischief, enjoying watching the boy from above ground sweat.

"Well, I am scared as hell! You exasperate me, Luke!"

"Look, Wade, I don't really see a problem here. All we have to do is sit here and wait for the water to push the door open. Right?"

It didn't matter whether he was right or not because at that moment we heard the *siss-s-s-s* sound of the approaching wave. It was only about eighteen inches high but it was powerful enough to knock us off our feet. It crashed into the iron door and curled back over the top of us embroiling us in a churning cauldron of foam.

The door didn't budge one inch.

I was more startled by how fast the wave had come than the getting knocked down part. Under any other circumstances, getting knocked down by a little old wave would have been fun. This was terrifying. Luke got back on his feet and helped pull me up. He was actually laughing. I couldn't believe it. I had gotten a mouth full of nasty water, swallowed some, foulness coating my tongue, and Luke is laughing like a drunken hyena. That ought to keep his catbirds away!

"Shut up!" I spluttered, choking and spitting out as much of the vile taste as I could.

"OK, OK. Are you all right?"

"NO! Damn, Luke! We're going to drown in here!"

I gagged and coughed, nearly threw up, while Luke calmly suggested that the next time I might want to close my mouth. Next time? The water was already up to Luke's waist and he still showed no signs of fear. Was there something wrong with me? Or, was my little brother insane?

"The door is going to push up any time now, Wade," he said calmly, and I realized then how quiet it was. Just the sound of thousands of bubbles rising and bursting at the surface. It was like being inside a big aquarium with a powerful aeration pump humming below. The water kept coming, and to make matters worse, the combination of the stress and the gag reflex from choking on the tunnel water had triggered a world class case of hiccups.

"I ho-u-pe! so Lu-u-ke!" I sounded like a sick Chihuahua.

My mental knot pulled tighter when it occurred to me that the door might have been damaged when the jack gave way. Maybe that was why it wasn't opening. I wanted to tell Luke what I was thinking so he could argue against it and make me feel better. I thought more of it though realizing the situation would be worse if I made him panic.

Just then the cast-iron jailer groaned. A burst of light showed from the bottom of the aquarium, the crescent moon of Atlantis offering rays of hope. Luke squealed, "I told you! I told you!" But the water kept rising. It was now up to the middle of Luke's chest. At least we wouldn't drown in the dark.

Back up the tunnel I could see many of the candles were still burning. Strange new multi-colored reflections played across the shrinking distance between the rippling water and the concave ceiling. It looked so weird, surrealistic—the tunnel, the water, the candles, the strange reflections. I imagined we were caught in the swamping passageway of an antediluvian monastery.

The door groaned again.

A waxing moon!

Yes!

Let the tides recede!

"Luke! Come close to the door." He splashed closer. "If it opens just a little more I think you can fit through." He was smiling again. "When I say go, take a deep breath, hold your nose, and push yourself down toward the light." He nodded agreeably, as if he were taking elementary instructions that he'd heard many times before. "As soon as it opens a little bit more, I'll come along right behind you."

"Sure. No problem, Wade." Luke was excited. Not scared in the least. Excited like at Disneyland with a whole book of "E" tickets in his hand. He was laughing again. "This is better than The Crippler ain't it, Wade!"

I was scared to death. "Much better," I said.

Another groan!

More light!

"GO! GO! GO!" I screamed.

Down Luke went in a furious whirlpool of bubbles. He disappeared faster than a scrap of bar soap being sucked down a bath tub drain. I screamed out victoriously and pictured him shooting out in a gusher on the other side. Luke had been born again unto the everlasting light of day!

Now I was alone with my fear. I was bigger than Luke. I hoped that the door would open wide enough to set me free, too. The candles extinguished one by one, no match against the rising tide. I wanted to let go, dive toward the light and push on the door, but I was afraid I would get hung up in the opening and drown. That would be my last option. Until then, I would wait and pray that the door would open further, in time for me. But I don't really know how to pray? I winged it. I prayed to God. I prayed to Jesus. I prayed to Poseidon and Neptune. And the water rose higher. I prayed to Johnny Weissmuller. I even prayed to Popeye, the Sailor Man. And the water rose higher. When the entombing liquid swelled up to my aching neck, I finally prayed to my highest power, The *Lord* of Flatbush, Duke Snider. Duke would save me. I was sure of it.

The prayer must have worked because my mind began to shut off the fear. I started to feel whoozie, buoyant. The water let go of me and gave way to a strange vision. The Stygian onslaught subsided, a Moses-like miracle, gone without so much as a puddle left behind. Down the passageway, coming slowly toward me, was a single file line of hooded monks. Each tapped lightly on a Tabor hanging from straps looped over their necks. They were singing, or more like chanting, a motet that was further complicated by a displeasing echo off the tunnel walls.

The monk at the front of the line was a high priest. He carried a swaying censer, the fumes from which confused me, first smelling of incense, then smelling like the wonderful, clean scent of Miss Cherry. The line of monks stopped at a distance and fell silent. The high priest came forward, pulled the cowl back from his mummified face and stared at me with rheumy, centuries-old eyes. Slowly, Pope-like, his arm raised up from his side and leveled at my face. As he scornfully wagged a bony, accusatory finger, his leathery, tightly pursed lips parted and spewed a raspy, penetrating, monotone utterance... *"Equus Asinus Gigantus."*

"Huh? I don't understand..." Bubbles gurgled from my lips. I strained upward, nose mashed against concrete, thieving one last deep breath. Moments strung together, links in a chain holding me under, the last breath tightening its grip in my chest, fighting to stay with me. Vaguely I sensed a gentle pulling at my feet, a comforting feeling that I did not resist. Slipping down, I heard the last candle extinguish with a kiss-like hiss, and the wet blackness became my friend. I embraced it with bleary passion.

sixteen

The dream was unpleasant, but not horrifying like most of the others:

Luke and I were postured together on a hard wooden bench. It was very uncomfortable. We waited faithfully in an anteroom adjoining the office of E. Townsend Parker, Esquire. We waited quietly, not talking, not fidgeting, behaving in strict accordance with the stern instructions given to us by an unfriendly secretary. We had arrived ten minutes early for our appointment, still we were told Mr. Parker would see us only if time permitted. Luke discreetly tugged at his stiffly starched collar, while I nervously glanced about the lavishly decorated room.

TWO HOURS LATER...

I looked up and saw ruby-red lips slowly pull taut in an ambidextrous smile. "I'm sorry, Master Wade, Master Luke, but your father will not be able to see you. He suggested that you make an appointment for sometime in your next life. Good day, boys."

We trudged out to a million dollar lobby and stood looking down into a marble fountain full of rare exotic fish. "I hope somebody hangs the prick," Luke said.

Embarrassed, tearful, I said nothing.

"Are you all right, Wade?" Luke said.

Fresh, after-rain air gorged my lungs, oxygenating my blood, restarting my brain, the sensation of light-headedness, faint, pleasurable.

"Are you all right, Wade?"

My eyes cracked open, billowing gray clouds bobbing in a sea of blue. *Am I dreaming?* Something shook me, perhaps was pulling my arm, I wasn't sure.

"Wade! Are you all right?"

Woof!

Not quite back over the line of consciousness, I thought the fish in the marble fountain were barking at me.

"Wade!" Luke yelled, slapping my face repeatedly.

I'm alive! I bolted up to a sitting position, looked quickly for the wizened, finger pointing monk, then started coughing uncontrollably.

Woof! Woof! Mac zealously informed Luke that I was all right. *Woof!* he said again, climbing on top of me and sloshing his tongue all over my face.

"OK, boy," I sputtered, trying to push him off. As I attempted to hold Mac away from my face, my eye caught something in the distance. I thought I saw a man hanging by the neck from the catwalk under the old A.T. & S.F. trestle. *Hang the prick?* Am I still dreaming? "Mac, quit!" He got off of me, reluctantly. I closed my eyes tight and rubbed the lids. When I opened them the man was not there. *Jeez.*

I looked at Luke and could tell he'd been crying. "I'm OK," I said, and gave him as much of a smile as I could.

He broke down completely, blubbering and shaking, deep breaths catching in his throat as he tried to talk and cry at the same time. "I–I–I thought you–you–you were dead!" he bawled. I pulled him down to me and put my arms around him. I felt him shudder hard, then surrender the tension in his body as he melted into me.

"I'm OK, I'm OK," I said, patting him on the back.

He whimpered, "I love you, Wade."

"I love you, too, Luke." I began to cry as I held him.

Mac sighed. He looked straight at me, as if to say, *I told you so*, then laid himself out across my legs. The stoic sentry was still doing his duty.

Over Luke's shoulder I saw our knapsack and the rest of our debris. Hundreds of candle remnants were scattered about like wreckage on a beach. We sat there huddled together, drenched, crying, splayed out on the wet concrete like worthless mullock discarded outside the mouth of a dangerous mine.

Cookie cutter shadows drifted over us, then bright sun and instant steam rising off the concrete, then subdued light again. The vacillating sky epitomized my entire state of affairs. *What do I do now? I'm not worth spit. God is punishing me for killing that man, I know he is.*

Whatever it was that had happened after I blacked out in the tunnel, it had left my body sapped, aching. The knot on the top of my head throbbed. At least I could remember how that had happened. My body would recover, and the emotional deadening I had experienced from the first near drowning at Three Ponds was worse; somehow this flogging by dunking seemed less severe. Was I building up a tolerance? Was I becoming immune? No. I had merely beat the odds. Blind luck. Nothing more. My will, my purpose of mind, wasn't even part of the equation. My will was locked in paralysis. My life, although apparently buoyant in the presence of water, was at a total standstill, as though the insidious roots of ataxia had riddled the soil of my very existence, and I had become nothing more than a stubborn, noxious weed, barely clinging to life.

The next few minutes were nearly unbearable as I listened to poor Luke, choked with emotion, relate how he had waited outside that stubborn metal hatchway. How he had prayed for me to be alive, and finally the door burst open and water gushed out like a giant garden hose. How I came shooting out of the hole and onto the deck as lifeless as a defeated salmon tossed to the rocks by a raging rapid. He told the whole story with a two-dimensional affection that made it sound like a violent, chimerical cartoon. But I knew better. My bumps and bruises, physical and mental, were real. The worst part was seeing how Luke had nearly died of sadness.

We slogged up from the arroyo on a slick, narrow, switchback. The path topped out at a brushy ridge straddled by a hole-ridden chain link fence. We breached the fence and appeared on the street, out of wind, looking like a couple of sewer rats seeking the safety of higher ground. I felt lousy. My legs were wobbly, my stomach even less steady, and my mind was knotted over what to make of the entire episode. I wished Festus and Jethro were there to tow me home and put me to bed. Luke, on the other hand, looked fit as a fiddle, fully recovered, ready to tackle the next adventure on the agenda.

"Luke, let's stop and sit down for a minute. I need to rest."

"Sure, Wade. You want me to go up to Kory's and get you a Royal Crown?"

"You have some money?"

He grinned. "Naw, but I can swipe some empties from around back and cash them in."

"That might work at Sal's Liquor Store, probably because Sal lets us get away with it, but don't try it at Kory's. We already have a bad name there. Thanks anyway. I just need to sit for a bit."

"OK," he said, and sat down on the curb next to me.

Mac had lagged behind us coming up the path. Now he sat down on the other side of me, rump on the curb, front legs in the gutter.

"Hi, boy," I said.

"Dern dog," Luke muttered. "He thinks he's a person sitting like us."

I gave Mac a long scratch behind both ears. "I think Mac may be smarter than both of us put together, Luke." Mac's tail started up acknowledging the compliment. He gave my cheek a lick which I took as forgiveness for ignoring his warnings about the storm drain.

Resting quietly at the curb, I thought about the Sergeant. *I failed to think clearly and realize the danger,* he had said. At least I was alive to have those words haunt me now. I dug my fingers into the furry folds of Mac's shoulders and massaged my way up his neck. "Good boy, good dog," I whispered. Mac may have forgiven me, but I had not forgiven myself. Contrition weighed heavy on my shoulders and no one was volunteering to massage mine.

The walk home had never been longer. Each step tread hard on what little was left of my failing, gossamer ego. I had evoked the wrath of God. Being driven out of Three Ponds and flushed out of Cavendish Caverns proved it. Superstitious worry had turned into wary veneration and now fear was compounding at an alarming rate, filling me with prognostications that the worst was yet to come.

I tried to banish that sinking feeling as I lay in bed that night, willing myself to think positive thoughts. Mental countermeasures. I imagined that I possessed an ampule of concentrated bravery, applied a tourniquet, found a vein and gave myself a massive dose. It put me to sleep. But I did not rest. The man reappeared, swinging like a pendulum from the catwalk under the train trestle. All through the fitful night, the rope groaned, calling my name. Mister Sand Man had nothing but bogus sand for me.

1962 took forever to come, or maybe it was 1961 that took forever to leave. Carl, the gun-toting baker, would have agreed with me. He was on probation for discharging a firearm within the city limits and for disturbing the peace. He had been looking long in the face, attending three AA meetings per week by order of the court. Lately his spirits had revived considerably thanks to Friendship 7 and John H. Glenn, Jr.

Maybe it was the spirits that had revived him. Carl claimed to have given up Blatz, implying that he had quit drinking, but Luke and I knew better. We saw him stashing several cases of Brew 102 behind the old fig tree in his back yard. He saw us peeking through the fence, then pretended that he hadn't seen us. "Bottled bread yeast," he sang out, plenty loud enough for us to hear.

Luke and I giggled and hunkered down behind the fence. "*FIG*-ure that," Luke whispered, his pun cracking me up to the point that I had to get up and run around to the other side of the house.

Carl had always been harmless, but I had been extra considerate of him ever since the day that he tried to shoot down the Russian cosmonaut. Looking back on it now, I doubt that Carl was any more unstable than I was, the only difference being that I hadn't yet learned how to drink. My time in the bars would come later, and the story of Carl-the-baker shooting at the Russians would be told at least a thousand times.

April Fool's Day 1962 found me prepared to thwart any attempt by Luke to trick me. I was sure he was trying to set me up for a fall of some kind. I was concentrating on his every action. My guard was up.

I had been struggling along, making it, so to speak, one day at a time. But today there was an invigorating newness about. I was enjoying the mood with good reason to be upbeat and happy. It was spring time. The smell of baseball was in the air.

I was sitting on the bedroom floor annoying Mac, who was in the middle of one of his random naps. Tickling the tufts of fur between the pads of his paws was one of my favorite past times. Suddenly Luke bounded into the bedroom. "Wade! Guess what? The Sergeant just pulled up out front—in Queenie!"

I looked at him cross-eyed. "You can do better than that, Luke."

"No, really. I'm not fooling," he said.

He looked as serious as an undertaker in dire need of business. I wasn't falling for it though, partly because Mac hadn't raised an eyebrow, a good indication that no interlopers had entered Parker territory.

"Yeah? Well, tell him Miss Cherry and I have gone to Hawaii on our honeymoon."

"OK," Luke said with a shrug. He spun on his heels and left the room as quickly as he'd come in. *Easily defeated twerp.*

Mac, growing more weary from my prolonged pestering, made a half-hearted attempt to nip my hand. He added a weak growl before laying his head back down on the floor. Then, with one eye closed, he watched me apply a piece of floor lint to the tip of his shiny black nose. His tolerance for this kind of abuse did have a limit. If I kept it up long enough he'd concede the space to me and retreat to another part of the house. End of game. Following him was not a good idea.

Something startled Mac. He snorted out a loud burst of air that sent the piece of lint sailing in a perfect loop-the-loop. In the same fraction of a second he was up on his feet displaying an erect ridge of fur down the length of his spine.

"Jeez, Mac. Take it easy, boy. I won't tease you anymore."

His deep brown eyes glared, piercing the space I occupied like parallel X-rays.

"Aloha. Thought you were in Hawaii, tough guy."

Scar.

Mac relaxed and put a little wag in his tail.

I turned around slowly.

Discomfited, I mouthed, "April fools?" at the same moment realizing it was too late to stop Luke.

He grinned that handsome grin. "How have you been, Wade?"

"Just fine, sir. How are you?"

Luke leaned his head in the door. "I told him what you said, Wade."

I gave Luke one of those looks that could kill. He stuck his tongue out at me. The Sergeant laughed.

"Got somebody out in the car that wants to see you guys."

Mac jumped up on the bed and peered through the window. His tail went into high gear and he started whining.

"Molly—uh—Mrs. Robinson's dog must be out there," I said.

"No—it's Cherry," the Sergeant said, nudging me with his elbow.

My jaw dropped. The mention of her name sent me reeling. My crush on Miss Cherry had been quiescent all this time. Now it came surging back. A trove of giddiness spilled forth and filled me with an urge to bolt and run. "Miss Cherry?" I said tentatively.

"Come on. It's not wise to keep a beautiful woman waiting. Remember that," he said, tugging me along by the arm.

seventeen

A debilitating bashfulness of the likes I had never experienced before came over me as we walked out onto the porch. There she was standing by Queenie, both of them radiating pulchritude in a dramatic shaft of afternoon sun. Miss Cherry smiled, Queenie shimmered, their stylish contours in perfect compliment. The picture could have come right out of a four-color Buick brochure—beautiful blond leaning against the comely-lined, four-wheeled work of art. Consanguineous objects of great desire. Commutable metaphors of male fantasy. The American man's dream. *Buy this car and you're sure to get a girl like this.* Subliminal message hell. This blonde was real and I wanted her all to myself.

I could feel her smile from all the way across the yard. I felt denuded, my wits stripped bare, something dashingly mature to say dangling just beyond my mind's reach. I tried to think faster.

Mac reached Miss Cherry first. His pretense was to assess her as a possible threat, but I didn't buy it for one minute. His behavior was farcical, although measurably better than my own. He gallantly tendered himself at her feet and gazed up with unabashed adoration. The scorpion of jealousy stung me in the heart as I watched him receive a caress for his adroit opportunism. Luke slipped under her other arm and confiscated a generous hug, as if he had preeminent rights. I made it to within six feet of her and stopped dead in my tracks. I fixed on the snug voluptuousness of her form fitting sweater and yearned for both of her arms to close tightly around me. Alas, profligate Parker just stood there, shamelessly staring, desperately stumped, profoundly mute.

"Hello, Wade."

The Goddess had spoken.

A reply was mandatory.

"Hello, ma'am—uh—you look—uh—real sharp, ma'am." *Oh God, what a doofus.*

She giggled. "You look pretty neato-keeno yourself."

I do? Blue jeans with patched knees, faded striped tee shirt, old sneakers caked with storm drain scum. I do?

"Gosh—uh, thank you, ma'am." My cheeks beamed pink. One shoe sort of dug its toe into the sidewalk.

"Well, come here. Don't you want a hug?" she pouted.

I stepped closer, biting my lip to stop myself from saying: That would be real sharp, ma'am. She let go of Luke and Mac and grabbed me, pulling me to her forcefully, aspersing me in an exhilarating, teddy bear embrace. Pressed tight to her sumptuous bosom, she dandled me, steeped me in stupendous rapture. I felt light-headed, flushed and strangely warm, though the proximate sensation wasn't quite sexual. I was blissfully drifting somewhere out in that sea of blithe confusion, that cocoon time between boyhood and manhood when female tenderness can turn gears that don't quite yet mesh.

She held me tight, lingering longer than I expected, pressing my face against fleshy waves of gentle ardor, rocking me in her arms from side to side, lulling me, freeing me from all of my unearned burdens. I wanted to say: I love you, Miss Cherry. Instead, I turned my head to the side and looked at the Sergeant. I fished for a semaphore expression, a wink, a nod, a raised eyebrow, a set to his jaw, anything that would tell me to bunt, take, or swing away. He only grinned, but I saw what I wanted most to see. He wasn't mad at me. At least that was my interpretation.

The hug was over and suddenly it was only half as long as it should have been. She stood me back from the car door. "Lyle and I brought you each a surprise, to show you how much we—well, how much we—*like* you," she said, her voice candied with a tantalizing lilt. She smiled. Her perfect set of pearly whites, gleaming behind full magenta lips, clicked softly to tease us further.

Luke squealed and dashed closer to her. "What surprise?" he gushed.

"Let's see," she said, feigning perplexity, "who should be first?" She was deliberately trying to build the suspense. My heart, for reasons having nothing to do with the order of receiving gifts, was already quivering at peak amplitude.

"Me first! Me-me-me!" Luke yipped. He skipped about in a wild caper and then pranced in front of Miss Cherry like he used to do outside the bathroom waiting for Earl to finish one of his marathon sessions.

The Sergeant started dancing, mimicking Luke. Miss Cherry swatted him, making him quit, but only after he clowned with her first, covering his face with his arms like a boxer inducing an opponent to waste punches. He settled himself down and then turned to me. "I talked to your mom about this, and she said it was OK," he said.

It surprised me that he would seek Lucinda's permission to give us presents. I was sure this was no big deal. Maybe some baseball cards, or a kite perhaps, something like that. Luke was a different story. He was really revved up now, high steppin' at 6,000 rpm. Put him in gear, pop his clutch and he'd burn rubber for a quarter of a mile.

"Better give Luke his present first, before he explodes," I said.

"Yes! Me-me-me!"

Luke had always been impossible to take on Christmas morning. I just wished I could be as free with my emotions as he was. Not me. Keep-it-all-inside Wade.

Miss Cherry opened the car door. I saw two brightly decorated packages sitting on the front seat. One was shoe box size, the other one smaller. She leaned inside the car and pulled out the shoe box. I watched her move—so lithe, so graceful, so incredibly beautiful. She handed the present to Luke. I had to consciously train my attention on Luke and his present.

Luke suddenly turned circumspect. He was staring at the package and I realized he was looking specifically at the designs on the wrapping paper. He looked extremely uncomfortable and I thought maybe he was about to cry. I touched his shoulder, and whispered, "What's the matter, Luke?"

"It's c-c-covered with—birds-*s-s*," he sputtered, the word *birds* hissing through his teeth with heavily salted disgust.

The Sergeant chortled but quickly put a hand over his mouth. Miss Cherry clipped short a peeplike chuckle and smiled sweetly.

Luke stood there ridged as a redwood. The effrontery had stolen his glee, and he held the offensive box away from his scowling face as if it were a poopie diaper. Miss Cherry's expression turned to regret, and I realized they had picked out the bird patterned paper as a joke. *Hey, wait a second. How did they know about Luke's mockingbird problem?* The Sergeant playing a joke was one thing, but Luke was too cute for Miss Cherry to tease like that. Birds, in the all inclusive sense, had become a very serious subject with Luke. Miss Cherry and the Sergeant obviously didn't realize that joking about it would be cruel. Now, seeing Luke's pained reaction, I think they wished the idea had not come up. It was an uncomfortable moment and they clearly didn't quite know what to say. They needed a little help.

I looked closer to inspect the feathered specimens and quickly noticed the design pattern was actually an array of game birds. "No catbirds, Luke. Only quail, pheasant, grouse, dove and—uh—uh —bobolink and cassowary," I rambled, pointing at the different shapes, spouting the names of whatever winged creatures came to mind. The truth was I didn't know a game bird from a parakeet.

"Oh...OK," Luke said, needing only to hear the right assurances from his big brother. I glanced at Miss Cherry and she gave me an appreciative wink. *Yes!* Luke ripped off the offending paper and threw it to the ground. It *was* a shoe box. He popped the lid, lifted back some tissue paper, and proudly removed a new baseball cap. He beamed in a flash, bright as a searchlight. "Wow-wee! Zow-wee! Look, Wade, a Georgia Bulldogs cap!" Suddenly the bird patterned paper made sense. He quickly snugged the cap down over his vulnerable, rubrical pate. Above the visor was a caricature of a muscular bulldog smiling shamelessly, as if he had just eaten, you guessed it, a catbird.

I finally surmised that Lucinda must have blabbed about Luke's mockingbird problem and offered some tips on what we would like for gifts. While, to the best of my knowledge, Lucinda knew nothing about our lives as storm drain troopers, she did know about Luke's desire to own a Bulldogs cap, and the hilarious reason why. I wondered what she might have told them to get for me?

Miss Cherry saw the opportunity for an apology. Donning the cap of a mediatrix, she spoke in an overly sympathetic voice. "Sorry about the wrapping paper, Luke. I hope you're not *too* upset with us." She was a little too contrite for the Sergeant and he rolled his eyes in disapproval. I thought she was just being nice, feminine, nurturing, motherly. Now Luke was glowing, sanguine-faced and fanciful, up beyond the clouds in a respite from worry, his new cap auguring a future free of attacks from on high. He hadn't heard a word Miss Cherry said.

I elbowed him, harder than I meant to. "What do you say?"

He turned on me. "Hey, you big donkey. Watch it!"

"Well, Miss Cherry was talking to you...and you didn't even say *thank you* for the cap."

He frowned at me and then turned and quietly said, "Thank you." Immediately his hands went up to touch and stroke his new hat, his new pet, his new defender. Seconds later he was gone again. Eyes glazed. Off in a mental utopia where, I envisaged, he sat around a campfire like a pompous nobleman, roasting mockingbirds on a wooden spit as he listened to his jowly bulldog bodyguard recite Churchillian parables in perfect King's English. Miss Cherry watched him slip back into his reverie. She smiled like the Madonna, pleased that he was so taken with his hat.

"Hey, what about Wade's present?" said the Sergeant.

"Well, well—*hmmm*. Let me see. What have we for Wade?" She reached back into the car and brought out the other gift. She handed it to me along with the blessing of one of her captivating smiles.

"Gee," I said stupidly.

"Hope you like it, Wade," she said. "Lyle picked it out. He said we had to get the best for Wade Parker."

I was so bewitched it could have been a box of snakes and I'd still embellish her with lavish appreciation. "Thank you, ma'am...and sir," I said, looking over at the Sergeant who was now sitting on the grass scratching Mac's belly.

"You're welcome, honey," Miss Cherry said. Her bedazzling blue eyes made me melt.

The gift was heavier than I expected. What would be in parity with a Bulldogs cap? I couldn't imagine. Then I felt a pinprick of caution. Seeing what they had used to wrap Luke's gift, I subconsciously scanned the box for renderings of the dead man of Three Ponds. *Whew!* Nothing but freeze-framed images of Emmett Kelly and friends engaging in various antics with balloons and seltzer water dispensers. I glanced at Luke and saw that he was facing toward me, but his eyes showed he was still frivoling in a fantasy dimension. His mind was hooked to a helium filled sonde and had not yet returned to earth. I shook the package and listened for telltale clues to its contents. Silence.

Luke returned from his coma-esque sojourn. "Just open it, Wade. Maybe they got you a cap too."

"Nah," I said coyly. "They know you're the hat wearer in the family, not me." I glanced at the Sergeant as I spoke. His supplicating smile should have eased me around the vague inquietudes that gnawed at the back of my mind. I couldn't suppress the thought of the last time he gave something to me. It turned out to be something spurious, not really a gift at all, more like a warning. That little chromium cipher he dropped in my hand had clung to me like a pilot fish ever since, and probably was the force that held me in the phantasmagoria of dreams that plagued me to this very day. I stood there looking askance at the clowns, hesitating, uncomfortable, like a confused ascetic troglodyte trying to abstain from pleasure, but not wishing to offend.

The Sergeant tried to goad me. "Maybe we should give it to Mac. Wade seems to think something's in there that's going to bite him."

Mac had been lounging indolently, preening his fur on the grass, relishing his belly rub. Now he sat up at attention, ready, willing and able to rip open a hand me down gift. He stretched out his legs, did one of those *get-the-kinks-out* whole body tremblers that starts at the head and flows like falling dominoes to the tip of the tail. He pranced spryly over to me, or rather to the gift I was holding, and promptly gave it a thorough sniffing. Finding no hint of edible treasure within, he shambled back to the Sergeant in hopes of continued tactile sustenance.

Oh, how I envied Mac his simple life. Many years later I heard a joke that summed it up perfectly. Let's see—how did it go? Oh yeah:

One warm summer day a father dog decides to take his young son with him on a run around the neighborhood. It was time to teach the young pup a few things about life. The father instructs junior to watch his every move. "Do like I do son and you'll grow up to be a good dog." At the end of the day junior had a few questions for the old man. "Hey pop, it made a lot of sense when you tipped over that trash can and found that big juicy steak bone, and I could definitely see that you were enjoying yourself when you mounted that beautiful golden retriever. What I don't get, though, is why you urinated on those shiny

hub caps we passed along the way. "Well son," the old man said, "it's
like this. If you can't eat it, or screw it, piss on it."

Not being born into a dog's life, and faced with no way to eschew
my own, I was left to observe Mac with envy and to vicariously
supplant my own tenebrous existence with wistful fantasies of a
carefree canine life. I stood there frozen in my own ridiculous reverie,
doing the same thing I had chastened Luke for only a few moments
earlier. Miss Cherry must have noticed a disturbing trend, a genetic
trait implanted in both Luke and I. *Parker's Syndrome: Stupidity in
the presence of gifts.* No doubt my eyes had glazed over, zapped by
Somnus and *Hypnos,* because Miss Cherry took hold of my arm and
gently pulled me out of my dingy stupor. I was completely silly with
infatuation. She was a seraph. Her auric smile comforted my soul.
Her preternatural touch was powerful enough to pull me up from the
depths of *Tartarus.* Her dominion over me was absolute. "It's OK,
honey. Go ahead and open it," she said.

The clowns were drawn and quartered with a minimum of effort.
Another wink from Miss Cherry, and I was the proud owner of a brand
new transistor radio. "Wow! Neat!" I exclaimed.

Mac's disappointment showed as he turned his head away.

"Hey, that's cool," Luke piped up. "Can you get Vin Scully on
that?"

"Sure can," answered the Sergeant. "Wolfman Jack, too. Clear as
a bell. All the way from Tijuana. I checked it over real good,
Wade—KRLA, KHJ, KFI, KNBC, KMPC—it picks up all of 'em,
static free."

I looked over the pudding box size receiver with the scrutiny of a
jeweler inspecting a new shipment of diamonds. It had the smell of
brand new—solder, wiring, plastic—and it seemed to be very well
made. Then I noticed the label on the back, *Made in Japan,* and I
frowned. To me that meant *throw this junk away.* I turned the radio
around and looked at the brand on the front. Westinghouse? I was
confused. "It says the Japs made this on the back," I stated, distaste
implicit in my tone.

I noticed that Carl-the-baker had come out of his house and was
sitting on the steps of his front porch. I saw him lean his head behind
the solid banister that encircled his porch and deduced he was nursing
a beer. He looked over at our little gathering and waved like a well
behaved and polite neighbor should. I waved back.

The Sergeant answered. "The Japanese are going to own the electronics market some day, Wade. Better get used to it. Fact is their quality has improved. Westinghouse wouldn't put their name on it if it wasn't any good."

"That so?" I said. My prejudice against the Japanese had come from Earl. He claimed to have been captured by the Japs during the war. I gathered they did not treat him kindly. Disdain for the Japanese—those sneaky, slanty-eyed bastards, as Earl had always called them—was about the only thing Earl ever gave me. Carl definitely had a beer hidden behind him. I saw him lean twice more. Come to think of it, speaking of the Japs, Carl once told us he lost a nephew at Pearl Harbor.

"In fact, some folks believe the Japs are going to own this country someday," the Sergeant continued.

A mischievous impulse clicked inside my head. Earl's racist imprint would be removed years later when I fell in love with a beautiful Japanese-American woman named Melissa, however, at that moment I couldn't wait to inform Carl that someday he'd be making his mortgage payments to the Bank of Hirohito. Just to get his mind off of the Russians, of course.

eighteen

We all sat around on the front lawn talking, Luke still on cloud nine with his new cap, me running up and down the dial finding more radio stations than I ever knew existed. Miss Cherry and Luke meandered over to the fence to chat with Carl. By now Carl had abandoned his effort to hide the beer. In another thirty minutes he'd be singing patriotic songs to the entire block. Mac had drifted off to sleep stretched out between the Sergeant and me, nap number five or six probably.

I had thoroughly enjoyed the surprise visit and was doubly pleased that they had decided to stay for the entire afternoon. The Sergeant seemed particularly relaxed. I noticed he carried an unusually nice tan for so early in the year. I wondered where he had been spending his days to get so brown. If he had been going to the beach I wished he would invite Luke and me to go with him.

The Sergeant and I were alone for the first time since they had arrived. It was great just to be sitting there sharing the same space with him, passing time together, enjoying each other's company, like a family. It also made me acutely aware of how much I had missed him. I couldn't help wondering if he had missed me too. Or whether or not he had even thought about me.

No one was more content than Mac. He was dreaming, whimering softly, feet twitching just like they did when I tickled them to annoy him.

I settled in on one radio station. After a while, the Sergeant got up and turned Queenie's radio on to the same station. "Hi-Fidelity sound," he said, as he settled back down next to me.

I smirked. "Enjoy it while you can. It won't be long before Carl's singing drowns out everything—and I mean everything."

"Maybe we'll just sing along with him then. You know, when they give you lemons—you make lemonade."

"Oh no, " I countered. "Carl's not a lemon. He has a very nice voice. It's just loud. Real loud."

The Sergeant laughed and rubbed the top of my head. Then out of the blue, he looked right at me and said, "You know, I kind of missed you, Wade."

My heart soared. "I missed you too, sir."

"You don't have to call me sir all the time. You can call me Lyle if you like."

"Yes, sir, I know that. Maybe to some people it's kind of corny, but I just like to call you sir—because I respect you—being a policeman and all."

His face instantly turned solemn, almost a show of shame, confusing me completely. He looked away as if to keep from revealing more. He didn't say anything. I was uncertain what, but something sure seemed wrong. My confidence faltered as a sail slackens in shifting wind.

He coughed, and I took it as the kind of cough you make when you want to change the subject. So I changed the subject, trying to keep the hurt out of my voice. "Where have you been all this time?"

Now he looked uncomfortable, skittish. "Well—uh—I had to go away on business for a few months."

I thought that was a little strange. A Los Angeles cop gone on business for months at a time? But I didn't have the nerve to question it. "Oh," I said, disgusted with my lack of courage. "I was afraid maybe...I was thinking maybe you were mad at me, and that was why you didn't come around."

"Why would I be mad at *you* ?"

He seemed genuinely surprised that I would think that. A ball of desperation clenched tight in my gut. I wanted so much to tell him the truth. That I knew he knew all about me killing that man. That I was glad that he didn't arrest me or turn me in. That I thought he was very mad at me and didn't want to see me because of what I had done. But I couldn't. *Coward!* "Well—uh—remember the last time we saw each other?"

"Yes...Rodney's funeral." His mood turned melancholy. I had dredged up unpleasant feelings.

"Well, remember when you dropped me off that day?"

"Yeah, sort of. What about it?"

I thought, *Jeepers, do I have to go through the whole thing?* And suddenly I remembered what I had told Luke to say to him when I thought Luke was just April foolin' me, about Miss Cherry and me being in Hawaii on our honeymoon. He must be playing dumb? Must be pulling my leg?

"Well, if you remember, I kind of, well, actually...I played a dirty trick on you."

Then, just as suddenly, I was painfully conscious of the possibility that he might have told Miss Cherry about that dirty trick, that I had claimed that she wanted to marry me. *Oh God!* Nervously, I glanced in her direction.

"A dirty trick? Gee, I don't remember," he said. His face was straight now and he seemed interested, as if this was the first he had heard about it.

I got up and moved around to the other side of him, positioning my back to Miss Cherry just to make sure she wouldn't hear me. I lowered my voice. "Don't you remember? We were sitting in Queenie." I pointed. "She was parked right there where she is now." I realized I was whispering, and didn't like that I was. The secretive vibration of my voice tantalized Mac out of his slumber. He didn't open his eyes, but rising brows and quivering ears were sure indications of eavesdropping.

"Yeah. So what? I always park there," the Sergeant said looking dumbly at Queenie.

I stared at him for a bit, looking for the crack of a smile, stalling for time. He didn't break. A Coca-Cola commercial playing on the radio ended and the disk jockey segued into *Poor Little Fool,* by Ricky Nelson: "*...and here's Ozzie and Harriet's little baby boy with an April Fool's Day lament...*" I glanced over my shoulder. Miss Cherry's hips were noticeably swaying to the music.

Carl had swallowed enough courage and was in the middle of telling Miss Cherry about his day of infamy and his unfortunate incarceration. He was getting louder, his arms darting about punctuating his speech with animated flair. Miss Cherry seemed to be enjoying Carl's lowbrow humor. Carl had been generous with his supplies. Now Miss Cherry cradled a beer of her own. He had also produced a cream soda for Luke. Out of the corner of my eye I saw Carl's poor wife peeking through a slit in the curtains. She deserved better, I thought.

I tapped the radio volume knob up, moved a little closer, and resumed whispering. "Come on. Don't you remember? I told you I had heard some talk at the Highland Park Police Station." He looked at me blankly. I was really beginning to become annoyed with his charade. I could tell Mac was becoming annoyed too. Ricky Nelson adequately obscured my voice, "...*ah-ha, oh-yeah, I was a fool...*" but I leaned in even closer. "You said you wanted to marry Miss Cherry and I told you that I had heard that she wanted to marry someone else."

He just stared and shrugged his shoulders. No memory whatsoever. Now I was exasperated. Ricky's final refrain faded to silence as I got to my feet, dizzy with frustration and completely unaware of the quiet lull. Out of control, I shouted, "I told you Miss Cherry wanted to marry me!"

The Sergeant's face jelled with pure pleasure as the heat of utter humiliation set mine ablaze. I glanced at Miss Cherry as my cue came over the pudding box radio...the intro to Del Shannon's *Runaway*. *"...As I walk alone...I wonder what went wrong..."* My brain said flee from this place of shame and confusion. *Run! Run! Run!* But my body couldn't respond. I was frozen solid, entrapped in a crystalline glacier that wasn't moving anywhere. On public display like a statue in the park. *Bring on the pigeons!* A second or two of eternal length expired before, at last, my synapses rejoined my legs with the will to move. But, alas, it was too late.

"April Fools!" the Sergeant bellowed. With lightning quickness he lunged, grabbing my legs and pulling me down on top of him. My humiliation flashed away in a frothing frenzy of uproarious laughter, hilarious squealing, and frantic attempts to escape. I was hopelessly ensnared in the powerful clutches of a human grizzly hell-bent to tickle me beyond the bounds of oblivion. He howled and roared, laughing equally as much as me. "I remember every word you said, you little rat fink! But I got you now!"

Miss Cherry and Luke ran over and jumped on the pile. Mac pranced and barked as he jumped in and out of the roiling ball of arms and legs. Carl laughed, and clapped, and whooped, and hollered as he danced a jig. The fence separated him from us but he was not to be left out of the merry scrum. His wife, still peeking through the drapes, seemed delighted to see him so energized and happy. So much so that she came out of the house and gave him a fresh bottle of ice cold contraband. Carl locked an arm around his wife's waist and waltzed her around his front yard until she finally squirmed free and scurried back inside the house, but not before collecting up an armful of empties.

My synapses eventually overloaded and I finally gave up the effort to get away. Batteries drained, limp as a tuckered out trout ready to be reeled in, I slumped into a wheezing, giggling mass of arms and legs. Just as tuckered out as I was, the Sergeant grinned and said, "We're even. But you did put up a heck of a fight." Relieved that my fears were unfounded, I squeaked out a breathless thank you.

Miss Cherry ended up next to me in the pile. Now we lay side by side on our backs looking up at the first twinkling hints of dusk. Luke untangled himself and restored his cap while the Sergeant sat up and brushed a few blades of dried grass from his hair. Mac wallowed on his back, snorting and snuffling in the grass, nuzzling the Sergeant's leg with his snout and the Sergeant obliged him with a firm caress behind the ears. As though in response to a conductor's baton, from the other side of the fence, Carl's beer-barrel baritone began a remarkably soft, dulcet rendition of *God Bless America.* It was strange how the ambiance had shifted from an almost violent caterwaul to sublime calm. Lying there so close to Miss Cherry, I felt like a circus tiger being soothed by the trusting presence of my trainer. As the sky blushed toward nightfall, Carl's ariose praise of God and Country was lifted up on a gentle breeze, a sweet gift to the neighborhood. We gazed above and beheld the most beautiful orchid sea and I was immersed in a wonderful sense of security. I felt so loved, a feeling I wanted to last forever, wanted to be real.

Miss Cherry took my hand in hers and suddenly I was arm in arm with a beautiful Roman goddess. She turned her head to me, her lips very close, and spoke with the tenderness of *Tellus.* "You know," she said barely above a whisper, "if I weren't already betrothed to Lyle, I'd marry you in a minute."

He did tell her.

I wanted to ask her what betrothed meant, erroneously figuring it was a term from the secret lexicon of undercover cops. Instead, I decided to ferret it out later. "That's real sharp, ma'am," I said, for the moment beguiled into feeling nothing at all like a doofus.

"Lyle and I won't be able to have children. I'm not capable. I love being around kids, especially you and Luke."

"Lucinda wouldn't mind sharing us with you," I happily volunteered.

The crickets of spring provided a cacophonous background score for Carl's loyalist medley. We lay there on our backs listening, enjoying, like patrons at an evening concert on the green. We gazed to the heavens with the same awe and wonder that human beings had been experiencing for thousands of years. To me the brightest stars were symbols of my private thoughts and I scanned from horizon to horizon reviewing the seminal events of the day. Like the earliest astronomers, I scoured the constellations in search of the paradigm that would make it all add up. I needed to find my guiding star, or at least a way to uncross my star-crossed life.

My biggest problem was that I was only eleven years old. And try as I might, I lacked the necessary intellectual maturity to solve the complex riddle of emotions that overflowed from every cell within me. The adults lying in the grass beside me had made an imprint, but I needed more. I needed them permanently engraved in my life. I just didn't know how to tell them. I wished it all to be so as I ruminated over the vast galaxy above. I sat up for a moment and roamed the sky. My lucky star had to be up there somewhere. I closed my eyes and pictured it twinkling, a stellar diamond reserved just for me. I made a silent vow and wished upon my star, wherever it was. In the form of a prayer, I proffered myself, a votive child, in exchange for bringing Miss Cherry and the Sergeant closer to me. For deep down in my lonely heart of hearts I knew that the exegesis I sought could not be found, or understood, without the abetting love of a mentor. I wanted to lie down and stay there next to them forever.

The moist chill of night had already fogged her windows when finally the Sergeant put the key in Queenie and fired her up. Luke and I stood at Miss Cherry's window, my heart weighing heavy in my chest as they prepared to drive away. Sadness accumulated with each breath as I struggled to accept their departure. It was awful not knowing when I might see them again. On top of that, there was no escaping the cowardice that had caused the missed opportunity to confess my sins to the Sergeant.

It had been a good day, the best in a long, long time. But the reality of April fools came like a slap in the face when Miss Cherry smiled, hugged me, and said good-bye. I tried my best to be a man, but I just couldn't stop the uncooperative tears that trickled loose and dripped down on the pudding box radio tucked snugly to my chest. I took a quick step back from the car and turned the radio up louder, desperately in need of a happy song to bring me back under control. I was in trouble from the opening drum roll. The greatest rock and roll crooner of all time opened my floodgates wide, his bitter-sweet empathy burning into me like lashes from a whip. He sang of the painful side of love, of desperate longing for things that can never be, of pitiful crying when pitiful crying is the soul's only defense against crushing abject sorrow.

A modicum of left over pride compelled me to turn away and walk toward the house, head down, Roy Orbison as my singing sherpa guide. I closed the front door and slumped to the floor. Tears flowed to beat the Arroyo Seco, and only Roy Orbison understood my misery.

nineteen

Luke had stayed by Queenie and handled the final good-byes. I turned off the radio, got up off of the living room floor, blew my nose, and was sitting on my bed when Luke finally meandered into the house. He was humming something upbeat and cheerful as he came over and sat down on his bed directly across from me. Two inches separated the toes of our sneakers. Mac strolled in and jumped up on the bed beside me. He quickly began licking my cheek. He wasn't being sympathetic or affectionate, he just liked the salty tear trails. Carl had stepped it up a notch and was now blasting out a thunderous interpretation of *Wild Blue Yonder*. He would usually finish up on a religious note. Tonight I was betting on *Onward Christian Soldiers*.

I was thinking...*What a way to live.* My life had become a topsy-turvy ride down a churning rapid of wild emotion. I wasn't living. I was existing, like a Nubian slave with no hope for a better future, for a better life. Except *my* master did not pop a bullwhip, or wield a club to beat me into submission. My master was a wicked trio of guilt, loneliness and heartache.

I knew that Lucinda loved me with all her heart. My condition was not the result of her failings. I did not begrudge my mother. If I was capable of blaming someone other than myself, it would be Earl; but I couldn't even blame him. I was my own worst enemy, and deep down I knew that I would have to find a way to negotiate an armistice with myself. I had enslaved myself. I must free myself. *Only the dead are not slaves*, the poet had said. I hoped that wasn't true.

I could handle the days. It was the nights, the dreams of Three Ponds that held me in a strangle. I needed healthy dreams to stave off the consuming madness. I needed to dream of Miss Cherry and the Sergeant. I would try to look forward. I would try to keep them with me at night, inside my closed eyes.

And still, as I sat there on my bed wrestling with my painful thoughts, I looked at Luke and saw that there was purpose and good in my life. If not for Luke, I reminded myself, I surely would have turned to dust long ago.

The silver ball bearing raged like a tempest in my pocket. It did not approve of my taking solace in brotherly love. It did not like me partaking of anything positive. Like a hexed amulet around my neck, it tenaciously throbbed with disapproval, refusing to let me forgive or forget.

The battle raged on.

It was obvious to Luke that I was upset. He sat quietly, patiently respecting my feelings. When finally I sighed and shifted my position on the bed, he spoke.

"They gave me this," he said, handing me a sealed, plain white, business size envelope. "They said to give it to you. That you should open it because you're the oldest."

I looked at the envelope, mistrusting, dubious.

A good-bye note?

A subpoena?

An arrest warrant?

It was killing Luke that he was not the one designated to open it. "They said we—uh—you I mean—could open it any time you want." His slip of the tongue was plainly intentional.

"Hum-m-m. What could it be, Mac?" I held the envelope to Mac's nose and let him sniff.

Luke was irritated that I hadn't immediately opened it. He complained, "Don't let the dern dog slobber on it."

Mac sneezed. I, too, had noticed the smell of Miss Cherry's perfume on the envelope.

A love note?

"Maybe it's money," I suggested, knowing it couldn't possibly be.

Luke couldn't contain himself. "Come on, open it!"

"Let's not be hasty—could be a trick or something." I almost laughed.

"Oh jeez!" he puffed, his face mantling under his new bulldog coronet.

Teasing and baiting Luke was good medicine for me. The bigger the rise I got out of him the more it recharged my batteries. I looked at him. He was glowing red as a beet, britches full of ants. Thanks to him, I felt a thousand percent better than I had five minutes earlier.

I looked at the envelope again. It was addressed to *Luke and Wade*. It was written in cursive with bright blue ink, definitely a feminine hand. Luke's name was before mine. "Here," I said, surprising the heck out of him, "you open it." Being the oldest carried with it an obligation to be magnanimous once in a while.

Then Luke surprised me. He pulled out his peewee pocket knife and carefully slit open the envelope, rather than the usual barbaric shredding that he was famous for. He removed a single trifolded sheet of bond paper and let the envelope fall to the floor. He unfolded the paper and held it out in front of him, carefully scrutinizing, as if he were censoring a note from his teacher to Lucinda. The top half of his occasionally cherubic face appeared above the sheet of paper. I watched his eyes. His expression changed from one of curiosity to either ecstasy or horror, I wasn't sure. The sheet of paper slipped down and joined the envelope at our feet.

In Luke's impish little hands were four, third base, box seat tickets for the opening game at the brand new, house that O'Malley built, Dodger Stadium. A million volts of *ec-c-c-static* electricity zapped through my body, making me screech, "WOW!" Luke screamed loud enough to drown out Carl, and Mac howled to his ancestors with the power of a hundred full moons. Luke leapt off of the bed and began hopping around the room. He whooped and squealed with the vehemence of a rainmaker challenging a ten year drought. Mac and I joined the rumpus in a wild, sequacious effort that was not to be outdone by Luke. I grabbed my new radio and cranked the volume knob all the way up just as Bobby Darin's *Splish Splash* came over the air.

Luke handed off two of the tickets to me and we paraded from room to room holding the tickets high like the honored regimental standards of a proud cavalry. Two uproarious bantlings we were, strutting peacocks, leprechauns flaunting the proverbial pot of gold. The radio blared out instructions like a coach on the sidelines inspiring his team to victory. We went crazy with excitement, dancing with each other, imitating what we'd seen on *American Bandstand*. The songs poured from the radio, and we responded accordingly, doing The Twist, standing side by side wiggling our behinds and snapping our fingers, pounding on our knees like make believe bongos, and slamming down imaginary shots of tequila. Finally, in one huge encore, Johnny and the Hurricanes sent us into a frenzy that completely wore us out. Exhausted, we crashed back on our beds where the lofty celebration had begun. Our private party had lasted for over an hour.

The sweat of our unbridled joy evaporated slowly, cooling me down, leaving more salt crystals for Mac. I watched Luke's chest rise and fall. He was fast asleep, probably deep into a catbird hunt with his new bully bird dog leading the way. He was smiling in his sleep as I worked at a stubborn knot in my shoelace.

I gently removed the tickets still clutched in his little pink hand and matched them with the ones that I'd been revering. I studied the four tickets, putting them in numerical order, reading and re-reading all of the information printed on the front and back, convincing myself that they were real. At length, I put them with my Duke Snider card collection that I kept in an old oxbow chest of drawers in the corner of the room. I safely tucked them under a pair of oversize corduroy pants that I had won years before in an audience raffle at the Pinky Lee Show.

I was debating whether to slip under the covers or wait up for Lucinda when I saw the sheet of paper and the envelope still lying on the floor. Mac jumped up on the bed as I picked up the paper. There was some writing on it that I hadn't noticed before:

> *Dear Wade,*
>
> > *Lucinda said it was OK. "C" and I will pick you guys up plenty early so you can watch the players take batting practice and warm up. We'll have a real blast!*
> >
> > > *Your friend,*
> > >
> > > > *Lyle*
> >
> > *PS. I have to go back to Miami for a few more days.*

(So that's where he got so tan, I thought.)

> > *PPS. Never look back, Wade.*

"Never look back." I read the words out loud.

They were Rodney's dying words, too. I thought of him and horsecakes and smiled. The front and back images of Doris also came to mind. I put the piece of paper into the envelope and put it in the drawer with Duke and the tickets.

"Never look back," I muttered to myself. *What does that mean?*

Mac watched me with droopy eyes.

"Move over, boy, I'm tired, too," I said, shucking out of my jeans. I turned out the light and slipped under the covers. Lucinda wouldn't mind if I didn't wait up for her tonight.

"What a day, Mac. What a day."

He thumped my leg with his tail and licked off some more salt.

Outside my window Carl crooned on.

I laid there in the dark listening to Carl sing. It was kind of sad, really. He needed to express himself, and had no audience. Somehow I identified with him. I reckoned we were both misunderstood souls, savants of the vespertine, forever seeking but never quite finding our place in the mysterious order of things—life. Then I decided I didn't like the thought of my being anything like Carl. He was a drunk, just like Earl. I certainly didn't ever want to become a drunk, like them.

I turned the radio on low and held it by my ear. As Santo and Johnny played *Sleep Walk* I drifted off in a dream of being there when Duke Snider hit three home runs in one game for the third time in his career. Briefly, my discontent and self-pity had been driven back into the closet.

Lucinda came home about an hour after Carl's vocal chords gave out. She wasn't alone. She and a "friend" tiptoed in as best as they could, but vigilant, radarmutt Mac detected them easily. He jerked up in bed on full alert, knocking the radio into my head and awakening me from a light, but highly vulnerary slumber.

"No barking," I whispered. "It's only Lucinda."

He settled down but wasn't happy about it. He knew someone else was out there besides Lucinda. A man.

Lights went on in the living room.

Muffled voices.

Giggling.

Three, two, one, the bedroom door opened. She looked in on us. I pretended to be asleep. She left the door open a crack as usual. Mac decided everything was copacetic and went back to sleep. More muffled noises from the living room.

This was the first time Lucinda had brought someone home with her, as far as I knew. I was a little perplexed. Not angry. More curious than anything. Earl had been gone for over two years now and in all that time Lucinda had not shown any interest in men. She was in love with her work, nothing more.

Curiosity got me out of bed. I listened at the door gaining little information—ice cubes tinkling, more giggling, and Lucinda's voice saying the name Ted. The living room lights went out. Fifteen seconds later I heard her bedroom door click shut.

My curiosity did not wane. In T-shirt and underpants, I crept out into the hall and tiptoed slowly down to Lucinda's door. The horizontal shaft of light under her door disappeared. I heard the man talking. *Ted who?* His voice sounded strangely familiar, but I couldn't place it. He said, "You're not going to say 'April Fools'...are you?" Lots more giggling. *Wait a second! That voice sounds just like that mean cop, Kowalski. Nah. No way. It can't be him. Now I'm playing April Fools tricks on myself.* I tiptoed back to the bedroom thinking I knew exactly what Ted, whoever he was, had meant. In the dark, I silently slid the dresser drawer open and felt under the corduroy... just to make sure.

Lieutenant Kowalski? Couldn't be.

twenty

I had risen up some from the nadir of my dilemma. After Luke flashed those Dodgers tickets I felt a little bit like Saint Peter had sent me a free pass to heaven. I checked under the corduroy pants no less than a dozen times per day until the drawer handle couldn't take it anymore. I tried to quiz Lucinda about the whole thing—Bulldogs cap, transistor radio, Dodgers tickets—but she was very hush-hush about it, except to say that she had approved. I found her behavior unsettling, the distant smile that seemed to hint regret, or camouflage hurt feelings. Lucinda had become so disengaged from our daily lives, never quite having returned to us since Matthew died, that it wouldn't have occurred to me she might have liked to go to the game with us. It was hard to get her to express her feelings.

I'm certain Luke and I never consciously excluded Lucinda from anything. We simply coexisted on parallel dimensions, and the independent nature of it obscured any thoughts of inclusion. It was beyond me to figure her out, though, so I didn't give it a lot of thought. Many years later, just before she died, Lucinda would tell me how sad she had felt that day. She said watching us drive away from the house with Miss Cherry and the Sergeant on our way to Dodger Stadium, seeing how happy we were, had made her feel she was losing us, too. In a way she was right, at least as far as it would turn out with me.

We arrived at Chavez Ravine two hours before game time. My stomach was plagued with butterflies over the possibility of seeing

Duke Snider up close. When Queenie sauntered up over the rise on Stadium Way my heart swelled with pride. That first glimpse of the new stadium structure caught me completely unprepared—a beautiful, gleaming, Brooklyn blue castle majestically shooting skyward, rocketing the dreams of Abner Doubleday far into the future.

The splendor of Dodger Stadium was equaled only by the stunning beauty of Miss Cherry. She rode in the front seat ahead of me, looking over her shoulder and smiling now and then. Each time her eyes met mine my heart sped up a little and my chest would tingle for a minute or two. I was unquestionably in love.

The stadium was so far beyond what I had pictured in my mind, I couldn't believe it. I was in awe, or perhaps in *Oz*. I thought, so this is how Dorothy felt when she first set eyes on the Emerald City. I peered out the car window at the newest wonder of the earth. "Man! This is as good as life gets!" I exclaimed, a feeling of utter bliss tickling my insides with a sugary rush of anticipation.

Luke was dumbfounded, too. " Ho-ly Mo-ley! Would you look at that!" he blurted.

"Absolutely magical" I concurred, knowing that *The Duke* was already sequestered somewhere inside the castle, royalty that he was.

Queenie hummed across a sea of newly laid blacktop, delivering us through a phalanx of wooden saw-horses and concrete barricades. She nosed her way up to a guarded gate upon which a sign hung that read: AUTHORIZED OFFICIALS AND PERSONNEL ONLY.

The Sergeant showed his police badge to a guard who seemed to recognize him. He immediately waved us through. As we moved past the smiling sentry the Sergeant glanced over his shoulder at me. "This is where the players park," he said, then nodding up ahead as he cranked the wheel to the right. "There's Duke Snider's Corvette over there."

A new tingle rattled down my spine and I began to giggle from an overflow of nervous energy. I never thought I'd get that close to Duke's Corvette. Two seasons earlier, Luke and I had ventured to the Coliseum for "Duke Snider Night" when he received the car and other gifts in honor of his outstanding career. 'I'll remember this night for the rest of my life,' he had said to the crowd. I stood in the stands and cried. My heart was filled with deep respect and honor for my great hero. 'I'll remember this night for the rest of my life, too, Duke,' I had called out to him from deep within the throng of over 51,000 admirers.

It was a double header. Duke didn't play in the first game. We got to see him hit a smash homer over the centerfield fence before an usher caught us and expelled us from the park. We didn't have tickets. We had managed to slip through the turnstile by crowding in with a family with a bunch of kids. We had used every penny we had for bus fare. It was worth it, though. It was a night I would never forget. As we rolled past the Duke's sporty carriage—it was almost close enough to touch—I felt compelled to bow and renew my pledge of fealty.

Queenie found a vacant stall and eased herself in. I opened the car door and hesitated for a moment before placing my feet on the pavement. I was about to step on hallowed ground, a humble believer savoring the final steps of a lifelong pilgrimage. I said a private entreaty of esteem and thanks, took a deep breath, and got out of the car.

"You're awfully quiet," the Sergeant said, sidling up next to me on the ramp climbing up from the parking lot.

I smiled as one might smile while beholding a renowned work of art. "This is the greatest day of my life," I said. He put his arm over my shoulders. "Thank you for making this possible, sir." He squeezed me in kind of a fatherly hug.

"My pleasure, son. I know this means a lot to you and Luke." He used the word *son.* It sounded wonderful. I tried it on for size, knowing full well he'd meant it just as figure of speech. It was only a generic term not intended to imbue the specialness of sonhood, if there was such a thing. He squeezed again. "I think you and Luke are in for a special day indeed." I caught that all knowing look again and wondered.

We walked to a turnstile with an overhead sign that read, VIP CHECK IN. A portly man dressed in bleach-white pants, equally bright starched white shirt, blue blazer and a dashing red tie gladly checked our tickets. Friendly as a car salesman, he said, "Field Level Box, row one, third base side." He laughed heartily, almost like Santa Claus, and gregariously chimed, "You'll be able to hear Mr. Alston *think* from these seats."

"Ho-ly Mo-ley!" Luke blurted.

I glanced up at the Sergeant's face, shock smeared all over mine, and mouthed, "Row one—dugout seats?" He nodded yes, grinning just the way he did at that cop, Lieutenant Kowalski, the night of the hazing on Billy Goat Hill. I did something totally out of character. I did a Luke. I squealed at the top of my lungs and danced in-place till my feet hurt.

Programs, popcorn and peanuts in hand, we gleefully headed into the infield tunnel. I was rapt with a feeling of homage and sincere aplomb, like one chosen for a private communion with the Pope. This was no storm drain, or subterranean dungeon, or illusory playground offering false hope to wayward souls. No flash flood. No miasma inhabited by apocalyptic hooded monks. The light at the end of this tunnel was brilliant with the beaming animus of baseball. Luminous enough to brighten my spirit and fill my needy heart with monumental satisfaction. Luke was beside himself, too. This was GREAT!

As we emerged from the interior portal, a whole new level of awe loomed forth. I was seized in the grip of epiphanic thralldom. My eyes roamed, omnivorous conductors flooding my already overloaded brain with images of a great Icon. My concept of *Oz* now appeared glamorously before my dazzled senses. A campo of emerald green abounded far and wide, a living carpet so rich and luxurious that only a wizard could have made it so. The sight of the infield made me giddy. Hybrid clay, groomed to perfection, warmed in the life giving sun, glowed with radiating tinges of conquistador copper. The base pads stood out like mother-of-pearl tuxedo buttons, formal, resolute, classy adornments in the sacred wreath of competition. Ivory talc rifle shots blazed out from home plate, a twin-tailed comet resting its head on the seat of business. And out in front, the pitcher's mound, a solitary naked rampart centered in the field of battle, fain to commence the cannonade.

Slowly I turned to take in the full panorama of Dodger Stadium. "Oh my gosh," I whispered, as my eyes filled with the massive decks, staggered four high, looming like a stair-stepped mountain behind home plate. The stands fanned out in a gargantuan horseshoe from foul line to foul line. Towering stanchions of artificial sun hovered around the glorious field. Bleacher sections, standing proudly left and right of centerfield, wore matching festoon scoreboards surmounted with giant orange Union 76 globes.

Bunting, elegantly draped from nearly every horizontal place, declared through its colors that we were in the land of the free and the home of the brave. Old glory, the California bear, and brightly colored baseball pennants everywhere, lazily waved in a gentle breeze. I viewed these accouterments with perfidious disinterest. Nice all right, but unnecessary carnival trappings, mere window dressing, as far as I was concerned.

If there was anything wrong at all it was the outfield wall. It was a pitcher's helper. No, not the distance. The color. Baby blue was too light. Of course, I favored the hitter. A hitter needs contrast in his field of vision. It's damn difficult enough to hit a small ball with a round stick when it's coming at you at 95 or 100 miles per hour. If it had been up to me, I would have painted the wall a darker blue. Duke will tell them, I thought.

It all seemed so perfect, antiseptically clean, comfortable, and secure. Heaven on earth. I felt safe. I *was* safe inside this temple of baseball, my new citadel. Nothing else mattered at the moment.

"We're this way," the Sergeant said, after consulting with a smartly dressed usher. "It's a ways down there, isn't it?" he added.

I traipsed along behind Miss Cherry, her form-fitting, apricot pedal pushers leading the way with a metronomic jiggle. Luke straggled along behind me. I glanced back at him often, remembering my own folly with Earl at the Rose Bowl seven years earlier. I didn't want to waste any time hunting for Luke today.

As we made our way down the aisle stairs, members of the Cincinnati Reds began to trickle out of the first base dugout and gather around the cage set up at home plate. "Batting practice," the Sergeant said.

About then a minor disaster occurred. My eyes were on the field instead of my footing. I stumbled going down the steeply paced steps and regained my balance by grabbing, more or less (more than less), Miss Cherry's most shapely derriere. It was an involuntary reflex, completely unintentional, and wholly embarrassing. Let's face it...I goosed her.

Miss Cherry squealed in a soprano shrill that echoed off the underside of the mezzanine deck like feedback from the public address system. Her popcorn shot up in a volcanic plume and showered down all around us like flash-cooled buttered pumice. Luke flinched hard, fearing for an instant that a squadron of deadly catbirds had amassed for an all out blitzkrieg. The Sergeant, caught at mid-sip, dumped half of his ice cold beer down the front of his shirt. And me, well, I did the only thing that made any sense under the circumstances; I sat down on the steps and laughed—nervously.

Miss Cherry turned around smiling, unflappably calm. She leaned over, bending at the waist, preparing, I feared, to vehemently chastise me for my ungentlemanly malefaction. I sensed a coming monsoon. Too late to skedaddle now. Her impressive, marzipan breasts, heaving mounds of mammary mistletoe, hung over me no more than half of a cubit off the tip of my nose. The delicious muenster twins, straining against their flimsy confinements, were so close my eyes crossed in a valiant effort to stay in focus. Of all things, the thought of marmalade dashed through my skein mind. I was mesmerized. Inside me somewhere, I sensed a sneaky warmth, the reward of ill gotten gains. And if this was my punishment, well, then Lord let me be bad all of the time. I hadn't fondled her on purpose, but if thoughts were sufficient grounds for conviction, I *now* was guilty of moral turpitude.

"No, no, no monsieur," Mademoiselle Cheri' admonished, playfully wagging the finger of shame in my face. I giggled at the popcorn decorating her new *Maienbad* coiffure. She had cut off her beautiful long hair in favor of a stylish look that I really didn't care for—short, straight, tucked behind the ear, swept across the forehead. The popcorn didn't help. I couldn't help it. I laughed more.

The Sergeant had been leading the way and now turned around toward the commotion. He was dripping beer, soaked from chin to crotch. One look at him and I laughed even harder. He started laughing, too, and I could see in his roaming eyes that he very much appreciated the view of Miss Cherry from his own vantage.

I fought to catch my breath. "I tripped," I said earnestly in my own defense.

"I 'yem not a demimondaine!" Miss Cherry proclaimed, chafing melodramatically, feigning great offense.

"A what?"

"She means don't grab her ass, Wade," the Sergeant boomed, the voice of Scar ringing loud and clear. He flashed a leering grin and wiggled his eyebrows just like Rodney Bernanos used to do. Luke busted a gut. He would have loved Rodney.

I spotted him immediately. He was very close, smiling, talking to Jim Gilliam. When he first walked onto the field I was startled to see just how gray his hair really was. He happened to remove his cap for a moment and the sun lit up his head in a flash of silver. I was sitting next to the Sergeant. He nudged me to make sure I had seen him. "There's the Dukester," he said. I was already working hard to contain the paroxysm inside me screaming to break out. "He's looking awfully gray around the muzzle, isn't he?"

"He's always been gray," I said testily.

The Sergeant looked at me a bit warily. "He's the pendragon this season. Did you know that?"

"No, sir. What is a pendragon?"

"It means he's been appointed team captain. That's one of the highest honors in team sports."

"Oh."

I was gazing. At one point Duke Snider looked in the direction of where we were sitting. He seemed to spot someone and waved. My heart pounded. The Sergeant saw me squirm. "Don't get too excited, Wade," he said. "His wife and kids are sitting behind us about four rows." I wanted to turn around and look but couldn't work up the nerve. I had started to sweat. My hero was only a few yards away. Restrained delirium best described my state of mind.

The Reds finished their batting practice. Now it was the Dodgers' turn. Tommy Davis, Frank Howard, Johnny Roseboro and Maury Wills took their turns in the cage. Then Willie Davis, Ron Fairly, Wally Moon, and Larry Burright. Duke Snider stood off to the side the whole time, watching like an omniscient fox nestled in the grass.

I noticed that each player made a point of talking to him after they finished their turn in the cage, no doubt checking with the master sage for any words of wisdom. Don Drysdale walked over to Duke and said something that made Duke double over with laughter. I found myself laughing along with them as if somehow I had been privy to the joke.

Soon it was time for *The Duke of Flatbush* to step into the cage. My heart raced a little faster. Yes, he looked a little long in the tooth, but tell that to the first ball that sizzled toward the plate. SMACK! There was no sweeter sound. "Incoming!" shouted one alert somebody standing among a group of blue-coveralled men huddling in the right field bull pen. Members of the grounds crew scattered like shadow spooked chicks in a barnyard as the leather-bound projectile slammed into the earth right where they had stood. Frank Howard, both Davis' and Wally Moon had gathered around the cage ostensibly to heckle their esteemed captain. Now they howled with delight.

Frank Howard, the giant power hitter, loved it. He grabbed the chain-link screen and shook it much like a caged gorilla might do to display his fearsome power. The Duke cracked up and aped back at his teammate.

Gradually, I noticed the laughter around me and realized I had jumped to my feet and put on quite a display of my own mimicking Frank "the gorilla" Howard. Instantly embarrassed, I sat down to the applause of a dozen fans that had filtered in behind us. Chagrin contained me for the next few minutes.

"Hey! There's my buddy, Leo!" The Sergeant scrambled to his feet. "Leo!" he shouted over the railing.

Leo "The Lip" Durocher heard his name called out and turned around. Recognizing the Sergeant, he grinned and came straight over to where the Sergeant was leaning over the railing. They shook hands, laughed, chatted, while I watched with great surprise. The Sergeant looked over his shoulder at me, then turned back and chatted some more, laughed some more, shook hands again, then came back to his seat and sat down.

"What was that about?" Miss Cherry asked.

"Leo's a friend of mine."

The Sergeant leaned close to Miss Cherry and whispered something in her ear. I never did like whispered secrets and this time was no exception. Miss Cherry squealed almost as loud as she did when I goosed her, but this time she clamped her own hand across her mouth.

"Really?" she asked out loud, catching her breath. But her curious excitement was not to be curtailed. The Sergeant nodded yes and Miss Cherry promptly planted a big kiss on his lips. *Very weird.* I sat and stewed, knowing it was no use asking them what was up.

Duke Snider kept swinging, making solid contact with nearly every pitch. Several more baseballs sailed over the right field wall. One threaded the bleachers in center field, bounced hard in the staging area some 450 feet from home plate, and rebounded over the outer fence into the parking lot. Quite a display of the awesome power still contained in the body of my hero. In my mind, I was swinging with him on every pitch.

When he finished tuning up his swing, Duke cradled the Louisville Slugger on his shoulder, bowed obsequiously to his youthful understudies and strolled with pavonine elegance toward the dugout. Leo Durocher intercepted him and the two legends stopped near the on deck circle and talked. Number four had his back to me, but I could see Mr. Durocher's face and could tell he was doing most of the talking. My eyes were riveted on them. I wished I could read Leo's lips but nobody had ever been able to do that.

I mused that Leo Durocher probably knew Duke's swing better than anyone. Since Duke was expected to play that day, Leo was no doubt mentioning some subtle nuance he had noticed in Duke's stance or swing. I studied them carefully and gamesomely fancied I was a child prodigy, a phenom, the youngest rookie in major league history. I stood beside them in full Dodgers battle dress, absorbing the wisdom of two of the greatest sages of the sacred realm of the holy diamond.

The opening day sun pushed through a diaphanous morning haze pouring its thermal blessing over the inaugural scene. I closed my eyes and turned my face up toward the warmth, feeling as though life above ground was good again, even if only for a day. My face began to glisten as I gave myself to the sun's goodness. A heady, pleasurable sensation merged into a feverishly sweet delirium, overpowering me, and I began to feel as though I were no longer in my seat, but floating. I became less and less aware of the other people around me—the murmur of the growing crowd, the touting cries of prowling vendors, all fading away. Slowly, gently, I felt my body deliquesce and flow into the ambient surroundings. Like a christening spirit establishing occupancy, I claimed my rightful place in the new milieu.

twenty-one

Leo Durocher pointed. Duke Snider turned around and stared. Leo Durocher made a beckoning wave with his arm. The Sergeant stood up. Miss Cherry squealed, again. And before you could say *Hokus-Pokus* I was being hoisted over the wall and down into the solid arms of Edwin Donald Snider, "Duke," the pride of Compton, the Silver Fox, the Duke of Flatbush, future Hall of Famer, and MY HERO! A snapshot impression sliced through time eternal.

Duke Snider sat me down on the field. "I hear you're my number one fan," he said, giving my hand a firm shake.

My feet and legs were functioning, but I felt as though my body was levitating. A grin wider than Los Angeles distorted my face. My bladder quivered, confused over what it thought was an emergency *pee or flee* signal from my brain, but was actually a combination of the *melvin* the Sergeant had given me when he picked me up by my belt loops, and the adrenaline that had temporarily displaced my blood supply. When Duke let go of my hand, my fingers instinctively toyed with the sticky, honey-like residue of pine tar. I could feel my head nodding up and down in the affirmative, and I heard someone that sounded just like me say, "You're the greatest, sir." I was hopelessly star struck.

Duke laughed shyly. There was an endearing modesty about him that I hadn't expected. He was human, just like me. "Let's hope Mr. O'Malley thinks so after the season is over." He winked at Mr. Durocher who was standing within earshot. Duke could see I was extremely nervous. He spoke in a calm, reassuring voice. "What's your name, son?"

It must have been the excitement, but now I really did have to go to the bathroom. I licked my dry lips. "Wade Parker...sir."

"No kidding. We've got a kid named Wes Parker in our farm system. We think he is going be a big star in a couple of years."

God, I can't believe this is really happening. I would be dancing like Luke again if I didn't do something soon to relieve the pressure in my bladder. "Duke—sir—uh, Mr. Snider, I mean..." I sounded like I had a mouth full of marbles. "...I have to go to the bathroom."

"No problem. Have you ever been in a big league clubhouse?"

"No, sir."

"OK. We'll pretend you're a sports writer or something."

My heart went into *stringendo* and my smile wrapped around to the back of my head as Duke Snider led me into the Dodgers' dugout. I saw Walter Alston talking on a telephone. He looked up and was obviously startled to see a shrimp like me standing there. "It's OK, Walt," Duke said. "He's a cub sports writer from *The Times*. He's with me." Mr. Alston nodded and kept talking into the phone.

We entered the clubhouse just as someone yelled: INFIELD PRACTICE! The booming voice startled me. Big men wearing baseball uniforms were coming my direction and I felt like an indecisive squirrel in the middle of a road, unsure which way to dart to avoid being run over. My senses were just beginning to stabilize when I bumped smack into Johnny Podres. "Sorry. Excuse me, sir," I mumbled shakily.

"Hey, kid, how are you doing?" Podres said.

"Fine, sir. Good luck today." He was pitching the historic first game in Dodger Stadium. It was quite an honor. Podres smiled and gave me the thumbs up.

It was now about an hour before the pregame festivities were scheduled to begin. Activity in the clubhouse was frenetic—ball players, trainers, real sports writers, team executives—all looking harried and ruffled as they scurried about with no evident organized purpose. I found the hubbub very exciting.

"The urinals are that way, Wade," Duke said, pointing beyond where I stood wide-eyed, marveling. "Go ahead. I'll wait right here for you." He smiled reassuringly.

I headed down a corridor past a dozen players, recognizing some, not recognizing others, and turned a corner into the bathroom/shower area. I stepped up to the trough and unzipped. Alone for the moment in the belly of Dodger Stadium, I tried to convince myself to be calm and accept that this was really happening. But after about ten seconds my euphoria burst out in a nervous giggle. *Who would believe it!*

Major league chatter, metal cleats gnashing on concrete, raucous laughter, a swear word here, a swear word there, the symphony of the locker room resonated off sparkling tile walls. I was so tight with amazement I had to concentrate hard to start the flow of urine. I thought, *This can't be a dream. If I were dreaming I would dream myself to be tall enough for a Major League urinal!* I had to reach up a little by standing on the balls of my feet, but I was almost positive I wasn't dreaming. A moment later an amiable voice startled me.

"Rookies are getting younger every year."

I turned my head toward the sound and then looked up—way up. Don Drysdale stood towering over the trough taking a leak less than ten feet away from me.

"No, sir, Mr. Drysdale. I'm not a rookie. I'm a reporter with *The Times.*"

I was so nervous I almost lost my balance. I dipped my knees to keep from rolling over backwards and splattered on the front lip of the porcelain trough. I looked like a newborn colt trying to stand up for the first time. There was nothing I could do to recover my dignity.

Drysdale chuckled. "You can't be a reporter, kid, you're much too polite." He winked, tucked in his jersey, cinched his belt tight and adjusted his cap. "Don't forget to wash your hands, kid," he said as he left.

Back out in the locker room, I found Duke talking with Sandy Koufax. A twinge of sadness scurried through me as I thought about how thrilled Luke would be if he were here with me now. Luke had been unhappy with the Dodgers since they traded Charlie Neal to the Mets, but he still thought a great deal of Sandy Koufax. Maybe, out of kindness, I wouldn't tell him I saw Sandy Koufax.

Duke saw me coming. "Hey, Wade, meet Sandy Koufax."

I stuck out my hand and realized too late that I hadn't rinsed all of the soap off. I wasn't accustomed to washing my hands after taking a leak, but wasn't about to go against Don Drysdale's orders. Koufax smiled warmly and shook my hand. If he noticed the soap, he didn't say anything. "I hear you're a reporter with *The Times.*"

"Naw, " I said grinning. "I'm too polite to be a reporter."

Duke and Sandy were momentarily speechless. They looked at each other and cracked up. Koufax patted me on the back. "You're all right, kid," he said. Still laughing, he rubbed the top of my closely cropped noggin and walked away shaking his head. "Hey, Perranoski!" he yelled. "Wait till you hear this one!"

Duke laughed some more as he led me back out to the dugout. Mr. Alston was still on the phone and didn't pay any attention to us. We walked back out into the warm sunshine. I felt charged up, rife with enthusiasm, really alive. And I wasn't nervous anymore. Mr. Durocher was over by the wall talking to the Sergeant. I looked up to the seats and saw Luke and Miss Cherry waving to me. I grinned, but was too cool to wave back.

Duke noticed them. "Is that your mom and your brother?"

Suddenly I felt uncomfortable, not quite sure how I wanted to respond. I liked the fact that he thought Miss Cherry was my mother. But it made me feel guilty, disloyal to Lucinda. "That's my brother Luke," I said, trying to ignore the other part.

"Your mom is very pretty. I'm not wild about her hairdo though."

I giggled in agreement. A couple of kernels of popcorn were still nested on top of Miss Cherry's head. "The lady isn't my mother. She's a real good friend of ours."

"Oh. Is that your dad there talking to Leo?"

He caught me off guard again. This time the question gave me a little stabbing feeling and I knew it was already too late to mask the pain. "No, sir. He's also a good friend. Earl—uh—our real father abandoned us a few years ago."

A sympathetic sadness showed in Duke's eyes as if he had gotten the whole picture from one word. He glanced up to the seats where his own family sat and seemed to empathize. I sensed he had some regrets about being away from his wife and kids so much. I stood there feeling like a textbook example of abandonment.

Duke put his hands on my shoulders and turned me around so I faced toward the field. The Dodgers' infielders had taken the field and were in the process of stretching and limbering up. One of the coaches was heading to the plate to hit some ground balls. Duke knelt down on one knee and put an arm around my waist. "Do you think you might want to play in the big leagues someday?"

"I don't think so. I'm just an average athlete. I think I might want to be a policeman, though."

"Police work can be kind of dangerous, don't you think?"

"Yes, sir. But not as dangerous as facing pitchers like Gibson or Drysdale."

His eyes got serious. "You've got a point there, my friend."

"My brother is a big fan of Charlie Neal." I chuckled. "He's not very happy with the Dodgers for trading him."

"Charlie's a friend of mine," Duke said. "Baseball is a tough business. Sometimes it happens. But going to the Mets wasn't necessarily a bad thing for Charlie. He's from Brooklyn. Charlie will help them win some games, but it'll be some years before the Mets are a competitive ball club."

"I hope they never trade you, Duke."

He smiled and gazed wistfully toward centerfield. "I'm a Dodger, Wade. I might not know how to play in any other uniform."

"I think you're the greatest centerfielder of all time, sir."

The silver fox grinned. "Think so?" he said, teasingly.

"Yep."

"Boy, I don't know about that," he said, his modesty showing a little again." There's some great ones in the game right now—Willie Mays and Mickey Mantle, for example."

"They're great, too. But I think you're a little better."

He smiled wide. "Boy, you are my biggest fan aren't you?"

"Yep."

"Well, I sure appreciate that, Wade. But just between you and me, strictly off the record, Joe DiMaggio is the best centerfielder of all time."

Duke stood up signaling the end of our chat. I saw him look over to Leo and the Sergeant and give them the high sign with his eyebrows. "You know, Wade," he said, "about your father and all. There's a little saying I learned along the way that has helped me. Sometimes I can be pretty hard on myself, and, well, this saying has some meaning for me: We must find a way to forgive or we only end up blaming ourselves."

Duke smiled as I pendently considered his meaning. *But Earl doesn't deserve forgiveness,* I thought to myself, missing the propitious fundamental of his point. I would have to chew on it...the image of Duke Snider suddenly dissolved.

"Wade!"

"Huh?" Startled, I jerked my head around.

"Are you all right, honey? You look a little pale," Miss Cherry said, as she placed the back of her hand on my forehead.

Dang! I was dreaming. "Ah, yeah. I'm OK. Sorry, I guess I was thinking too hard or something."

"I guess so, sweetie. Lyle's been calling you. He wants you to come over there by him." She pointed and nudged me out of my seat.

I saw the Sergeant motioning to me to come to him. Miss Cherry looked electric with pent up enthusiasm, like she was in on a big secret. I picked a popcorn kernel out of her hair as I slipped by her toward the open aisle. I looked back at her and Luke once more, then cautiously made my way over to the Sergeant.

I was still numb from my midday fantasy as I approached the Sergeant, but perked up some as I came under the influence of his captivating grin. I stood next to him and put my hand on the railing. "Yes sir?" I said.

"Wade, I'd like you to meet—Duke Snider."

I started to slump to the floor and had to grip the railing with my other hand to steady myself. My heart clattered like a motor with a bad case of engine knock. I blinked hard, swallowed harder, and peered over the railing straight down into the face of my real live hero. He stuck his hand up. "Hello, Wade. I'm Duke Snider. Glad to meet you."

I still had enough sense about me to reach over the rail and take his hand. I squeezed firmly and ground as much pine tar into my pores as I could, planning to never wash my hand again.

"It's a great honor, sir," I said, in a surprisingly clear and forceful voice. I immediately noticed the bat he had used for batting practice was still resting on his shoulder.

The Sergeant piped up. "Wade here is going to be twelve years old next month, Duke. My fiancee and I brought him and his brother to the opener as a treat, and kind of an early birthday present for Wade."

"No kidding," Duke said. "What day is your birthday, Wade?"

"May 30th, sir."

Duke warmed with an obvious twinkle in his eye. "You know something, Wade? May 30, 1950 was a darn good day for both of us."

"Yes, sir, it sure was," I said proudly. "You hit three home runs in the second game of a doubleheader against the Phillies at Ebbets

Field that day. And the Dodgers won. It was a Tuesday."

Duke's mouth hung open in amazement.

"Pretty special kid, huh, Duke?" the Sergeant said.

"I'll say. It seems that Wade and I are kind of connected." His words made me light headed. "I've been blessed with a lot of good fans, especially back in Brooklyn. You're right up there with the best of them, Wade."

My heart soared up around the lights. "I think you're the greatest centerfielder of all time, Duke."

Those words of praise rang forth like a familiar echo. It seemed to me I had rehearsed that line just a minute or two before. Duke's winning grin was even bigger and better than the Sergeant's best grin.

"Tell you what, Wade. How would you like to have this bat..." He handed it up. "...as an early birthday present?"

"Wow! Really?" I beamed ecstatically and my hand grasped the handle of the bat as quickly as a frog snatches a fly from mid air. "Thank you!" I gushed.

"You're welcome, son. Happy birthday."

Suddenly my eyes pooled up, like a very happy woman. Embarrassed and confused, my male conditioning quickly checked the outburst, and for a moment I questioned myself. *Is this really happening? Or am I still drifting in a daydream?* But the Duke's regal scepter, tightly gripped in my sweaty hands, was real. It pealed as true as a lover's promise as I tapped it firmly on the concrete deck. A therapeutic vibration traveled up my arm and rippled across my chest, magically giving me power. The sound and the feel of that simple shaft of lathed wood instantly filled a good portion of the bleak void in my soul.

Since long before Earl ran off to Barstow, a dearth of love had battered my psyche and had left my heart raw as an open wound. Mind and body had been festering ever since. Now a gift from the noblest of all royalty commenced a painless debridement of my wounds. At last the tide was turning. At last I was moving in the right direction. At last my wounds had begun to heal.

The Sergeant brushed his hand over the top of my head. His reassuring touch triggered the tears again. Overpowered by the joy, I broke down completely. Through eyes blurred like rain streaked windows, I gazed down at Duke Snider. Glorious sunshine poured across his mirth-filled face and glistened off his silver stubbled cheeks like glitter. His compassionate smile said everything was going to be OK. The message was implicit: *I must find a way to forgive or I'll only end up blaming myself.* But to me this was a conundrum of untold scale.

The Dodgers lost the opener 6 to 3. I was so enamored with the bat I didn't care who won or lost. Guess which Dodger got the historical first hit in Chavez Ravine? I'll give you a hint: he also hit the last two home runs at Ebbets Field. How sweet it was that day!

Hero worship had a short term therapeutic benefit. But even after all that, the little silver sphere would come back around with the certitude of an orbiting planet ruled by the unyielding laws of physics. My gloom probably gave it its energy. I had just experienced the greatest day of my life and still I was depressed, tangled in a web of oppressive guilt. I couldn't help thinking about the dead man. Because of me he never got to see Dodger Stadium. It was all too much for the bruised mind of a boy not yet twelve.

And yet, by now the instinct to survive had made me a master cunctator, and an artist of denial. But bad dreams cannot be offset by fantasies forever. Even by fantasies come true. Something had to give soon. And when it did, I would feel as though it were the end of the world.

The missiles in Cuba couldn't begin to compare.

twenty-two

Seven years later...1969

John Fogerty's lamenting voice, strong and clear, floated around the moonlit room, evoking my soul, beseeching me like a sportive wraith beckoning from the shadows. Creedence Clearwater Revival, mixed with a quart or so of Red Mountain wine, stirred lightly—my recipe for passage into the special zone of subconsciousness wherein I'd been tarrying more and more of late. Music and alcohol. In them, their combination, I had found a form of sympathy. Artificial, yes, but better than no sympathy at all.

In the dimness, the transistor radio still looked new. Seven years had gone by and still every time I looked at the radio I thought of the Sergeant. I guess his claim that the Japanese had achieved an acceptable level of quality had been correct after all. I wondered where he and Miss Cherry were, hoped they were OK. I smiled sardonically, the wine buzzing just right, and reasoned the radio signal was so clear because I'd never used the *fm* function all those years. Now *fm* had become the rage. They called it *Underground Radio,* a term which seemed to speak directly to me. The MADE IN JAPAN sticker was long gone, but I hadn't progressed at all.

Melissa loved to use my arm as a pillow. Not wanting to wake her, I had resisted moving my arm as long as I could; slowly my hand went numb, like my mind on the wine, and now my whole arm felt cold and prickly. Time to turn over.

"Ouch! Damn it!" My shoulder length blond locks were always getting caught in the wickerwork headboard.

"Huh-h-h?" Melissa mumbled.

I whispered, "Nothing. Go back to sleep, babe." She turned over, mumbled femininely, and snuggled closer. Ten thousand pins slowly left my arm in search of another cushion.

Moonlight sifted in through the window bathing the bed in a subdued, lambent glow, tantalizing and energizing the natural violet highlights in her raven hair. Soft and herbal smelling, it shimmered iridescently against the whiteness of the pillow, beguiling me, deluding me in the most pleasurable sense.

Melissa's long, beautiful hair had sparked my initial attraction to her. I enjoyed creative fantasies about how it would feel draped over my body. I loved most everything about her. But her physical beauty could not be broken down into individual attributes, though when combined with her transcendent personality, she was the sum total of any man's notion of the perfect woman.

The sheer curtains in the bedroom had not been my choice. Melissa had insisted that she be in charge of decorating the bedroom, and I soon found out why. Melissa's sexual passion escalated in the moonlight. Now I loved the curtains. She said the moon was a mysterious orb, that it made her feel erotic, swelled with urge, fierce, like a wolf in estrus prowling the night. Those were her exact words. Precise. Direct. She was a wolfish lover, indeed. Moonlight was her aphrodisiac. Full moons were wild, at times even dangerous.

Often I would lie awake at night and watch her sleep, enchanted with her warmth, her scent, the soothing rhythm of her breathing. She was unaware of my voyeuristic proclivity, a well kept secret, and now was no exception. With tender fascination, I watched the beat of her heart, pulsating quivers gently ebbing at the delicate dip between her collar bones.

I had been crazy about Melissa from the start. She thought I *was* crazy, but I sensed in her an interest that she wished to explore. I had become a shameful purloiner of female affection before Melissa came along. I admit it. I was love starved and love shy at the same time, which I'm sure had everything to do with Lucinda's treason, and the trauma of suddenly losing contact with Miss Cherry, the only two women I had ever been close to. Consequently, my relationships with females had been episodic, compulsive and neurotic, and, in hindsight, unhealthy. Melissa suspected much about my sexual escapades, which made it tough for me in the beginning. As time went by she began to see through the case-hardened exterior that I lugged around like a full plate suit of armor. One night early in our courtship she discovered a small chink in my breastplate.

We were sitting in a pizza parlor, both feeling uneasy, self-conscious, not chewing our pizza the way pizza was meant to be chewed. Conversation had been strained, a little too forced, superficial at best. We tentatively probed for themes of common ground. She flirted with her eyes, I with my voice. We had replowed some of the same ground from our previous date and I was slipping into self-defeating doubt that she would ever decide she liked me.

"What's your favorite movie?" she asked.

I smiled. New ground.

"You mean of all time?"

"No, only those made between 1960 and 1965," she playfully taunted me. "Of course of all time."

Her smile was a carbon copy of Miss Cherry's smile. I had been noticing how much she reminded me of Miss Cherry. Except for the hair color and skin tone, they could easily pass for mother and daughter.

"No question about it, my favorite movie of all time is *The Wizard Of Oz.*"

Her eyes shimmered with approval. "You're kidding?"

"Your favorite, too?"

She nodded yes and smiled a little more invitingly than she had before. My radar blipped in reaction to an alluring shift in her body language. "I love *The Wizard Of Oz,* " she said huskily. Strong encouragement. Inside my chest the coney of desire thumped hard with both hind feet, built-in good luck charms that I didn't know I had, until Melissa. My blood stirred and my temperature tweaked upward.

It turned out we were an incredible match on *Oz* trivia. Neither could stump the other. We dazzled each other with knowledge of obscure details. We even agreed on the most controversial aspect of the movie. The shift from black and white to color was a stroke of genius. Inhibitions dissolved, we bartered back and forth over who should eat the last slice of pizza. I negotiated hard for a passionate, pepperoni flavored kiss.

Later that night we made love for the first time. Matched halves of a wondrous geode. Perfect similitude. Sensual symbiosis. Spiritual affinity. I remember lying there sharing Melissa's moonlight, filled to repletion, aching memories distanced, supplanted by the calming intensity of her. Melissa slept, as I learned she always would after we made love. She called it "recharging."

Now, watching her sleep, the satiated wolf reposing under her lunar blanket, her skin rippling in hues of gray with the breezy shifts of the curtain, I thought only of the good things from my past and smiled at the ceiling. It had been that way since that first night, her sleeping, me watching her and feeling wonderful.

Melissa had guessed correctly. I identified with the Tin Man. I *was* the Tin Man. Jack Haley did a perfect rendition of me. Melissa took me into her heart that first night. She had more than enough heart for both of us. Many times since, I have mused over how she had so skillfully pressed me to reveal my feelings.

While she had busied herself with that last slice of pizza, I gobbled up the attention as any fool would have done, but soon I feared that I had made a real fool of myself. She loved the Tin Man, of course she did, she was the embodiment of Dorothy, and her Dorothy-like sweetness and empathy had overwhelmed me. It had never happened before—she had me in tears. The Tin Man character was a metaphor of my life and I was so emotionally rusted I couldn't move. Then Melissa came along with the oil can.

She shifted in her sleep again, the she-wolf spontaneously stirring, primordial instinct warming her blood. The sheet fell away leaving her lean beauty uncovered. The moon painted her with magic, cupping her perfect, full breasts with subtle rays borrowed from the sun. With the awe of a mortal amid a divine contact, I watched.

It was in this same bed that we had made love that first night. For a long time after, we huddled in the sweet afterglow, our spent bodies glistening with the moisture of perfectly choreographed chaos, our heightened minds in a rapturous union beyond anything I had ever thought possible. When later she awoke, I talked for hours as she listened with a disciple's faith.

I told her everything.

She understood...everything.

Earl..

Lucinda.

The murder.

The Sergeant.

Miss Cherry.

All of my misgivings, failings, guilt—all of it—vented like lava, spewing from deep within my tormented core, burning everything in its path, flowing into my sea of ruin, churning furiously, boiling an ocean of pain into steam. I felt as if she had been there with me through it all as she held me tight and took it all in. God, that's what I never had!

And her eyes were so comforting. Windows of wisdom. Pools of compassion. Two-way mirrors that both absorbed and reflected my deepest feelings. Her loving eyes took my spirit deep into hers. It was left unspoken, but I truly felt she had been there with me through all those years, sharing my losses, my pain, my need. The only time she cried, and even then she did it with great strength, was when I completely broke down in a cataclysm of emotion and told her how Mac had died.

Mac's heroic death had nearly killed me. It happened the last night before we moved away from Ruby Place. Luke and I were very angry because Lucinda had announced—and it was just that...an announcement—that we were moving from Ruby Place right away. And almost as an afterthought, she said we couldn't see the Sergeant and Miss Cherry anymore. I reasoned that she was jealous of them after all. Lucinda, our own mother, now a traitor, had viciously turned against us. No consultation. No questions allowed. We were moving. Period!

Out of pure defiance, Luke and I had snuck out for one last hurrah at Billy Goat Hill. We came home at 4:30 in the morning to a very scary scene out in front of the house—four police cars, lights ablaze, neighbors milling around in their robes and slippers. Luke went into a stupor over the flashing lights. I rushed into the house and found Lucinda crying hysterically. A policeman was trying to calm her. Dazed by confusion and disbelief, I turned around in a panic and saw him. The tiny little light left in my soul was savagely snuffed out by a massive sigh of pitiful desperation. Mac, my great protector, my true soul mate, was lying dead on the floor, his tongue lolling from his mouth in a circle of blood that he'd coughed up with his last dying breath. He had been shot once in the chest. The whole thing was horrible, way out of control.

Something evil had broken into our house in the middle of the night. Mac had died protecting Lucinda from an intruder. I couldn't believe it. An intruder on Ruby Place? To my knowledge, there had never been a burglary in our neighborhood. Lucinda had nearly gone insane when she couldn't find us. She had it in her mind that we were dead or had been kidnapped. I could make no sense of any of it. I wanted to run away from everything, but I couldn't.

I have no memory of the actual move. I just remember swallowing the rage. It was like Lucinda had shut down, there physically, but her spirit gone elsewhere, searching harder than ever for Matthew, I told myself. She wouldn't communicate. Soon, an impenetrable distance, into which a coolness settled, defined the relationship between us. I'd never even heard of Glendora before and with only a few day's notice we were living there. I had questions, lots of questions, all prefixed with the word why.

Why did we have to move?

Why the hurry?

Why Glendora?

Why did Mac have to die*?*

Why can't I see the Sergeant anymore?

Why can't I see Miss Cherry anymore?

Why won't you answer me?

Many ugly battles followed. Lucinda always ended up in tears, but she never once gave me a plausible answer to any of the core questions. Luke tried his best to stay out of it. Worst of all, I never heard from the Sergeant or Miss Cherry again. I obeyed Lucinda and did not try to contact them. For a while, I harbored hope they would find me and do something about the terrible travesty. I thought they would help me, but months went by during which every ring of the telephone, every knock at the door, sent my heart skipping with the hope that it would be them. They never called. They never came. Not even a note in the mail. Eventually, my pride kicked in. I lied to myself and said I didn't need them.

The initial shock slowly wore off, but I was left with a residue of resentment that wouldn't go away. I no longer trusted Lucinda, or anybody else, for that matter. For a long time after that, I tried to accept things as they were and make it work. But after everything else that had happened, my litany of misfortune, I couldn't help seeing Lucinda as the bad guy, the one that had ripped me up by my precious few roots and brusquely jammed me into another universe without so much as one word of explanation. The stress began to mount, and over time my bitterness grew.

Lucinda seemed to age ten years overnight, but I felt no compassion for her. Frustrated and hamstrung by her derisive silence, I knowingly, ever so gradually, separated myself from her, until it became clear we were living in opposing camps. To me, Lucinda had become the enemy.

My only power in the whole mess had come when I absolutely refused to go along with her ridiculous proclamation that, coinciding with the move, we would have to start going by a different last name.

"What do you mean we have to change our name?"

No answer.

"What do you mean from now on our last name is Gelson?"

No answer.

"Bullshit, Lucinda! Earl was an asshole, but I'm not changing my name from Parker to Gelson! No way! What in the hell is going on?"

No answer.

For a while after the move Lucinda tried to spend more time with us, saying she now could afford not to work so many hours. I wondered how that could be? She had the same job, as far as I knew. I didn't bother to ask. She wouldn't tell me anyway. She seemed always on edge. We all felt the tremors building toward a cataclysmic convulsion. Our new home in Glendora became a darkening sky. The showdown was coming. The fuse of rebellion had been lit and it sizzled and sputtered irrevocably for four long years, until finally I just couldn't take it any longer. I thought I was doing myself, and probably Lucinda, too, a big favor. I had to target my anger somewhere and Lucinda was the bull's eye. Two days after my sixteenth birthday, June 1, 1966, I emancipated myself. I ran away from home, and unlike most kids—I never went back.

The worst of it was the sting of missing Luke and the shame I put on myself for running out on him. Luke suffered from the separation as much as I did. Linked sprites pulled apart by a cruel mystery. It was never quite the same between Luke and me after that.

With me gone, Luke caught the brunt of Lucinda's reaction. She became paranoid that he would leave her, too. I talked to him now and then, that is, whenever Lucinda the grimalkin didn't answer the phone. It was very rough for the next two, long, experience making years.

Then I met Melissa, and for the first time since the tragedy of Three Ponds I had someone I trusted. Someone that I believed could and would still love me after learning of my unspeakable secret. I confided my sin to Melissa. She didn't question any of it. She simply understood. Melissa loved me, period. I had survived the rebellion. I would be OK now, as long as I didn't lose Melissa.

Her breathing played upon my ears like a lullaby. The rise and fall of her breasts coquetted with the moon shadows. She was beautiful, very smart, incredibly sensual, honest, sensitive and kind. But in my entrenched mode of self-punishment, I struggled not to think of her, her loving me, as an undeserved gift. I lay there next to her, counting my blessings, thankful for having her—but I could not pretend that everything was OK. I knew full well that Melissa's loving me did not mean that I was "healed." Even with Melissa and everything she represented as good in my life, I still found myself coveting the childhood that I had lost. As cancer is to tissue, unshriven sin is to the psyche. And not even Melissa could absolve me of that.

The radio sat next to me on the night stand. I remembered how I had kept it on my pillow that April Fools night when Luke and I celebrated our good fortune—the Dodgers tickets. I treasured the radio, most of the time, as a symbol of the precious times, the minority memories that were forever seeking to be heard over the clamor of guilt, resentment and regret. It was also capable of conjuring up painful images from the past. I had come close to smashing it to bits more than once. An inanimate object made in Japan, *well made* in Japan the Sergeant had argued, whose mere existence was an act of complicity in the perpetual haunting of Wade Parker.

A far more dependable friend was leaning in the corner of the room. A friend as faithful as Mac ever was, always within arms reach, the bat that Duke Snider gave to me. I could just make it out in the shadows. I smiled as the images of that glorious day played in my mind. The bat was a symbol, too. It stood for truth and virtue. It was my private treasure, my personal proof that some dreams can come true. I wondered what Duke Snider would say if he knew the bat had been used for more than just hitting baseballs? I smiled at the ceiling again.

The Huntington Car Wash in Monrovia had provided everything I needed to survive. A job. It had taken me six weeks at the car wash to scrape up enough money to put a roof over my head. The third night after I ran away from home I knew it was going to rain. I had gathered up as much cardboard as I could find, and under an overhanging bush, against a cinder block wall backed up to the railroad tracks, I made my nest. The rain came. So did the trains every couple of hours. Soon the cardboard soaked through and sagged down all around me. Wet, cold, and very lonely, I thought about quitting and going home.

Dozing fitfully about an hour before daybreak, something suddenly grabbed the front of my jacket and jerked me up to my feet. A hulking, penumbral form towered over me, its foul breath of cheap wine and rotting teeth, stinging my nostrils. One huge, gnarled paw closed around my neck. I couldn't breathe. I was terrified that the dead man of Three Ponds had returned to carry out his revenge. I was sure a third eye of wicked silver was staring, with sinister clarity, deep into my psyche.

A voice, barely human, hissed like a serpent selling the original sin. "Got any—money-y-y—or stash—boy-y-y-y?"

In a reflex of its own, the Louisville slugger came up from my side, up, over, and down with such savage power that it must have stored the awesome energy of the Duke's last swing. The serpent went down hard and slumped with a horrible hiss against the wall, a murky, dark ooze tracing down its neck.

My compressed larynx spasmed and then relaxed allowing me to gasp in some air, and then scream out, "Mother Fucker!" I kicked the slumping torso as hard as I could, slipping in the process and falling down next to it. I screamed again, I thought, then realized another train was screaming by at sixty miles per hour a few short yards away. I ran, bat in hand, as fast as my trembling legs would take me. I was thankful for the miracle of Duke's gift, without which the serpent would have surely eaten me.

Three hours later I was in the Car Wash owner's office begging for as many hours as possible. I desperately needed to earn enough money so I could afford to sleep behind the safety of a locked door. Six weeks was a long, long time.

It was during that first six weeks, suffering from loneliness and a longing that had never really gone away, that I tried to find the Sergeant and Miss Cherry. On a rainy summer day, when car wash labor wasn't needed, I thumbed my way west on Colorado Boulevard from Monrovia, through Pasadena, over Suicide Bridge, down past Eagle Rock to Highland Park. It took all day, but the last ride dropped me off right in front of the police station. I was a nervous wreck, very tired, and too scared to go inside. I hung around outside the police station for over an hour hoping one of them would come out. Finally, I went in and planted myself at the front counter.

"What can I do for you, kid?" said a burly desk sergeant.

"Well, I was wondering if it would be possible to see Sergeant Cavendish, or, Officer—uh—I'm not sure about her last name, but her first name is Cherry—uh—please, sir."

He gave me a long look. "Webster."

"Pardon?"

"Webster. Cherry's last name was Webster. Cavendish and Webster." He scratched his forehead. "What do you want with those two?"

"Nothing. They're old friends of mine. I would just like to see them—please."

"I'm afraid you're a few years too late, kid."

"What do you mean?"

"They don't work for the department anymore."

My heart sank. "Why not?"

"Well, now. That's really none of your business, kid. Anything else I can help you with?"

"Do you know where they live?"

"Couldn't tell you if I did. Department policy."

I must have looked pitiful as I started to turn away, because he leaned forward across the counter, glanced around, and then whispered to me, "You best forget about those two, son. They both got into some very serious trouble back in '65. Big secret investigation. Whole lotta trouble for a lot of people. You seem like a good kid. Best you don't have anything to do with those two."

"Fuck you!" I said angrily.

I was in tears before I got outside. I didn't want to believe him. *They're O.C.I.U. Undercover. Can't tell me the truth about them.*

Near dark, I found myself walking up the hill at Ruby Place. Molly, her muzzle now a wintry gray, barely able to walk, no longer cared about barking at passersby. She looked at me with sad disinterest. It seemed, other than Molly, not a soul who ever knew me still lived in the neighborhood. I sat down on the curb in front of our old house. The place needed paint, needed Carl to sing a song, needed Mac to snooze on the porch. No lights on. Nobody home. My misplaced childhood was a thing of the distant past.

I tried again, and again, and again. But two years later I gave up my search for the Sergeant and Miss Cherry.

Booze seemed to help.

In her sleep, Melissa turned again. This time she fussed like a snoozy feline until she got comfortable lying on her stomach. The view was equally intoxicating, loin rousing. The way she shifted around in her sleep amused me. She was a beautiful, nocturnal nudist seeking an even moon tan. As if on a timer, she made sure the moonlight touched all of her.

As John Fogerty worked on a chilling crescendo, I wondered about Miss Cherry and the Sergeant. I thought of them often, as I did now lying there in the dark, toying with the little silver ball bearing. When pocketless bell-bottom pants came into style, I drilled a hole through the ball bearing and turned it into a piece of jewelry, wearing it around my neck on a leather thong. Melissa liked the way it danced on her skin when I hovered over her in the dark.

She knew all about the ball bearing, and wasn't afraid of it at all. "Superstition," she had said, "is born of ignorance."

I took another swig of Red Mountain and glanced over at the bat. A sudden rush of sorrow. Duke Snider hadn't made it to the Hall of Fame. I had wanted him to be elected in his first year of eligibility. *Damn sports writers have their heads up their asses!* Another big gulp of wine pushed me beyond the special zone.

My pattern of self-punishment was becoming pathetically formulaic. My drinking was steadily getting worse and I seemed powerless to do anything about it. It was not for the lack of a good woman that I could not heal my pillaged spirit. That much had been

177 / Mark Stanleigh

established way back when Miss Cherry had been involved in my life. Yet, if there was no cure for me, at least watching Melissa sleep was a temporary remedy. It treated my symptoms.

While men were walking on the moon, I thanked God for my one special blessing—Melissa.

She turned over again, the arc of her body brushing already hardened nipples across my still tingling arm. This time she grinned and slowly opened her moon-filled eyes.

"Hi there, handsome man," she whispered with artful ingratiation. Her hand slowly slid down over my belly and staked a lustful claim. Melissa always knew what she wanted. As for me, another much needed respite from what ailed me.

I smiled back and softly slurred, "I love you."

"I'm fully recharged," she purred.

The wine had its hold on me, too, but I needed no wheedling, under the light of the full moon.

twenty-three

Sometimes certain things you hear will stick in your mind and won't go away, ever, even when you're drunk. There was a guy I used to know, a drinking acquaintance, who, while sitting at the bar one night, turned to me and said, "Booze is a strange poison—*Sip*—Short of causing you to run your car into an abutment or a tree, it kills you slowly, while—*Sip*—being your very best friend." Later that night, that same guy flipped his car into a ditch and broke his neck. He left behind a loving wife and five wonderful kids. I, too, had become a husband, and father, but I kept drinking.

By 1975, alcohol had become a ubiquitous force in my life. In a vicious partnership with the nightmares that never went away, it had seized control of me. My existence had gradually filtered down to the dregs of saloon culture, one step above, but only a short stagger away from the gutter. Melissa, my wife of three years now, proved her love for me on a daily basis. She was a persistent soul, driving me up the wall at times with her constant urging that I get some counseling. My argument was steadfast and logical. 'I don't believe in psychology. It's nothing but unscientific mumbo jumbo, a so called *profession* teeming with mendacious charlatans more twisted than I'. Any treatment of what ailed me—whether by a shrink, a priest, a gypsy, or an extraterrestrial being—would require my confessing that I had committed the heinous crime of murder. No. *The Atrocity At Three*

Ponds, as I had come to think of it, would remain an unconfessed sin. It sounded like the title of a true crime novel—THE ATROCITY AT THREE PONDS. It sickened me to think that I could easily be the villain in one of those sensationalistic, blood and gore diatribes.

So, I was left to run with the boys in the bottle—Beam, Walker, Grand-Dad, Turkey, and Parker, the den of fools—until something, somebody, someday, would rip my wings off and put me inside the bottle, like the insect that I had become. There was no question about it, I was the offspring of Earl Parker. Earl, the drunk. And now, ladies and gentlemen, I give you Wade, the drunk. I tried not to think about turning out just like Earl. In the comparison I found a brutal shiv of truth, a razor sharp burr cutting away at my heart, unraveling my poorly knitted pride.

On the outside I was, of course, the life of the party: Oh, yes, the classic alcoholic. Only Melissa—my sweet, beautiful, kind, loving Melissa—knew of the demons that held the mortgage on my sanity, and cruelly shuffled the index of my dreams. At times I felt that even Duke Snider, along with the Sergeant and Miss Cherry, had abandoned me. I thought of all of them often, especially at night as I struggled against my dreams. Sometimes I imagined they were my guardians, my protectors. I made them into powerful scarecrows and stationed them around my field of slumber. They were supposed to ward off the incessant, airborne carnivores that fed on my mind and robbed me of my much needed rest, much like Luke's mockingbirds had swarmed about his crimson crown.

My rapacious oppressors were crow-like thieves, attracted to all things shiny—silverware, jewelry, buttons—and the omnipresent ball bearing which hung from my neck on a sterling silver chain. One of the worst nightmares involved a hideous, foul smelling vulture whose head was that of the dead man of Three Ponds. The vulture would circle me for hours, days, tormenting me from the sky, its shadow looping around me, around and around, hypnotizing me, until finally I could no longer stay awake. Then, in the dream, I would dream that the huge vulture landed on me, its talons pinning me to the ground, ripping the tendons out of my neck as it attempted to swallow the shiny ballbearing. I would wake up from the dream inside a dream screaming through a terrible, jagged gash in my throat and the dead man vulture would laugh at me. If only I could remove that damned symbol of my crime and cast it into the sea. Maybe then I would be free of my sinful past?

The only thing "in the past" was the medicinal value of the alcohol. Now the booze acted as a turbo-charger in my brain, a distilled catalyst inciting my nightmares to a heightened level of torture. Even during my waking hours I was slipping deeper and deeper into a semilucid, anchoritelike withdrawal. I was teetering dangerously on the psychotic. Melissa continued to urge counseling. After a close call with a telephone pole one blurry night, I promised Melissa I wouldn't drink and drive anymore. An ulterior motive lurked within the promise. It meant that she would have to come to the bar with me, and this pleased me immensely. Except for a sip or two of wine at home, Melissa didn't drink. She was the ideal chaperone for a fun craving twenty-five-year-old drunk.

Melissa got pregnant and gave birth to a baby girl the year before we got married. Now our four-year-old daughter, Kate, spent more time with Luke and his new bride, Trish, than she spent with us. They found out Luke was sterile shortly after they got married. Luke had almost seemed relieved. He laughed it off, proclaiming himself to be the last in the Parker line to suffer the curse of the mockingbirds. Uncle Luke adored Kate, and sometimes she seemed to be more theirs than ours. And the free supply of baby-sitting gave Melissa complete freedom to baby-sit me.

I was a happy drunk and usually harmless, except perhaps to myself. I did, however, end up in the drunk tank sometimes when Melissa wasn't available to accompany me. Booze is a strange poison and its insidious cumulative wear was taking its toll.

They say a drunk has to hit bottom before he can start to climb back up. I hit the bottom one night at a place called *Buster's Bar,* a classic American watering hole in San Dimas. I can remember the bartender, Buster, swearing he would have cut me off a long time ago if Melissa hadn't been there baby-sitting me. I remember Buster's disapproving frown only amused me. With another refill in hand, I turned around and shouted across the crowded bar to Melissa, "R-r-rack'm up baby!" and then had to steady myself to keep from falling down. I can remember that much. My inebriated gyroscope was bumping strangely and for a moment there was a babel of confusion, something popping in my head like bad static. Finally, I seemed to get my coordinates set and I shuffled back over to the pool table.

"Come on, honey, maybe it's about time we headed for home," Melissa urged, for the tenth time. "It's a full moon," she added, her eyes twinkling solicitously.

She tried everything she could think of to gain my cooperation. But her best efforts were all in vain. I was too far over the edge. On that night I couldn't be charmed, or reasoned with. In the larger context, deep down I felt I was too far gone to be saved, period. Even worse, I didn't believe I deserved to be saved. The curse of man, the liquid destroyer, the poisonous genie of blended grain mash was out of the bottle big time that night. And nobody, not even sweet, loving, wonderful Melissa, had the power to put the genie back in the bottle.

I brushed her off and drew back my pool stick, eyes blinking to find some focus. I let her rip, nearly falling down in the process. The cue ball slammed into the wedge just as Melissa removed the rack. Sixteen billiard balls collided in a nuclear carom. The sound of the impact clanged off the walls and reverberated with the pounding beat of the jukebox. Melissa flinched and cursed at me, her patience dwindling and then gone. She glared across the table, angry as a carny working the midway caught in the line of fire by an impatient kid hungry for the big prize.

Nearly as jangling as the scattering of the billiard balls, my senses collided, throwing my already anesthetized perception into total disarray. Something was wrong. I felt queer, amiss. Palpable tremors signaled through my bones sending crabs of alarm scurrying around in my gut. The room began to move, a slow spin, like the feel of a merry-go-round starting up, and the jukebox began to wail an ominous warning. An eerie message thumped throughout the smoke filled bar, a musical harbinger announcing the accession of an alcoholic's madness. *Mama Told Me Not To Come,* by Three Dog Night, blared from the far end of the bar:

> "*...Wash your whisky in your water, sugar in your tea, what's all these crazy questions they're asking me? This is the craziest party there could ever be. Don't turn on the lights cause I don't wanna see.*
>
> *Mama told me not to come!...*"

The room tilted sharply, a spine-jarring jolt that caused my legs to buckle. The billiard balls toppled off the table. Like oversize marbles, they clunked hard on the floor and dispersed randomly around the barroom. Squinting through the smoke laden air, I watched in disbelief as the balls, now far more than sixteen in number, began to scrabble around and arrange themselves at my feet.

To me, the floor appeared as a muddy flat. I recoiled and gasped for air as the balls slowly shifted into forms, shapes, characters—letters of the alphabet. First an "M," then an "I," then an "S," until finally the word *Mississippi* held static, coagulated in a pastelike, muddy gruel. Then suddenly, in a dizzying, anagramatic, kaleidoscopic swirl, the balls reconfigured to form the word...*MURDERER!*

I stepped back trying to shake off the vision, but it wouldn't go away. Then, as suddenly as before, the balls raised up from the floor and hovered miraculously in a precision "V" formation two feet above the pool table.

> "*...Open up the window let some air into this room. I think I'm almost choking from the smell of stale perfume. And that cigarette you're smoking is about to scare me half to death. Open up the window, sucker, let me catch my breath.*
> *Mama told me not to come!...*"

I weaved back and forth, my legs wobbling, barely holding me up, as I rubbed my red-rimmed eyes, trying to clear away the apparition. But my fatigued eyes grew wide as the numbers and colors dripped off of the billiard balls and down onto the table like melting wax, leaving behind blinding-silver metallic eyes that taunted me with sporadic charges forward and back. My hallucination was as real as the panic sweating out of my cramping body.

In a fit of terror induced rage, I drunkenly lunged forward and wildly swung my cue stick at the ghostly balls. They scattered about like plump rats evading an attacking broom. The cue stick shattered on the edge of the pool table, a large splinter rebounding up to the ceiling where it stuck like an arrow meeting its mark.

Now my darkening fate loomed all around me as the silver balls took up a radial formation and began circling, like blood-sniffing sharks. They poised to strike at any moment, filling me with dread, pushing me down, down, deep inside the fear. I blubbered out a cowardly whine and then screamed out violently, cursing incoherently at the demons only I could see. "Ahg-g-g-g!"

"...The radio is blasting, someone's knocking at the door. I'm looking at my girlfriend, she's passed out on the floor. I've seen so many things I ain't never seen before. Don't know what it is, I don't want to see no more.

Mama told me not to come!..."

My face was white with panic and wet with the desperation of brain infesting fright. I wrenched myself around in a spastic turn and lurched toward the door, sure that the army of silver fiendish eyes would chase me to my death. Insane from the sickness consuming me, I stumbled through the crowded bar knocking aside people, chairs and drink-laden tables in my path. I was frantic to make it to my car, to the trunk, to the only weapon that offered a defense against my helpless paranoia.

"...That ain't the *way to have fun, Son!..."*

The music kept at me, pounding its prophetic message into my boozie head. But the silver balls did not follow me outside the bar. Instead, I feared, they had tricked me into my retreat, only to take my precious Melissa prisoner. The warped manifestations of my hounding insecurity had come to strip me of my only link with reality—my Melissa!

"...That ain't the way to have fun, Son!..."

From out of the trunk came the holy Excalibur, the magic sword of The Duke of Flatbush. In my muddled mind, I recalled how it had been handed down from a Royal Duke to an innocent, peasant child, a fatherless ghetto rube, whose lonely destiny had been forged in the heartless shires of The City of Angels. Like the sacred sword, I had been heated white hot and hammered true on the anvil-like hill of the sacrificial goat, and quenched in the second of three baptismal ponds, and blessed by the High Priest of the Caverns of Cavendish.

"...That ain't the way to have fun, Son!..."

I stood there shivering, cowering in the dark, my alcoholized blood oxidizing with each rapid gulp of night chilled air. Alone and scared, I began to mutter fragments of the *Paternoster,* as a believer might do in preparation for death. Slowly I began to focus my mind. With all of my might, I gripped the bat in both hands and pleaded for an end to my madness. A faint electric hum began emanating from the bat. The tingling hum entered my hands and climbed up my arms. Growing in intensity, the energy marched across my chest, swelling my muscles, then jolting me with a strange surge of rejuvenating power. Instantly I was cleansed of my fear, washed in heavenly light through which I now saw with brilliant clarity. An alcoholic's pathetic nirvana flooded into my heart.

My psychosis took me on a quantum leap, propelling me beyond the present, into the future, toward my manifest destiny. I was born to be Melissa's savior—Melissa's knight in shining armor. I clutched the wooden avenger firmly and felt my strength swell ten fold. Empowered with newfound courage, I prepared to answer the call to glory. Excalibur hoisted to the heavens, poised to sever the head of the dragon called guilt, I charged back into the smoke filled abyss.

Booze gave breath to my battle cry. "I'll save you fair Mi-s-s-sala!" I slobbered.

I, Sir Wade of Ruby Place, stumbled forth in need of a drink, but determined to rescue the beautiful maid in distress—my darling, sweet, beautiful, loving Melissa.

"...That ain't the way to have fun, Son!..."

twenty-four

"Hey, Parker!"

The clamp around my skull instantly twisted a full turn tighter. "Jesus," I croaked. An astringent belch made its way to freedom. "What?"

"Rise and shine, Wade. This ain't a goddamn motel."

With considerable effort, I slowly raised my face off of a mattressless, fiberglass plank. A gelatinous string of drool stretched between the plank and my swollen lower lip. My eyes focused enough to make out a human form. I was pretty sure it belonged with the voice.

"God, Bob...is that you? Am I in the drunk tank again?"

Deputy Bob Smith, an unusually tolerant friend, intentionally clanged his collection of keys on the steel cell door. I could see enough to tell his bushy, black mustache was turned down in a severe frown.

"I'm afraid so," he said, absent his normal convivial tone.

Bob Smith and I became close friends back in 1973. One night he and his partner did a walk-through at Buster's Bar. Buster's had long before become my home-sweet-home away from home. We talked that night at the bar, and he came back later, without his uniform. Bob started hanging out at Buster's, I soon found out, after his daughter died of leukemia. All of the regulars at Buster's were friends of mine and Bob was no exception.

"Easy with the keys—please."

"Oops," Bob said, banging the keys again, except harder.

I wiped a bare forearm across my mouth. The spittle left a gooey, snail-trail smear from elbow to wrist that instantly began to dry. The way my head was throbbing, much less the damage to my face, I knew it must have been a bad one.

"Did I hurt anybody?"

Bob swung the jail door open and stepped inside the tank. "Yes, well—uh—not seriously, anyway. Melissa's feelings are a different story, though."

I looked up at Bob. "Aw, she's OK. Probably won't talk to me for a day is all, maybe two."

My bloodshot eyes cleared enough to see the disgust plastered all over Bob's face. He couldn't resist taking a jab. "You don't deserve a woman like Melissa." He was right, but it wasn't the first time he'd said that.

"Shit, Bob. I don't deserve a friend like you either. Do I?"

My lip was badly swollen. The grin I gave him wasn't worth the pain, but it did force his stern-set gaze to give way to a half-smile. "Nope, you sure don't."

I wanted to lay my head back down, but I was afraid to give Bob another reason to yell or bang his keys. Grunting, I hauled myself up to a sitting position. "Did I do any damage?"

Bob hooked both thumbs in his gunless gun belt, the holster empty in accordance with jail rules. "According to Buster you owe him three bills."

The skull clamp tightened another turn.

"Damn. What'd I break this time."

"You don't remember any of it—do you?"

There was a suggestion of pity in Bob's voice that I didn't care for. I guess a part of my ego wasn't fully pickled yet. I shook my head and felt a stiffness in my neck. "No, Bob. I don't remember a damn thing."

He sighed and clenched his jaw. "Christ, Wade, you really outdid yourself this time. According to forty-plus witnesses, you went out to your car, got that damn bat of yours, and proceeded to belt a billiard ball through every one of Buster's windows."

"Cleared the place out did I?"

"Yep. And when you finally ran out of balls, you went outside and tried to get everybody to sing *Take Me Out To The Ball Game* with you."

"Good grief," I said, wearily trying to rub the kink out of my neck.

"You caused some grief all right. The watch commander says I have to charge you this time." I closed my eyes and willed against a sudden pang of nausea. "You know how many times you've laid on that bench sleeping it off?" I shook my head no and started to tune him out. His message already sounded too much like a lecture. "Nine drunk and disorderly arrests in the last two years," he said, with poorly veiled disdain.

I knew it would sound stupid, but I said it anyway. "I'm sorry, Bob."

"That ain't all."

Jesus, give me a break. "What?"

"Buster says you damn near took Melissa's head off with that damn bat of yours." I felt the blood drain from my face. "That's right...you should be scared. Apparently she tried to stop you. You were out of control—and everybody knows you didn't mean it, they all know how much you love her—but Jesus Christ, Wade, you could have killed her." He clenched his jaw again, signaling something worse than unpleasant was coming.

"What? Tell me," I said.

"Buster said the bat clipped one of Melissa's pierced earrings and ripped her ear lobe in half." Panic flooded my veins. I struggled to get up on my feet. "Sit the fuck down!" Bob yelled.

"Huh?"

"You haven't heard the worst of it yet." Now I saw pain in Bob's face. He looked away as he said the words. "Melissa took off. She's left you."

I started to my feet again, but a sledge hammer of dread hit me in the solar plexus. The blow knocked the wind out of me. I couldn't breathe. Bob said something about bail being a thousand dollars and then disappeared leaving the jail door standing wide. He returned with a Dixie cup of water and handed it to me. In shock, I took the cup and then dropped it. The water splattered back up in my face. Bob backed out of the cell again, but I didn't notice. I slipped off the bench to the floor, the water dripping from my face. In my mind I was suddenly lying in the bottom of the middle pond. I frantically ripped at my pockets as if they were full of deadly ball bearings, holding me down, drowning me. Then my hands were stuck. I couldn't get them out of my pockets. And this time I knew Mac couldn't save me. He'd been dead for thirteen years!

"Here," Bob said, handing me another cup."

"Huh—what?"

"Come on, damn it! Don't spill it. Christ, Wade, you're shaking like a wino."

I managed to raise the cup to my mouth but couldn't drink. To me the water looked as green as the water in Three Ponds. I set the cup down on the floor. Bob grabbed me under the arms and raised me back up on the bench.

"I'm sorry," I mumbled again. All Bob heard was a muffled whimper. He sat down next to me and handed the cup to me again. This time the water looked potable. I downed it. *God, I need a drink,* I thought, but didn't dare say it out loud.

"Wade, you're better than this," Bob said, now with the consoling tone of a friend. "I know you've heard me say this before, but, goddamit man, you've got to get yourself straightened out. Come to a meeting with me." He looked me straight in the eye. "AA saved my life, Wade. I lost my wife because I didn't get help soon enough. It's not too late to get Melissa back, but you've got to get some help."

I'd heard him make this pitch a half dozen times before. He'd even told me his whole story, how he was about to be kicked off of the Sheriff's Department and the staff psychologist finally told him he didn't have a choice, go to AA or get fired. I sat there letting what Bob said soak in, remembering the last time I talked to Luke when he had made a similar speech. 'I hate to say it, Wade,' Luke had said, 'but you're turning into a drunk. You're starting to remind me of Earl.'

'Shit, Luke, you were too young to remember anything about Earl,' I had argued, knowing full well if I remembered Earl's drunken tirades, Luke remembered them, too.

"What time is it?" I asked.

"Trying to change the subject?"

"Give me a break, will you."

My fat lipped grin wore him down some. "Two in the afternoon. It's Sunday, in case you're wondering. Know what month it is?"

Another turn on the clamp. "Jeez, why didn't you rouse me earlier?"

"You got bail money on you?"

"No."

"There's your answer."

"Shit," was all I could think to say.

Bob was right. I had to do something about the drinking. But not AA for Christ sake. *Hello. My name is Wade. I'm an alcoholic. HI, WADE!* "Shit," I said, again.

Bob sat next to me patiently waiting, allowing me to think. "Did you see Melissa?" I finally asked him.

"Yep."

"Did she say she was going to her mom's house?"

"Nope. She mentioned San Diego, though."

"Yeah, her mom lives in San Diego."

"Good," Bob said.

At least I knew where to find her. Her mom didn't like me much before, and I figured this debacle would drop me about fifty rungs on the ladder with her.

"How much is my bail again?"

"A grand."

Assuming Melissa hadn't cleaned out the bank account, I figured I could probably get my hands on about two hundred. "Which bondsman will cover me if you tell them I'm your friend?"

"Bonds-*woman*, you mean." He smiled. "The lady I'm seeing these days would do it. But you don't need her. Your bail has already been made."

"By who?"

"A woman. She's waiting outside for you."

"What woman?"

"A friend of mine. I know her from AA. She's a recovering alcoholic. Maybe she can do you some good."

"Jeez, Bob."

Bob grinned again. "I thought you'd say that."

I stood up, my stomach reminding me just how much poison was still in me. Wino shakes turned into nervous shakes as I tried to focus my mind on Melissa. Out in the hallway, I spotted myself in a polished metal mirror. I looked like a badly trampled throwaway from some skid row alley. "Can I borrow your comb, Bob? I guess if some woman I don't even know is bailing me out of jail, the least I can do is show a little respect and comb my hair."

Bob reluctantly reached into his back pocket and gave me his comb. "In case you were wondering, nobody hit you in the mouth.

You banged your lip on the bench last night, *after* we put you in the tank."

"What? No police brutality?" I showed him a real grin.

He shook his head implying I was hopeless. I handed the comb back to him. He nudged me toward the cell door. "Get out of here!" he barked. "And remember, AA, a meeting. I'll take you any time you're ready. You just say when."

"Thanks, Bob. I'll give it some thought. I promise, I'll really give it some serious thought."

"You better."

I took a deep breath and walked out into the holding area. Another deputy handed me a manila envelope that had my name printed on it, had me sign a receipt book, then gave me the pink copy of what I signed. Bob walked me to the rear door of the jail.

I stopped suddenly at the door, my heart kicking even harder from a new jolt of panic. I turned back to Bob, my red eyes pleading, hoping. "Do you know what happened to—my bat?"

He shook his head and gave me a look that strongly suggested I was pathetic. "I was hoping you'd forget about that godforsaken bat."

"Never," I said.

"It should be locked up in evidence, but I put it in the trunk of your car last night. It's still parked in front of Buster's. Your keys are in the envelope."

"Thank you, Bob."

"You can thank me by going to a meeting with me."

"I'll do whatever it takes to get Melissa back," I said. He swatted the back of my head and backed away giving me my leave. I stood at the back door of the jail shaking enough to rattle the keys in the envelope.

"She's right outside the door, Wade. She's been waiting for almost an hour. Go on," Bob nudged.

I pushed on the door.

"Good luck," Bob called, from the echoing innards of the jail.

My breath caught in my throat. She was standing twenty feet away with her back to the jail door. She turned. She smiled. It was her.

"Miss Cherry?"

I quickly assessed she looked much older, but still exquisite. I pictured her as I saw her that first night on Billy Goat Hill, climbing off that motorcycle, standing in the circle of headlights. God, she had looked like a beautiful angel descending from paradise. I could still feel the rhapsody of her first words. 'How old are you, honey?' she had asked. Jeez, that was sixteen or seventeen odd years ago. The smell of her perfume, stored away in a mental vial somewhere deep in my brain, now flooded my olfactories. I breathed deeply, her scent vividly recalling the pleasure, and the terror, of that first encounter. The mix of emotion was the same at this very moment. I had longed to see her, as a lost toddler must long to be reunited with its mother.

"It's been a long time, Wade. How do I look?"

Her voice was the same, so familiar that the years of separation seemed hardly more than a week. I was speechless. My brain couldn't process what was happening fast enough. I had wanted to go and immediately find Melissa, beg for forgiveness, but this was such a shock my priorities were suddenly all tangled up, conflicted.

I damn near said, *Real sharp, ma'am,* but finally came out with, "As beautiful as in all of my dreams."

She giggled girlishly.

"I can't say the same about you, young man. You've grown into a handsome prince. Except, right now you look like you've been to hell and back."

"Maybe I have," I said, meeting her eyes squarely.

She hugged me. It was a strange feeling. I was much taller than her now, the reverse of the last time she hugged me.

"Thanks for bailing me out."

"I want to hear all about it," she said.

"Ha, ha! How much time have you got. It's a very long story."

She grinned. It was a serious grin. "For you, I've got the rest of my life."

With less than a modicum of shame, I asked, "Would you like to go have a drink somewhere?"

"I can see we really have our work cut out for us, don't we?" she replied

"I need to find my wife. I need a drink. I need to apologize to Buster. And I need to get my car. Maybe not exactly in that order, though." God, my mind was spinning.

"Come on," she said, taking my hand. "My car's over that way. You can show me the way to Buster's. I guess we can accomplish three of those things at one place, huh."

"I really screwed up this time. They say I beaned my wife with a bat, but she's supposedly OK. I must have completely lost it. I don't remember a thing."

"I know. Your wife told me what happened."

"Really? You've talked to her?"

"Yes—At length. She's wonderful."

"I know. But how did you know about this? I mean this is too good to be true."

"I'm an investigator, or was, anyway."

That angered me. "No way, ma'am. Not good enough. That's what the Sergeant always used to tell me. I'm sure as hell not a dumb, naive kid anymore. Well, not a naive kid, anyway."

She looked me dead in the eye. "I'll tell you this much, Wade. You need some serious help. And I think maybe I can help you, if you're willing. Your wife asked me to bail you out, but she's not coming back to you—not just yet, anyway. She and your daughter are staying with your mother-in-law. She doesn't want to talk to you, so it looks like you're stuck with me for the moment. OK?"

Feeling pissed off and powerless, I looked away from her. "Yeah? Well, where have *you* been all these years?"

"Not far away."

"Doing what?"

"Trying to keep my head on straight. Staying sober."

"So it's true, then. You're not a cop anymore?"

"That's right."

"Why?"

"I'm sorry, Wade, but I can't really talk about that."

I felt like walking away from her, leaving her right there in the parking lot. She was sounding too much like Lucinda. No answers. But it was impossible for me to stay angry with her. I turned to look at her again.

"How about the Sergeant, then? Do you happen to know anything about him...that you care to share with me, that is?"

Now she looked away. "No. We split up long ago."

"I tried for years to find you and the Sergeant. The way things happened—really hurt me. Now, after all these years, you find me. It's too much to comprehend."

"We have all the time in the world to get to know each other again. Come on," she said, tugging me toward her car. "Tell me how to get to this bar of yours."

Her hand was warm and soft just as I had remembered it. I planned to call Luke later. There was much I needed to talk about.

The way Luke said hello, practically shouting into the phone, made it pretty clear he was mad at me. I figured he'd heard about the show at Buster's, and was ready to ream me good. Miss Cherry stood by me at the open phone booth door, lending moral support. It felt like she'd always been there.

"Where in the hell have you been, Wade?"

"I know, I know. I really screwed up this time. You've been right all along. I'm just like Earl was. I gotta do something, AA maybe."

"What are you talking about?"

"Yeah, right—like you didn't hear what I did to Melissa? I think I'm gonna need your help this time, Luke."

"I've been trying to find you, Wade. You haven't answered your phone. I went by your house and left a note on your front door."

Good. He's already talked to *Melissa.* "I know she's probably so pissed off right now she won't talk to me. But she'll listen to you. I need you to tell her how sorry I am. And you're never gonna believe who bailed me out of jail." I looked at Miss Cherry, both of us anxious to tell Luke.

"Wade!"

"What?"

"I don't have a clue what you're talking about."

"Come on, Luke. Don't mess with me. I've had a rough weekend. You said you left a note for me. What? Have you heard from Melissa?"

"No. I haven't been able to reach her either."

"Shit. I guess she's really pissed. It's gonna take some real doing to get back on her good side."

"What did you do?"

"You mean you really haven't heard what happened at Buster's?" Miss Cherry's eyes offered encouragement. She nodded her head, gently nudging. "I figured word would be all over town by now. Me and my bat put on quite a show, so I've heard, anyway."

"No, Wade. Nobody said a word about that. I've been all over God's green earth trying to find you."

"What?" It finally sunk in that something other than my idiotic behavior was on his mind.

"Wade?"

"Yeah, Luke."

"I'm afraid I've got some real bad news." The cracking edge to his voice scared me. Miss Cherry took my hand, sensing the wrongness of the conversation.

"What is it? Tell me."

"Lucinda—is dead."

twenty-five

Melissa came home right away. A death in the family, funerals, as unpleasant as they are, bring people together who otherwise would not acknowledge a need to speak to each other. It was my mother's final kindness to me. Melissa's only condition was that I join AA. I joined AA, but it took a while to fully win her back.

My jagged estrangement from Lucinda had ended several months before she died. The ameliorating influence of time had brought me around to a let-bygones-be-bygones frame of mind. I invited her out to dinner one rainy night and the dinner went reasonably well. There was a calm after the storm. We had enjoyed several subsequent visits before her accident froze the status of our relationship where it stood, midway to full reconciliation.

A drunk driver had mistaken an off-ramp for an on-ramp and hit her head-on on the San Bernardino Freeway near the top of Kellogg Pass. There must have been a preceding moment of horror, but save that, her demise had been instantaneous and painless. There was the added sting of irony when I learned that she had been killed by a drunk driver, a member of my own dangerous legion. As a part of my program in AA, I met with, and forgave, the young woman that had taken Lucinda's life. That was 1978. I've been sober just over two years now. One day at a time, as we recovering alcoholics say.

I was grateful that I was no longer angry with Lucinda. We hadn't really gotten to know each other again, but at least she didn't go to her grave as a total stranger to me. Still, the door on the "Lucinda" part of my life would not quite close. All those years of anger had been replaced by a nagging feeling that she was trying to work up the courage to tell me something. Important stuff. And now I would never know what was bothering her. It added to the already burdensome feeling that my whole life was based on some arcane punishment, that there were events, circumstances, people, things of mystery that were far bigger and far more complex than slingshots and mockingbird feathers. The feeling that one too many things didn't add up was always there, deep inside my head. An unscratchable itch. It kept me in a state of unease which had become the baseline for everything about my existence. Since I could do nothing to change it, I endured it. I made it a way of life. I had become an expert at that.

Miss Cherry had all but replaced Lucinda as a mother figure to me. She encouraged me to reconcile my thoughts about Lucinda, to let go of the bad and keep only the good. I gradually acceded to Miss Cherry's wishes, and with Lucinda gone, Miss Cherry became all the more important in my life. Melissa and Kate loved her.

Deputy Bob Smith and Miss Cherry were my sponsors in Alcoholics Anonymous. With their help, I eventually admitted I was powerless over alcohol. Empowered by their friendship, and Melissa's love, I was able to realize just how unmanageable my life had become. As the haze of booze slowly evaporated allowing hindsight to become clearer and clearer, I began to see just how hard I had slammed on the bottom. And I began to see how lucky I was to be in recovery. When I accepted the truth about that strange, poisonous, deceitful friend—that it had defeated me—only then had I taken my first step toward liberation.

In the beginning it was humiliating.

'Hi—my name is Wade—I'M AN ALCOHOLIC!'

But I learned there was noble virtue in humility, not in humiliation. I became more like Luke, a philosopher. I learned the only true form of peace comes not from the feckless friendship of alcohol, but from within one's own self, and the belief in, and reliance on, a higher power. The process of recovery was slow but sure. I was learning.

Miss Cherry played a pivotal role in my recovery. Our one-on-one testimonial sessions created open-mindedness. She told me of her struggle with the pressures of police life. And, in an oblique manner, she told me of her eventual breakup with the Sergeant. She said that there had been other boyfriends, but that no other man had been able to take the Sergeant's place in her heart. She often spoke of the breakup in terms of its consequences. She had left him, that much she made clear. But her life after him was often equated in terms that I found—well—very curious. It was almost as if the downturn of her life had been expected, part of a deal, the agreed upon price that had to be paid. Sometimes she described herself and her "consequences" in such a way that I euphemistically thought of her as a soldier that had been asked to do something that exceeded her conscience, and then rather than carry out her duty, or perhaps stop carrying out her duty, she resigned in shame. What ever it was, it had taken its toll, exacted its price.

I could tell that her conscience was bothering her. About what I did not know. Something though, perhaps an unspeakable dark secret like my own, was eating away at her, making her empty and aching inside. She remained beautiful on the outside, like a lovely shell, a pearly nautilus. But loneliness, the unscratchable itch, had crept inside and taken up residence in the beautiful shell. I found it very easy to relate to her. She told me how her drinking had gradually gotten out of control and finally landed her in Alcoholics Anonymous. Now I was embracing that same outcome, which doubly rooted our camaraderie in a common history.

We talked about many things. However, on the subject of the Sergeant she remained guarded. When my probing went too deep she would change the subject, just enough to keep from turning me off, or discouraging me during my quest for sobriety.

She wasn't the only one to hold back feelings. I was equally incomplete with my candidness. I resisted crossing the big line when rambling about the past. It was crazy how adept we both were at walking that line, even dancing on it once or twice—never crossing over.

As the years passed by, she and I whittled away at the layers of our history, waxing profound on the memories we shared. I remained mired in the perspective of the boy infatuated with the beautiful, unattainable, older woman. And she rode the track of the ladycop career woman concerned about the welfare of two young hooligans naive of the hazards on wrong side of the tracks.

A hundred times we talked into the wee hours of the morning, long after Melissa and Kate had gone to bed. We whittled, and whittled, and whittled. And always I was left with a ponderous feeling, a sense of mystery. It was just like my impression that Lucinda had wanted to tell me something. I couldn't shake it—there was something more about those years, something vital to my existence that she wanted to, but wasn't, telling me. And, of course, there was an entire chapter I wasn't telling her either. Unspoken words are like spirits stuck in limbo.

My secret life as a *Murderer* stayed buried, an indelible tattoo that my timeless timidity had conspired to embosk under layer upon layer of scar tissue. For five years we whittled away at that scar, but I never could bear to let Miss Cherry see the tattoo. It was quite a dance.

Sometimes our talks became nebulously Byzantine, esoteric, as we delved beyond our own understanding into all manner of temporal and spiritual subjects. We'd cycle through a topic from top to bottom, usually serious, but sometimes entertaining each other with made up profundity. Like long-term passengers in a private elevator, together we rode, up and down, down and up, sharing the ride with great mutual affection. Almost always having fun. Almost like a loving mother and an adoring son dancing every dance at a fairy tale ball. But never ever did we stop on that certain forbidden floor where the devil called a do-si-do for erstwhile dancers with sub rosa pasts.

Sunday afternoon had been chosen to celebrate Kate's fifth birthday. She'd actually turned five the Wednesday before but wanted to wait for the weekend so Miss Cherry could be there. Miss Cherry's car was in the shop over the weekend and I had picked her up early to allow us to go present shopping. I had to tell Kate a little fib about why she couldn't come with me to get Miss Cherry.

"How's Luke these days?" Miss Cherry asked, as we headed home with presents galore safely snugged in the trunk. She had complained of a headache when we were browsing in the toy store and had taken something for it. I was a little concerned, but knew she was a trooper.

"Luke is Luke, fine all the time." She nodded, but didn't smile.

"Head feeling any better?"

"Worse."

"Maybe I should take you home. Kate will get over it. One look at all these presents and she'll be oblivious anyway."

"No. I'll be OK. Just takes a while for the aspirin to work."

I glanced at her, saw her jaw clenching, her knuckles turning white. "Miss Cherry?" She gasped and put her hands to her head. I reached across the seat, put my hand on her shoulder, felt the tremor moving her against her will. I turned the car around, instantly desperate, furious that the nearest hospital was at least ten minutes away. I tried to keep her talking, the pain in her head making that impossible. She screamed out twice, tears streaming, hands pressed tight to her temples, until, still more than a mile from the hospital, she slumped unconscious against the car door.

Everything had seemed so right that morning. Kate had put us in a celebration mood at the crack of dawn by jumping up on our bed and making us all sing *Happy Birthday*. Slowly, the day unfurled its fronds of trickery, intimating nothing coming of extraordinary magnitude. Sneaking killer earthquakes give little or no warning. It had never once crossed my mind that a time might come when it would be too late to tell Miss Cherry everything. Now faced with that daunting possibility, I felt as if I had been banished from the elevator, stranded in a stairwell that climbed or descended but never ended in either direction.

I sat across the desk from Miss Cherry's doctor staring blankly past him at rain streaked windows. I was embarrassed. I had been fine when I first shook his hand and introduced myself. Then something about his position of authority—his officiary comportment, the massive desk, the expansive collection of books lining the shelves, the plaques and certificates adorning the walls—gave me permission to drop my guard. The drizzle had set me up. I couldn't help myself. I let it out in a downpour. The doctor sat quietly, unaffected, professional, while I reined in my sorrow.

When finally I spoke, my throat was still tight, constricted by heavy-heartedness. "She's only forty-eight years old, doctor. I thought strokes were something only old people had." I looked around the doctor's office, absorbed in my frustration, despondent. A single unforeseen event had brought back old devils: powerlessness and despair. The urge to take a drink waged a dishonorable war against my weakened resolve. I fought the war with the only weapon I had, the one Miss Cherry had helped me to obtain: three AA meetings per day for the past fourteen days—the most powerful medicine for a most powerful disease. Miss Cherry would be proud of me.

The doctor tapped a pencil on the file that lay open before him.

"Yes, Mr. Parker, strokes are generally associated with the aged, but there are many different causes of stroke. In your aunt's case..." I had told him I was Miss Cherry's nephew and only living relative. A lie, but not too far from the truth. "...we believe the weakness in the blood vessel in her brain was due to a congenital defect, something she was born with. Her hypertension no doubt contributed to the stroke."

The doctor's bearing was forthright and businesslike, which I appreciated. At the same time, I was a little put off by the clinical detachment in his tone. After all, we were discussing the condition of Miss Cherry, someone I loved. Not a damaged car that had been towed in for repair.

"I didn't know she had high blood pressure."

"Nor did she, apparently. That's the terrible thing about high blood pressure. Often there are no symptoms."

My mind drifted momentarily. I felt angry that something like this should happen to her, especially after she had worked so hard to kick the booze habit.

"It's been two weeks now, doctor. What is your assessment of her condition—uh—her long term prognosis, I mean?"

I had spent every evening at her bedside since the day of the stroke. The entire right side of her body, her leg, her arm, even her facial muscles, were paralyzed. Her once perfect face now listed to one side in a dour snarl that seemed, to me, to be getting worse. She couldn't talk, although it was clear she could still hear and, to some extent, understand. We had worked out a rudimentary way to communicate. With considerable effort, she could answer simple questions with yes or no responses by extending one or two fingers on her left hand. I had to keep my chatter very simple, almost childlike phrasing, or she didn't seem to comprehend. It upset me that she wasn't improving. I was very discouraged.

"It's very difficult to know with any certainty how any stroke patient will recover," the doctor answered. "Statistically speaking, we know that some patients will recover some, if not all, lost motor skills. Speech can also return to normal. I believe your aunt's condition is stable and that she will survive this terrible ordeal. As for her medical treatment and outlook for recovery, we'll just have to wait and see. Time will tell."

I listened carefully, doing my best to understand and accept what had happened to Miss Cherry. But I couldn't help but concede that the bottom line was clear. Miss Cherry might not recover from the stroke. She might be stuck in a semi-vegetative quagmire for as long as she lived.

I must have sat there looking as stoic as a stroke patient myself, because after some indeterminate period of time the doctor escorted me out of his office and back to Miss Cherry's room.

"It's good that you are spending so much time with her, Mr. Parker. I'm a strong believer in fostering the will to recover. Sometimes I think we practitioners of modern medicine have barely scratched the surface of the science of healing." He chuckled. "The human brain is an amazing organ. We should never underestimate it. Keep talking to her, Mr. Parker. I know it does her a lot of good." The doctor patted me reassuringly on the shoulder and left the room.

I returned to the familiar chair next to Miss Cherry's bed and quietly sat down. I carefully lifted her delicate hand into mine. She looked pale. Her hand felt cool, almost lifeless, frail as a baby bird fallen from its nest. Clear plastic tubing disappeared into both of her nostrils giving her enriched oxygen to breathe. Saliva tended to pool at the unnatural, downturned corner of her mouth, which I dabbed occasionally with a tissue. I doted over her for hours at a time. Her once lovely face, contorted to one side as though some silent hurricane force wind tugged at the flesh covering her skull, still was beautiful to my love blind eyes.

To me she remained as enchanting as the day she appeared at Ruby Place and surprised Luke and I with unexpected treasures. I still saw her, envisioned her, as that beautiful angel standing beside Queenie, bathed in a shaft of afternoon sun. And though I knew I could never go back, my mind allowed time to fold back on itself. For brief, merciful moments I was that little boy again, securely embosomed by a kind and beautiful angel.

I softly stroked the back of her hand as I recalled the silly, anxious, throbbing heart of that naive, bashful boy. I remembered exactly the butterfly feelings as I hesitated gazing from the front porch that day long ago. The fool of April, spun like virgin wool yarn around a spool of adolescent fantasy. Lord knows an ocean of water had passed under the bridge since then.

The Bridge?

My breathing held still. My God, I hadn't thought about the bridge, in what, maybe five years? I stopped rubbing Miss Cherry's hand and just held it for a little while. It scared me to think about how close I had come to jumping to my death. I shuddered as a picture of me on the bridge looking down into the lonely mist flashed through my mind. I remembered how Mac had whimpered when I slid the bedroom window shut and began my morbid march in the dark.

I thought about all of the stuff that I would have missed. Mostly bad stuff, but a lot of good stuff, too. Luke and I enjoyed our share of brotherly fun, and certainly there was wonderful Melissa, and my adorable daughter, Kate. Yes, there had been a lot of good. I realized I held some of it in my hand right then. I looked at Miss Cherry lying there helpless and vulnerable, as much so as I had been, way back then.

Tears welled up again as I thought about how she had come along as a salving force, nursing me along with her personality, her attention, her caring. I was wreckage in need of salvage and she was a vital part of the team that had collected my scattered pieces from along the shore of my life. She and the Sergeant, working in tandem, had quickened the rebonding of my pieces.

Man, what a day we had at Dodger Stadium. That was far and away the best day of my entire childhood. Mental snapshots of that blessed event had flashed through my mind every day of my life since. I owed Miss Cherry my life at that point, if not by the time she reentered my life to help me break with my pathetic reliance on the poison in the bottle.

Miss Cherry was my reformation. Without her taking an interest in my life, as she did, I would have always thought of myself only as the murderer kid that never got caught, never was punished, never did his time in the reformatory where he belonged.

In the disturbing quiet of the hospital room, I ran it through my mind again. I killed a human being. There had been no arrest, no confession, no punishment, and no forgiveness. How could that be? There was no answer. Perhaps that was why I had worked so hard at punishing myself. How unmerciful I had been in my masochistic campaign of self-torture, a relentless psychological blooding intended to purge the guilt that could never quite be eliminated. And it seemed that no matter what I did to myself, I could not repay my debt. The man that I had killed remained dead forever. From that fact I could not escape.

Was Miss Cherry's stroke part of my punishment?

It was a miracle when Miss Cherry came back into my life. She had reappeared to embrocate my churlish spirit. Her miraculous timing must have been marked by God's own omnipotent chronometer. She understood my pain, without, I believed, understanding its real cause. Only God could do something like that. Now as she laid there before me, helpless as I had been, I feared that I would never be able to tell her the whole truth, to reveal the true source of my guilt—and, I reasoned, only God could do that.

God is fickle.

I wished that I could perform a miracle for Miss Cherry. I wished I could lay my hands on her and make her well. Instead, a new sense of guilt began to seep into me. I owed Miss Cherry everything, and now, worst of all, I might never get the chance to repay her. *Why would God do that?*

'Keep talking to her, Mr. Parker. I know it does her a lot of good.' The doctor's voice echoed through my mind. *But can she understand me? Can she really understand me?*

Unconsciously, I fondled the keys in my pocket, my fingers toying with the silver ball bearing which now hung from my key ring on a loop of its own. Subliminal impulses traveled up my arm and blew in my ear like the voice of a gremlin perched on my shoulder. It was an old familiar voice.

Where is the Sergeant now?

Would he come to Miss Cherry if he knew of her plight?

Would she want him to come?

Should I try to find him?

I shook off the gremlin. These ridiculous thoughts were nothing more than the ruminations of a desperate man. As always, the ball bearing offered no helpful advice. Its signals, if there were any signals, were only in my mind. And they were always questions, or painful reminders, never any answers. Fabian tactics for a slow, punishing defeat.

I dabbed Miss Cherry's mouth with the tissue. Watching her lying there, so frail, so defenseless, so much in need—I thought, *I can't let these devils cower me now. Miss Cherry needs me.* Then, with the silly innocence of that lost little boy of so long ago, now a man, but perhaps still just as lost, I thought, *What would Duke Snider do now? For one thing, he would have gotten rid of that cursed silver ball bearing a long, long time ago.* I wondered about that one for a while and then gave up. There was nothing I could do but sit next to Miss Cherry, hold her hand, and for the moment give in to my anguish. Then another frantic thought—*I could call Luke, just to hear his voice, maybe try to make him laugh.* He was prematurely balding now and wide open for mockingbird jokes. I tried to make myself smile, but I couldn't even get up from the chair. Despair had seized me again. Sadly, I had not yet fully learned the strength-giving value of prayer.

I couldn't manage a real smile until the following August, and only then it was as I watched Duke Snider on TV as he was inducted into the Baseball Hall of Fame at Cooperstown, New York. With the smile there were tears.

Way to go, Duke!

twenty-six

The past few years had brought a deeper mellowing. Absent a conscious awareness of it happening, I had begun to accept the things that I could not change. I abstractly gleaned the concept from the *Serenity Prayer*, an important part of the AA tradition. If my past was to be shrouded in mystery, so be it. Ever so gradually, I forced myself into a deliberate state of mind, one that allowed for the unsolved riddle of my Chinese puzzle youth. A state of mind arrived at only after an arduous battle with my own ego. But the important thing was that I had chosen it. The bad dreams were still there, though much less frequent, and therefore much less disturbing. Brooking the night-mares of darkness no longer entailed sleep deprivation.

Approaching middle age, where the road is smoother but seemingly faster, I found that I had much to be thankful for. Fourteen years of marriage to Melissa, sweet and beautiful as ever, was more than any man deserved. And, with the grace of God, I was in my twelfth year of sobriety. And Luke and I were about to celebrate five years in partnership as proud owners of a thriving travel agency.

My daughter, Kate, a beauty to rival her mother, had just turned sixteen. Kate was very excited about starting her junior year in high school. She was carrying a 4.0 grade point average. Confident thoughts of scholarships glimmered in her beautiful blue eyes. She had my eyes and her mother's hair. She looked like a sixteen-year-old Connie Selleca. And, although the brain damage had left Miss Cherry permanently disabled and relegated to live out her remaining years in a rest home, she had survived her stroke and was doing well. Indeed, there was much to be thankful for.

Saturday morning...

I was lounging on the back patio of our new Upper Bradbury home, enjoying the blessings of the summer morning sun as it rode the ridge line of the steadfast San Gabriel mountains. Early shadows leaned toward the Pacific making their steady crawl east toward day's end. My first cup of steaming, black coffee pleasantly warmed my insides as I lazily scanned over a printout of the prior week's bookings. Luke and I were promoting an Australia vacation package. Sales were brisk, thanks to Paul Hogan and Crocodile Dundee.

As often happened, that first sip of coffee stimulated welcome flashes of Rodney Bernanos. *Cackle!* I skirted around the pain of his heart attack and gave some thought to that little puppy, Kirk, wondering what ever became of him. Kate opened the slider and strolled out to refill my cup. My nostalgic interlude evaporated when Kate purposefully cleared her throat to get my attention.

"Daddy, can I use the Chevy this afternoon? Christina and I want to rent a video, probably that Sally Field movie, *Places In The Heart*, and watch it over at her house."

I looked up from my printouts. "Thanks for the refill, honey."

She leaned against the recliner I had been cozily occupying, bumping it softly with her hip, teasing me as I raised the hot laden cup to my lips. "I'm being extra nice, so you'll let me use the car, Daddy," she said pointedly. The ink was still wet on Kate's new driver's license. Walking had suddenly gone out of style.

My free hand sneaked up and tickled her behind her bare knee. "Creepy mouse," I said, reciting a piece of the tickle song she loved so much when she was a little girl. She giggled and backed away, the coffee in the pot sloshing, but steady in her hand. She smiled as she always did whenever her daddy gave her some attention.

Kate's smile was just like her mom's, and therefore just like Miss Cherry's before her stroke took it away. Those three heavenly smiles, gifts from the Almighty, were the sustaining blessings of my life. The sun backlit Kate's raven hair, the natural violet highlights shimmering iridescently, the wonder of genetics on display. "I ever tell you how pretty you are?" I said.

Her smile took on an added glow. "About ten times a day..." she said, adding coyly, "...but I'll creepy mouse *you*—unless, of course, you say I can use the car."

Her mother also contributed a monster gene containing the genetic code for relentless persistence. I smiled...after all, it was her mother's stubborn love for me that had held our marriage together through the bad years, before Miss Cherry came along and cajoled me into joining AA. For the rest of my life, I'll always be trying to make up those years for Melissa, and I'll always be grateful to Miss Cherry.

"Uncle Luke and I are going to visit Miss Cherry this afternoon. I'm sure he won't mind picking me up. I'll call him in a few minutes just to make sure."

Kate took that as a yes, her eyes glimmering accordingly. With step one successfully completed, she now hit me with step two.

"I might want to spend the night at Christina's," she said, trying her best to make it sound like an incidental thought. "Her mom already said it was OK. And mom says it's fine with her, if you say it's OK." She giggled surreptitiously and softened her voice. "I think mom wants to spend a cozy night at home alone with you."

Kate was very clever. I already felt for the poor young man that wins her heart. I gave her a smile that told her I was on to her, but that I admired the ruse. Inside I was smiling, too, but for a very different reason. Having memorized the lunar chart out to the year 2020, I knew a big, fat, full one was due in town tonight.

"If you bring me one more refill in a little while, you can stay over at Christina's..." My voice dropped down to the octave of doting sternness. "...with one very important condition."

Her dangerously innocent eyes brightened devilishly. "A proviso, you mean?"

"Yes, that too. You have to stay put. No running around in the car, OK?"

"OK, Daddy. I promise."

In the house the phone began to ring. Kate scampered to answer it, then reappeared at the door a minute later. "Daddy, it's for you. It's Uncle Luke. I already asked him if he could pick you up and he said 'fine'."

An opportunist, just like her mom. "OK, sweetie, please tell him I'll be right there."

A hawk hovering high above appeared not to be moving, in total command of the thermal riding up the pocked, barren slope that ascended sharply from our rear property line. He was looking for a meal, a mouse maybe, or perhaps a little red-headed boy. I was glad not to be a creepy mouse with red hair as I got up and went into the safe cover of the house. Kate eagerly handed me the phone. I gave her a lightning fast tickle making her squeal and squirm away. "Creepy mouse," she cursed playfully.

"Hello."

"Uh, yes, hello—Mr. Wade Parker?"

The voice was all too familiar.

"Yes, Wade Parker here."

"Wade, this is Duke Snider calling."

Yeah right. "Gee, Mr. Snider, you sound more like Charlie Neal."

"Ha, ha. How would you know what Charlie Neal sounds like?"

"Actually, I don't know, Luke. Could be Charlie's pushing up daisies by now."

"Well, that's a pleasant thought."

"Sorry about that. I'm sure old Charlie is doing fine. I know Duke Snider is doing well. I heard he's working on his autobiography—supposed to be published sometime next year."

"Oh jeez," Luke moaned. "The way you've lugged around that bat he gave you for the past twenty-five years, you better buy a bunch of copies of his book. Books aren't as durable as bats you know."

"I've already put in an advance order for a dozen copies," I said proudly, and then listened to Luke groan on the other end of the line. "Hey, come on, Red. If it wasn't for Duke Snider I probably wouldn't be here talking to you now."

Luke laughed. "Yeah, and if it wasn't for Duke Snider, Buster wouldn't have had to replace all of those windows in his bar either."

"Aw, heck, those windows were old anyway."

"Yeah, right. Old glass, broken or not, needs to be replaced. So tell me, Wade, who do you think is better..."

"Drysdale or Koufax?" I interjected, filling in the blank.

Luke jived, "What are you gonna do, big guy, throw me in the pond again?"

Luke liked to joke about the negative highlights of our past, but

209 / Mark Stanleigh

even the slightest reference to Three Ponds could still give me a chill, possibly even ruin my day. I quickly changed the subject.

"So, little brother, I understand your niece conned you into picking me up this afternoon."

"Sure. No problem. Trish won't need the van, she's going to the mall with the new gal from across the street. She's the one I was telling you about the other day. The one with the big gazzangas. Oh, and get this—is this spooky or what? She's got a seven year old son named Jake. Last name's not Blume though, it's Kimball. Of course she calls him Jakey."

"What color is his hair?"

He laughed. "I knew you'd ask. Blonder than yours, but the name Jakey and the big gazzangas is a real blast from the past, ain't it?"

"Yeah...real," I said, annoyed that I still couldn't touch on such things with the lighthearted zeal that Luke could. "Luke, let's be serious for a minute. I'm glad you're going with me today. She called me twice to remind me to be sure I brought you with me today. I don't know why today is so important, but it evidently means a lot to her that we're both coming. She's been asking why you haven't been to see her in a while. I know you don't feel as close to her as I do, but it really means more to her to see you than you think. It's kind of like the Smothers Brothers. I think she always liked you best."

"Well, of course."

"No, really, Luke. You were only six years old that first night on Billy Goat Hill. She's never forgotten that. If she only knew you were tougher than me, even then, maybe she would have liked me best."

"You're full of shit, Wade."

"Always have been, Luke."

"I'll pick you up at three-thirty, big brother."

"I'll be ready. See ya."

"Wait a second, Wade!"

He caught me just before I hung up the phone. I put the receiver back to my ear. "Yeah?"

"How long do you think Mac would have lived, I mean, you know, if he hadn't got killed?"

His question caught me completely off guard. "Well—uh—I guess fifteen, maybe twenty years at the most. Why?" I flashed on a picture of Mac climbing all over me as I woke up outside the mouth of Cavendish Caverns.

Softly, with a poignant touch of painful longing, Luke said, "Aw—I miss that dern dog sometimes."

My heart quavered in-between beats. Hearing him say it just that way pulled at something deep in my buried core, choking me up. My eyes turned glassy and I had to clear my throat. "Yeah—*ahem*—I think about him sometimes, too. A lot, actually. I know he probably saved Lucinda's life, but, well, as terrible as it sounds, for a long time I wished that he'd come with us to Billy Goat Hill that night."

"Yeah. Well, the reason I brought it up is because Trish and I have been thinking about getting a dog. We went to the Glendale Animal Shelter yesterday to look around. There's a dog there that could pass for Mac, if she was a male and didn't have any spots, that is."

I wonder if...naw, it can't be. I smiled and didn't say it. "Luke, I have the strangest feeling that you should go back to the pound and get that dog."

"Really? That's what Trish said."

"Yeah. I have a strong feeling you should have that dog."

"I think you're right. There was something special about her."

"Can I suggest a name?"

"Sure."

"How about—Antoinette? Uh—you could call her Toni, for short, maybe?"

"Yeah, Antoinette. That's what I was thinking."

He did remember. I was pleased.

"Wade?"

"Yeah, Red?"

"I'm glad you're my big brother. I love you. See you around three-thirty."

He hung up before I could respond. *I love you, too, Luke.*

Kate came in from the patio carrying the coffee pot. "I warmed your coffee for you, Daddy." She noticed the moisture in my eyes. "What's the matter, Daddy? Did Uncle Luke tell you another one of his funny stories?"

"Naw, I must have—uh—I think I just got something in my eyes, honey."

"Yeah," she said, beginning to tear up. "I think I got something in my eyes, too."

Kate put her face to my chest and gave me a hug worth millions.

Across the room, Melissa, beautiful and loving as ever, watched with great satisfaction.

One of the many reasons *Parker's Travel Agency* was a success was Luke's willingness to work Saturdays. The office was in Covina, I lived in Bradbury, and Luke lived in Glendale not far from where Rodney Bernanos had lived all those years ago. Lorrie, our senior travel agent, and another important reason for our success, agreed to cover things so Luke could leave early to pick me up by three-thirty. Bradbury was roughly halfway between the office and Rosewood Manor of Altadena, the retirement home where Miss Cherry had been living since being released from the hospital back in 1980. I knew the place well.

Before we even made it down the hill from my house to the 210 freeway, we had a brotherly spat over what music we were going to listen to on the way to visit Miss Cherry. I had remained a traditionalist with a strong preference for pre-1975 classic rock and roll. Luke had gone astray years before during the so called glitter rock phase. Lately he had a taste for what I imputed to be ethereal jazz. I had smuggled a Creedence Clearwater Revival tape into his van, but he caught me before I could slip it into the player. "Uh, uh," he scolded. "I'm providing the transportation so we listen to my music. Here..." He handed me a cassette. "...put this in. You might even like it."

"I doubt it," I said, and wanly inserted the tape in the slot. I read the cassette jacket. *Andreas Vollenweider, Down To The Moon.* "What in the hell is a *Vollenweider*?"

"Just listen, you big donkey."

The music started. Luke turned up the volume. The van filled with hip harp music. I gave it a fair listen for a few minutes and decided it couldn't hurt me. When the first song finished, Luke asked, "What do you think? Kind of nice, isn't it? Light, unobtrusive, soothing."

"Probably what they play in elevators in heaven," I muttered.

"I'll take that as a compliment, Wade." He flashed a grin and changed lanes to let someone in more of a hurry than us pass by.

If my options ever narrowed down to living in a rest home, I'd pick Rosewood Manor. At $1,500 a month it was a helluva deal.

Fifty-two very fortunate seniors lived in idyllic surroundings under the care of a well-trained and compassionate staff. Visitors were encouraged to come at meal times and were welcome to eat with the residents at no charge. The food was varied and quite good. After a couple of years, I found myself arranging my visits to straddle the lunch or dinner hour.

The cook was a woman by the name of Marge McZilkie. She liked me and made a point of saving me servings of her specialty, a raspberry cobbler so good that thoughts of visiting Miss Cherry released a Pavlovian dribble. Miss Cherry and Marge McZilkie had been at Rosewood Manor longer than any of the current employees and residents. They were the same age and had become the best of friends. I could count on Marge to let me know if Miss Cherry was having any problems or if she needed anything. Marge knew that Luke and I paid the resident fee in excess of that covered by Miss Cherry's monthly social security payment.

Marge McZilkie had called me the day before to make sure I was coming. She was concerned about Miss Cherry's spirits of late. She said Miss Cherry seemed down about something, just what she really couldn't say for sure. All she knew was that Miss Cherry had received a letter recently. The letter had come by special courier, which was enough to give me concern. Marge suspected something in the letter had upset her.

Miss Cherry sat in her wheelchair in the sunny, west garden of the rest home. Parked next to her was a tiny black woman who appeared to be no less than a hundred years young. They looked like salt and pepper figurines, frail breakables cushioned by profuse clusters of surrounding jasmine and bougainvillaea. From the distance, I could tell they were locked in serious discourse, the old lady seemingly engaged in dispensing some worldly advice. Miss Cherry was nodding, one half of her face expressing agreement, or perhaps acceptance, the other half incapable of concurring. She held her shriveled hand in her good one.

Luke and I made our way across an expansive lawn, as green and well-groomed as the grass of Dodger Stadium. As we came close, Miss Cherry noticed us and waved. I noted it was not her usual happy wave. The tiny black woman stiffly turned her head to see the approaching Parker brothers. I smiled and gave Miss Cherry my mainstay greeting. "How's my best girl today?" I kissed her cheek and gave her a soft hug.

Miss Cherry dutifully dabbed at the perpetually moist downturned side of her mouth with an embroidered handkerchief, her *Satchmo*, as she had come to call it in honor of Louis Armstrong's trademark hankie.

"I'm fine, sweetie. Hi, Luke. I'm glad you came, honey," she said. I doubted Luke noticed it, he'd spent one tenth the amount of time with her that I had, but there was a faint selvage of trepidation in her voice that gave me concern. Luke bent down and hugged and kissed her.

"Boys, this is my friend, Emma. She just moved in last week, and we're already good friends."

The old woman smiled and offered her hand to me. I took it, carefully. "Nice to meet you, ma'am."

Luke echoed me.

"You boys are very special," Emma said, her voice not much more than a parched, high-pitched whisper. "Miss Cherry done told me all 'bout her two best heroes. I'm real proud to mee'cha both. Ya'll go 'head now and have yo'selves a nice visit. Maybe I'll see ya'll at supper." She winked at me and said, "I hear we're havin' raspberry cobbler for *dee*-zert." With that she pushed a lever on her wheelchair and an electric hum carried her off across the lawn.

Luke chuckled. "Emma's got your number, bro."

Miss Cherry rode her wheelchair over to a nearby bench where Luke and I could sit down. She looked drained and her eyes were a bit puffy, as though she might have been crying recently. I looked at Luke and now saw a concurring expression of gravity on his face. Luke and I sat next to each other on the bench while she maneuvered the wheelchair around to face us. I felt strange, as though we were about to be lectured for some wrong that we had done. I didn't say anything. It was clear this was to be her show.

It was just my imagination, but it seemed as though Luke was trying to squeeze himself behind me, like he did that night on Billy Goat Hill when we were awakened by that gang of policemen-bikers. With effort, Miss Cherry cleared her throat and dabbed her mouth. Her friend Emma now gone, she made no effort to mask the pain in her eyes. She took a deep breath and began.

"I love you boys more than anything in this world—and—and I would never want to do anything to hurt you."

"We love you, too, Miss Cherry," Luke said. I nodded in agreement, feeling concerned, uncertain.

"I just hope..." She dabbed the handkerchief at one eye, but a tear ran down her other cheek. "...after what I have to tell you, you'll still love me enough to forgive me."

"Why, don't be silly, we'll always love you," I said. "What is it? What's wrong?" She looked away across to the far side of the lawn toward the spot her friend Emma had just reached. Her forlorn gaze seemed to be imploring the old woman to come back and help her. I got up from the bench and kneeled down beside her wheelchair. "Whatever it is, there isn't anything that would cause me to stop loving you. I know Luke feels the same. I owe you my life. If you hadn't come and bailed me out of jail that time I hate to think where I might be now. I doubt I'd be sober. Why hell, I'd probably be dead by now. You deserve most of the credit for the happiness in my life."

Her handkerchief fell to the ground as she reached up and touched my face. "You were such sweet little boys. I didn't mean for any of it to happen. I should have had the courage to stop it—but I couldn't—I didn't—I wasn't strong enough. I'm so sorry. I'm so very sorry." She was weeping now. I put my arms around her and looked to Luke for any sign of comprehension, but he just shrugged his shoulders. He was as baffled as I was. The three of us did nothing until the emotional impasse was finally broken by Miss Cherry. She exhaled a heavy sigh, and struggled with her thoughts before finally saying, "Lyle Cavendish—is dying of cancer—and he wants you both to come and see him in the hospital."

I raised myself upright, slowly, with forced calm, until, without realizing it, I loomed over her. Suddenly she looked as old as Emma and as vulnerable as young boys prowling the darkness of Billy Goat Hill. "You mean...the Sergeant?"

She looked up at me, shame distorting her face beyond its normal contortion. "Yes. I've remained in contact with him all these years, Wade. I'm sorry—I lied to you."

My stomach teetering with restiveness, I asked, "Why? Why would you keep it a secret?"

She knew how I had longed for years to see him again, how the rawness in my heart had never been able to heal. How could she have lied to me about something as important as all that? Luke had gotten up and now had his hand on my shoulder.

She was crying hard now, trembling. She gasped as she spoke. "Mostly—I lied to you mostly because I promised Lyle. There's much more to it, though. Oh, God—parts of the story, the reasons—I don't even know everything." She tried to reach down to pick up the handkerchief but couldn't quite reach it. Luke quickly picked it up for her. She dabbed her eyes and nose trying to regain some composure. Somehow she managed a little smile, half of a smile. "We all were part, are part, of something—something bad. You boys were, of course, completely innocent. You did nothing wrong. I wish I could say the same for myself. But I guess God found a way to punish me for what I did."

Starting to break down, dizzy, clammy, I held back against a giant rush of confused emotion. I forcibly calmed myself. "Punish you for what?" I said, almost too softly, too compassionately. "Your stroke was caused by high blood pressure and a weak artery in your brain, weak from birth, according to your doctor. You know that. I don't think God had planned to punish you for something before you were even born?" She looked up at me, her eyes red and weary, pleading for something, what I couldn't discern. "What's this all about, Miss Cherry?"

"You have to go see Lyle," she blurted. "He has to tell you. He *needs* to tell you—before he dies. Then, if you still want to, come back and we'll talk."

It was all I could do to keep from screaming out. Luke knew, and was patting my back now, desperate in his own way, fearing the situation could disintegrate to the level of ugliness. I felt nauseous, my shirt had soaked through, and far back within the forbidden recesses of my mind, subliminal suspicions undulated like voracious maggots awakening from a long, forced hibernation. All those years of hard earned progress—checked fears, subjugated cravings, buried nightmares—came crashing back, demanding reprisal. I desperately wanted a drink. Luke's reassuring hand suddenly felt more like the rabid monkey of addiction sinking its fangs deep into my shoulder.

"Is this about—Three Ponds?" I couldn't believe I said the words. Luke was shocked, but stood firm, his hand now still, bracing me up.

Her eyes, filled with soul-crushing guilt, forebode of repressed horror clambering to break free of long held silence. "Yes," she said weakly. "And much, much more."

Outwardly I appeared, at worst, numb. But deep inside a creepy mouse rode the back of the hawk, razor sharp talons clawing, jagged teeth gnawing, floating on a thermal of quivering viscera and quaking bone, my stalled heart laid bare for the feast. From my pocketed key ring the ball bearing cried out mordantly, mocking, taunting, drilling its message into a thousand holes in my vermiculated, threadbare mind: ...*Know ye all men by these presents... Victims, perpetrators, accusers all...are summoned forth to the judgement ball!* Luke held my arm tight as I slumped to the ground. The assault on my stomach came up in one violent contraction, raspberry red with the blood of a decades old ulcer.

Miss Cherry cried out, "God forgive me! Wade!"

Silently I pleaded...*Help me, Duke!*

twenty-seven

I never liked hospitals.

They made me uncomfortable—the peculiar smells, the maze of unfriendly hallways, the not knowing quite how to behave when face to face with someone injured or ill. Only once did I enter a hospital for a positive reason. That was when Kate was born. It occurred to me how unusual it must be that I had never been hospitalized. No diseases, no surgeries, no broken bones. What were the odds? Broken hearts and guilty consciences, my pestilence, never brought me under the purview of modern medicine, or I would have spent a lifetime in the hospital. And now here I was, summoned by a ghost from the infinite past, preparing to enter Saint Mary's Hospital in Long Beach. The irony was like a poorly told bad joke. I tried to smile.

Luke stood by me in the parking lot as I stared at the sterile structure rising high above us. A man I once knew, the most important man I ever knew, was dying inside that building; and, for reasons I dared not to think about, he had petitioned me to appear at his deathbed. Nothing and everything filled me with apprehension, occluding all efforts to prepare for the emotional riptide swelling within me like a tsunami approaching landfall.

Entering the building, I felt grateful to have Luke there pacing alongside me; still, I felt alone, as far from my element as a sailor a thousand miles away from the sea. A bizarre, convoluted stream of antiquated images whirled like a dust devil in my head.

* * * * *

We had left Miss Cherry whimpering at the gate of her own drowsy hell, her doctor having been called to authorize a strong sedative. Marge McZilkie found me a bottle of Malox. She also found the letter in Miss Cherry's closet, neatly folded, tucked in a box filled with keepsakes, mostly pictures of Luke and me. Prominent in the stack of snapshots was the photo the Sergeant had taken of Luke and me standing in front of Queenie. A magenta lipstick kiss mark adorned the picture, a sacred seal of authenticity. The picture had made me smile for a moment.

Marge had been right about the letter.

> *Dear Cherry,*
>
> *I'm sorry it's been so long, and that I have only bad news to give you. It's been a hard trip through this life, lots of regrets, but none about you. You were my best gal, the only woman I ever loved. I only wish I had listened to you more. I was a good cop. So were you. I know now that I wasn't good enough. I know now how wrong I was. I know now...*
>
> *The boys have a right to know, too. I'm at Saint Mary's Hospital in Long Beach...CANCER. Please ask them to come right away. I've had them cut way back on the morphine so I can make some sense when they come. Can't hold out for long, though.*
>
> *Except for seeing them, I've taken care of all my affairs. I've tried to set things right. After I'm gone, a Mr. Corsetti will contact you.*
>
> *I never stopped loving you,*
> *Lyle*

As always, Luke was philosophical, stronger than me. On the way to Long Beach he had done his best to mollify my fears, but he was nervous, too. At one point he looked at me and grinned. "We're a long way from Billy Goat Hill, ain't we, bro?" he said.

"Light years," I replied.

"Trish wanted to come. I think she wanted to satisfy her curiosity about the Sergeant."

"So did Melissa. But I thought it should be just the two of us."

"Me, too," Luke said.

While riding along on the freeway, listening to harp music, it occurred to me how fortunate Luke and I were to be married to women that loved us, that we trusted, that we could talk to. After getting Miss Cherry settled, we had both called our wives. That was what we had needed when we were kids; a close trusting relationship with someone who loved us, someone we could talk to no matter what the problem was. Deprived of that essential thing, and when confronted with a very serious problem, we floundered. We are not born into a perfect world, that's for sure, but no kid should have to deal with that by himself. Calling our wives, wanting to tell them about this news, hearing their compassionate voices, was about as perfect as the world can get. Wonderful, calming thoughts.

Then Luke interrupted my reverie. "Don't you think we should talk about it before we see the Sergeant?"

"Talk about what, that he's dying of cancer?"

"No—about what happened all those years ago. That's what he wants to talk about, isn't it?"

"I guess so." I didn't want to talk about it though, and Luke knew why.

"Wade...it was an *accident*."

A lump in my throat was swelling fast. "Yes, but..."

"There are no buts about it, Wade. It was as much my fault as it was yours. If I hadn't been such a wimp about those freakin mockingbirds—well, things would have been different is all. Maybe worse. Who knows?"

"That's not it, Luke. We should have told somebody. I should have told somebody."

"Who?"

"Lucinda, Reverend Bonner, Jake-the-barber maybe?"

He thought about it for a moment. "Naw," he said. "There was really only one person who would have truly understood, and might even have known what to do."

"Who?"

He started to giggle. "Carl-the-baker."

We laughed for the next ten miles. Luke had done his duty, God love him.

Dark solemnity had returned by the time we found ourselves standing outside the Sergeant's 6th floor room.

"Look at that," Luke said, pointing above the door. The Sergeant was in room 6-060. We had lived at 6060 Ruby Place. "Good sign or bad sign?" Luke said.

"Let's find out," I said, sounding far more confident than I felt.

Together, we pushed the heavy, hospital door open. I wasn't prepared for what I saw. A voice covered with cobwebs came weakly from across the room, like a ghostly memory. "I'm glad you came, boys."

It was him, or, more accurately, what was left of him. It was obvious his battle with cancer had wound down to the last salvo. Staring at a skeleton, I wondered whether he'd make it through the night. A gaunt, yellow, translucent shell of the person I had once revered motioned with his sunken eyes for us to sit down beside the bed. Two chairs had been purposefully positioned for the occasion. We sat down, Luke taking the chair closest to him.

Straight in front of me a catheter bag hung from a metal bed rung. It was half full of urine tinged brown with blood. Scabs that didn't look like normal scabs dotted his skin, like the spots of a leprous leopard. His hair was gone except for two strange clumps above one ear. The ear looked dry and shriveled as though it could fall off at any time. I doubted that he weighed a hundred pounds. It was shocking.

His lips were dry, badly cracked, hardened. They should have been bleeding but weren't. They parted like the bill of a bird as he spoke, his tongue dark and swollen. "How is Cherry?"

"Not good," I said, being truthful, not morose.

He nodded as if that was what he'd expected. "I have no family. No children. Life insurance is to be split between you boys and Miss Cherry."

It was an abrupt start. He wanted that much on the table right up front. I started to say, "No, I don't think that would be..." but he shifted his hand dissuasively. The movement was obviously painful for him.

"It's yours. Give it to charity if you wish. But I know you both have been subsidizing Cherry for quite some time. It's an expensive world we live in. The money is yours."

"OK...sir," I said.

He nodded slightly that it was done. "Luke, I'm dry," he said. "Give me a little squirt." A squeeze bottle marked *Water* sat on the bed stand next to Luke. Luke put the plastic tip to the Sergeant's mouth and gently squeezed. A small amount of water trickled down the Sergeant's chin onto his pale green gown. He nodded thank you to Luke.

His jaundiced eyes seemed to sparkle faintly. "We had a great time at Dodger Stadium that day, didn't we?"

I smiled. "Yes sir, we sure did." Luke echoed me. "I still have the bat, sir," I said proudly.

"I never could get you to stop calling me—*Sir*, could I?"

"No—Sir—uh..." I smiled. "Just a matter of respect, Sir. I guess I've always felt that way about you."

His failing, desiccated body appeared incapable of producing tears, but his once powerful eyes began to spill over. He looked away from me, thankfully, for I was very close to losing it. The love I had always felt for this man was welling up fast from the deepest holds of long imprisoned memory. I felt awkward, off balance and I glanced at Luke, hoping for strength, but could see he was already straining under the weight of his own emotion.

The Sergeant gathered some strength. "I wanted, needed, you boys to come, because I want to apologize to you for the thing I did that I regret more than anything in my life." I gave Luke a confused look. This didn't feel at all like what I had been expecting. *Why would he need to apologize to us? I killed the man—not him.* "Please hear me out, if you can. I don't think I have enough left in me to go through this more than once."

I nodded tenuously, uncomfortable. Luke nodded just as uneasily. The Sergeant motioned for more water. Luke gave him some.

"First, I want you both to know I am very sorry, especially to you, Wade."

Out of habit from attending to Miss Cherry for so long, I took a tissue and stretched to dab the tears from his face, then caught myself. "Go ahead," I said. Whatever was bothering him, he was a dying man, I couldn't help wanting to give him some encouragement.

"In the late 1950's the police department went through a period of heightened paranoia about the increasing presence of east coast organized crime families in Los Angeles. The OCIU, a small, elite group of prima donna detectives, including Miss Cherry and me..." He sighed. "...were running too fast and too loose with our tactics. An even smaller group within the OCIU had begun to carry out covert actions, many of which were never even revealed to the mayor or any other elected official, making them extralegal, if not illegal. Most of the cops were good cops doing what they believed to be the right thing."

He paused for another sip of water.

"One cop in particular, Lieutenant Theodore Kowalski, took it upon himself to rid the city of all perceived scourges. Ted was a real piece of work. You guys might remember him from that night on Billy Goat Hill."

"I remember him," I said, from an almost trance like quarter.

"He tried to punch you that night," Luke said.

I thought the Sergeant might have smiled, perhaps inside. Outside it was a wincing grimace, the cancer taking another bite of something still alive with nerves.

"You were supposed to forget about that, Luke," I said, nervously scrounging for levity.

"I forgot to forget."

The Sergeant continued, "Lieutenant Kowalski was responsible for the murder of four reputed mobsters, all sent, one after the other, from Miami to set up a west coast operation. Kowalski was sick, a cunning loose cannon with a conviction that he had been put on this earth to liquidate organized crime. He was assassinating these guys and making the hits look like they were done by a particular local gang whose death signature was a single bullet between the eyes. They were known to fiercely protect their turf from any foreign competition. It took balls for the third and fourth explorers to take up the challenge." He paused to breathe. Speaking was difficult labor, each word like pressing three hundred pounds of dead weight.

Something ticked in the back of my brain, the germination of a vague but very unpleasant thought. I shifted in the chair, fidgeting, crossing my legs, then recrossing them. Luke seemed fascinated with the story, like when he listened to the Sergeant tell the saga of Jakey Blume.

"Kowalski's first two hits went like clockwork. He had the whole unit crowing over the dumb goons killing each other off. Then he got a little cocky. He ran into some trouble on the third killing, and we caught him in the act of committing the fourth one."

"What trouble did he run into on the third one?" Luke asked.

The Sergeant looked directly at me. "He made the mistake of dumping the body—in the wrong place."

Luke stiffened on the edge of his seat, suddenly agitated. "What? Wait a second. Where did he dump the body? You don't mean at Three Ponds?"

The Sergeant nodded yes.

I nearly choked, feverish realization beading all over my face. Then instantly I got the picture.

Luke scrambled out of his chair, rage igniting his firecracker blood. He railed the Sergeant at the top of his lungs. "Christ! I don't fucking believe it! You mean you let my brother suffer his whole goddamed life thinking he killed that man?"

I was up beside him. "Luke! It's OK. Take it easy." I grabbed him by the shoulders. "It's OK. Calm down." I hadn't seen him this angry since we were kids. I tried to ease him back down in the chair, but he pushed me off.

"What do you mean, it's OK? It's not fucking OK. This son-of-a-bitch deserves to have cancer! Fucking cop, my ass! You're a goddam child abuser, for crying out loud!" There was fire in his eyes, his shock and anger fomenting, seething. "Shit! Do you have any idea what Wade has been through all these years? Do you? You're scum, Sergeant Cavendish! You hear me? FILTHY FUCKING SCUM!"

There was a knock at the door. A nurse stepped in. "Just checking," she said sheepishly. "Is everything OK in here?"

The Sergeant waved her away.

"Yes, ma'am," I said. "Just some understandable emotion is all. We're fine. Aren't we, Luke? We're OK, Luke. We're fine, Luke." The nurse did not seem satisfied but she quietly backed out of the room. She did not close the door all the way, though.

Luke wanted to hit something. He took a deep breath and jammed his hands in his pockets. Disgusted, he stepped away from the bed and stared out the window at nothing. The Sergeant was no longer fit to look at as far as he was concerned. I went over to the window and stood by him.

My germinating thought had exploded into a thousand urgent questions, all of which seemed inconsequential when weighed against the tons of guilt that had suddenly been lifted from my shoulders. I was in shock, too, my mind racing at the speed of light, struggling to fathom a lifetime of crisscrossed meaning.

Finally, I lamely said, "Thank you for telling me. My life was already on a good track. Now it's better."

"There's more to the story, Wade," the Sergeant whispered.

I looked at Luke. His face tightened but he didn't turn around. I left him standing at the window to sort through his own feelings and sat down where he had been sitting, in the chair closest to the Sergeant. I gave him some more water. He looked paler, weaker, closer to death. "Go ahead, tell me," I said.

He closed his eyes, conserving energy.

"Kowalski evidently dumped the body sometime shortly after sunrise because he met me for breakfast and we were together the entire day working on paperwork at the Highland Park station. He left in the late afternoon to get ready for a dinner party he and his wife were to attend that evening. About fifteen minutes after he left, I got an anonymous phone tip that the body of Johnny "Bloody John" Giacometti could be found near the middle pond of the area unofficially known as *Three Ponds*."

The face of Bloody John glared at me. I shook as a chill whipsawed down my spine. Luke came back over and sat down, his anger left somewhere outside the window. I gave the Sergeant more water.

"Not being far away from Three Ponds, and feeling somewhat skeptical of the phone call, I went out there to take a look by myself. As I made the turn from York Boulevard onto San Pasqual Avenue, I saw Luke, barefoot and hatless, running for home like he was late for dinner. A few minutes later, I found his Dodger cap floating in the water in the lower pond. That's when I started to worry. Then I heard Mac yowling farther up the draw. When I got up to the middle pond," he opened his eyes to look at me, "I saw the—ball bearings..."

My heart jumped. The ball bearing that had haunted me for twenty-seven years was in my pocket, and now back within two feet of the man that had dropped it into my sweaty, trembling, guilty hand.

"...in the mud spelling out the word *Mississippi*.."

"The dot was missing from the second *I*," I said, the memory, stark, vivid.

Cadaverous eyes, vestiges of his burned out soul, burrowed into me. "Yes," he said, "from the second *I*." His gaze flared, then dulled as he focussed on Luke. "I followed the sound of Mac and came upon Wade lying unconscious next to Kowalski's victim number three. Mac wouldn't let me near your brother at first."

Luke clenched his fists, eyes watering at the mention of Mac. "Our dog was the best fuckin' dog that ever lived. I always..." He choked to a stop, his control poisoned by a flood of emotion. I put my hand on his shoulder, felt him trembling. He sighed deeply and hung his head down. "I didn't mean to run away. I was scared. I didn't know what to do." Luke looked up, eyes pooled, long repressed regret tightening his mouth in a pained smile. "By God, Mac didn't run though, did he?"

I patted his shoulder. "No, he didn't, Luke."

The Sergeant, listless, degrading rapidly, focussed on me again. "You had a nasty bump on your forehead," he said sorrowfully. "But you were breathing normally. It didn't take long to figure out what had happened—the sling shot floating in the pond, feathers strewn about, the hole in the cardboard, and victim number three with a shiny musket ball jammed between his eyes."

God, I wished he hadn't put it that way. My stomach tightened.

The Sergeant closed his eyes again. "I panicked, just like you, Luke," he said. "I didn't do the right thing. I didn't think it out." Speckles of sympathy appeared on Luke's drained face.

"I woke up out by San Pasqual Road with Mac standing over me," I said. "How did I get from—how did I get there?"

"I carried you."

"Why? Why did you leave me there like that?"

The Sergeant seemed to rally slightly, a ripple of new energy. "After the murder of the first hood from Miami, they sent a replacement, a heathen by the name of Carlo Puzzi. I had some nagging doubts about Kowalski when he miraculously discovered Puzzi's body over by Franklin High School and called it in himself. It was too neat. He over played it, crowing on about how the gangsters were killing each other off. I had no proof, though. And part of me felt like if it was Kowalski doing the killings he was doing us all a big favor. These were rotten guys he was bumping off."

"But why leave me lying in the dirt with a knot on my head?"

"I wanted to protect the OCIU. There had been rumors that Chief Parker was thinking about shutting down the unit. I didn't want that to happen. It was politics pure and simple. We were engaged in some very important work, national security stuff, and some internal matters involving corruption within the Los Angeles Police Department. A scandal involving an OCIU operative committing vigilante style murders would have devastated our operation for sure.

"When I received the phone call at the Highland Park Station tipping me to the body at Three Ponds, there were some things that pointed to Kowalski being the caller. The call came from outside to the Highland Park Station, through the switchboard, not to the OCIU downtown where I would normally be reached. I was pretty sure only three people knew I was at the Highland Park Station that afternoon, Cherry, Rodney Bernanos and Kowalski. The caller asked for me by name. He also made a mistake. He referred to Johnny Giacometti as "mutt number three" a label a few of us put on Giacometti when he first arrived from Miami. I had spent time in Miami working under cover and knew a little about Giacometti before his bosses picked him for the assignment."

"I remember how tan you were. Your note with the Dodgers tickets mentioned Miami and I thought that was strange."

His eye lids drifted down. "I shouldn't have done that. Stupid slip."

Luke had been listening quietly. Now he spoke up. "There's a lot you shouldn't have done, Sergeant."

"There's a lot I should have done, too, Luke. But there's more to this story. I want you to know the whole story." He raised his hand to his mouth and coughed. He trailed his fingers on the sheet leaving a streak of bright red blood. "I carried you out to the road, made sure you were still breathing, and ordered Mac to stay with you. I went to a phone booth and made an anonymous call to the station that someone was lying by the road. I quickly drove back arriving just as you and Mac came up onto the road. You looked pretty good, from a distance anyway. I watched you start walking up San Pasqual and saw the patrol car stop and talk to you."

A full-color memory played in my head as he slowly recounted what had happened.

"Then I called Cherry."

I was disheartened to hear that. "Miss Cherry knew about the whole thing?"

"No. She didn't know about you boys, about you discovering Giacometti's body, until later. Luke's Dodger hat, two pairs of tennis shoes, a sling shot, and the ball bearings were in my car under the seat before she arrived at Three Ponds." He coughed again, grimacing, and wiped more blood on the sheet. "I got rid of the cardboard, too," he

227 / Mark Stanleigh

said, looking straight at me. "And, I dug the ball bearing out of his head." Shuddering, I closed my eyes. In my pocket the ball bearing squirmed. "Cherry and I removed and disposed of the body and set out to trap Kowalski. But even at that point, I had no idea how crazy and dangerous he really was."

"I think you all were crazy," Luke said.

Again, the Sergeant nodded. "Cherry and I were in love. But, please believe me, she had nothing to do with the early decisions. She trusted me. I was senior to her in the chain of command. She was a damn good cop, doing her job, following orders. Cherry and I thought we had figured out how to nail Kowalski. We took our story to our Captain and he went to the Chief. A plan was put in place."

"So the cover-up went all the way up to the Chief of Police?" Luke said.

"I believe so, but I still hadn't told anyone about you boys finding the body. I was hoping you were scared enough to keep your mouths shut."

Luke expelled a mouth full of invective. "We never told a soul, officer."

The Sergeant almost looked angry. "I know you didn't."

"What would have happened if we had told?" I asked.

Luke answered, "He had it all figured out, big brother." He turned his angry stare on the Sergeant. "Didn't you, cop? No one would have believed us. Would they? Just two little jerks making up a wild story. Two fatherless, latchkey lunatics starving for some attention. Is that about the way you figured it—huh, Sergeant?"

The Sergeant's eyes fluttered weakly. "That's the way I figured it, Luke. You're right."

"So you kinda just left us swinging on our own rope then, didn't you?" Luke was heating up again.

"You said the whole story, right?" I numbly said. The Sergeant nodded. Then it spilled out, the one thing I had never told Luke. "I was sure I killed that man. So sure, I almost committed suicide over it?"

Luke was aghast. "What!"

"That morning I found you on the bridge," the Sergeant replied. "Yes."

New tears spilled down the Sergeant's sallow cheeks. "That's when I realized what a terrible mistake I'd made. But I couldn't tell you anything. It was too late to turn back things that had already been set in motion."

"You almost jumped off a bridge?" Luke couldn't believe it.

I ignored Luke. "You could have told me anything, sir. I idolized you. I would have believed anything you said."

A pain worse than cancer showed in his eyes. "I turned to Rodney for advice," he said.

God, not Rodney, too? "You mean Rodney knew?"

"No. I confided many things to Rodney, he was like a father to me. But he did not approve of my activities with the OCIU. He tried to convince me to transfer out of the unit. Rodney wasn't an American citizen. He was French and had been involved in the Underground Resistance against the German occupancy during World War Two. He felt the OCIU was dark, dangerous like the Nazis, a potential threat to civil liberty, and would eventually lead to my downfall as a police officer. He was right, of course. I knew he would have considered my judgment at the time I found you lying by the body, and my decision to leave things as they were, to let you continue to believe you killed the guy, not only despicable, but Gestapo-like. I only told him you were a troubled kid—like me when I was your age.

"Rodney fell in love with you from the start. You reminded him of me when I was a kid—the son he never had, like in the movies, I guess. I knew if he took you under his wing you'd be OK. But, I finally broke down and told him the whole story, the truth, just before he died."

I was in tears now, too. "You used Rodney?"

The Sergeant twinged. "Yes."

"Goddam," Luke grumbled.

"Rodney was outraged when I told him the whole story. He was ashamed that I could do such a thing. He even slapped my face, something he never once did when I was growing up." *Yes, the slap—I did see it.* "He said he was going to tell you the whole story himself. I was scared, but I thought it was better for you to hear it from him anyway. I was sure he was going to talk to you about it that day you kids came to visit him at his house, the day he had the—heart attack." More tears came in a rush. "I think the stress killed him."

"Man, this is only getting worse," Luke muttered, shaking his head solemnly.

"The Sergeant saved my life, Luke. I'm pretty sure I would have jumped from the bridge if he hadn't come along."

"It was only luck," the Sergeant said, refusing undeserved clemencies.

Luke hissed, "Boy, it turns out Lucinda was right all along. Not letting us see this low down dog anymore was the best thing she ever did. And poor Miss Cherry, he ruined her life, too."

"There's more," said the Sergeant.

Luke stood up. "Great! Fucking great! What now? Are you gonna tell us you're the one that broke into our house and shot Mac!"

The Sergeant closed his eyes. "No. Kowalski did that."

Luke turned white and slumped back down in the chair. I had begun to shake. My head was pounding.

"Kowalski found out you guys knew about the body. Later we were able to piece together that one of his cohorts overheard Cherry's end of an argument she and I had on the telephone. An argument, like many we had, over whether or not to tell you boys the truth. Part of her spirit died when she found out she was the source of the leak that almost..." He didn't finish the thought. "The irony was Kowalski didn't know you thought you killed Giacometti. It spooked him when the body disappeared from Three Ponds. He became paranoid, obsessed. When he later found out you boys knew about the body, I think he convinced himself that you had seen him dump the body in the first place, and had recognized him from that night on Billy Goat Hill. He lost it. He completely snapped. And we didn't know—he'd started—seeing your mom."

I jerked out of my seat, my body rigid, my memory on fire, sucking like a vacuum back in time. *She came in late—Mac awoke with a start—laughter—ice tinkling—Ted? She called him Ted! My God, he was the man she brought home with her that night!* Icily, I said, "He came to kill...us?"

"We had suspicions he'd recruited a few other officers into his cabal and that they were planning something. We had Kowalski and several others under surveillance and discovered he was dating Lucinda. That's when we realized he must have found out you knew about the body at Three Ponds. We, Cherry and I, immediately went to your mother and told her everything. Your mother was amazing. She could have turned on us, gone to the District Attorney, the FBI—but she didn't. She believed in us and backed us all the way. We agreed on a plan to protect you boys, to give us time to discover all of the officers involved with Kowalski, and to keep it all quiet. Cherry and I gave Lucinda $7,000 we had saved for our wedding."

"That's why we moved so suddenly?" Luke asked.

"Not suddenly enough," I said.

The Sergeant went on, "Kowalski's luck finally ran out. Lucinda had tactfully broken it off with him. But he'd already been in your house. He knew the layout, which was all he'd wanted in the first place. The night before you were to move to Glendora, he came to the house intent on shooting all three of you as you slept in your beds. He had a silencer. We found it later."

"Good Lord," Luke said.

"He came to the house at about three in the morning. He entered the front door with a key we figured he'd stolen from your mom. It was dark, of course, and once inside it must have taken a minute for his eyes to adjust. The inside of the house was in disarray, moving cartons strewn about, furniture shifted around. He must have tripped or bumped against something, who knows. The important thing is the dog heard him. You know the rest."

"Twelve more hours and we would have been gone. Mac would have lived," I said.

The room fell silent except for the awful rasp of the Sergeant's erratic gasping for air. He stared at the ceiling, devoid, empty, depleted, but looking strangely satisfied, relieved. I could see it clearly, understand it clearly. I knew exactly how he felt, burdens lifted, ready to move on.

"What ever happened to Kowalski?" Luke asked.

"He was shot and killed six days later. Kowalski, along with two other renegade cops, made a hit on Giacometti's replacement at a warehouse in North Hollywood. For what it's worth, Cherry's the one who shot him. Kowalski had a hunk of meat missing from his shoulder, too. It wasn't healing. Must have been terribly painful. I figure Mac got in a good lick before Kowalski shot him.

"Officially, Kowalski died in a boating mishap. The sharks must have got the body. He was never found."

The Sergeant looked completely drained. He closed his eyes, the lids quivering strangely. We were all quiet for a little while longer, the undertow of rampant emotion pulling us down below the tumultuous surface. Luke got up and walked slowly to the window. I followed him with my eyes. I wanted him to turn around with a fresh

Lukeism and brighten the room. But he didn't turn around. My little brother had run out of words. We all had. The window held him there, offering him a glimpse into his own past, a view full of ugly clarity, yet beautiful with the shine of new found truth.

"Hey, Luke," I said, after a little while. "Wanna find some cardboard and sneak out to Billy Goat Hill tonight?"

"Maybe we better stay in—feels like a bad moon rising," he said, staring out the window.

I got up and walked over next to him. "Wha-cha lookin' at, Red?"

He turned to me, tears running down his face. "See down there in the parking lot, the blue pickup." I looked and found the truck. In the bed of the pickup were two little boys, one blond, one redhead. They were spittin' images of the man sitting between them. The man had his arms around their shoulders.

A few more quiet minutes went by. The Sergeant rested. I stood at the window with Luke, my arm across his shoulders, my mind in a surrealistic drift shifting between images of the past and visions of the future. Lucinda? It pained me to think how hard on her I had been. And Miss Cherry? All those years carrying that burden—maybe it did cause her stroke. We were all in it together, but not "together" in it. If there had only been more trust, better communication? It was the question, and answer, for most of the worlds problems, I mused.

From across the room, my gaze still fixed on the parking lot below, I asked the Sergeant, "Why did you give me that ball bearing?" My hand was in my pocket stroking that singular silver ball like a worry bead. He didn't immediately respond. I assumed he was thinking.

The nurse reappeared, her stockings swishing quietly behind us. A long moment passed while she checked over the Sergeant. "I'm very sorry, gentlemen," she finally said. "I think Mr. Cavendish has slipped into a coma."

The Sergeant never regained consciousness. He passed away four days later. I was at his side when he died. Sadly, I felt as though he'd been dead for a long, long time. We should have talked a lifetime ago. So much could have been different.

I loved him.

epilogue

The years have passed quickly since we buried the Sergeant in accordance with his wishes, at Forest Lawn, next to Rodney Bernanos. Time, the indefatigable healer, has slowly worked its magic. The travel agency has grown, eight offices now, and more profitable than we had ever dreamed. The insurance money we received from the Sergeant was put to good use. Luke bought an airplane and learned to fly, his way of defeating the mockingbirds, I guess. After many years of part-time effort, I completed a master's degree in English literature. And Melissa and I bought a cabin on the west shore of Lake Tahoe at Rubicon. We modified it to be wheel chair friendly for Miss Cherry. Captain Luke regularly flies us all up to the cabin, where we celebrate all things as a family.

Luke and I sometimes make trips to Rubicon alone. Sojourns to talk, just us brothers, still linked sprites. The cabin is a great place to relax and ruminate. The pine scented seclusion offers a kind of therapy, a natural easing of inhibitions that somehow makes me more comfortable with thoughts about the past. The entire structure projects out over a magnificent grouping of boulders that cling precariously along a thin strip of emerald shoreline. A short way out from the water's edge, shimmering emerald plunges straight down into an infinite chasm of frigid cobalt blue. Breathtaking.

We are here now, brothers Parker, sitting out on the veranda overlooking the splendor and vastness of Lake Tahoe, enjoying the late afternoon sun. Luke, ever the philosopher, is waxing profound as we lounge next to an iron railing separating us mere mortals from a heavenly, alpine sky.

"Rubicon," he proclaims, gesturing to the chilly depths below.

"Rubicon," I answer, encouraging him.

"It drops off nearly vertical for hundreds of feet. Throw a penny out there and your wish will come true before it hits bottom."

A rippling veneer lays like a shimmering cloak over the glacial depths.

"Tell me more," I say.

"Rubicon," he repeats, this time with more fervor. "It means..." he extends his arm and slices it down toward the water's surface some fifty odd feet below, "...to be decisive. To take irrevocable steps, like Caesar did when he crossed the river Rubicon between Cisalpine Gaul and Italy to march against Pompey."

"Very impressive."

Luke's eyes brighten with passion, bore into me as if making a challenge. "To conquer or perish!" he roars. I nod. Grinning inscrutably, he adds, "Something to think about, isn't it?"

"I've been thinking about a lot of things lately, Luke."

"It's this place," he says. "The Indians believe Lake Tahoe is one of the earth's spiritual centers."

I muse for a moment. "It's remarkable how full it is again, after all these years of drought."

Luke agrees. "Back up to its natural rim. Its abundance is once again flowing into the Truckee River."

"Kind of amazing, really, if you think about it. After suffering years of deprivation, the lake is full again, even has more than it needs."

"Just like us, huh?" Luke says.

I glance at him. "Hadn't thought of us that way." He winks.

Sitting there, the lake doing its spiritual number on me, I'm thinking about all of them—Matthew, Lucinda, Earl, Carl, Jake, Kowalski, Duke, Mac, Miss Cherry, and especially the Sergeant. All, but Miss Cherry and Duke Snider, are fading pictures, images and sounds floating in a river of memories turbulent with the eddies of my dreams. Now and then I hear Mac barking, though faint, far away.

To the west behind me, the sun is fast slipping down into the cradle of evening, its ebbing sliver setting ablaze the windows of cabins far across the lake along the Nevada shoreline. As I looked up, the orange flares of mirrored light seem to douse all at once, as if, at long last, the flaming quintessence of the Sergeant has been extinguished. I close my eyes, and except for feeling lonely for Melissa, stillness and quiet dwell comfortably within me.

Luke gets up and reappears with a glass of ice tea for me and a beer for himself. He settles into the deeply cushioned chaise lounge next to me and raises his beer, signaling a toast. I raise my glass.

"I want to say something I've never said before."

"What's that, Luke."

"Thank you for watching out for me when we were kids. You had to do everything. I know it wasn't easy." He gazes at me, his bright eyes serene, glimmering.

He's always been able to sneak up on me like that. Never see it coming. My chest warms. "I couldn't have made it without you, Luke."

As we sit there enjoying the unwinding mood of dusk a gray dove glides down and alights on the deck in front of us. "Not a mockingbird," I say.

Luke smiles and coos at the dove. "Mockingbirds are for kids, big brother."

I nod speculatively as my mind drifts back to the beginning, to a time when pedantic adultism is a quality yet to be learned; to a place where grand adventures fill our indulgent hearts and courage courses through our veins with the merciful blue blood of innocence; to a microworld full of excitement and risk where even the smallest occurrence is important, serious, and equally free of lasting consequence. Something indefinable, deep inside me, still longs for those days before the Sergeant and Miss Cherry. That shortlived period of family life that existed before Matthew died. Before Earl ran off to Barstow leaving us ill prepared to deal with most things, much less the worst of things. The hole in me still needs mending, maybe always will.

"Wade?"

"Yeah?"

"If they made a movie about us, about our lives, what would they call it?"

Feigning sarcasm, I say, "How about...*Life's A Bitch*."

Luke unleashes a hearty laugh. "Naw," he says. "I see it more as...*The King Of Billy Goat Hill,* starring Wade Parker."

I was the king of Billy Goat Hill. I had a kingdom once and then life dethroned me, exiled me.

We both sit quietly for a few more minutes, being together, thinking our own thoughts. The dove hops up on the lounge near Luke's feet, fluffs out its feathers, and lowers its body comfortably down over its legs and feet, as though it plans to spend the night right there. I feel that secure with Luke, too. The dove sleepily closes its eyes.

The lake works on me some more, brings up thoughts of Duke Snider, opening day at Dodger Stadium, my day dream about going down into the club house with him, then him giving me the bat for real. In my heart, I feel Duke really would have said something like what I had imagined he had said that day. Without realizing it, I say the words out loud. "We must find a way to forgive or we only end up blaming ourselves."

"What?" Luke says.

"Nothing. Just thinking out loud."

I go inside the cabin and return with the bat that Duke Snider gave to me.

"Not the bat," Luke complains.

"You've never even touched this thing, have you?"

"You never let me. You used to threaten me with death if I got anywhere near it."

"Here," I say, handing it to him.

Luke stands away from me and raises the bat over his shoulder. Beaming just like the freckle-faced kid he was long ago, he takes a swing toward Nevada. "Damn, it gives you chills doesn't it?"

"I get chills just looking at it," I say, and for a moment we are boys again, best pals, kindred spirits transcending the purlieus of time, metaphysically joined by the lasting magnificence of Duke Snider's benevolence.

He swings the bat again, this time with much more vitality. "Kinda makes you feel powerful, too."

In a flash of clarity I know what needs to be done. I take the key ring out of my pocket and remove the ball bearing. Luke smiles knowingly and hands me the bat. "To conquer or perish," he gently admonishes, and squares up his shoulders as though preparing to advance on Pompey.

I step to the lake-most point of the veranda and gaze out over the Rubicon, my heart filling with the spirit of Lake Tahoe shimmering under vestiges of a warm cinnamon sunset. With closed eyes, I visualize little Wade Parker, and Luke. I say a silent prayer for all children who need someone to trust, someone to care enough to understand.

Then I do what I know Duke Snider would do. I toss the ball bearing up in the pine scented air, swing the bat with my arms fully extended, and cream that sucker on the sweet spot with everything I have.

"Your dream will come true before it hits bottom," Luke says, grinning.

Never look back, Wade, the Sergeant whispers from the twinkling heavens.

For the first time in my life I feel like everything is right. I leave the bat with Luke and go inside to call Melissa. I want to tell her about an idea I have to start a foundation to help troubled kids, maybe build a shelter for runaways. She'll think I'm crazy, of course, and then she'll help me with everything she has to give. *I know she will.*

about the author

Mark Stanleigh was a Chief Executive Officer and Marketing Specialist in California where he worked in engineering disciplines for government and private enterprises. Born in Pasadena, California, he spent his childhood in northeast Los Angeles and resided for a period of years in the San Francisco Bay Area. He now makes his home in central Oregon with his wife, and son, and has two grown daughters living in Los Angeles. *The King of Billy Goat Hill* was written while he lived in Nevada at Lake Tahoe. He is presently working on three books.

-Mark Stanleigh-

If you are experiencing difficulty getting copies of this or any other FPG book through your local book retailer, please feel free to order direct from the publisher.

Please call 1-800-352-8173, mention interest code KBH-996, and use your credit card. Or use this coupon to order by mail.

<u># Copies</u>

_____   THE KING OF BILLY GOAT HILL
                ISBN 0-9652888-0-3 $13.00

_____   THE INTRIGANTES (Coming Fall 1997)
                ISBN 0-9652888-1-1 $13.95

<u>Watch For These Future Releases By Mark Stanleigh:</u>

Deadly Nightshade
The Seventh Generation
Savants of the Vespertine

Name
_____

Address
_____

City _____ State _____ Zip _____

Please send me the Fallbrook Publishing Group books I have indicated above. I am enclosing $_____. (Please add $3.00 for the first book and $1.00 for each additional book for postage and handling.) Send Check or money order (No cash or C.O.D.) to Fallbrook Publishing Group, P.O. Box 3623, Sunriver, Oregon 97707-9998. Please allow 3-4 weeks for delivery.

Prices and numbers subject to change without notice. Valid in the U. S. only. All orders subject to availability.   KBH-996